Happy Readin,

FOUR
MORE
words

Aurora

Stenulson

♡

[signature]

ISBN: 978-1-0882-0917-2

For all those who have loved through the hurt.

And for my younger brother, Hayden.

CONTENTS

PART ONE:

UNFOLDING ADORATION

ONE

"Don't move, Christine. Your head is bleeding."

I place my hand on the back of my throbbing skull. When I pull my hand up in front of my face, it's smudged with blood.

I begin to sit up, but Avery quickly pushes my shoulders back down against the frozen cement. "I said don't move," she says this with a panicked overreaction. "You might have a concussion."

I lay still, even though I'm sure I'm fine. I just don't want to generate any more unnecessary hysteria in Avery's tiny body. I wouldn't want to cause her to explode from the melodrama.

She scans the campus, then calls out in the snowfall, "Help!" I would honestly call this flurry a whiteout since I can barely see fifty feet in front of us.

I close my eyes, trying to keep myself from rolling them. "Avery, I only slipped on the ice. I'm sure I'm fine to walk."

"Somebody! Help!" she calls out again, ignoring me. Maybe if we hadn't shown up thirty minutes early, there would be someone to answer her chirring.

The puffy snowflakes are melting as they hit my face. I lift my arm to shield myself, then say, "Could someone help my cousin before she gives herself an aneurysm?" This is my attempt at humor. I even chuckle to myself a little because since we were two years old, Avery has somehow managed to turn every event into theatrics.

1

For example, when *my* parents divorced when we were in seventh grade, Avery took two weeks off from school to mourn the experience. I didn't even consider missing school as an option. Although I anticipated the divorce was coming. Then, when I moved away with my brothers and my mom, Avery called me every day to tell me how sad *she* was.

But I love her anyway.

"*Help! Please!*" I don't have to uncover my eyes to know she's released the waterworks.

Crunching snow under heavy feet approaches us, followed by a man's voice. "What happened?"

I feel him kneeling next to me.

At this point I'm sort of mortified that I've allowed Avery to take the situation this far. But now that I've committed to her antics, I'm curious to see how this plays out—so I keep myself still and my arm over my face.

Avery chokes, *dramatically*, on her words. "She slipped on the ice and hit her head. There's blood everywhere."

"I can see blood, but…" I hear him shift as if he's trying to find the rest of the exaggerated and imaginary blood Avery is talking about, "…it's not much."

"I'll call the ambulance," Avery says directly.

"Why don't we take her to the college health center? It's right there and," he takes my arm and begins to lift it, "is she unconscious?"

When our eyes meet, I'm equally horrified and relieved. Horrified because I realize I probably seem as strange as Avery for lying on the sidewalk in silence for this long. And relieved because I recognize the man kneeling over me. But now that I'm considering what's happened, I could also be feeling horrified that I do recognize him as well.

He tilts his head and the corners of his eyes crinkle with his knowing grin. "Christine?"

"Declan…" I'm sure it's him, but since we haven't seen each other since high school I say his name with lacking assurance.

Avery tries to push me down again. As I sit up, she says to Declan, "And I'm Avery. Now that we all know each other, help me keep her from moving."

I push Avery's hands off me. "Stop, I just need a band aide."

"You have a concussion!"

2

I widen my eyes at her with warning, and clench my jaw to keep myself from saying something I might regret.

"Did you lose consciousness?" We flip our heads to face Declan, his tone and posture are both stoic.

Avery's eyes widen more with each word when she says, "For like, two seconds she did."

Declan nods slowly, chewing on the information. Then he drops his gaze to mine, as if after knowing Avery for twenty seconds he already doesn't trust her and needs my confirmation.

I shake my head. "I never lost consciousness." Which is true.

Avery scoffs and drops her mouth open. Her words are spilling out when Declan talks over her, saying, "I don't think you have a concussion."

Avery is steaming now that she realizes she's been ignored by both me and Declan.

I have to remind myself that I'm a twenty-two-year-old grad student and it would be incredibly immature of me to stick my tongue out at Avery right now. Even though she deserves it.

"But…" he says, dragging his word as he inspects the back of my head. He gently tugs at the strands of hair around my open wound, then finishes his statement, "You probably need stitches."

I drag in a breath and drop my head back between my shoulders before blowing a cloud of steam up into the snow-covered sky.

This couldn't have happened at a more inconvenient time on a more inconvenient day. I have a project to present and it's essentially my entire grade for the semester. I don't have time for doctors or stitches.

Declan rises, taking my hands in his leather gloves and helping me to my feet. The head-rush causes me to stumble back a little. But enough that Declan grips my shoulders to steady me.

"See," Avery says. "Concussion."

I narrow my eyes in her direction. "I stood up too fast."

Declan draws his head back and considers me, then says, "Nonetheless, you should get checked out at the health center." He lifts his satchel in Avery's direction. "Will you carry this so I can carry her?"

Before Declan's statement registers in my jostled mind, he drops his satchel in Avery's hands then tucks one of his arms around my torso and lifts my legs in one swoop with his other arm.

I'm sure most women would be thrilled to be in my position. But

3

I'm not most women. And I feel slightly disturbed Declan feels so comfortable putting his hands around me without permission. Especially since he barely spoke two words to me in high school. Even though he was at my house every day hanging out with my brothers, he seemed to pay zero attention to me.

"I can walk," I say.

He's already headed for the health center. "I know," his warm breath billows out in a foggy puff against the cold air.

My eyes are fixed on him, even though I'm awkwardly aware of how close our faces are. "Then put me down so I can walk."

He glances at me and the corners of his mouth curl up as he says, "I'd rather be cautionary and make sure you don't have a concussion first."

Despite my intense desire to be set down, I can't ignore that my head trauma, as miniscule as it is, is affecting me. I also can't ignore the fact that I'm positioned unwillingly in his arms. Which sends a quiver through my stomach.

Avery is fumbling behind us. "I knew you had a concussion," she says. She has to jog three paces just to keep in stride with Declan.

The falling snowflakes have muffled the sounds around us except for the squeaking crunch of the snow under Avery and Declan's shoes, and the quiet grunting exhale from Declan's throat.

"I'll get the door," Avery says, rushing towards us from several steps behind.

Declan doesn't wait for her. Instead, with the momentum of his stride, he flips around to enter the health center by thrusting his back against the door and pressing on. I tuck my feet under myself to keep from hitting them on the doorframe.

Avery rushes through the door behind us. "Or not," she mumbles. She doesn't like being ignored. And more so, she despises feeling useless in distressing situations like this one.

Declan gently places me in a chair, then takes a seat next to me while Avery is discussing my fall with the most traumatic description to the medical clerk. Hopefully it allows her to regain any lost sense of self she's experienced from the moment Declan scooped me up until he set me down.

I adjust myself in my seat and notice Declan is leaning back against his chair, extending his neck while examining the back of my head. He removes his gloves and tucks them in his jacket pocket. "Here," he says, handing me a wad of Kleenex from the table. "Head injuries tend to bleed excessively."

I take the Kleenex and press it against the back of my head.

I must have a misgiving expression on my face since he quickly adds, "Even if the lesion is insignificant."

"*Insignificant?*" I repeat. If the fall didn't send my mind into a whirlwind, his vocabulary could create an eruption in my brain.

He lets out a rush of air through his nose and considers me for a moment before elaborating on his statement. "Even small head wounds seem to bleed more than they should."

"Oh," I nod, feeling like I might need a dictionary to understand the rest of our conversation.

Part of me wants to ostensibly point out that I remember him hitting his head and almost drowning at the pool. Which is how he would know about an excessively bleeding head wound. But I don't, because I know the events that unfolded after that were most likely traumatic for him. We don't know each other well enough for me to open that scar up.

Now that we are sitting here. Waiting. It's starting to sink that Declan Price and his mysterious vanishing are all sitting right next to me in a clinic waiting room chair.

It's strange that he's here. Surreal too, since we both somehow managed to be in the same place at the same time six-hundred miles from where we grew up. The last time I saw him was the summer after he graduated high school. He's so different now. I guess it's probably surreal for him to see me too since I was barely sixteen the last time we saw each other.

"Do you still play guitar?" he says curiously.

This catches me by surprise. At first, I give him a perplexed expression since no one remembers me for playing the guitar. If anyone were to remember me playing an instrument, it would be the flute in the pep band or keyboard in jazz band.

Then it registers, that he would remember me playing the guitar only if he was paying close attention to the talent show my sophomore year of high school.

I smirk, then say, "Sometimes." I shake my head, wanting to direct the conversation back to him. "Are you in grad school here?" I'm trying to come up with a way to begin filling in the blanks of his life over the last six years.

He draws his leg up by placing his shoe against his knee and arching his leg in an L-shape. It's the first time I notice that he's

5

wearing pressed pants and a charcoal sport coat that looks like it was just pulled from a rack at Bloomingdale's. His entire ensemble resembles the slacks and blazers most of the professors on campus wear. I'm certain that even the way he's sitting screams *professor* confidence.

"No," he says frowning but not in a sad way. His frown is natural against his pouting lips, and his mouth is slightly hidden behind his manicured facial hair. If it weren't for his same deep brown eyes, I might not have recognized the man he's transformed into.

"Are you a teacher?" I can almost answer that for myself after my subtle assessment of him.

He shakes his head. "No."

"No?" I tilt my chin up and run my tongue along the front of my teeth behind my lip in thought. After a moment I adjust my gaze over my shoulder to check on Avery who seems to be filling out my paperwork for me, then facing him again I say, "You could have fooled me."

He looks amused at my flustered state. "Why is that?"

"Well," I drag my eyes over his clothing and motion my hand in the same direction. "You're dressed like any other respectable professor. You're on campus, but apparently not a grad student. And your grammar and posture seem...smart."

He presses his mouth together until releasing it as his full grin spreads across his face. "Wow," he blinks, raising his eyebrows like he's satisfied with my remark. "I have intelligent posture, huh?"

I roll my eyes. *Why did I say that?*

"Actually," he says, his eyes fixed on mine. Very fixed. In a way that makes the quiver return to my stomach. "I work at the museum, but occasionally I do research on campus. That's where I was headed before I saw you."

"Really?" I raise my eyebrows, interested. And ignoring my fluttering insides. "What sort of research?" I sink into my chair, hoping it will relax the blizzard in my core.

"Linguistics," he says without missing a beat.

Well that would explain why he's such a logophile with his expanding vocabulary.

Avery plops in a chair next to me, handing the satchel back to Declan. "Linguistics?" She nudges me with her shoulder. "That's in the humanities building, isn't it? Linguistic anthropology or something?"

6

I'm nodding at her correct assumption when Declan says, "Are you both grad students?"

Avery nods vigorously, then pointing to herself she says, "Marine biology," then swinging her finger in my direction, she says, "Anthropology."

This intrigues him, but before he can open his mouth to speak, the nurse calls my name.

I begin to sit up, but Avery says, "Stay." Then she marches over to the nurse and says, "Is there a wheelchair? She has a concussion. They told you she hit her head on the ice, right?"

Declan rises to his feet and says, "It was good to see you, Christine."

"You too," I say.

"And I'm sure they'll take good care of you. You'll be healed up in no time," he winks before giving Avery a brief farewell wave. I'm taken aback by his unsubtle confidence. Maybe it just goes along with everything else he's developed himself into. I guess he always was confident when we were teenagers, but there's a new sense of confidence he has that I can't quite find a word for.

He heads for the exit but doubles back right as Avery is shoving a wheelchair in my direction.

"Oh, and Christine?" he says, pulling his gloves from his pocket. I give him a look of anticipation. "Yes?"

"Tell your brothers *hi* for me, would you?" Then without letting me answer, he turns back to the exit. Disappearing into the whiteout.

I squint my eyes at the, now, vacant entrance. Not because I'm blinded by the snow shining through the window. Maybe a little from the blinding snow. But mostly because I wasn't expecting him to say what he said.

I know he played sports with my brothers in high school and might want to reconnect with them. But in order to do that he would need my number, or at least theirs. Or tell me to come by the research department so we could catch up. He didn't even give me a chance to suggest we should get together.

Maybe he didn't want to see me again.

But I'm interested in talking with him. I'm interested in his work and intrigued by his profession. I would like to know more about what he's doing with it all. And I could tell he was interested that I'm in the anthropology program. It would make sense for us to see each other again. Maybe we'll run into each other when he's researching

7

on campus.

I've thought about him on occasion over the years, and this would have been the perfect opportunity to ease my curiosity. Especially because I've always wondered where he went after what happened at the pool that summer.

TWO

Eleven months later.

Scratching.

Or crunching sounds, rather, wakes my mind while my eyes refuse to open.

My eyes don't want to open because I know when they do, I'm going to have a mess to deal with.

"Princess," I say, with an apparent impassive tone to my sleepy voice.

There's a rapid scuffle then Princess paws down the hall to my doorway and barks without entering. She's not the brightest dog, but at least she knows she's not allowed in my bedroom.

"What did you do?" When I ask her this, I half expect her to respond even though I know she can't.

Instead of talking, she responds with another shrill bark. And I'm certain she does this because she likes me about as much as I like her. Which is not very much at all. I wonder if my voice is as painful on her ears and her barking is on mine.

I finally sit up and Princess runs back down the hall. So I follow her into the bathroom, which is where I find garbage strewn all over the floor.

I look at Princess, who is now sitting in the hallway like she's proud of herself, with an unimpressed expression. I look back at the garbage. Then once more at Princess.

"I'm not cleaning that up." I shut the bathroom door. Then Princess scurries to Avery's bedroom where she jumps up then lays in the middle of Avery's bed on alert.

Without being completely awake yet, I close Avery's door too,

9

keeping Princess locked away until Avery gets home to deal with her. *I need coffee.*

At least I'll be done with grad school in another six months. Then I won't have to deal with Princess' outbursts, and I'll have my own place. I've contemplated that I might be lonely living on my own, but after living with Avery and her tiny temperamental dog for the last five and half years, a quiet space of my own couldn't be more enticing.

My phone is flashing and vibrating on my bedside table when I return to my bedroom, so I quickly fumble over my bed to retrieve it and answer.

"Hello?" I say a little out of breath from the fumbling.

"Hello! This is Bianca from the fellowship department at the University. I'm looking for Christine Malloy?"

"This is her."

Continuing her chipper tone, she says, "Hello, Christine, I was just calling to let you know your application for the research fellowship in Papua New Guinea has been approved for this fall."

My mouth falls open, shocked that the application has already been approved. "That's great!"

"I'll send the rest of the information to you in an email, if that's alright?"

"Yes, that would be great. Thank you so much."

She sounds as if she's smiling as big as I am when she says, "Congratulations, Christine. Please give me a call if you have any questions. And have a nice rest of your day."

With my shocked exhale I say, "You too."

Then I hang up with a massive grin on my face and a soul excited for the future.

The front door opens, followed by Avery's voice. "Christine! I have a surprise for you!"

I'm not sure if she will care about the surprise I have for her. The one about me moving to the other side of the world.

Princess barks from the other side of Avery's closed bedroom door as I walk by.

When I get to the living room, Avery points toward her bedroom with a concerned expression. "Was that...?" She lets her words trail like she can't believe I might be capable of stuffing her dog away in her bedroom.

I shrug, innocently. Even though I'm not innocent. But neither

10

is Princess. I think the punishment fits the crime and I don't feel bad she's locked in Avery's room.

"I'm going to Papua New Guinea in the fall." The statement is supposed to pull her attention from the noises in her bedroom. But she doesn't seem to hear me.

She draws her eyebrows together and purses her lips before rushing to open the door. Obviously unimpressed by my dog handling skills. Or lack thereof.

She and Princess greet each other in a dance. *"Did that mean Christine lock you in my room?"* She's using one of the voices people use when they talk to animals or babies. Princess is jumping and scratching at Avery with as much energy as Avery is releasing. If I were a dog owner, I wouldn't encourage that sort of obnoxious behavior. Maybe if she didn't treat Princess like a toddler, Princess wouldn't act like a toddler and make a mess of our house all the time.

She holds Princess in her arms and I'm certain they are both masked in identical judgmental expression when they look at me. "Did you lock Princess in my room?" she asks.

I lift my gaze up to the ceiling and shift my mouth to one side, then say, "She destroyed the bathroom again."

When she sets Princess down, Princess runs in a circle around Avery's feet. "She's a dog, Christine."

"So that makes it okay for her to ruin the bathroom?"

"It's normal dog behavior," she says dismissing my question.

Releasing a long breath to calm myself and determined to get out of this conversation, I say, "Did you say you had a surprise?"

Deterring the conversation works. Avery raises her eyebrows up and down rapidly before digging in her purse. She hands me a paper with her name and contact information along with the word *Winner* written across the top. "I won!" she says.

"I see that." I flip the card around, searching for some sort of indication of what exactly she's won. "What's it for?"

"Bikram."

I crease my forehead, confused, and search her face for an answer while Princess is jumping at her legs again.

Picking up Princess, she says, "It's like yoga but they turn the heat up to like one hundred degrees."

"Sounds awful." My negative response is reminding me that I still haven't had my coffee yet and I should probably stop talking until I do. I gave all my positive energy to Bianca on our short phone call.

Avery follows me into the kitchen. "It's not awful at all. It's amazing and it's good for you."

I pour water into the coffee machine and press the start button. "Well, congratulations." I'm trying my best to be positive. In my defense, her dog did ruin the bathroom. And I might be taking it out on Avery a little bit.

"Where did you win that from anyway?" I say.

"They had a drawing at the coffee shop."

"And you're the lucky winner. Good for you."

"We both are."

I tilt my head. The aroma of the coffee brewing just isn't enough to get my brain cells working quite yet since I can't figure out if she's talking about her and Princess or her and me. "*We* are the winners?"

She nods and nuzzles Princess. "Yep," she flashes her eyes at me. "One winner and a guest. And you're my guest." Her face falls flat when I don't respond. "You're welcome."

I shake my head. "I don't want to go. Take Brent."

She blows raspberries and scrunches her nose. "Brent would hate it."

I widen my eyes and bore them into her. "So would I!"

Ignoring my emotionally infused comment, she says, "Brent is busy anyway." She retrieves Princess' leash and hooks it to her collar. "I'll take Princess for her walk, and we can go when I get back. So get dressed."

"I'm sorry, I'm not going with you. Find another guest."

I'm standing on a faded purple and blue striped beach towel in a room that's somehow acquired the heat and humidity of muggy east Texas air in the middle of August.

"Isn't this place so cute?" Avery says sprawling across her yoga mat. "The heat feels so good after being out in the cold, doesn't it?"

I give her a sad attempt at a smile.

I could walk out right now. But that would only encourage her to try harder to get me to stay. So, I give her my best attempt at a sincere smile to satisfy her expectations of me.

It seems to work since she smiles back and then turns her attention to herself in the mirror, stretching her arms over her head.

After a moment, the instructor strides to the front of the room. He's wearing what I would describe as nothing more than underwear and he's already sweating. When I look in the massive mirror at the front of the room, I realize I am too.

Note to self, never wear grey cotton if you're trying to hide the fact that you're perspiring.

The instructor jumps right into it.

I admit, the first few stretches feel great. I also surprise myself at how flexible I am, even though this is a beginner class. Avery must be surprised too because I notice her trying to push herself a little deeper in each pose, which is a quick indication that she's trying to compete with me.

Then, the instructor motions us to follow him into a pretzel. I forget what the move is really called but the twist in my torso, along with the thick humid heat, is enough to force my morning coffee up into my throat.

I cover my mouth and stand straight up.

"Christine?" Avery whispers over the ethereal music with a furrowed brow.

A guy with dreads next to Avery glances at me with a frown, like I'm interrupting the entire class by feeling sick.

I steady myself, swallow hard, and then place my hands on my hips. I quietly say, "I'll be right back."

She doesn't question me, and folds back over into the pose.

I weave through the people in their half cactus poses. Wobbly cactuses. Then I make my way out to the lobby.

The young girl at the front desk looks up at me but doesn't say anything when I rush to gather my boots and head outside.

I rest my back against the brick building once I'm outside and close my eyes while I steady all the nauseated pulsing in my body with each deep exhale. I don't mind that it's November and basically winter in Washington. My body is responding much better to the frigid temperature than to whatever weather they were trying to recreate in that room.

"Christine?"

I open my eyes.

"You're going to get hypothermia dressed like that."

Declan is standing in front of me with a similar expression as the one he had a year ago when I slipped on the ice. And my eyes are flashing open in the same surprised way as they did then too.

I assess myself and can see how concerning my appearance looks since I'm wearing sweaty grey shorts, a tank-top, and snow boots while the temperature is well under forty degrees.

I point down to the entrance of the Bikram building. "Avery made me come with her to yoga on steroids. It made me sick."

He looks at the entrance then drags his eyes down my front. "It must be terrible if you'd rather be standing out here in the cold."

"That's an understatement. I think I sweat my entire cheeseburger from last night out of my pores while I was in there." I quickly wish I hadn't said that. Especially because I'm not sure how he will take my humor.

He's unzipping the front of his coat as his eyes scan the building. "I've walked past this place every day for the last three years and never once considered what they were doing in there." He pulls his coat off as his eyes land on mine. "But now I'm curious to see what everyone else is sweating out of their pores."

I let out a short laugh with my breath. I'm also more intrigued by him now that I know he's witty.

Declan motions for me to move closer, so I pull myself from the wall and approach him. "Here," he says, wrapping me in his coat. "You wouldn't want to catch a cold before the holidays."

I adjust his coat, unsure of how I feel about the way he's so comfortable offering it to me in this familiar way.

"Yeah," I say with hesitation. "Or finals."

He folds his arms over his chest and drags his tongue across his bottom lip, considering me. "That's right, you said you were in the anthropology department, didn't you?"

I nod, feeling strange; consumed by the warmth of his coat. "Social-cultural anthropology. And I'm headed to Papua New Guinea for fieldwork in the fall."

He considers me without words. Which returns the quiver to my stomach he somehow manages to thrust at me with his heavy gaze.

I squeeze my arms around myself, forcing my body to return to its normal un-quivering state. "Which is probably why I haven't seen you," I say. "Linguistics seems like an entirely different department."

His smile lines dent into his face. "That, and I haven't been doing much research in the last year." I'm not sure why that statement accompanies a grin like the one he's giving me.

"Why not?" I hope that question doesn't sound too intrusive, but I'm honestly curious.

His grin shifts down as he tightens his jaw subtly, but enough to indicate he might not want to share that information. With an exhale, he says, "There's a lot going on at work right now that keeps me preoccupied and I'm working on another project in my free time."

I nod, unsatisfied with his general response.

His posture relaxes as he changes the attention from himself to me. "How's everything with you?" He lifts his chin, and extends his neck, searching the place where I hit the back of my head, without moving from his position. "Looks like they fixed your head injury."

"Yeah, five staples later."

"Staples? Ouch."

"Yeah, I guess it's faster than stitches." I touch the hidden scar. "Plus, my hair covers it, so it didn't need to heal pretty."

The door opens and I flip my head toward the sound.

A woman exits the building with a yoga mat, followed moments later by a young man with a tattoo sleeve covering his leg.

At least I'm not the only one in shorts out here.

"I guess I missed the class," I say with a shrug.

Declan hasn't pulled his eyes from me. He doesn't respond to my comment and instead says, "Did you tell your brothers *hi* for me?"

I shake my head. I'm surprised he remembered that he had said that since it's been almost an entire year since I've seen him. "I will though." I laugh nervously with my smile. "I have to warn you, they might try to sell you something or get you to join their cult."

He draws his head back, raising one brow. "Their cult? Really?"

I roll my eyes. "It's not really a cult. They are entrepreneurs and run a pyramid scheme together."

He folds his mouth for a moment, then drops his head with his laughter. It makes me laugh too.

"But when they're not trying to sell you shaving cream," I say. "They're still the same as you probably remember."

He's coming down from his laughter when he says, "Are they in Washington too?"

I shake my head. "Nope, still in Nevada with my mom." I tilt my head realizing how that sounds. "Well, they have their own houses, but live on the other side of town as my mom." I don't want him to think my brothers are running a multilevel marketing company in my mother's basement.

The way the door bursts open and hits the side of the building makes me wish this moment wasn't about to be interrupted by Avery.

I close my eyes gently as I prepare for whatever she's about to say.

She thrusts my rolled beach towel at my sternum. "You said you would be right back," she announces to the entire block.

"Sorry, it made me sick to be in there." I motion to Declan. "Then I ran into Declan and we were catching up and sharing what's new." I guess I've been the only one catching Declan up on my life. Not by choice, Declan seems like he doesn't want to share much.

She nods with narrowed eyes shifting between me and Declan before she says, "And apparently sharing clothing too."

I drag Declan's coat from my shoulders and hold it out for him, hoping Avery chokes on her words.

He takes the coat, and instead of putting it back on, he folds it over his arm then places his hands into his pants pockets. "Nice to see you again, Avery."

Her eyes are still narrowed when her grin beams up at him. "You too, *Declan*." The way she annunciates his name is a sure indication that she's going to do everything in her power to set us up. "What are you doing on this side of town?"

He shifts his torso and nods in the direction of the street. "I work at the museum, there." He tips his head in the opposite direction. "And I like to have breakfast at the bistro down the street before work."

I'm watching their body language and interested to see how Declan declines her set up once he realizes where she's taking this conversation.

Avery raises her brow, assessing his response. "Mmm hmm, okay." She's also nodding, and it's beginning to annoy me.

Declan doesn't blink. As if he's anticipating more interrogation from her. *And welcoming it.*

I take my coat from Avery and slip it on. It fits much better than Declan's coat that was like a blanket over my shoulders, but my coat doesn't smell as nice as his.

"Do you have a girlfriend?" she finally asks. Honestly, it surprises me that it took her so long to insert this question. It's as if she's made it her mission to set me up with every single guy we come in close contact with. Although, it is a little mortifying that she's asking someone I know this time. But it also makes me more curious to know his answer.

"No, I don't have a girlfriend," he says, as if he's just been asked a common mundane question.

"Wife?"

16

"No."

"Secret mistress?"

I smack her arm with the back of my hand. "Stop," I say, only because I must remind myself that I'm not doing anthropological fieldwork right now and I'm allowed to intervene on behalf of poor Declan who is at the mercy of Avery and her insanity.

She ignores me. "You two knew each other in high school, right?"

I'm biting the inside of my bottom lip now, because I'm hoping she doesn't bring up the incident at the pool which I had mentioned to her in a brief conversation after our encounter with Declan last year.

He nods with a grin full of intrigue.

"So it totally wouldn't be weird if she brought you as her date to my boyfriend's New Year's Eve party?" She beams with anticipation.

I release my breath. *She's not going to bring up the pool thing.*

I quickly prepare my mind to accept his decline to her ridiculous invitation.

Declan is still looking at Avery with the same interested expression, when he glances at me before saying, "Not weird at all. I'd love to."

"No," I say instinctually. "Seriously, I'm fine going stag. You probably have plans already." I face Avery. "Could you stop meddling?" I say with clenched teeth.

Avery pulls her phone from her pocket and begins tapping and swiping at the screen. "I need to tell Brent you found a date." She hugs her phone against her ear. "Meet you at the car," she says to me as she heads for the street. Before she reaches the car, she waves at Declan and says, "See you at the party!"

I'm normally much better at these situations Avery puts me in. They always end the same.

She'll invite a guy to take me out. He declines by coming up with an absurd excuse or tries to reschedule but never follows up.

It's not a big deal. I have more to look forward to in life than dating.

And normally, I'm not very interested in them to start with.

But this isn't *normally.*

This isn't a random guy.

This is *Declan staring down at me with a smug grin.*

I try to give him an out. "Really, you don't have to—"

17

"I want to," he interjects, gently.

I narrow my gaze, trying to figure him out. It's something I do without even realizing. Like all the textbooks, fieldwork, and projects I've invested myself in over the last five and a half years are branded into my responses. And right now, my analyzing is telling me that Declan is either that lonely—that he would spend his New Year's Eve with a person like me. A young woman with a dull life who can't even handle ten minutes of Bikram yoga without having a nauseated reaction. Or he's looking for something from me that I don't think I can offer him.

Either way, I stuff down the fact that I'm a little excited to be going to a party with someone as handsome and intelligent as Declan Price.

At least with him by my side I'll look like I belong there.

"I'll give you my number," he says.

I hand him my phone and watch as his smile grows while he adds his contact information.

Handing me my phone, he says, "I'll see you on New Year's Eve."

"That's more than a month away," I say. "Should I call you? Or text you a reminder?" Can he tell I've never been on a date before?

He's sliding his arms back into his coat sleeves now. "Sure," he says, as I notice his shoulders look like they might burst the seams of his coat.

"Okay," I lift my phone above my head as he begins walking backwards with his eyes on me and the same grin on his face that causes my stomach to quiver. "I'll call you."

Before he flips around, he says, "It was good to see you again, Christine."

"You too," I say, unsettled. Then I watch him with interest. Not just because he's indescribably attractive, but also because he seems to leave me with more questions after our encounters. And I wish I could get some answers to those questions.

Like, *what happened to you after high school?*

And, *how did you end up here working at a museum?*

And, *why linguistics?*

And, *why me?*

And, *what are you thinking when you look at me like that?*

Just before I open the door to Avery's car, I look at his contact on my phone. Which causes me to glance up once more to see

Declan's silhouette shrinking into the distance. But not before he looks back over his shoulder at me. It sends a jolt down my ribcage, and I suck in an unexpected rush of air. I'm not sure how to take his behavior. No guy that compelling could be interested in a girl like me.

I put my seatbelt on and shift in my seat. Unsettled by the unfolding events of the last thirty seconds.

"What?" Avery says as I climb into her car.

I press the button to turn my heat seat on. "What do you mean, *what?*"

"You look all…" she twists her face, "…bothered."

I tip my head towards her and blink, unimpressed. "Bothered?"

"Yeah, like…" her expression falls, and she says, "Oh no, did he decide not to go with you to the party?" Then she sits up abruptly, and her voice hardens. "Or you convinced him not to go with you? Christine, if you rejected him—"

"I didn't," I say. "He's taking me to the party."

She smiles and her voice goes back to normal. "Oh good." She faces traffic but waits for the light to change before putting her car into gear. "Then what's the problem? He's like an Italian Armani Exchange model with a brain."

I laugh, because it's unbelievable how correct her statement is. But I'm not going to tell her that she's also correct about me feeling bothered.

"Also, there's this." I lift my phone in front of her so she can see his contact.

Her eyes widen, then flash up at me. "Are you kidding me?"

THREE

"Whipped cream?" my mother asks, hovering the tub above my head.

I nod. Then she plops a massive spoonful on top of my slice of pumpkin pie. "Thanks," I say.

She continues around the table, making sure everyone is served diabetes inducing amounts of whipped cream over their Thanksgiving pie. I'm at the age now where I wonder why we aren't allowed to serve ourselves. But for as long as I can remember—and for every meal—my mom has made sure to serve us in this same way. Although, she was typically only serving my brothers and me. Now, she's challenging her skills and quick serving abilities with a full table seated with nine relatives, in total.

Uncle Drew doesn't bother trying to convince my mother otherwise. I have to wonder if maybe her traditional behavior is something she learned from their mother—my grandmother—and Uncle Drew just thinks my mother's acting normal.

"How's the pie?" my mother says, finally taking her seat.

We nod with delightful moans through our mouthfuls. My mother couldn't look more thrilled. Even though she's an attorney with thick courtroom verbiage, and a voice that carries, she seems to keep her heart at home in the kitchen with her family.

Avery sips her drink, then, to my mother, says, "Aunt Diane, has Christine told you about her boyfriend?"

I'm immediately aware of how unnoticed I normally am at family gatherings when I realize this is the first time my entire family has given their full attention at once.

I keep my eyes fixed on Avery. "I don't have a boyfriend."

"Yet," she adds with sass.

I will never understand Avery's intense need to recreate the truth. Thankfully, my family is fully aware of her amplified tendencies. So I don't have to elaborate on Avery's exaggeration. Although I want to.

My brothers are both smacking their mouths as they chew their food. It's one of their many twin mannerisms.

Our mother hands Tallen a napkin and says, "Give that to Parker, he's made a mess of his face already."

Typically, her comment is something that's saved for young children, but my mother has been saying this same statement to my adult brothers since I can remember.

Instead of handing the napkin to Parker like a normal human being, Tallen presses the napkin into Parker's face and smears the whipped cream around. Maybe the distraction of my brothers will pull everyone's attention away from me.

Parker shoves the napkin away and it falls to the floor, so he leans down to pick it up. "You're such a tool," he says to Tallen.

But when he sits back up, Tallen holds Parker's head down and says, *"Clean your face Parker, you're a mess."* Mimicking our mother's voice.

Parker takes Tallen's arm and pulls himself free. "I'm about to make a mess of your face," he says aggressively locking his free arm around Tallen's head and bumping into the table which causes the glasses to teeter.

Before they can turn their behavior into a full-blown wrestling match, our mom claps her hands together and says, "Boys, knock it off! You're about to break my table." Another statement not meant to be used on grown men.

They quickly release each other and return to their food as if nothing happened. I'm not sure when brothers are supposed to grow out of rough housing, but my brothers seem to regress every time we're home and especially if there's an audience. Not that their behavior is new to any of us, aside from Brent who seems to be avoiding eye contact with everyone at the table—understandably.

Sometimes when my brothers are selling shaving cream and wearing suits while talking to clients, I don't even recognize them. It was the same in high school, they were a team that was against the world when they were in public.

But at home, it's another story.

My mom rests her chin in her hand and turns her attention back

21

to me. "Christine," she says when I don't say anything.

I fork a piece of pie into my mouth, hoping it will give me time to come up with something to divert the attention on something else besides me.

Aunt Milly, who managed to infuse her personality into Avery while she was still in her womb, says, "Christine, your mother asked you a question."

My mom didn't ask me anything. But I'm not going to argue with Aunt Milly, because for how much Avery annoys me, her mother scares me that much more.

I sip my water, then say, "Sorry, I wasn't trying to be rude. There's just nothing to tell."

Avery raises her eyebrows with her eyes focused on her plate. "That's not what your cell phone says." It's a shame we're not allowed to choose who we're related to. Sometimes I wonder if I would even be friends with Avery if we weren't cousins.

It takes Parker two seconds to decide to snatch my phone and begin punching numbers on my lock screen. "What's your password?" he says.

I let him continue his failing attempt to crack the code on my phone.

Tallen nods in my direction. "What's on your cell phone, Chris?"

I shrug. "Nothing."

"Liar," Avery says, still without looking at me. Probably because she knows she's the *liar*. She nudges Brent, who is sitting next to her. "Tell them Brent! You saw it too."

Brent's blue eyes widen like a deer in the headlights. Poor guy. I have to feel sorry for him since our family is worse than a Kardashian episode. I'll be surprised if he stays with Avery after tonight.

Avery nudges him again. "Brent," she says, as if she's warning him.

Brent searches the table with his eyes, then drags his words out when he says, "I don't feel comfortable talking about it."

Parker instantly tosses my phone at me. It hits me in the arm before dropping to the floor.

I face him with a blasé expression. "Did you have to throw it at me like that?" I'm starting to wish I had stayed at my tiny town house with a bowl of cereal for Thanksgiving.

"Sorry, Brent's comment was…alarming," Parker says.

"Why's that?" I'm not sure why I'm entertaining whatever game he's playing.

Parker continues, "I was worried if I got into your phone, I was going to see something I didn't want to see."

"Like what?" Tallen says curiously.

Parker gives him a knowing look.

Tallen glances at me, then back to Parker and they both make a disgusted face, before saying, "*Nudes*," in unison. I'm not sure if talking at the same time is one of their twin superpowers, or one of the most irritating attributes about them.

Avery's mouth opens, *again*, and she begins to say, "Her boyfriend put—"

But my mom raises her hand in Avery's direction, and says, "Hush, Avery, no one asked you."

Aunt Milly and Avery share a wide-eyed look, as their blonde hair shifts over their shoulders with their turning heads. Even though they seem offended, they both know not to challenge my mother.

I want to laugh, but I'd rather not make Avery upset with me. So I retrieve my phone from under the table and unlock the screen. "It's nothing, really." I open my contacts and flip my phone around to show my screen to my mom and Uncle Drew, who are sitting next to each other and just so happen to be the only two people at this table with any sort of social intelligence at all.

Uncle Drew raises his salt and pepper-colored brows and nods at me. "It's about time, Christine." It makes me a little sad that he says this. Like everyone has been waiting my whole life for a guy to be interested in me.

My mom gives me an endearing smile, then says, "Well, if it blooms into something, I'd love to meet him."

"You already have," I say. "It's Declan Price, from high school."

Parker takes my phone again, *without asking*, and hovers it in front of his and Tallen's faces. "Declan Price is your boyfriend?" he says with astonishment to my phone screen.

"He's not my boyfriend." I correct.

Tallen leans around Parker to look at me better. "Does Declan know that?"

Avery chimes in with, "I'm not so sure he does."

Aunt Milly's eyes are fixed on my phone, but she's on the other side of the table so she has no idea what they're looking at. "What is it?" she says failing at trying not to sound too nosey. The fact that she's feeling left out makes me a little bit happier, which I know is wrong. But I like to marinate in these moments for every time she was ever too nosey or passive aggressive toward me.

Being submerged in my family is like its own culture. It almost feels like fieldwork observing them. And what I've learned from fieldwork is that sometimes, if you wait long enough, bullies get what they deserve. And that's sort of what is happening now with Aunt Milly.

Avery faces her prying mother, and when they lock eyes, she says, "He put a poem as his contact name in her phone."

Aunt Milly perks up. "A poem? What does it say?"

I bite at my lip for a moment, remembering the words I've shamefully read a thousand times over on my phone since Declan put it in there a week ago. Then, with my gaze fixed on nothing in particular in front of me but deep within my mind at the memory of Declan looking back at me from the sidewalk, I say, "*Of all forms of caution, caution in love is perhaps the most fatal to true happiness.*"

"He wrote that?" Aunt Milly says, dumbfounded.

"No," I shake my head. "Bertrand Russell did." I only know this fact because a quick google search told me.

"Well," she blinks arrogantly. "I don't see how a stolen poem is so special."

Avery rolls her eyes. "It's the thought, Mom. And the fact that he memorized it and put it in her phone in a split second. It's nothing short of a dream." This is a dramatic truth from Avery that I'm willing to accept.

"Oh," Aunt Milly says, with a cheek full of pie. Then pointing her fork to Brent, she says, "Why didn't you think of doing that for Avery?"

Uncle Drew finally looks up from his plate to his wife, and says, "Milly, no man is that romantic." This makes me feel better. Like I've won a prize by receiving poetry from Declan.

Parker hands my phone back to me. "Apparently, Declan Price is." To me, he says, "How's he doing anyway? I haven't seen him in years."

I place my phone on my lap where Parker can't snatch it again. "He's good. He works at the museum."

Everyone is nodding with intrigue, waiting for more.

I continue, "He studied linguistics at the University. The same building I'm in, actually." I can't help but smile knowing Declan has walked through the same entrance as I have. Maybe if we were the same age, we would have taken some classes together.

My mother looks impressed. "Really?"

Tallen grins, like he's just learned the truth about a secret he always suspected of Declan. "That explains the poetry." Even though my brothers are twins, Tallen has always been the more grounded and accepting of the two.

Aunt Milly tilts her head in confusion, then says, "Linguistics?"

My mom must sense Avery is about to spew something regrettable to Aunt Milly, because she quickly says, "It's the study of language." Then to me she says, "How long have you two been talking?"

"She still hasn't texted him," Avery interjects before I can answer.

I narrow my eyes at her in place of rolling them. Which somehow still feels immature.

Tallen scoots his empty plate, making room to set his arms on the table in front of him and focuses in on me. "Chris, don't be rude. Text the guy back before he thinks you're not interested."

Parker nudges me with a grin in Tallen's direction. "She probably doesn't know how to text a guy since she's never had a boyfriend."

"Not by choice," I say defensively.

Parker tilts his head, like I've just given him a false statement. "It kind of is, since you bury yourself in school. I mean, have you even looked in the mirror lately?"

My mom begins gathering the empty plates from the table, and defends me with, "Academics are a priority in this family."

"I'm not saying they're not," Parker says. "But there's got to be balance."

"I have balance," I say. "Sometimes I wear jeans and fix my hair. And I have friends from my study group that I hang out with all the time."

My brothers dip their chins in unison, unimpressed, since technically hanging out with my study group friends falls under the same category as school.

"I went to yoga with Avery last week," I say more defensively.

They look at Avery for reassurance, since they know yoga isn't something I would normally do.

"That's true," she says. "Although you left and never came back because you were preoccupied with *Declan*."

Tallen smacks his hand on the table. "Text him."

"He told me to tell you guys *hi*," I say.

25

"*Text him*," both Tallen and Parker say this at the same time. Which makes me let out a deep exhale and retrieve my phone from my lap.

I turn my phone screen off and tuck it under my leg since I don't trust Parker's grabby hands. And I know they're not going to give this up easily. At least with my phone hidden, they won't be able to snatch it from me again. "It's Thanksgiving, he's probably with his family," I say trying to end the conversation.

"Which means he's probably in town," Tallen says.

So much for ending the conversation.

Parker shakes his head at me. Like he's disappointed and thinks I should be beyond where I'm at in life. "Chris, you need to take care of yourself and live a little."

Harsh. But I'm used to his blunt words. "I live a lot," I say. "And I like my life just the way it is."

"If there's any guy I would be happy for you to be with, it would be Declan," Parker says. "So, start brushing your hair and don't screw it up."

Without facing us, Tallen says, "She's right." His comment seems out of place, but I notice his phone in his hands and his eyes glued to the screen.

I'm instantly suspicious of what he's doing. I narrow my eyes in his direction, waiting for an explanation.

"He's with his family," Tallen says with a proud grin.

I don't return the smile he's giving, because I hope it will deter him from pushing this whole thing with Declan any further.

Parker leans over to see what Tallen is staring at, then says, "Invite him over."

My face goes hot. Because I know exactly what Tallen is doing. "Please don't," I beg Tallen.

He turns his phone off and grins at me again, this time showing me all the teeth in his mouth with his smile. "Too late."

"Did you just text Declan?" Avery says in shock.

Tallen shakes his head and blows raspberries. "No, I'm not going to steal his number from my sister's phone and text him. That would be creepy." Because he's my brother, and I've witnessed this same facial expression from him my entire life, I know he's partially telling the truth. Which means the other part is a big fat lie and he's done the unthinkable and somehow contacted Declan.

Parker leans closer to Tallen and says, "Maybe we could get him to sign up for Shaven?"

Tallen nods. "Good idea."

"You didn't text him?" Avery creases her brows. "Then how do you know he's with his family and how did you invite him over to join your pyramid scheme?"

"*MLM*," they respond to her in unison.

She must be over this discussion, since she says, "You two are unbelievable." She shakes her head and rises from the table with Brent following in step. "I'm going to take Princess for a walk."

My mother and Aunt Milly begin clearing the table and start on the dishes while Uncle Drew flips the TV on and sits on the couch.

I keep myself seated at the table. Fumbling my phone in my hands and periodically searching Declan's contact; re-reading the poem. Contemplating what to do next. This entire situation has my pulse throbbing like a fifteen-year-old. I can admit that Declan has always been easy to look at, but when we were in high school, I never saw him without a girlfriend. And his type of girl beamed with blonde highlights and winged eyeliner. He didn't pay attention to ordinary girls like me. Which is probably why I'm keeping him at arms-length now. As if I'm waiting for this to be some sort of strange dream, or worse, a humiliating nightmare.

Tallen and Parker are in the front room, already discussing how they're going to coax Declan into joining Shaven, their organic shaving cream brand they curated after completing business school.

I smash myself between them on the loveseat without a word. It's the same behavior I've done on countless occasions, and especially when they are causing havoc in my life.

"Chris, you're kind of interrupting us right now," Parker says, as his smile falls flat. As if I didn't know what I was doing. He scoots away from me, and I sink further into the loveseat.

"I think she's still mad," Tallen says leaning forward and looking around me at Parker. Then to me he says, "Why aren't you happy? You know we're doing you a favor, right?"

I give him my best grumpy-pouting face.

He grins. "Come on, Chris. In our defense, we were friends with him first. It's not random if we reach out to him and invite him over."

I guess that's true. But they were friends with him *before* he liked me, and *before* I had his phone number, and *before* we were adults.

"You stole his number from my phone," I say. "That's wrong,

whether you were friends first or not."

He shakes his head. "No, I wouldn't do that to you." I can tell his statement is honest.

I blink, waiting for him to elaborate.

He lets out a defeated breath, then, "Instagram."

I scrunch my nose. *"Ta-a-allen..."* My voice is slightly whiney when I say this. Mostly because I can't accept that this is happening, and I want to restart the entire evening. If time travel were a thing, instead of allowing Avery to open her mouth, I would have tossed my pie at her face which would have redirected the entire events that unfolded this evening.

"What?" he says with a complacent grin.

"Stalking him on Instagram is worse." I drag my hands down my face in horror because somehow my brothers always seem to cause unnecessary stress in my life. No matter how old we are. I blink up at him. "You really DM'd him on Instagram?"

He nods, matter of factly. "I did."

"You invited him over after I basically ghosted him for a week?" This is exactly why I keep myself submerged in my studies.

"I did."

"But I ghosted him."

He tilts his head and looks up, thinking. "That's your fault, not mine."

"Did you really invite him over?"

"I did."

"Did he DM you back?"

"He did."

"And he's coming over?"

He nods. "He is."

I make a groaning sound and flop my arms over my face. "Tallen, why do you act like your actions have no consequences?"

"Hey," Parker says. "Look at the bright side. Now you can apologize to Declan's face for ignoring him after he wrote you a love poem."

I punch his arm playfully. "Do you guys understand how mortifying this is for me?"

They look at each other. Smile. Then, *"Yes."*

I sit up and motion toward the stairs where the bedrooms are. Because if Declan Price is coming over to my childhood home, my place of comfort and rest, I better make myself look more presentable than the last two run ins I've had with him.

But before I reach the stairway, before I'm able to fix my hair or change into something other than the sweatpants I've been wearing for the last two days, and before I can prepare myself mentally for this moment—Declan has approached the house and is looking at me through the window at the entrance door.

FOUR

When I realize there's nothing I can do. That retreating to my old bedroom would only make this situation worse. And that the longer I stare at Declan through the window, the stranger I will appear. I decide to open the door, and let him in.

"Hey," he says with a friendly smile. He looks just as polished and fresh as the other times I've seen him. It's the opposite of how I maintain myself when I'm home visiting my family. Which is why I'm in the same t-shirt and sweats from yesterday.

"Come in," I say, opening the door wider, allowing him to step through. I'm hyperaware of the fact that I'm slouching. As if slouching is going to hide my grungy appearance.

When he passes me, I get a whiff of the same fragrance that consumed the coat he draped over my shoulders last week.

He narrows his eyes at me with his grin. "I honestly thought I would hear from you before one of your brothers reached out to me."

My mouth falls open. But nothing comes out.

I hoped we would both ignore that fact. But here he is, standing in front of me, addressing the elephant in the room as if it's no big deal.

I'm sure, despite how confident he is, I managed to impair his pride by not texting him. Especially after the poem.

"I-I'm sorry," I say, gently bumping into the entryway table. "I was going to text you. But I've been busy with school, and then thanksgiving, and—"

"You've been on my mind," he says blatantly.

I swallow hard. His statement hits my stomach. And I'm not sure how to decipher it. With widened eyes, I say, "I have?"

He closes the space between us with the same gripping expression he's had since he walked through the door. "It was troubling not hearing from you."

I search his expression, unsure how to respond. No one has ever treated me like this before. So, if it's flirting he's after, I don't have a clue what to say, or do, or even think right now.

His jaw tightens briefly before he says, "Wouldn't you worry if the last two times you saw me, I experienced a head injury and then was standing partially clothed in the cold?"

But before I can answer, not that I know how I would answer that question mostly because of the honeyed sound his voice is making in my ears, Parker's—not so honeyed—voice infuses the entrance pulling my attention from Declan. "Is that Declan Price, already?" he says.

I glance back at Declan for a moment, but I fall stricken when his gaze is still pasted on me.

Tallen follows in step with Parker.

"It's been a minute, hasn't it?" Tallen says. "You look good, man."

Declan finally releases the tension I'm feeling by turning and acknowledging my brothers.

The trio greet each other, and I have a sudden urge to escape before my brothers humiliate me any further.

※

"That poem was an impressive tactic," Aunt Milly's voice somehow carries from all the way downstairs in the kitchen up to my old bedroom where I'm hiding. "Where'd you learn that trick?" she asks Declan.

I.

Could.

Die.

I'm fully regretting sharing that poem with Avery. And my brothers. And especially Aunt Milly.

"Leave the man alone," my mother says, knowing all too well that Aunt Milly will press an uncomfortable subject until a person is so red in the face that bystanders experience secondhand embarrassment.

Everyone has made their rounds with Declan. First my brothers. Understandably. They needed to catch up and reminisce about their high school days playing football and basketball together. Uncle

31

Drew said *hello*, Declan said *hey*. When Avery came back from her dog walk, she introduced Brent. Declan focused on Brent's life and was impressed by how Brent accidently got rich investing in Amazon in its early development. Which was right around the time my mother and Aunt Milly laser focused in on how *handsome* Declan is.

And *smart*.

And *driven*.

And *romantic*.

Ugh.

They did not just call him *romantic*. And all these words are echoing up to my bedroom. Making it that much harder to want to face him.

I.

Could.

Die.

"You know you're making this a lot more awkward by hiding out in your room, right?" Avery enters my bedroom, with a searching finger scanning across my bookshelf.

"I should've just texted him." I fall back on my bed and cover my face with my pillow.

Avery makes a sound in her throat in place of saying I-told-you-so, then flips a book open.

I pull the pillow from my face and turn to my side, bunching the pillow under my head. I've contemplated changing and putting some mascara on, but that feels even more awkward. And knowing my family, they would comment about it in front of Declan. Making this whole situation worse. If that's possible.

How has a relaxing Thanksgiving with my family turned into a stress induced experience?

She looks back at me briefly with a mischievous expression, then sits on the edge of my bed. "*Declan Price*," she says, sitting up a little straighter with each annunciated syllable. "*Homecoming King*."

I sit up, peering over her shoulder at my old sophomore yearbook. Which means it was Declan's senior year. There's a photo of him and Timber Stein at halftime during the football game. Both have crowns on their heads and smiles plastered on their faces.

What's not pictured, but is still very much there in my memory, is his girlfriend, runner-up Jess Thompson's scowling face. And just ten feet to the right of her was me in the front row of the pep band playing my flute to the melody of *I Love Rock and Roll* by The Hit

Crew, right before we transitioned into *The Hey Song* as the football players returned to the field.

"I bet he was Prom King too," she says without looking up.

I reach over and flip to the back of the yearbook. Skipping over the prom photos of Declan and Timber crowned Prom King and Queen.

"Oooo, Senior Survey," Avery says raising her eyebrows up and down. "Declan Price and Timber Stein, *Best Looking*." She rolls her eyes. "That's not a surprise. Homecoming royalty and best-looking go hand and hand. Do they really need to credit them for being ridiculously attractive?"

I nudge her with a smile. "Keep going."

She clears her throat with a giddy grin that takes me right back to when we were in middle school before my parents' divorce. Like we are a couple of silly tween girls searching Tallen and Parker's year books and giggling over their friends.

She points to the picture of Declan and Jess. "Declan Price and Jessica Thompson, *most likely to vote for themselves*."

We laugh.

Although, I'm not sure Declan is at all that self-absorbed now.

Avery reads on, skipping the girls in the photo and instead skimming through each page and naming Declan's successes on the Senior Survey. "Declan Price, *most likely to succeed*."

I read the next one. "Declan Price, *most muscular*."

"Declan Price, *best storyteller*."

"Declan Price, *most athletic*."

"Declan Price, *biggest flirt*."

We cut our eyes to each other.

We don't have to say anything to know we both have the same thought. But Avery opens her mouth anyway. Probably because she was born without the cognitive ability to filter her thoughts before they come shooting out of her mouth. "You don't think that he wrote that poem because he's just a flirt trying to get into your pants, do you?"

Before I can speak, Declan clears his throat. He leans a shoulder on the doorframe, crossing his arms over his thick chest when we face him.

Avery closes the yearbook with a slap and does the most disloyal thing she can do, and says, "Well I'm going to see if Dad...needs help...with..."

Her words are broken as Declan's head is turning with his stare that's following her movements out of the room, anticipating her to finish her statement.

When she doesn't, I say, "You really think your dad needs help watching TV?" I might be trying to get her to shoot some more words out of her mouth. Or at least stay in this room a little longer so the fact that Declan standing in the threshold of my bedroom can sink in before she leaves.

But instead, Avery mouths *sorry* to me then disappears around Declan and down the hall.

Then, I'm alone.

With Declan.

I like being alone with Declan. But I don't know *how* to be alone with Declan.

He stays in position, leaning on the doorframe.

I hope he didn't hear us talking about his superlative achievements in the yearbook. "How was your Thanksgiving?" I say, biting at the inside of my cheek so I don't smile too much.

"It was good. My parents made a ham. My sister and her family were there most of the day, so I got to play with my nephews." I feel my heart melt at the imaginary images in my mind of him and his nephews playing together. "And my brother gets to spend the rest of the holiday with us until school starts up again on Monday."

I squint, trying to remember his brother. "You have a brother?"

He nods. "Younger. He's thirteen."

I don't know much about his family. I mean, I barely knew his older sister, Winnie. So it wouldn't be strange if I never met his brother.

"I didn't know your parents had a kid that young."

"They didn't." He says this so clipped that I get the sense that he doesn't want to talk about why his brother is thirteen years old and thirteen years younger than him. Or why his brother *gets* to spend the holiday with his parents. Insinuating that he's not normally at their house.

I decide to change the subject from his brother to him. "You can come in," I say, avoiding his eyes. Now that he's shown he's interested in me—I mean I think that's what he's shown with his acceptance as my date to the New Year's Eve party, the poem, and the intensity behind his eyes when he looks at me—I can't figure out where to focus my eyes.

Suddenly he unfolds his arms, tucking his hands into his pockets, and enters my bedroom. His eyes are fixed on the yearbook on my bed. Then he says, "Is it weird that I feel like I'm going to get in trouble for being in your room?"

A soft laugh escapes my nose. "Yeah, a little weird."

He untucks his hands from his pockets, picks up the yearbook and begins flipping through, scanning his eyes across the pages. Then he says, "You mean I shouldn't be afraid your brothers are going to beat me up, cancel our friendship, and take back the shaving cream they just sold me?"

I give him a wide-eyed animated expression and pop my jaw open. "They didn't!"

"They did." The only part of him that changes from its position are his eyes when they flash down at mine and hold my gaze in that heavy way they've been doing since he got here.

I'm pretty sure we can both hear my pulsing heart. So, to cover up whatever this is I'm experiencing by just being in the presence of Declan Price, homecoming king and best-looking on the Senior Survey, I say, "If anything, I'd say that buying shaving cream from them has to be some sort of insurance towards your friendship. And you'd only need that sort of insurance if my brothers were to be upset that you were in here. Which they wouldn't be because they never cared about my life when I was in high school, so I'm pretty sure they don't care about it now."

This causes him to lift his face and draw his head back. I'm not sure if his gesture is confusion or surprise. He narrows his eyes considering me for a moment, then lifts his brow. "Are you trying to humor me right now?"

My eyes search around my bedroom, perplexed by what he's insinuating. Which is that he believes my brothers do care about a guy in my bedroom. Then I get a quick glance of myself in the mirror and realize my top knot is a hot mess. I look back at him and start pulling at my hair to fix it.

With my scrunchy in my mouth and my hands acting as a brush for my bed head, I say, "Why would I joke about that?"

He rolls his head back and releases a breath of disbelief with his smile. "Did you ever wonder why you never had a boyfriend in high school?"

I stop short on my breath because he noticed I didn't have a boyfriend in high school. Which means he was paying closer attention to me than I realized. Once I can breathe again. *And think again.* I want to say, of course I wondered about that all the time. What awkward band girl doesn't? Instead of speaking, I twist my hair into a braid, securing the bottom with my oversized scrunchy.

When I don't answer his slightly bizarre question. He looks at me dumbfounded and says, "You're a Malloy."

I tilt my head, confused.

He slaps the yearbook closed and tosses it on my bed, backing up against my dresser and bracing himself with his hands. "You're a Malloy," he repeats. Except this time, he's saying it like he's also warning himself.

"You said that," I say. There's something shifting in him and I'm not sure I like it. I cross my legs and pull them under me, making room on my bed. I pat the corner. "Sit," I say.

He searches my expression curiously then sits down closer to me than I thought he would. He clasps his hands behind his neck. Rolling his head in my direction and locking his apologetic eyes on mine, as he says, "You're a Malloy, Christine. You're Christine Malloy."

"Okay?" I say, wondering how a guy that's studied words for the last eight years is falling short of them.

He flips his head around toward my door, then back to me. With a quiet voice he says, "Your brothers would have killed anyone that set foot in this bedroom when we were in high school."

I purse my lips and pull my brows together. I'm not sure if he's exaggerating. My brothers were well liked in high school, popular, jocks, and got good grades. They weren't the type to cause negative disruptions or get into fights. They could be disruptive with their pranks, but never did they injure anyone...outside of the football field. The last thing on their minds was *me*.

"They never said anything to me about it," I say.

"They didn't have to say anything to you." His eyes are fixed on mine, and he doesn't seem as disheveled anymore. "It was a long time ago," he says. "But they made sure every guy knew you were off limits."

"It probably didn't take much," I say with a stiff laugh. "I was a band geek."

"A stunning band geek."

I gasp. But only a little. But also enough to make Declan look down at my mouth.

"What is it?" I say, wiping at the corner of my mouth just in case he's staring at a pie crumb on my face. He may be used to looking at me in my hot mess appearance by now, but I'm curious if he can sense that he's turned my insides into a hot mess too.

His eyes flash between mine, and he raises his hand as if he's about to touch me. After what feels like an eternity in this tension, he closes his eyes tightly, folds his mouth in and closes his hand into a fist, dropping it at his side.

He shakes his head with a laugh as he blinks up at the ceiling. "You're Christine Malloy." He says this to himself more than to me.

I'm so confused. "So, I'm Christine Malloy. What about it?"

He clasps his hands together and braces his elbows on his spread knees. His back expands with his inhale, then with his exhale he says, "Your brothers were my best friends in high school. The first rule was, keep my eyes off their sister. So I made sure you were invisible to me. Even if that meant dating girls I wasn't that interested in. Your mother is a respectable lawyer and quite frankly, she's intimidating as hell. Your father, although I've never met him, has been one of my favorite sports anchors since I can remember. Your family has created a force field around you. Even if I tried, I couldn't get close enough to you to have a conversation." He faces me with a gentle and hopeful expression. "But now that we're adults, and that force field is apparently dissolving since your entire family is very interested in whatever this is between us, and I can confidently say that I have a chance with you. Something in me tells me that I don't deserve you."

I blink. Shocked.

My heart and lungs and stomach have leapt so far up into my throat that I can't breathe.

Or comprehend what's just been said to me.

"Declan!" Parker calls from the stairway.

Declan stays seated but faces the doorway. It's strange seeing him like this. Slightly unnerved to be in my bedroom with my entire family just below us.

Locking eyes with me again, in that intense way he does, he says, "And for the record, I've never left a poem on another woman's phone before. It's not a tactic or way I flirt with women. What I did was deliberate. And it was meant for *only* you."

Everything, starting at my throat, through my chest, past my stomach, and down into my legs, tightens.

He rises, backs out of my room, and meets my brother in the hall.

Declan Price, homecoming king and best-looking on the Senior Survey, just confessed the poetic words he plugged into my phone for his contact were meant for me, geeky band girl and apparently off limits, Christine Malloy.

Declan Price, linguistics historian and manicured man, called me, Christine Malloy, hot mess in a pair of sweats, stunning.

FIVE

I slip the strap of my black dress around my shoulder.

Avery has been in Seattle with Brent since he asked her to marry him during Christmas break. Tallen and Parker have been crashing in Avery's room and on my couch while expanding their Shaven brand between here and Seattle. And I've been thinking about my portfolio. And completing the paperwork for funding for my research I plan to do in Papa New Guinea in the fall.

And more than anything, I've been avoiding my phone.

And more than avoiding my phone, I've been suppressing the flooding thoughts of Declan revolving around and around and around in my head.

Because I don't know how to do any of this. Dating. Flirting. Thing.

I'm dedicated to my school.

I'm going to leave for Papa New Guinea.

And even beginning to entertain any sort of thoughts about Declan has revealed that it would be impossible to include him in my life.

He works here.

I want to travel.

He lives here.

I want to move.

He wants to have a girlfriend.

I've never even kissed a guy.

We just won't work.

I realized all this once Thanksgiving was over. Declan said goodbye to my family and eyed me intently before exiting our home. As if he was trying to tell me to call him without using the words to do so.

I was flattered for the first time in my life.

And then I came back to Washington. To school. To my house. In the real world. Where I'm not looking to add any more commitments, mentally or emotionally, to my life.

Which is why I still haven't contacted Declan. And also why I only limit myself to reading the words from Bertrand Russell's poem he left on my phone five times a day. And even though my brothers colluded a plan to pick up Declan on the way to Brent's New Year's Eve party, I've already decided to tell Declan that I won't be seeing him again after tonight.

Buzzing. My phone is buzzing on my dresser.

I answer. "Hey, Tallen."

"Chris." He says my name with intensity.

"Yeah?" I sit on my bed and begin to wiggle my foot into my strappy black heel.

He lets out a sigh. "We're gonna be late."

I slump. Dropping my foot mid shoeing along with my tone. "How late?"

I hear him mumble something to Parker and Parker mumble something back. Then, "An hour."

"An hour? It takes an hour to get there. We'll miss the ball drop and I didn't really want to stay there too late." There's a slight pouting to my voice that I don't bother correcting. "We should just bag it. It's cold and snowing like crazy anyway."

"No!" Parker is on the phone now. "We're not bailing. There's just a change of plans."

"Okay," I begin to shove my other foot into the second heel. "What's the plan now?"

Tallen's voice is rumbling in the background and I'm starting to sense that they are up to something.

"Parker-r…" I drag his name out like it's a warning.

His muffled voice says something to Tallen, then to me he says, "Instead of us all riding together, Declan is going to pick you up so you're not late. He could have called you himself, but we're all trying to respect whatever you're doing by not giving him your number. Don't get mad, I'm just the messenger."

"Tell me you're joking."

"Not a joke."

My eyes widen. Not that Parker can see my facial expression or tell that his annoying change of plans is ruining my whole *avoiding Declan* thing.

"Thanks for letting me know," I say with bitterness. Then I hang up. An entirely new sense of disquiet emerges.

But I shove it down.

Along with the parts of me that are hanging on to Declan's words. The one's that said things like, *You're stunning*. And, *Now that I have a chance with you...*

The doorbell rings and I already know it's going to be Declan, so my pulse speeds up and rushes into my stomach.

I swing the door open.

The first thing I notice is his fresh haircut.

And I instantly revert back to the flute playing wallflower hidden in the band section of the football game, geeky teenager from eight years ago. Only this time, the Declan that is staring back at me is *more* confident, *more* put together, *more* attractive, and *more* than the king he was on homecoming night.

And he's holding an elegantly potted ivy plant.

"Wow," he says, stepping through the threshold and closing the door behind himself. "You look beautiful, Christine." He has to say that because I'm put together for the first time since...ever.

The drafting cold air rushes against me. Which is exactly what I need to chill the heat he's creating in my bones.

I give him an awkward smile. Because I don't know what to say. I don't know how to speak. I've always considered myself quite confident in who I am and confident in my ability to speak. But somehow his presence is making me forget that I decided to stop having contact with him after tonight.

His eyes are fixed on *all* of me. "This is for you," he lifts the potted plant slightly. "It's ivy."

I know it's ivy. It's strange that it's ivy. I love ivy. I love house plants. Especially ivy because it has an incredible resiliency to the ever-changing temperature in our home that is directly affected by the weather outside. It also seems to live without water for weeks at a time, which is the perfect sort of plant for a neglectful person like me. And the reason I would never own a pet, since they need water and attention more often than I can give. Which is why I love ivy.

"Thank you." I reach out to take the potted plant but he's already shouldering past me and apparently searching for the kitchen.

He spots the counter and places the ivy there. His eyes begin to scan the scattered house plants decorating the shelves. "Looks like you already know how to take care of plants."

I inhale slowly, trying to steady the trembling that my hands are doing. Maybe if I had gone on a date before, or had a boyfriend at any point in my life, my body wouldn't be responding in this ridiculous way right now. Like a teenager. And I would understand how to be in the presence of a man I like with my normal calm and confident demeanor. *I blame my intimidating family.*

"You know," he says, walking around the kitchen and into the living room still searching the house plants. "Ivy is significant in many cultures for its symbolism of fidelity and friendship."

Of course I know that. I've been studying culture for six years straight. But I don't tell him I know that. And I also don't tell him that I know ivy's symbolism is also for love and affection since I can tell by the slight grin emerging on his face that he probably already knows that too. Maybe he even knows that I know that.

I avert my eyes to the chair that my coat is draped over and focus on putting it on. "Ready to go?" I ask, my heels clicking over the tile as I make my way to the door.

I don't have to look at him to know he was hoping for more out of our conversation. His voice tells me when he says, "Why didn't you call?"

I've already opened the door to exit, but his words have me at a standstill. And now I feel bad. My own nerves and inability to think straight when my thoughts are consumed with him, are all getting in the way of my ability to see him as a person.

With feelings.

And emotions.

He's right behind me now, gently pressing the door closed with his hand. "Did you know that your brothers told me to pick you up tonight? When they learned that I hadn't heard from you since Thanksgiving, they insisted I come get you instead of us all riding together."

I knew they were scheming something.

When I face him, he doesn't waste a second to lock his heavy eyes into mine. It makes me catch my breath.

I don't know what to say, so I try to take a move out of Avery's book and say the first thing that comes to mind. "Your eyes are brown."

He tilts his head and blinks. Understandably confused.

"Your brown eyes are the same color as mine," I say, feeling more and more regretful of doing the one thing that annoys me about Avery and spilling words out of my mouth. "We have the same brown eye color."

A hint of a smile appears in the corner of his mouth. "So we do."

I blow a thick breath out. When it doesn't settle my nerves. I blow out another one. If my statement about his eye color didn't make me a complete nutcase, then my intense breathing has.

"Are you okay?" he says.

I shake my head. I look down at my painted toes. They're red. My mother told me to paint them red because *red is a sophisticated color*, she said. And *red is confident*, she said. But I don't feel either of those things when I'm around Declan. No matter how red my toes are.

"I don't know how to do this," I say in a whisper, my eyes still in a daze staring at my red toenails.

"No one really does."

This pulls my gaze up to meet his.

He shrugs and even though he's not smiling, his eyes are. "We're getting to know each other, right?"

I nod slowly.

"So you can relax a little bit. There's no pressure for anything. And if I've done something or said something to intimidate you or make you feel uncomfortable, tell me."

He hasn't done anything to make me feel that way. It's all the things in my head. Maybe it's because I always had him up on a pedestal. It's difficult not to put him there, honestly. He was always above me. Beyond me. And it sort of feels like he still is.

"I've never had a boyfriend," I say, making sure he knows what he's in for.

"I know."

I pull my dark hair over one shoulder and twirl one of the ringlets around my finger. "And I've never kissed a guy."

"I know."

"You know?" I crease my forehead, confused. "How?"

He drags his hand through the top of his hair. Then with a stifled grin, he says, "In the last month that you continued to ghost me, I've had many interesting conversations with your brothers."

I feel the embarrassing heat begin in my chest and rise up my neck. I place my hand there, hoping it will stop it from continuing up into my face.

He dips his head, closing the space between us more. "And despite the fact that they are still very much, and understandably, protective of you, they seem to be relieved that the guy trying to pursue you is *me.*"

I swallow, moving my heart out of my throat. "They said that?"

He squints and shifts his head from side to side. "Not exactly," he locks his eyes on mine again, "but I could tell they were trying to say that."

I press my mouth together in thought. Then, "So, I guess this means they weren't running late?"

He shakes his head. "Not at all. I wouldn't be surprised if they're already at the party."

I shift my mouth to one side, then say, "I guess we should probably get there too then."

He nods with a grin and motions for the door.

I lock up and follow him to his car where he opens the door for me and closes it once I'm in. It's a nice car. Clean. Maintained. Just like him.

When he's seated, he turns to retrieve his seatbelt, and I notice a scar on the back of his head where hair normally would cover it. But since his recent haircut, the scar is visible and pulling at my curiosity.

"What happened?" I say.

He faces me.

I point to his head and elaborate. "You have a scar on the back of your head."

He slaps his hand to the back of his head. "I forget that's there."

I would too. Who spends time making the effort to examine the back of their own head?

"What happened?" I repeat in a softer tone.

He focuses on plugging in the address to the party on his GPS. "I hit my head a long time ago." Then he pulls onto the road.

I wonder if it's from the summer he disappeared, then I say, "Is it from the pool?"

When he looks at me his expression is hard. The same way it was when I asked about his parents having another kid.

"No," he says flatly. Then he shifts the top of his combed hair to one side and leans his head in my direction, exposing another bald scar on his head, and says, "This one is from the pool." He says this like it's the only thing he's planning to say about it.

I don't know how to take his reaction. Or how to bring up what

44

happened after he hit his head at the pool. So, I don't say anything.

With a soft exhale, he says, "The scar on the back of my head is from flipping over my bike handlebars as a kid and cutting my head open on a rock."

I think about this for a moment, then say, "Staples or stitches?"

His expression lightens. With his eyes forward on the traffic, he says, "Stitches. And a concussion."

I want to ask if he got stitches or staples with his other scar from the pool, but he made it clear he doesn't want to elaborate on it with the way he seemed put off when I mentioned it before.

"So," I say, not knowing what I have planned to say after the word *so* but not wanting to sit in the uneasy silence of his pool memory.

"So," he says. And to my relief he continues the statement with, "What's new since Thanksgiving?"

I smile. "Nothing."

He glances at me then back to the road. "We're supposed to be getting to know each other, right?"

"Right," I say, knowing that I'm terrible at this.

"Well, when you get to know someone, you give them answers to their questions and gather information about them. It's sort of like fieldwork." Now he's speaking my language.

Before the stop light turns green, he winks at me.

My mouth goes dry, but I don't want to seem like a complete child in his presence. So, I force some words out. "Well, I presented a final project in class at the beginning of December. And I've been thinking about my end of the year project due in the spring. And I've figured out funding for my research in Papua New Guinea this fall."

He nods slowly, digesting the information.

"What about you?" I say, "What have you been up to?"

He glances at his mirror and merges over in the passing lane. "I've been working on some stuff in D.C."

"Washington, D.C.?"

He nods. Checking his mirror again and merging back over as the car wheels under us make a crunching noise over a patch of packed snow. "I've been doing a lot of planning for it since last year. I'm part of constructing this new idea for a museum there."

I'm intrigued. "What kind of museum?"

He looks over at me with confidence and intrigue. "It's a linguistics museum like no one has ever seen before."

I smile, as he veers around a bend in the road.

The red glow from the stacked taillights are the first thing I notice to illuminate his face before I flip my head forward and realize the traffic in front of us is at a standstill.

His eyes widen as his arm shoots across my chest instinctually, bracing me like a metal bar on a roller coaster ride.

He hits the brakes, and the car immediately begins circling.

He probably didn't consider in the split second that he had to react, that the roads were icy.

We seem to spin for an eternity. I'm pressing my heels into the floorboard, as if there's an imaginary brake pedal that's going to stop the car from twirling. The entire time I'm thinking about how much pain we're going to be in once we collide into another vehicle and my body tenses even more.

But we don't.

We glide, winding off the road and end up sideways in the snow covered median.

Once the car is at a standstill. All I can hear is our heavy breathing and my throbbing heartbeat.

Declan faces me. "Are you okay?" he says between his breaths. His arm is still bracing me.

I nod despite my shock. "I'm okay."

He shifts the arm that's bracing me back over to his side and runs his hand through his hair. "I can't believe that just happened."

My breathing is starting to steady, and I see a man exit his semi-truck, holding onto the door as he jumps down onto the slick road.

Since the traffic is at a standstill, he abandons his truck and meets us on the median.

I wind my window down as he approaches.

"You two okay?" the semi driver says in a raspy breathless voice as he ducks his head down to look inside the vehicle.

We nod.

He throws his thumb over his shoulder. "On the CB radio they're sayin' there's a big wreck up ahead."

"Is everyone okay?" Declan asks.

The guy shakes his head with remorse. "It just happened, but it doesn't sound good. A couple kids ejected from the car. That's all I know."

"That's horrible," Declan says shaking his head in disbelief

Then the man says, "You need some help out of this snow drift?"

Declan nods with a polite smile. "That would be great, thanks."

With the help of a few good Samaritans, Declan's car is freed. But we're still at the mercy of the standstill traffic.

"We should have had them help us get on the other side of the interstate," Declan says with a smile. "Then I could have at least driven you back home. It doesn't look like we're going to get to the party in time."

"Yeah," I dig in my coat pocket for my phone. "I better call Avery and let her know we're not going to make it."

He nods, checking his own phone briefly before placing it in the cup holder.

Avery picks up on the first ring. "Where are you guys?" she says over the humming sound of people talking and music playing in the background.

"We're not going to make it."

"What? Why not?"

"We're fine." I start with this, so she doesn't freak out when I say the next part. "There was a car accident and traffic is at a standstill." I don't mention that we slid off the road since that truth would send her into a conniption fit.

"Oh my gosh, are you okay?" The noise becomes instantly silent, like she's gone into a quiet room, but she's still yelling when she speaks.

"Yes, that's why I said we're fine." I exhale with regret. "But there's nowhere to get turned around so we're going to be stuck here for a while and I think it would be better to go back home than try and brave the icy road conditions."

She makes a sound in her throat indicating she agrees but isn't happy about it. "Well tell your brothers to drive safe and text me when you guys are home."

"My brothers aren't with me. They took a car and I rode with Declan." I feel a slight disturbance in my stomach when I say, "I thought they'd be at the party by now."

"They're not here," she says. I can hear Brent's voice and Avery tell him she'll be right there. Then, "I gotta go. Text me when you're home!"

She hangs up before I can say goodbye.

When I face Declan, he has a troubled expression covering his face. I'm sure he's thinking the same thing I am. Since I'm sure he couldn't help but hear the conversation I just had with Avery.

As if we have twin superpowers that allow us to read each other's thoughts, he says, "I'll call Tallen," in the same breath that I say, "I'll call Parker."

Parker's phone goes straight to voicemail. Which isn't out of the ordinary since Parker keeps his phone on *do not disturb* and prefers to be the one making the phone calls on his terms.

Declan releases a relieved rush of air when his phone call is answered. "Hey, man—" he begins to say, but his face drops when his greeting is cut short.

He glances at me, then back to his hand that's now tapping on the steering wheel.

I'm being as quiet as possible, but I'm unable to hear the other side of his conversation. All I know is that Declan isn't speaking with my brother.

My heart accelerates in my chest and feels like it's spinning in the same way Declan's car was just doing across the icy road.

He ends the call and holds his phone in front of him. Seeming usure of where to place it or what to do next.

I'm hoping he keeps staring at his phone, so he doesn't look at me. Because after that phone call, I know when he finally looks at me, I'll be able to tell he just received bad news.

He looks at me.

Don't look at me like that.

"Christine…"

Don't say my name like that.

"I'm so sorry."

Don't apologize like that.

He takes my trembling hands in his. I look down at the way his hands encapsulate mine, vanishing them. If this were two minutes ago, my hands would be trembling for the sole reason that Declan Price was gripping them. But because I know Declan Price is gripping my hands because he's *sorry*, is making my hands tremble for an entirely different reason.

And it's not a good one.

"That was the police," his voice turns into a whisper on the last word.

I slap my hand over my gasping mouth.

I hate that the unraveling of whatever he's trying to say is hurting him. *And me.*

His voice is gentle, but I can hear his fear when he continues,

48

"The officer said a first responder found the phone. He said we can pick it up at the station." He swallows hard, and I look up just in time to see his throat roll and his eyes shine before he says, "He doesn't have many details besides that three people were dead on the scene and two were severely injured."

I blink at the confused tears in my eyes.

My heart is hammering. The thudding feels like it might beat its way right through my sternum.

"What kind of people?" I say, knowing my words aren't coming out the way I want them to.

My eyes are searching his. He pulls his brow down, confused. "What kind of people?" he repeats under his breath. I'm sure he's trying not to offend me and my inability to communicate appropriately right now.

I already know that if a police officer has my brother's phone, that my brother was in the accident. But I don't know if he's one of the injured or one of the deceased. And I'm not sure how to ask Declan if he knows which group of people my brother belongs to.

So, I say, "Was it men? Or women? Or—"

He's already nodding in understanding and beginning to speak before I'm done with my sentence. "The injured were two men, and the people that aren't alive anymore were a man and two women."

As if saying *aren't alive* anymore is any less painful than saying *dead*. I nod.

I want to be hopeful, but I can't focus on anything hopeful right now. All I can focus on is who that dead man is and if it's one of my brothers.

I pull my gaze from Declan's concerned expression and blink the tears away. "I should call my parents." I say this while finding my mother's contact.

Declan nods and faces forward again.

The stillness is too quiet.

And the quiet is alarming.

I don't know how he planned for this night to go.

But I'm certain it wasn't like this.

SIX

Parker is dead.

Those words continue to reverberate through my mind.

Coursing in my heart like poison I can't get rid of.

Tallen is paralyzed.

Why are there not easier words to describe what has happened to my brothers?

Why do medical professionals use such direct terms when delivering such unbearable news?

When the doctors informed us, it hit our family like being buried in an avalanche. It was unbearable when the sentence was effortlessly given to us, *"We're so sorry, Parker is dead."* It must be some kind of medical regulation that they have to be as straight forward as possible so there is no room for confusion.

It wasn't any better when they told us Tallen was paralyzed from the waist down due to a spinal injury during the accident.

And now, there's a weight that's fallen over my mother's house like never before.

And it feels like my world is in pieces.

The shock of it all has faded. And the reality set in as soon as I hugged Parker's lifeless body one last time before they closed his casket at his funeral.

And I hate that Tallen is in the hospital and didn't even get to say goodbye to Parker.

Everything I look at reminds me of them. Everything I do feels more difficult knowing my life is a little more unsteady without them in it. Without Parker ever again. Without Tallen whole.

My heart has never felt so broken.

Nothing compares to this heavy feeling.

No one really knows what it's like to lose a sibling unless they've experienced it.

It hurts.

Beyond words.

My heart feels like it's connected to a fifty-pound weight that I'm dragging around and can't get rid of.

"She should be mingling with her family," my father's voice says from the hall. "We're still here. She's still here. Tallen is still here. It could be so much worse."

My mother's voice is not hiding her irritation when she says, "She's just lost her brother. I don't think anyone is expecting her to be *mingling* any time soon."

"And I lost my son."

"*Our* son," my mother corrects.

My father's voice rises when he says, "She can't stay in her room, *Diane*."

"She can do whatever the hell she wants, *Steve*."

I press the tears away and scoot off my bed to meet them in the hall. "Even though you're divorced, you guys argue the *exact* same way," I say softly in passing.

My father's footsteps are closing in behind me as I cascade down the stairs.

"Chris, wait a minute." He stops me at the bottom of the stairs by gripping my shoulders firmly. "I didn't know you could hear us." As if that's a reasonable excuse for him to say what he did.

He releases his grip when he realizes that people are watching us. When he realizes that people are watching *him*. His voice is low when he says, "There's a standard I need to uphold."

I've heard this speech a hundred times. So his egotistical remark doesn't faze me much. I keep myself from rolling my eyes and say, "I know. You have a professional appearance to maintain. As if your grieving daughter is somehow a stain to your perfect appearance, you want me to mingle and chat and accept everyone's condolences to make you look good." My voice breaks. "Forgive me for taking a minute to cry alone in my room while one of my brothers is stuck at the hospital, unable to move his legs. And my other brother is…" I pinch my shuddering mouth closed for a moment with my breaking voice.

My father's eyes glisten with the slightest hint of remorse, which is the first time I've seen him show any signs of mourning thus far.

"And my other brother is…dead." My voice is not low anymore when I say this.

I don't have to look to know that everyone's heads are turned in our direction.

I can hear it in the way the house goes quiet.

I can see it in the way my father peers over my shoulder with his veneered smile and soft chuckle.

Fake chuckle. As fake as his teeth.

He's my father. I love him. I really do. I also know there are parts of him I don't particularly care for. He's imperfect. I know he's selfish. Which is what ended my parents' marriage.

But right now, I don't like him.

At all.

I can't help but say, "Why don't you mingle with Parker's friends if you're so worried about appearance?" I immediately regret my words. But I'm exhausted. I'm tired from staying up and crying. I'm weak and starving from having no appetite. And I'm in my mother's home which is my place of comfort and rest but is filled with so much sadness right now, I could crumble. My mother's home, which is the same place filled with all of my memories of my brothers.

My brothers, who are supposed to be here. Together. Who are supposed to be whole and alive. Who are supposed to be joking, and playing pranks, and making fun of me, and talking for each other.

I'm hurting.

And I'm taking it out on my father.

I bury my face into my hands and the sobs choke out of my throat. *"I'm sorry,"* I manage to whisper. I am sorry for acting like this. Like an unstable human. I know my father is hurting too, somewhere deep down in his tiny self-centered heart. And in his defense, he's not acting any different than he normally does. I should expect his behavior and ignore it like I normally do. It's just harder to do when my soul is cracked in half.

My father pats my shoulder. In a gentle voice, he says, "Maybe you can go sit in the garage until you're more composed?"

Go into the *garage*?

Like unwanted decorations or a disruptive pet?

I think I may have been completely wrong. Right now, he really doesn't care about anything but his image and how I'm somehow making him look bad by causing a scene.

I look up at him and my anguish shifts into anger at his complete lack of compassion. Even this remark is more narcissistic than usual. I clench my jaw and pinch my mouth, then say, "You're such an a—"

"Disappointment," Declan's voice smooths over my fury.

I'm still clenching my jaw and giving my father the most repulsed expression I've ever given, when Declan slips his hand around my waist. I can't even feel excited his hand is comforting me in this way because I'm so heartbroken by my life and my father.

"Excuse us," he says to my father as he guides me out of my mother's home, draping his coat over my shoulders as we enter the cold outside and make our way to his car.

We don't say anything.

The tears streak down my face.

The tears haven't stopped flooding.

They haven't stopped since we got to the hospital.

They haven't stopped since we were told Parker died receiving CPR in the ambulance truck.

They haven't stopped since we saw Tallen's mangled body and learned he would never walk again.

We're in Declan's car now and I sniff back the snot that's been plaguing my nose for as long as the tears have been falling from my eyes.

"Here," he says, digging in the pocket of his coat draped over me. He hands me a small plastic bag of Kleenex.

"Thank you," I say, looking up at him briefly.

Only when I do, I'm broken all over again. Like I've just learned that Declan Price, authentic gift giver and shoulder to cry on, is as much of a wreck as I am, Christine Malloy, sad selfish sister of the former Parker Malloy.

How have I not considered that this has been as painful for him as it's been for me.

"Oh, Declan," I say with remorse.

The tears are welling in his eyes. But he holds his composure when he shakes his head. Looking down, he says, "He was your brother."

"He was your friend!" I burst the words out as if they are justification for him. Because they are. They are justification for him to be allowed to cry over this horrific experience with my brother. His friend.

"I'm really going to miss him," he says quickly with his wavering voice.

I take his hand. "Me too."

He locks his tearing eyes on mine. Like he's saying something with his eyes. He *is* saying something with his eyes, and I don't know how I feel about knowing what he's saying. But I do what his eyes are telling me to do and shift in my seat. Then without hesitation he grips me in his arms, and I grip him back.

We stay in this position for a long time.

Hugging.

Hurting.

Crying.

My sobs are in his neck and his are in my shoulder.

Hugging him feels better than any security blanket I've ever owned.

He feels more like home than being in my own mother's house.

After several minutes, I let out a deep exhale.

Our sobs gentle.

Our tight grips relax.

He blows out a pained breath. A steadying breath.

We finally release each other.

Still not okay, but better now that we were able to release our pain.

Together.

I hand him the Kleenex.

"Thanks," he says taking it with a halfhearted smile.

I look at him for the first time since he made it known that he liked me, without a nervousness shivering in my core. I look at him with gratitude.

"Thank you for bringing me out here," I say.

He shifts in his seat to look at me better. "Want to go back inside?"

"I'd rather get out of here, honestly."

"I think I can help you with that." He's trying to smile, but then he looks back at my mother's house and frowns. "Your dad," he says shaking his head.

"He can be a jerk," I say. "I've learned to deal with it. He's always put himself first."

"You shouldn't have to *deal* with that." Declan turns the car on and shifts to glance at his rear window before backing out of the driveway. "It was disappointing seeing one of my favorite sports anchors overlook his daughter's pain and grief in front of all their grieving friends and family like that."

This truth stabs at my heart, like a butcher knife has been thrown at my chest. When he puts it that way, I'm disappointed in my father too.

He's still shaking his head. "I respected your dad so much before today."

"I'm sorry," I say. "It can be really hard realizing the guy you idolized on TV is an egocentric dolt in real life."

"Egocentric *dolt?*" His eyes are forward as he nods with a satisfied smile. "I like that."

I gently laugh at myself. Then, "It's true. He's always put himself first and acted like we were his puppets. It's what forced my mother to leave him. But, one thing my father taught me, just through observing his existence, is never to put a person on a pedestal. I can at least give him credit for that."

"I think he taught me that lesson today too," I can hear the disappointment in his voice.

I give him a half smile. It's a bittersweet lesson to learn, but one that's essential for accepting people for who they are. Not for who we *want* them to be.

We sit in the quiet of his car as we pass through the city. I'm sure Declan is doing the same thing as me and rewinding his mind back to all his memories with my brothers.

Even though Tallen is still alive, it still hurts knowing that his life will never feel as full as it did with Parker by his side. It hurts knowing that every moment of his life will be a reminder of Parker's absence. And it hurts knowing that even though Tallen is alive, he's going to wish every day that he could take Parker's place in that car accident.

As we make our way through Reno and into California, I say, "Where are we going?"

He shrugs. "Where do you want to go?"

"I don't know, but I wasn't expecting to cross state lines."

His eyes flash at mine. "We're cruising. We could end up anywhere."

I like his confidence.

I glance at the stereo. "Shouldn't we listen to music if we're going to be cruising?"

"We can." He turns the volume up on the radio and skips to a station. I'm surprised he doesn't have his Bluetooth on. "I don't usually listen to the radio. So if there's something in particular you'd like, by all means the radio's yours."

I smile. "This station is fine."

I take my phone out and text my mom.

Me: Sorry I left. I needed some space away from Dad.
Mom: That's understandable. Are you okay?
Me: Cruising with Declan.
Mom: Good. See you tonight.

I move to the next contact that I want to text and let out a small laugh at the way his name invades my screen. Invades is an understatement to the way his *name* takes over my phone. I send the text. Finally ready to share my number with him.

Declan's phone dings and he lifts it from his cup holder. I watch as a smile spreads across his face. In one swift motion he unlocks the screen, opens the message, and hands his phone to me.

"Could you text her back?" he says with a beaming grin.

"Sure." I smile knowing the *her* he is talking about is me. "And say what?"

He laughs. "Tell her," he raises one eyebrow and glances at me with a smirk that melts my core, "*thanks.*"

This makes me laugh. I set his phone back in his cup holder and Declan takes my hand in his.

I peer down at the message I receive on my phone and continue the laughter that I can't stop. Which is ironically the same laughter that finally brings my uncontrollable tears to a stop.

Me: Hey ♥
Of all forms of caution, caution in love is perhaps the most fatal to true happiness: Thanks.

His contact name is absurd.

Ridiculous.

Thoughtful.

And perfect.

I love it. And I love that, even though my heart is broken from the loss of Parker, I seem to be able to find comfort by just being in the presence of Declan Price, unconditionally kind and superbly thoughtful best friend of my brothers, and potential beau to me, Christine Malloy.

SEVEN

I press the power button, then the start button. But the same error flashes across the screen of my washing machine that's been flashing the last several times I've repeated this process.

I look up at the ceiling and raise my hands. Then I let out a very frustrated and quiet, "Why-y?"

I repeat this same process several times again before calling out to Avery for help. She parks herself in the doorway of our miniature garage, Princess at her feet, and says, "Is it still not working?"

"No," my voice is harsh. Harsher than necessary, but I'm feeling frustrated. I'm running out of clean laundry and too proud to run down to the laundry mat.

I drag my hands down my face. "Could you see if Brent knows how to fix it?"

She nods, pulling her phone out and dialing him. "Hey, babe," she says when he answers. "Do you know anything about washing machine repair?" She enters the garage and turns the machine on, presses start, then when it flashes the error she says, "That didn't work....yeah...okay...thanks, babe. Love you."

My mouth gapes open. I'm perplexed by the lack of effort put into that conversation.

She shrugs. "Sorry, he didn't know. You could try YouTubing how to fix it?"

"Thanks." My voice is pinched. I have to bite my bottom lip when I force my smile to contain my true thoughts from escaping.

Princess barks at me. Like she doesn't like that I'm unimpressed by her owner's lack of effort or assistance.

I narrow my eyes at Princess as Avery picks her up. "Try Declan," she says in a nonchalant manner.

The door slams behind her and I'm contemplating what she's said. I take my phone from my pocket, find his contact, and shake my head.

I don't want to call him asking for help. That feels rude.

He's probably busy working anyway.

So far, we've only had coffee at the bistro by his work twice. He's given me a brief tour of the museum that he works at, but that was cut short by my class schedule. We both happened to visit Tallen at the hospital at the same time. Twice. And we've had many *Hey, how's your day going* texts that don't elude to much depth.

It's understandable.

We're both busy.

We're both getting back to normal life after grief.

We're getting to know each other.

Slowly.

Painfully slow...

My phone vibrates and I check it.

Avery: Text. Him.

She couldn't have said that to me? She had to text it? I guess she did tell me to *try* him. Which is less direct than her text message. *She knows me too well.*

Me: Why?
Avery: Do you want to smell like fishy onions or see if he can fix the washer?

She has a point.

Avery: Text him. I'm taking Princess to the groomers.

I tap the side of my phone. Maybe I'll send a quick text. Or I could call. I'm equally nervous as I am giddy that he might answer if I call. And if he answers and comes over, we would be alone since Avery is leaving. This realization also makes me giddy and nervous.

I opt for calling since if he doesn't answer, I won't have to feel disappointed like I would if he left me on *read* in a text. Since this is the first time I'm calling unscheduled, he probably won't answer.

It rings twice, then, "Christine, hello." There's surprise in his voice. The good kind. Which makes all the nerves drown out of me and become replaced by the giddiness tickling my soul.

"Heyyy," I say, drawing out my greeting since I wasn't quite prepared for him to actually answer.

"How are you?" I can tell by his voice that he's smiling.

I can't figure out how to respond because his voice is better than any song I've ever listened to, and I don't want it to stop playing through my phone and into my ear.

I'm stricken with silence.

"Christine?"

His voice is consuming. It makes my throat tighten and my entire chest swell with a sensation I've never felt before. I could laugh and cry all at the same time.

What is his voice doing to me?

"Christine?" The melody he's singing is confused now. "Are you still there?"

I shake my head, trying to jostle my brain back into place since it seems to escape me when he speaks. "Yes, I'm here. I uh…"

He gently clears his throat like he's waiting for me to finish my statement.

"Are you busy?" I say.

"Nope, and I'm off the next two days."

Is this an invitation?

I laugh at myself because I'm starting to feel stupid for calling and feeling so many erratic emotions. "So, my washing machine has been on the fritz and I'm pretty sure I killed it today."

I can tell he's still smiling when he says, "Are you asking for my help?"

My heart bounces in my chest. Like it grew into the size of a basketball and won't stop crushing my lungs.

But then it halts immediately when I hear the voice of someone in the background ask him who he's talking to.

"*My friend's washing machine broke,*" he says to the person with a noticeably feminine voice. "*She needs my help fixing it.*" Then to me he says, "I'll be right over, Christine. See you in a bit."

Then he hangs up.

But I'm still standing in the garage, in front of my dying washer, with my phone pressed against my ear.

I don't know why I'm disappointed he has a woman at his house. We never talked about being exclusive. Afterall, he is Declan Price,

most likely to vote for himself and biggest flirt on the Senior Survey.
I let out a sad sigh and wait inside where I contemplate on how
I'm going to force a smile when he gets here.

※

I count to ten before opening the door after the doorbell rings. I
don't want him to think I've been by the door nervously pacing the
three-by-three tile in the entryway since I got off the phone with him.
I swing the door open. Expecting to see Declan in his all to
familiar put together appearance, but instead I'm met by the bright
blue eyes of a prepubescent boy.

"What's up?" Blue eyed boy says.

My mouth opens but nothing comes out, at first. I give him a
confused expression and say, "Are you selling something?"

He twists his face like my question is stupid and says, "What?"

"Fundraising?" I ask.

"No. I'm not trying to get your money." He swings his arm to
his side and points down the street. "Declan's my brother. He said
you called for help with your washer."

Relief rolls over every inch of my body, starting in the center of
my heart and pulsing its way through my veins. "Declan's brother,"
I say with a smile wider than necessary for this moment. "I'm
Christine," I say waving him inside.

He makes his way in, saying, "I know. Declan told me." I quickly
realize how his voice could be mistaken over the phone for a
woman's.

I like a kid with no problems talking to adults, even if it's in a
slightly abrasive manner. It makes communicating a lot easier.
"What's your name?" I say.

He doesn't have to answer, since Declan is scaling the stairs now.
"Maverick, I told you to wait for me." He shifts his eyes to me,
saying, "Sorry, Maverick only has half his brain cells since his
prefrontal cortex is under construction until he turns eighteen." It
seems like he might be saying this more for Maverick to hear than
me.

"Shut up," Maverick says without looking at him.

Declan shoots an apologetic look in my direction. To Maverick,
he says, "What'd I say about saying *shut up*?"

"*What'd I say about saying shut up.*" Maverick mocks.

It's hilarious.

I have to fold my mouth together to keep from laughing and to keep from encouraging Maverick's behavior.

The anthropologist in me is both humored and intrigued by them. Especially because despite the shape of their facial features, they don't look anything alike.

Maverick is already wandering around inspecting my house. It makes me smile since Declan did the same thing the first time he was in my home too.

I close the door and motion for Declan to follow.

"Don't get into stuff," Declan commands in an almost fatherly tone to Maverick.

"*Don't get into stuff,*" Maverick mocks again.

Declan gives me another apologetic expression. Following me into the garage he says, "Teenagers." Like the word itself is an understood explanation for Maverick's behavior.

Once he spots the washing machine, he begins pressing buttons. "My parents had a washing machine just like this when I was growing up."

"Are you trying to outdate my washing machine?" I say joking.

"Well, they don't last forever." He smiles. "Do you have paper towels and a garbage?"

I nod, then head back inside to retrieve paper towels and the garbage can. And notice my piano is playing in my bedroom. I'm sure it's Maverick so I ignore it, happy he's found something productive to do while he's waiting.

When I enter the garage, Declan is on his knees in front of the washing machine and there's a pile of highlighters, pens, and money next to him. The debris is mixed together with soggy lint and a pair of unmatched socks.

"Yikes," I say, handing him the paper towels. "That's gross and a little embarrassing."

He retrieves a discolored sock and tosses it into the garbage. "Don't worry about it. Same thing used to happen to my parents' washer." He pauses, glancing at me. "Only it was toy cars, Legos, and crayons jamming ours."

"It wouldn't be so bad if they weren't covered in gunk," I say.

"It's a lot easier if you just empty your pockets before you wash your clothes," he says with a wink.

"That would be too easy," I tease.

I begin to toss the ruined pens and highlighters into the garbage while Declan wipes out the inside of the rubber seal that seems to have been clogged by debris.

"Thanks for doing this," I say. "If I had known you were hanging out with your brother, I wouldn't have interrupted your day."

He closes the door and hits the power button with his thumb. "You weren't interrupting. We needed a reason to get out of the apartment anyway. There's only so much time Maverick can spend with me before he starts to lose his mind and starts acting like...well, a teenager."

He flips the knob to *cotton* and starts the machine. It makes a noise, indicating it's successfully working.

"You fixed it," I say, my expression beaming. And thankful.

He wipes his hands on a paper towel and tosses it into the garbage. "You might need to clean the filter out soon, but it should be fine for a few cycles."

I tilt my head. "The filter?"

He raises his brow. "You've never cleaned your filter?"

I shake my head. "I thought air conditioners and cars were the only things with a filter."

His grin spreads across his face. "Call me the next time you get an error and I'll show you how to clean the filter."

I can't help but feel like he's not cleaning the filter now just so he has a reason to come back to my house again.

He takes the garbage and I follow him back inside.

The blissful sound of the piano is pouring through the house as soon as we open the door. It's amazing to hear that that kind of beautiful melody can come from such a moody teenager.

Declan drops his head, then facing me with a mixed expression, he says, "Sorry, he loves playing."

"No, it's completely fine." I take the garbage and place it back in its spot. "I'm sure my piano is happy to get some use."

I wash my hands at the kitchen sink and Declan copies me. "You don't play anymore?" His voice is less disappointed and more curious.

"I do."

His fingers gently graze mine before I finish rinsing. The unexpectedness makes me suck in a rush of air. I quickly compose myself, so I don't seem like a novice girlfriend to him. Not that I'm his girlfriend.

I retrieve the towel from the stove handle and continue as if our hands didn't just touch. "Just not as much as I probably should." I hand him the towel. "It keeps me sane when I'm about to break. But the sad part is that I don't play unless I'm already broken."

He leans around me to place the towel back. Almost touching me, but not quite. I can feel the warmth of his body he's so close. Then in a deep and low voice, he says, "What breaks you?"

"I don't know," I say, unable to look at him because he's so close to me. "I guess losing Parker was the last time I played."

I don't know what his expression is doing because my eyes are concentrating on the jeans he's wearing. It's not the typical way he dresses, but I think I like the casual look better. Not that any of this is enough to distract me from how close he is right now.

"And before that?" he says, closing the space between us a little more.

I shrug. My heart is pounding in my throat. "Before finals last year." I say this more as a question because I'm not sure if there was a time I played between finals and losing Parker.

The piano stops and Declan takes a step back. Like he was in a trance with the melody playing through the house and once it stopped he was brought back to reality. And aware of the way we were almost touching.

"I should make sure he's not getting into anything," he says.

I smile, motioning for him to follow me toward my bedroom. "The piano's this way."

When Declan realizes that Maverick was in my bedroom playing the piano, he says, "You can't just wander into women's bedrooms."

"I didn't put the keyboard in her bedroom," Maverick says.

Declan faces me. "Sorry about him."

I'm absolutely in love with witnessing their relationship. It's so interesting. And humorous. "It's really okay," I say.

Maverick sits on the edge of my bed and takes his phone out. Without looking at us he says, "Are we going to eat soon? I'm starving."

"We just had breakfast," Declan says. "And don't sit on her bed, it's rude."

Still with his eyes on his phone, Maverick ignores Declan's instructions and says, "Breakfast was like two hours ago."

Declan checks the time on his phone. "I don't know any places serving lunch this early."

"We can have second breakfast." Maverick glances at us, then lifting one shoulder he says, "Or brunch. Whatever, I'm not picky."

Declan gently takes my hand in his. Effortlessly. A rush of warmth floods my stomach when he says, "Do you want to have second breakfast with us?"

My eyes flick between his brown eyes. Out of all the shades of brown, it amazes me that we both share the same color. "I want to."

The crinkling at the edges of his eyes smooths. "Why do I feel a *but* coming on?"

I slump and shift my mouth to one side, but my expression couldn't be farther from the elated feeling inside of my body. "I should probably do my laundry," I say, making sure my grip doesn't slide from his hand. "And I have a paper I need to do some research for."

The wrinkles return around his eyes as he smiles. "How about dinner?"

Maverick is shifting his eyes between me and Declan. Then, he says, "Is she your girlfriend?"

Declan looks at me and smiles, then back to Maverick. "No, she's not my girlfriend."

My face goes hot.

I'm sure if I looked in the mirror, I wouldn't recognize myself. I'm not someone who gets flushed by a man's voice. Or giddy by his hand laced in mine. Or mortified that he used the word *girlfriend* in a sentence about me.

Maverick smirks. "She's your girlfriend." Then he brushes past us, exiting the bedroom.

Declan gives me a look. One that makes me melt into lava on the floor. I could burn a hole right through the carpet with the heat resonating from my body.

I swallow hard, allowing my body parts to go back into place before saying, "Dinner sounds nice."

"Great. I'll text you my address," he says with confidence.

I draw in a ridiculously shuddered and unnecessary breath. *What is he doing to me?* And how is this conversation causing me to lose control of myself?

He runs his tongue across his bottom lip, then locks his eyes on mine. Smiling, as if he knows what he's doing to me, and says, "I'll have dinner ready at 6:30, if that works for you?"

I have to look down to focus when I say, "It does. But shouldn't I cook you a *thank you* dinner? I mean, you just fixed my washer for free."

65

He shakes his head then begins to back away. Ignoring my statement, he says, "I'll see you at 6:30, Christine."

I can't move.

I can't even walk him out or say goodbye.

Not even thirty seconds passes after the front door closes before I receive a text message from him.

Of all forms of caution, caution in love is perhaps the most fatal to true happiness: 15 Parks Ave. #22.

I have got to change his contact name.

I quickly edit his name.

Then another text comes in.

Declan: Do you like seafood?
Me: I love it.

I flop back against my bed and let out a sigh of giddy-girly-feelings that I still can't believe I'm experiencing at twenty-three years old.

I text Avery.

Me: Declan fixed the washer.
Avery: You know what that means.
Me: No...
Avery: Now you owe him.
Me: He's making dinner for us at his place tonight.
Avery: OoooOoooOoo! I can't wait for all the deets!
Me: There won't be any to report since his brother is there.

I stand outside his apartment door with the dessert I picked up from the grocery store bakery. I knock three times and Declan swings the door open.

The aroma that hits me instantly makes me feel like my dessert is mediocre compared to whatever he's created in his kitchen.

"I brought dessert," I say lifting the bready mound.

"Thanks. Come in. You didn't have to bring anything," he says, inviting me in and taking the dessert in its plastic container. "I hope you like steak and lobster."

I pull my coat off. "I'm impressed you know how to cook

lobster."

He takes my coat, hanging it in his closet. "If you watch enough cooking shows, you can cook anything."

I follow him into the kitchen where Maverick is seated at the table with his phone in his face. He looks up briefly and nods when he sees me.

I smile in return.

"It smells like heaven in here," I say, leaning my hip into the counter while I watch Declan pull a pan of roasted vegetables from the oven. He makes cooking look easy *and* attractive.

"Thanks," he says, taking three plates from the cupboard and handing them to me. "Do you mind?"

"Not at all." I set the plates at the table, wondering if there is a certain seating arrangement that these two brothers normally have. I opt for placing one at the head of the table, one in front of Maverick and one across from him.

I help Declan carry the food to the table where I'm mesmerized by the way he dishes up each plate.

"Are you sure you didn't miss your calling as a chef?" I ask.

Maverick tilts his head at me. "You haven't even tried it yet. How do you know he's any good at cooking?"

I shrug. "It looks and smells better than any food I've eaten in the last few months."

"You know," Declan says, pulling the chair out for me in front of the spot at the table I reserved for myself, "what your eyes see on a dinner plate affects the way it tastes?"

Maverick frowns. "No it doesn't."

"It really does, look it up."

"How?" Maverick says.

"Your eyes tell your mouth the texture of the food before you eat it. The more pleasing the display is, the more appealing your brain tells your mouth it's going to be." I wonder what other facts Declan knows; and I can't wait to find out.

Maverick forks a bite of steak into his mouth. "That's not true."

Declan raises his brow in Maverick's direction. "Have I ever given you false information?"

"Well," Maverick searches the thoughts in his mind by looking up at the ceiling. "No, I guess not."

"That's because I want you to know I'm giving you legitimate sources of information." Declan glances at me. "And I want you to trust me."

His comment makes me feel like he wasn't just reassuring Maverick.

"So," Maverick says, with a mouthful. "How did you guys meet each other?"

Declan smiles at me, then takes a bite of his lobster. I take this gesture as an invitation for me to explain the details of our history.

So I say, "Your brother was kind enough to carry me to the clinic after I slipped and hit my head on the ice before class last year." I scrunch my nose and smile, waiting for Maverick's reaction.

But before he can say anything, Declan is shaking his head and saying, "No, we actually met before that."

I shift my head from one shoulder to the other, shifting my mind back as far as I can to the first time I can remember meeting Declan. "I guess you're right. I think the first time we met was after a football game when you got a ride with us in high school."

He's still confidently shaking his head no. Like I've given an incorrect answer to a trivia question. We never formally met, he was just always at our house. So I don't remember the first time we met each other, if there ever was one.

"No, that still wasn't the first time," he says.

Maverick takes this opportunity to shovel his vegetables onto Declan's plate while Declan is looking at me. It makes it hard not to laugh, especially because Declan is being so serious about the details of when we met.

Declan flips his head in Maverick's direction, who has an incriminating look to his blue eyes. I'm certain he's hoping Declan doesn't notice the extra helping of vegetables that's magically appeared on his plate.

"She was my best friends' little sister," he says to Maverick.

Maverick nods. But I can tell he's not very interested in this story anymore.

Declan continues anyway, saying, "The first time I met her, was at her house." He leans against the back of his chair and folds his mouth in with his thoughts.

I give him my full attention even though he's not looking at me.

"It was one of the first times I had been to her house. I was hanging out with her brothers upstairs." He wipes his hand over his mouth. I'm not sure if he's making sure he doesn't have butter on his face, or if he's trying to keep his composure talking about my brothers.

He continues, "I went to use the bathroom and heard her playing the piano in the living room. I went down the hall and stopped at the top of the stairs, looking down at her in the living room from the tread."

Now I'm completely intrigued, mostly because I've never heard this story before.

"She was playing Rihanna's *Stay*. But the way she played it was like an indie cover. Slowed, drawing out every lyric, only lifting the sustain pedal after each chord progression. I was mesmerized." He blinks and shifts his eyes to mine. "It was an incredibly mature song for a teenage girl to be singing so well."

Instead of feeling like a burning mess on the floor, I feel known. It's an odd sensation. Especially since I thought I was invisible to him all those years. He never said more than a few words to me. Such as, *Hey, are your brothers home?* He seemed like a cool jock that was too full of himself to even look at me when we were younger.

I hold his gaze. Wondering how many times he stood at the top of the stairs listening to me play. Wondering how many times I didn't have a clue he was there.

"That doesn't count as meeting her if she didn't know you were there," Maverick says.

Declan draws in a slow breath of air through his nose and says, "I wanted to walk down those stairs. But Parker approached me in the hall when I had been gone for a while."

"Parker?" Maverick says.

"My brother," I say, swallowing my words; unsure if I should bring up the fact that Parker is no longer alive.

Maverick nods, then drinks his water. "Gotcha," he says becoming more interested in the story. "Then what happened?" he says to Declan.

Declan raises his brow and smiles at me. Then to Maverick he says, "Parker asked what I was doing. I ignored him and said that she was incredible at singing and playing piano. I thought Parker would be happy I said that, since I assumed that she was his sister and I was only giving her a compliment. Instead, Parker got right in my face and backed me up to the wall and said, *That's my little sister. And if you ever talk about her again, I'll curb stomp your teeth in.* I didn't want to risk losing the only real friends I had, so I made no effort to get to know her."

69

My eyes widen as my stomach drops at his comment.

He stabs the heaping pile of vegetables on his plate. Then he continues, "He walked me back to the bedroom where their brother, Tallen, made sure I wasn't allowed to even say their sister's name without regretting it. So, I followed their rules, and had a great friendship with them. But that was the first time I ever saw Christine, and the last time I ever looked at her until I saw her lying on the sidewalk at the university last year."

Maverick lets out a noise in his throat, which sounds like an indication that he's done listening to this story. "So, Christine?" he says.

"Yes?" I gently smile at Maverick, but inside of my body I'm shaken by the reality of Declan's story. The way he told it, made it seem like he regretted never talking to me. Like he was so desperate to be friends with my brothers that he would sacrifice anything for them. Including any sort of association with me.

"Did you bring dessert?" Maverick says with the first smile I've seen on his face, which I quickly realize is the same shape as Declan's smile.

"I did."

I begin to rise from my chair to retrieve it, but Declan gets up. "I can get it. Is it a bundt cake?"

I shrug. "Your guess is as good as mine." Then I fork at my lobster for a buttery bite.

Declan slides the dessert from the plastic container onto a round plate from the cabinet. Reading the bakery label, he says, "Chocolate fudge bundt cake." He glances at me, lifting one brow. "You know, chocolate is an aphrodisiac?"

I nearly choke on my lobster when he says this. His smirk shows me that he's satisfied with my reaction.

"What's an aphrodisiac?" Maverick says, eyeing the cake Declan places on the table between us.

When no one answers his question, Maverick's expression grows concerned and he looks at me and says, "Do you know what an aphrodisiac is? Or is my brother just trying to sound cool by using big words in front of you?"

Declan slides into his chair and cups his chin into his palm while eyeing me. Completely smitten by the commotion he's caused.

I take this as an invitation to elaborate on the term. "It's a word that describes the way chocolate can make people feel in… certain situations." My face is flushed knowing Declan knows a better definition which involves vocabulary words I would never use in front of a thirteen-year-old.

Declan tucks his bottom lip into his mouth as a smile emerges. As if he's pleased by my reaction. "That's pretty close," he says. "But not the way I would have defined it."

I raise my brows and narrow my eyes. Challenging him. "How would you define it in front of your little brother?"

Maverick flips his head between us. "You guys are lying." Then, "Hey Siri, what's an aphrodisiac?"

Siri responds with, "An aphrodisiac is something that increases s—"

Declan snatches the phone from Maverick's grip before Siri can finish. "No phones at the table."

Maverick scrunches his nose and drops his jaw, offended. "Since when?"

Declan hands the phone back to Maverick. "Since now. Put it away until you're finished eating."

Maverick scoffs. "You're always on your phone when we eat." Then without breaking eye contact with Declan, he picks up the slice of cake in his hand and eats it in three bites. Then he rinses his plate at the sink and before completely disappearing into the depths of the apartment, he says, "Thanks for dessert, Christine."

"You're welcome," I say, but I'm not sure if he heard me since he was already out of view when I responded.

When I face Declan, he's leaning back in his chair with his arms folded over his chest, inspecting me with a curious expression.

I stifle my grin, then say, "What?"

"Do you still sing?"

I'm taken aback by his question. "I guess. I mean, sometimes. Not for real or anything."

He tilts his head, still smiling. Then, "What do you mean, *not for real?*"

I shrug. Then searching the ceiling, I say, "In high school, I played music and sang for concerts and talent shows. There was always a purpose, or a goal that I was working towards with my music. Now, I play and sing more as an outlet."

He's nodding as he gently says, "Me too."

I narrow my gaze. Interested in his comment. "You play?"

He nods, with a smug and ridiculously attractive grin.

71

"And sing?" I add in disbelief. I can't even imagine him playing an instrument, let alone *singing*.

He nods. "Want to hear?"

My eyes widen with fascination. "Uh, yes please."

He's already leaving the table for the living room where he retrieves a guitar that's hanging hidden on the wall.

I follow, finding a seat on the edge of the tufted leather couch.

As he checks the strings, and tunes the guitar, I scan the room and what I can see of the hallway. His entire apartment screams *bachelor* but in an exceptionally sophisticated way. Everything from the dark leather tufted sofa and matching chair to the Enrique Chagoya artwork and miniature Egyptian sculpture tucked between several linguistics books on his shelves. The dark browns, blacks and whites ornamenting the interior of his home are luxurious compared to the faded yellow couch, house plants, and dog hair decorating my house.

"What are you in the mood for?" He says this as he strums his thumb down the strings.

I can't stop my smile from spreading across my face. I don't know what mood to choose, since mine are all over the place. Is giddy-anxious-intrigued-aroused-weak-in-the-knees a mood?

"What are my mood choices?" I say, biting my smile.

His eyes crinkle in the corners and he looks down with a laugh, then immediately flashes his eyes up to lock on mine. "Fun and loud. Gentle and quiet. Sad and somber. Sentimental. Or, romantic."

I suck in a rush of air at his last word and blink.

His smile is so wide and so pleased by my reaction I could sink into the sofa and die from self-abasement.

With his satisfied grin, he says, "I think you just answered my question."

He sits on the opposite side of the sofa and strums a chord. As he begins to play, I can tell what song he's singing.

It makes me smile.

Then laugh.

I can't believe I'm sitting in Declan's apartment while he serenades me with a song.

And as he transitions into the chorus, I can't help but join in.

I feel so untouched.
And I want you so much.

That I just can't resist you.
It's not enough to say that I miss you.

Because the song he's singing is *Untouched* by The Veronicas.

Which was the song I played at the talent show with my friend, Lacey, who was into alternative rock in high school. I played the guitar and sang backup to Lacey. She got her boyfriend to play the drums and we quickly had a band. It lasted until the end of high school. Aside from the end of the year talent shows, our only audience was the three walls and door to Lacey's garage.

But now, hearing Declan play a slowed acoustic version of a teen-girl rock band cover takes me right back to that high school talent show.

I feel so untouched, right now.
Need you so much.
Somehow, I can't forget you.
Going crazy from the moment I met you.

There's something so fluid about our voices together.

There's also something so fun about singing with someone again.

When we finish the song, I can feel my face beaming.

"Well," Declan says, pausing to run his tongue across his bottom lip as he considers me for a moment. Then, "That was exciting, I've never sang with anyone like that before."

"Really? I couldn't tell." I release a soft laugh, then, "And I can't believe you learned the lyrics to that song so well." I place both my hands on my cheeks, dumbfounded by his ability to keep in time while leading the vocals to one of the girliest rock songs ever. "Where did you learn to sing like that?"

He's gently strumming to one of my favorite Tegan and Sara songs I used to belt out in my bedroom. Like he's trying to tell me how much he was paying attention to me while following my brothers' instructions to ignore me all those years.

"My parents," he says. "They made us take music lessons when we were kids. My sister chose the piano, and I learned the guitar. Two years of private lessons." He fixes his eyes on mine. "The singing part just happened once I started playing songs I liked."

"Well, your self-taught vocals are impressive," I say.

Wrinkles outline his smile. "Want to sing another song?" I could drown in his voice.

"Please don't," Maverick says this in passing from the hallway to the kitchen.

"Back for more cake?" Declan says.

"Not after I looked up what an aphrodisiac was," Maverick says filling a glass of water.

His comment makes me laugh.

Declan looks back at me and winks.

It makes my stomach quiver. In a good way.

Maverick crosses the living room back to his bedroom again, and says, "You guys aren't terrible at singing, but I'm trying to watch Stranger Things and I can't hear what they're saying with your voices in the background."

"Subtitles," Declan says.

"*Subtitles*," Maverick mocks, closing his door.

Declan looks at me. "Aside from his snarky comment, I'd say that was a decent compliment."

"You guys are hilarious to watch," I say. "Where did he get his blue eyes and blond hair from?" Declan and his family all have olive skin, dark hair, and brown eyes. Maverick apparently acquired a recessive gene.

Declan averts his gaze when he says. "His mother."

I crease my forehead. Confused. I'm not sure what to say since he doesn't seem very happy about Maverick's mother.

He must notice my bewilderment, since he says, "My dad." He shakes his head, like he's disappointed. Then he lowers his voice and continues, "He had an affair when I was thirteen."

I lift my hand to my mouth. "Oh, Declan, I'm sorry. I had no idea. I wouldn't have mentioned it if I knew."

"Don't apologize," he says with a small smile. Then his face shifts downcast again. "He didn't know she was pregnant. The affair didn't last long before he was so riddled with guilt, that he confessed everything to my mom. They decided that it would be better if they brushed the entire thing under the rug, pretending it never happened so they could focus on their marriage again. And our family."

He runs his hand down his face and drags in a breath before saying, "But it all surfaced when Maverick's mother showed up at my dad's work with four-year-old Maverick in hand. She demanded child support, and my dad demanded partial custody. They compromised and Maverick started spending holidays and weekends with us. We all loved him instantly. But I've always noticed a hint of pain in my mother's expression when he's visiting. Like Maverick's existence is a reminder of my father's betrayal. Or maybe that's me looking too much into things." He shakes his head. "Anyway, even though I loved Maverick and wanted to be a good brother to him, finding out my dad, my hero, had created a whole and complete love child behind our backs really messed me up. My entire senior year was kind of a blur."

I want to jump into his arms and hug him. What a confusing thing to experience. I'm sure there's so much to unpack with that that he's probably still dealing with some unresolved issues. But I'm glad he's stepped up now, and has been such a good role model and big brother to Maverick.

Picking at the guitar strings he says, "I don't know why I'm the one still feeling shame and trying to cover it up."

I shake my head. "Of course you feel that way, he's your dad. I would feel that way too if it had happened to my family. And if I'm being honest, even though I was expecting my parents' divorce, I still felt shame that I was growing up in a broken home. When our parents fail, it kind of affects us too. Even if it's only inadvertently."

He sets the guitar down, leaning it against the sofa and faces me. "Thank you," he says, taking my hand in his. "For the validation. No one's ever said anything like that to me before."

"Everyone needs to be understood by somebody," I say, my heart shredded for him.

Looking from my eyes to my mouth and back to my eyes, he says, "I'm grateful that you're the *somebody* that understands me."

I want to cave to his yearning eyes. But since I'm twenty-three and never kissed a guy before, and I don't even know if we're dating. I pull my eyes down to our hands and give his hand a gentle squeeze, then say, "I should probably go. I really need to get some research done."

When I begin to release my grip, he doesn't let my hand go. Which forces me to secure my eyes to his.

"Christine." The quiet way he glides my name past his lips weakens me. "You know my brain is like an encyclopedia, right?"

I smile. "I'm sure it is, but I need to get some studying done too."

He lifts his chin and raises one brow. "I'm insulted," he says, teasing me. "Not only am I full of information, I can also teach you my secret study techniques."

I sigh. Check the time. Then bite my bottom lip for a moment as he regards me silently before I say, "You have ten minutes to prove yourself."

And he does.

I half expected him to be bluffing just to keep me in his apartment long enough to kiss me.

But he doesn't try to kiss me at all. As if he can sense my lacking confidence in that department, and instead, he teaches me one of the most invaluable study techniques that causes me to feel convicted for knowing it. Like I've just robbed him of his knowledge.

He's just given me the upper hand in the classroom, and I only wish I had known these study techniques sooner.

I'm sure I'll think of something to reimburse him with later.

He deserves it.

EIGHT

"Heads or tails?"

I tilt my head to the side in thought. "Are you going to catch it and flip it over on top of your hand or let it drop to the ground?"

He narrows his eyes with a smug grin. It's a grin that I love more than any grin from any mouth I've ever seen. "Does it matter?"

I nod and flash him my smuggest grin in return to his. "It does."

"I'll catch it," he says studying me peculiarly.

I shake my head. "I don't like that way."

He laughs through his smile, like I'm being ridiculous, then says, "Alright, I'll let it drop."

I narrow my gaze at him. Challenging him. "Tails."

He flicks the coin off his finger, up into the air. It hits the ground with a ping and spins for a moment before collapsing. We both lean over to see what it is.

"Heads," he says, picking it up. He raises his brow. "I win."

Before I can fold my arms over my chest, he takes my hand in his. "Please tell me your choice was taking me to the museum for the day."

He shakes his head. "Nope."

"Well, that's what my choice was going to be if I won."

"That's not what mine is. I spend enough of my time at the museum, I don't want to spend my day off there."

He tries to get me to follow him, but I grip his hand tighter to stop him. "Then where are we going?" I say.

He faces me then runs the tip of his tongue against his bottom lip as he considers me for a moment. Or considers whether he wants to tell me what his choice is. Maybe he doesn't have an idea on where he wants to spend the only day we've both had off at the same time in a month.

We've managed to coordinate lunches, and prioritize dinner on the weekends. But we haven't spent an entire day together since Parker's funeral.

"We're going to the beach," he says with a wink, then pulls me down the sidewalk to his car.

"I don't even think the beaches in California would be any fun this time of year," I say, keeping my eyes fixed on the dense tree line out my passenger window. "It's too cold to swim," I say glancing at him, unsure why he's determined to spend our day on a cold beach at the end of winter.

Declan keeps a loose hand on the steering wheel and slips the other hand under my knee. "We're not going to the beach to swim."

I know if I ask him why we're going he won't tell me. He's being secretive. And I kind of like it. It's fun.

I roll my head against the back of my seat to face him completely. "Where do you see yourself in ten years?"

His mouth is firm while his thoughts are moving in his mind. "That's a good question."

I adjust myself so I'm leaning over the middle console. I want to be closer to him. Every one of my senses wants to be invaded by him. But since we're driving, I'll settle for where I'm at.

"It can be anything," I say noticing he's having trouble formulating an answer. "It doesn't even have to be something that will ever happen in real life. It can be a fantasy. I'm just trying to pass the time since you don't like listening to the radio."

He smiles. "Okay, where do I see myself in the unrealistic fantasy future?" He taps his steering wheel with his thumb, then, "I suppose I will have become a world leader and re-established hieroglyphs for a means of worldwide communication."

My laughter cracks so loud that I think I may have burst Declan's eardrum. "What else?" I say still laughing.

He adjusts himself. Sitting up straighter. Then with a grin he says, "I will be rich and disperse my income so that no one would be poor, and I would mandate that all the rich men trying to control the world would have to do the same with their money."

"I like that," I say, feeling a sudden urge to kiss the side of his face. "Is that all? Am I around in this future fantasy."

He forces a rush of air out of his nose. "Absolutely," he says drawing his head back as if I should have known this. "You will be at my side, leading the society we created that's dedicated to infusing peace in the world through our good deeds and morality."

I'm nodding, like I can't wait to be there with him.

He continues, "And we'll sing songs together and the whole world will join in. We'll have one voice. Together." He glances at me with a raised eyebrow. "It will be so magnificent, the angels in heaven will hear and join in."

I lean my forehead against his shoulder and close my eyes. Letting the images from his imagination run wild in my mind. As if there's a possibility it could really happen.

"What about you?" he says. "Where are you in ten years?"

I toss out every thought I've ever had about my future and say, "Singing songs that reach the heavens with you."

His smile widens. "I think you just became my girlfriend."

His words hit my sternum, blast through my chest, and explode into my heart. I close my eyes and smile. Taking a mental picture of this monumental moment and implausible instance.

"I think I did too," I finally say with the most fantastic grin that has ever masked my face as my heart doubles in size.

I'm still leaning on his shoulder when he gently presses his mouth against the top of my head, which shoots an earthquake down my ribcage and releases a tidal wave into my stomach because it's the first time he's kissed me. Even if it was on the top of my head, I still consider it the first kiss. It's the first kiss he's given me anyway. And I wish I could get a tattoo there as a reminder of it.

"You should have been a writer," I say. "Your mind is very creative."

His voice is steady when he says, "I am a writer."

I lift my head up, facing him. "Really?"

"Yeah," he nods. "I've been writing my entire life."

"What kind of writing?" I'm intrigued. Infatuated. And it's evident in my tone.

He scratches the stubble that's grown along the side of his jaw when he says, "Lyrics. Poems. Essays. But mostly journaling."

How does a guy with this much muscle mass have the confidence to admit he writes poetry? And *lyrics*? *And journals*?

"I'd love to read some of it," I say with sincerity.

He glances down at my eyes, and I see an affectionate flicker in his eyes when he says, "You will." He's turning my insides to mush.

79

We veer around a bend where a sign depicts the ocean we're about to infiltrate. We find parking and Declan is already out of the car before I can zip up my jacket.

"Come on, come on." His words and energy are equally enthusiastic and hurried.

I can already hear the roar of the ocean and crashing waves against the rocky shore.

He takes my hand as we abandon the picnic bag at the car. Not that the weather is picnic friendly right now.

The trees uncover a uniquely beautiful display of massive logs washed up on the shore and even greater rock formations protruding out of the ocean. Like they dropped from the sky and have been hostage to the water ever since.

"Here," he says, motioning us to a hammock amongst the trees. It's positioned in a place where large rocks and dense trees break the rushing wind.

"Did you put this here?" I ask as I plop myself into the swinging hammock.

He watches me intently as I swing. "No, it's always been here."

"I like it," I say with a smile. It's quieter behind the natural barricade. I use my best sophisticated voice when I say, "Is this a place you frequent often?"

"Is that a pickup line?" He leans his shoulder into the base of a tree as his mouth curls up on one side.

I laugh. "Well, do you?"

"Yeah." He raises his brows. "I love it here."

"Why?" I can't imagine anyone would voluntarily come here. It's nothing like the California beaches. No one is here. It's windy, cold, and rocky. I would much rather lay out on the sand and people watch in the warm sunshine.

"I can think here." When he says this, his eyes shift and his mouth falls into a firm line. As if he's just reached far back into his mind for a lost memory.

"What do you think about?"

His eyes move from his memory and fix on me. "Everything," he says softly.

"Apparently not where you'll be in ten years," I say joking.

"Yeah," he says with a halfhearted smile that makes me wonder what he does think about out here. And if it's anything I might be interested in knowing.

"So," I say.

"So," he repeats, fixing his gaze on me.

Since he's not going to talk about whatever is locked up in his mind. I say, "Can I ask you something?"

He's watching me swing back and forth like I'm the only and most interesting person he's ever seen. "Anything." He looks down at my swinging feet.

I scrunch my nose. Knowing what I'm about to ask is going to change the way he's looking at me. And a part of me regrets what I want to say, but the other part needs to know. "Remember when you used to lifeguard at the pool?"

His eyes cut to mine and hold an expression that looks as if I've just betrayed him in some way.

Even though I was partly expecting his expression, it still makes me wince when he reveals it to me.

He's quietly considering my question.

I take his silence as an opportunity to further explore the continuous knocking this question has been doing in my mind.

I gently lay out my words for him. "I was there that day," I say, dragging my feet to stop myself from swinging. "I used to go to the pool every day—"

"At one o'clock," he finishes my statement for me without taking his eyes off me.

I pull my eyebrows together, realizing he was paying more attention to me than I thought. "You noticed?"

He nods, still with a very serious expression. "I was always paying attention to you, Christine."

"But you always had a girlfriend. And you never talked to me." I know my brothers forbid him from me, but I still don't understand how that was enough to keep him from even speaking to me.

This causes him to approach me. He reaches for my hands and pulls me out of the swing. Without letting go of my grip, he says, "To distract myself. I had other girlfriends as a distraction. I know that's wrong. But it's the truth. I avoided you because your brothers told me to. If I hadn't been so worried about losing my friends, believe me, I wouldn't have distracted myself from you."

The quiver returns to my stomach and shivers up into my throat. I can't speak.

He drops his head back, looking up into the waving tree limbs dancing above our heads. "And distracting myself from my life. And my family. From the reality of my dad's affair." He shakes his head and looks back down at me. "That day at the pool. I was hungover. I hate to admit it, but I was probably still drunk. It's by far the worst day of my life."

An unexpected gasp shoots through my mouth. Because I think I might know where this is going, and it hurts me. Not personally. But it hurts me because I know it's been hurting Declan. For years.

He swallows hard. "I've relived that day over and over. Wishing I could change something. Wishing I could take it back."

My voice is a whisper when I say, "It wasn't your fault."

He shakes his head, exhaling. Then he faces the ocean and pulls me in to hug me tightly. Wrapping his arms around me entirely. It's as if he's using me to comfort himself. But I don't mind.

"It feels like it's my fault."

I press my cheek into his chest. "Have you talked about it with anyone?"

"No," he makes a sort of laughing sound. Masking his feelings. "It's not something I'm proud of. At all. Or want to share with anyone."

"Maybe talking about it would help? You can talk to me. I still don't know what really happened that day."

He pulls back and flicks his eyes between mine as if he's both eager to get the words out, and equally terrified. "What do you know?"

I press my mouth together, gathering my thoughts into words that will hopefully come out of my mouth in a way that doesn't hurt him as much as he's been tormenting himself.

I exhale through my nose. Nervous to get into this because I don't know how he's going to respond. But anxious to be the person that he opens up to.

I keep the side of my face pressed to his chest when I say, "I know that you were working that day. I know that you dove into the pool to save that kid that was drowning. I know I didn't get to swim that day because they closed the pool before I got there." I inhale and I'm surprised that my voice is shaky when I say, "I know you hit your head and have a scar from it now. And I just learned that you were hungover that day which means you probably weren't as responsive as you would have liked to be."

I feel his arms gently tighten around me.

I don't want him to keep falling into this circular pattern of reliving the worst day of his life over and over.

I pull my arms free and cup his face in my hands to make sure I have his full attention when I say, "And I know that if you could, you would change that day. I know that you blame yourself and you don't have to. I know that you were a teenager, and you have to forgive yourself. And I know that talking to me will help you."

His firm expression shifts into sorrow. "How do you know?"

I hug him around his neck, burying my face into his shoulder. Wanting to prove he can trust me. "I just know." I hate that he's keeping this inside himself. "I'll always be the somebody that understands you."

He rests in my hug for a moment. Breathing into my neck. When he releases me, he keeps his hands on my waist. Then, "The day before that happened, my parents had been arguing. They argued a lot that year. Understandably, after everything with Maverick and his mom. And after everything we learned about my dad's affair. We were all in a transition. I think we were all grieving the family we thought we were a little bit too. But I didn't want to feel it, so I partied and got too drunk too often. My sister was away at college. Your brothers had graduated the year before. I didn't really have anyone to keep me in check."

Forcing a breath out of his mouth, he continues, "I shouldn't have gone to work. But I did. The pool was busy that morning. We had three lifeguards on watch. I thought I could doze off for a minute behind my sunglasses. I thought if something happened another lifeguard would take care of it. I thought a kid that young would have his parents there paying attention to him. And I've wished every morning that I might wake up and find out it's all just been a horrible nightmare."

His expression grows firm as his jaw tenses. He blinks, looking past me, as if he's reliving it again. As if he's seeing it all unravel in front of his eyes and there's nothing he can do to stop it. Then he says, "I don't understand how saying something so horrible is going to help me."

I gentle my voice, seeing how difficult this is for him to talk about. "I don't understand either, but I promise it will help if you release it."

He meets my eyes. "Okay," he says with quiet uncertainty.

"Okay," I say with expectancy.

Gently resting his forehead on mine. He closes his eyes, and begins unraveling the trauma he's shoved down inside himself. "At first, I heard someone yelling. And because I had dozed off, it took a second for my mind to catch up with what I was hearing in my ears. But once it registered that they were yelling that a kid was drowning, I blew my whistle and shot out of my post into the pool. I didn't bring my floatation device. We were trained to bring it, and I just left it at my chair. Stupid. Everything went black after I hit my head. I was gagging on water when I came to. I must have been down long enough to run out of air. I instinctively rushed up for a breath and in that split second that I was above water, I could hear the chaos. I could hear the panic. I didn't notice the red hue masking my vision was my own blood running into my eyes. I filled my lungs with air and went back down to retrieve the kid. I didn't know how long he had been down there, but I knew something was off as soon as I touched him. Like I could tell he wasn't there anymore. Even in those short moments it took to retrieve him and hand him to the other lifeguards. I stood helplessly as they took turns giving him chest compressions. And once my adrenaline settled, I passed out and hit my head again. I woke up in my own vomit on a stretcher. After I was evaluated, they weren't sure if my concussion was from hitting my head during the first dive into the pool or from when I passed out. I was in pain. But nothing hurt worse than when I was told that poor kid drowned. Because of me."

I don't understand how he's not in tears. I hug him ferociously. This time I'm hugging him because I need it. The tears spill from the corners of my eyes. After hearing that story from his perspective, I'm shattered.

"I'm so sorry that happened to you, Declan. I'm really sorry." My words seem inadequate compared to the heaviness he's carried for so long.

"It makes me never want to bring another human into this world." His arms consume me, hugging me completely with every fiber. His breath is heavy as it hits the side of my face. Like he's just run the hardest uphill race of his life. "Honestly, I don't understand how anyone could bring a child into this broken world."

After a long moment, I say, "I never saw you again."

Without letting go of me, he says, "That's because I left. I packed a bag, wrote a note, left it on the kitchen counter, and left home. I didn't know what to do, so I ran. I spent two months living out of my car. I picked up fast food jobs to put some quick cash in my pocket. And I traveled. I made friends with strangers. I loved it because I could be anyone I wanted to be. I didn't have to be the lifeguard that let a kid drown ever again. All I had to do was keep running."

I pull myself away and face him. I don't know how to take his expression. But I've also never been in the presence of someone explaining the most painful parts of their life before, so I'm not sure what expression is normal for this situation.

"What made you come back?" I say, hesitant to push him too much.

He shrugs. "I'm not sure. Something just clicked. I knew I needed to come home to let my family know I was okay. I wanted to go to college. I knew what I was doing would only get harder and harder. And I couldn't leave my brother and sister like that forever. So, I came back. And my family was so relieved when I showed up that no one even questioned why I left the way I did. Except Winnie."

I tilt my head. "Your sister?"

He nods with a smile. "She's the only person that really knows me and calls me out on my foolishness."

His glistening eyes tell me there's more to that statement that he might not be ready to share yet, but I'm glad he's telling me what he can. And I'm glad he has her. "She doesn't seem like someone that would put up with much crap."

"She's not," he says, dropping his hands to lock around mine.

I grin. "I'm glad you came back."

The corners of his eyes wrinkle with his smile. "Me too." Then he pulls his hand up to meet the side of my face. "Thank you for being my *somebody* that understands." He grazes my cheek with his thumb, then, "I feel like I can tell you anything."

My voice is weak when I say, "You can." Then I give him an inviting look. One that portrays the way I want him to close the space between us.

His eyes fix on my mouth. He begins to meet my lips with his, but then he hesitates. I can feel the electricity between us, but he stops it. And I don't understand why. He's been stealing glances at my mouth since he came back into my life. Isn't this what he wants?

Pressing his forehead to mine, he lets out a breath through his nose then draws himself back to look at me.

"I want to kiss you," he says with a groan. Like he's pained by his own actions.

"I want you to kiss me," I reassure him.

He touches the corner of my mouth with the tip of his nose and brushes it against my bottom lip, then, "I feel like if I kiss you, I would be dishonoring your brothers in some way. I know we're adults, but you'll always be their little sister. And I want to do everything right with you. I want to be intentional with you."

I feel my expression shift into remorse.

"It feels like if I kiss you," he continues, "you would have to marry me."

The remorse I was feeling is replaced by the shockwave that his statement sends through me.

I pull away and blink at him. "You want to marry me?" I just became his girlfriend, and now he's ready for marriage. In his defense he has been secretly wanting to be with me since high school.

"What I mean is, it wouldn't feel right to kiss you before I married you," he says this from the side of his grinning mouth, like he's overconfident that I would marry him right now if a clergy person were nearby.

"You really want to marry me?" I repeat. Stunned. *Scared.* My reaction to him is making me wonder if I have my own set of issues I need to face. Like maybe my parents' divorce has affected me on a subconscious level that I wasn't aware of until now. When the mention of a potential committed relationship is presented before me, my mind tells my heart to *put my guard up.* And that can't be a healthy reaction.

"I don't want to scare you with my answer to that question," he says this unfazed by my unsettled reaction but he's also being cautious as not to run me off with a more certain response. "But for now," he says, tucking his index finger under my chin and raising it gently so our eyes meet, "I'll wait a lifetime for you if that's what you need."

NINE

"Take this exit," Tallen says motioning his hand at the windshield.

I'm already passing the exit when I say, "The GPS told me to take the next one."

"The GPS doesn't know. That way is faster," he says pulling aggressively at his seatbelt until it locks. "And safer."

He's developed a few of these habits. Locking his seatbelt. Keeping his seat as far away from the dash as possible. Triple checking the tire pressure before going anywhere. And making demands of the driver.

The driver, being me.

This outing is part of his recovery therapy. We were supposed to drive fifteen miles to Bellevue then back to the rehabilitation center in Seattle without Tallen expressing any signs of compulsive behaviors.

He made it almost eight minutes before making demands. Which is not much progress from the last time we were in the car together.

"Don't you want to go home?" I say. "Aren't you tired of being here? If you just ride in the car silently for thirty minutes, they will clear you to go home."

His voice is stern when he says, "You don't think I know that Chris? I can't help that every time I get in a car I feel like I'm going to get into another accident. I feel secure locking my seatbelt around my body. This body that only functions on the top half. I feel better when the driver listens to my directions. I feel better knowing I'm getting into a functioning vehicle. I have lost partial control of my body and all control over what happens to me while I'm a passenger in a car."

"Okay," I say, trying to stop him from continuing because I know his words are hurting both of us. "I'm sorry. You're right. You should have some control over your life."

When I glance at him, he looks defeated. I hate that Parker isn't here to lighten Tallen's mood. I hate that Tallen has to miss Parker every day of the rest of his life. I hate that Tallen's world is full of so many unnecessary hurdles.

I park the car and face him. "Want me to tell your doctor that you passed with flying colors?"

He unbuckles himself and opens the door. "Can you hand me my wheelchair?" he says, ignoring my question.

"If I tell them you completed their checklist, you'll be free to continue your therapies from the comfort of your home back in Nevada."

When I don't immediately do as he asks, he turns around without looking at me and begins dragging his wheelchair from the backseat.

I let out a breath, but I'm not going to give up on him.

I exit the car and meet him on the other side as he's getting ready to adjust himself from the car to his chair.

"It would be easier for you. You wouldn't be alone. Mom would be right down the road for your every need," I say, hopeful.

When he moves to his chair, he doesn't have enough momentum which causes him to slip from the chair seat into a stranded pile on the pavement.

The sight of his helpless body makes my heart sink. He lifts his upper half with his arms, but his legs look like they belong to a rag doll.

I don't know if I'm supposed to help him, or just watch. I've never had to help him. Not one time. He's helped me countless times. Picked me up when I've fallen down, not before making fun of me of course. But he's never needed me to pick him up. I've never seen him this helpless and I don't know how I'm supposed to respond.

"Damnit, Chris!" He's yelling at me, but I don't care. I know this is so hard for him and if yelling at me is what he needs to do right now, then I'll take it. "Why do you have to act like that?" His tone hurts worse than his words.

I blink the tears away because I know if he sees me cry it will only make it worse on his pride. "I'm trying to help you get out of this place," I say, finally approaching him. "I'm trying to give you some hope and optimism."

He pulls himself into the chair that I'm now gripping so it doesn't move. "Did you ever think I might not want to go home?" His words cut through me.

"Why wouldn't you want to go home?"

Unlocking the brake on his chair, he says, "I'm not ready." Then he pushes the wheels and moves forward toward the sidewalk.

"Why not?" I press him with my words and close the passenger door before following him.

He ignores me, continuing toward the building.

"What will make you ready?" I say, begging him with my words. "Whatever you need, I'm here to help you." I know our relationship has been built on jokes and lighthearted fun, but I want him to know that I'm willing to do anything for him. He's my brother. My only living brother. And he needs help more than ever.

He stops and with a sad unsteadiness to his movements that breaks my heart, he turns his chair around to face me. It takes several long seconds until he's fully facing me. "I'm six foot five, Chris." His voice is low, but still has a sting to it.

"I know," I say with a broken whisper.

His nostrils flare with his breath. "In this chair, I'm not even five feet." His jaw is set, and his brows are pulled together so hard they've created two wrinkles between them. "I'll never see the world at six feet again. Home will never feel like home at this level. Looking up at you will never feel right. Hugging mom from this chair will never feel normal."

I cover my mouth with my hands and slowly drop to my knees so he can at the very least look down at me again. "I'm so—"

"Don't," he says. "Don't say you're sorry." His shoulders are rising with each bitterly heavy breath.

I don't speak.

I'm afraid anything I say at this point will just upset him more.

He continues, "And the worst part of being forced to endure life at this level, is that Parker will never be in my view again."

With that, he turns back around and enters the building.

I rise from my knees.

Lift my head.

And make my way to my car where I grip my face in my palms and cry.

I miss my brothers.

I miss Parker.

I miss Tallen.

I miss my brothers, *together.*

I wish I could do something to make it better. I wish I could figure out how to help Tallen through this. I wish I knew what he needed.

Grief is a wicked thing. But it doesn't have to be. I just wish I could get Tallen to see that.

The ringtone of the facetime call jars me. It's Avery. I know this because she's the only person that ever facetimes me.

I sit up in my seat, turn the car on, answer the call, and place my phone in the cupholder as I pull out of the parking lot. She shouldn't be able to tell I've been crying from her view in the cupholder.

"Still on for the dress fitting?" Her voice is chipper. And I'm thankful since it seems to avert my mood.

"Yes, I just dropped Tallen off so I'm headed your way now," I smile, even though I can still feel the corners of my mouth refusing to shift from their frown. But Avery can't tell I'm upset from where I've placed her.

She's quieter when she says, "How'd it go?" The concern in her voice makes me want to cry again.

Thankfully I don't have to discuss anything since the doorbell rings and Princess starts barking in the background.

"That's the designer now," Avery says with delight. "Fill me in when you get here. I've got to go. See you soon."

The call ends and I'm debating on crying again. But since I'm spending the rest of the afternoon with Avery, I settle for blasting the Yeah Yeah Yeahs through the car speakers and pretending I'm excited to try on dresses.

"I hate it," Avery says holding Princess under one arm and giving the wine-colored dress I'm wearing a disgusted look.

The designer flips her head around. "This was designed to resemble Vera Wang's Manuella bridesmaid dress."

Avery scrunches her nose. "I don't care if Monique Lhuillier made it herself, it's too boxy and I don't like it." Then she blinks at me with a smile. "You're the best."

I know this is her way of telling me to change into another dress. I thought I would be measured, try on a few dresses, then be on my way home. But it's been hours and all I can think about is how I'm starving. And I'm probably going to be too tired to drive home tonight which means I'll be crashing here. And if I don't get some food soon, I'm afraid I'm going to turn into a bridesmaid-zilla.

When I reveal the next dress, which looks like someone shredded fabric and then sewed it all back together, Avery's eyes light up. "Yes!" She jumps when she says this and thrusts her arms in my direction. To the designer she says, "This is exactly what I imagined." The designer slumps into a chair. "Finally." I feel sorry for her having to listen to her work be criticized by a miniature woman with a huge attitude, and obviously no taste in design. Even I can tell this dress was saved as a last resort because it's so hideous.

"Thank you so much," she says to the designer who is suddenly packing her things as if she can't wait to get out of here.

Avery is eyeing me when she makes one last demand from the designer. "Could you change up the straps on every dress? I think it would look better if the dresses were different in some way."

The designer is unzipping the back of my dress as if she's forcing me out of it, when she says, "I'll make a note."

After I change into my normal clothes. I help the designer take her things to her car and repeatedly apologize for Avery since I know she has to come back in a few weeks to help Avery pick out a bridal gown. I can't help but wonder if Uncle Drew knows what he's paying for since Avery hired a designer to come to her apartment for the dress fittings. That can't be affordable. But then again, Avery is Uncle Drew's only daughter *and* only child.

As I head for the elevator, the doors begin to close. I can see that someone is standing in the elevator, so I say, "Hold it, please!"

The doors pop back open, and I rush inside. I'm relieved to see Brent. And more relieved to see he's carrying two bags of takeout with the Wild Ginger logo on the side.

"That smells amazing," I say.

He grins. "There's some peanut sea bass in here with your name on it," he says this as he lifts the bag in my direction.

"Avery doesn't deserve you," I tease, taking the bag from him to peek inside the container.

He lets out a short laugh.

"It took her seven hours to pick out a dress," I say. "I don't know how you're going to handle her for the rest of your life."

The elevator doors open, and we file out toward the apartment door. "You know the saying, *when you know, you know*?" he says.

91

"Yeah, I've heard it. But it doesn't make any sense."

"Well, that's how I feel about Avery." He unlocks the door, but before opening it he looks up at the doorframe in thought and says, "And I don't think it's supposed to make sense until you're with someone that it makes sense with."

The simple way he describes love has me reeling over my last discussion with Declan about marriage.

When Brent opens the door, Avery rushes to him and greets him with a kiss. "Thanks, baby," she says, taking the bags of food from his grip and whisking it away to the kitchen.

I place the bag I'm holding on the counter and watch as Brent and Avery discuss their day to each other. There's nothing exciting about the conversation but they both seem interested in what the other has to say. They also spin around the kitchen effortlessly as they get plates from the cabinet, wine glasses from the rack, and spoon food out onto three plates together.

The familiarity between Brent and Avery is something I've only seen on TV shows. I can't remember a day my parents weren't arguing. It's a miracle that I even exist. I mean, even Uncle Drew and Aunt Milly aren't this connected where they can meander around their kitchen together in a silent dance. If anything, Uncle Drew seems like he would rather be doing anything else than be in the same room as his wife.

But Brent and Avery are showing me that there can be a special connection between two completely opposite people. Witnessing the mundane parts of their love makes me think about what Declan said again. That he didn't want to scare me away with the fact that he would marry me in a heartbeat.

It's as if he was telling me that he's ready to fully commit, but he knows I'm not and he respects that so much that he refuses to say something that might disrupt the harmony in our relationship.

It makes me smile just thinking about how he considers my feelings, and fears, in such a deep way.

It makes me less afraid to hand my heart over to him too.

And it makes me want to experience the mundane everyday activities *with* him next to me.

"What are you thinking about?" Avery says, setting a plate and glass of wine in front of me.

"Nothing," I say.

She tilts her head. "Maybe the better question is *who* are you thinking about?"

I cover my smile with the back of my hand.

"I can't believe you were just thinking about Declan while I am serving you food!" She teases.

"I wasn't." *I was.*

I suddenly want to talk to him. To hear his voice at the very least. I'm consumed by the need to confess how much I care about him. Consumed by the desire to take a step closer to him in our relationship.

I take a quick bite and head for the balcony with my phone in hand.

Avery lifts her arms in confusion. "Where are you going?"

Brent sits next to her and gently tugs at her arm so she'll sit down too.

I slide the glass door open.

Avery laughs, astonished at my behavior. "What? You need to cool yourself off after just thinking about him?"

"Have you seen the guy?" Brent says to her. "I might need to go cool myself off after thinking about him too."

I see Avery whack his arm playfully, then dig into her plate as I slide the door closed and lean against the railing on my forearms.

I drag in a deep breath of the crisp evening air.

Just as the early spring night brings hope for warmer days, I feel hope for my relationship with Declan. It's a kind of hope that makes me hear a wedding march and see him with grey hair.

I text him while I'm feeling brave with my uplifted and sentimental mood.

Me: I miss you.
Declan: You just made my day with that message.
Me: I wish I could come over right now.
Declan: I don't know what's stopping you.
Me: I'm still in Seattle 😞
Declan: Are you busy?
Me: Not really.

My phone begins to ring.

My heart jumps up into my throat when I see Declan's name.

"Hi," I say with a knowing tone.

His voice is thick and smooth when he says, "It seemed like you wanted to tell me something important."

A gentle laugh accompanies the smile his voice creates on my face. "I don't think I said anything about needing to talk."

"You didn't have to." I sense my voice makes him smile too. "I could tell by the way you wanted to see me. Right. Now."

I laugh again.

"So," he says. "What urgent matter is boggling your mind this evening?"

I inhale deeply then release it out slowly as I process. "Remember when we talked about marriage?"

"I remember you wanting to avoid talking about marriage, yes." He's trying to be funny. And he is funny. And I like it. I like that he can see through me too.

I roll my eyes with a smile. "Well," I say hanging on to the word for a moment. "I wanted to tell you that I can see myself married to you. *Someday.*"

"Someday, huh?" He breathes a short breath of laughter through the phone, then, "I'll be looking forward to *someday* every single day."

How is he my first and only boyfriend?

He's perfect.

I look up at the moon and the only star that seems visible in the darkening sky is the north star. "Are you looking out your window?"

I can hear him moving around. "I am now."

"Do you see the north star?"

"I do."

"It kind of feels like we're together when I can hear your voice and know you're looking at the same sky as I am."

He chuckles. "It does."

"This moment just made up for the lousy day I had."

"What made it lousy?" He knows I was going to Seattle to try on dresses and visit Tallen today.

"It didn't go so well with Tallen this morning."

He makes a subtle utterance. Like he's listening intently and wants me to elaborate.

I exhale. "He's still in a dark place and I don't know what more I can do for him. Have you talked with him lately?"

I hope he has. He's visited Tallen when he can, and I know they've gotten closer since the rekindling of their friendship after Thanksgiving.

"Yeah," he says, downcast. "He's beating himself up for the

accident. I'm sure he has some survivor's guilt along with the frustrations of being newly paralyzed. I mean, he and Parker were kind of a package deal and incredibly active. It's a huge change and adjustment for him, you know?"

"That's true." I hadn't thought about how survivor's guilt might be plaguing his emotions and ability to function. "But I still think he would recover better at home and he's refusing to make any effort to leave."

"Christine," *I'll never stop swooning over the way he says my name*, "I think I can help you with that."

"Really?"

He's quiet for a moment, then, "We'll write a song and sing it for him."

TEN

"He doesn't want any visitors," the nurse says with her eyes fixed on her computer screen.

"Yes," I say, plastering a smile on my face as I try to keep my composure. "I know he doesn't want visitors. Which is why I'm trying to discuss some sort of compromise with you about how I can speak with him for two seconds."

"We accommodate to the patient," she glances at me, then back to her computer, "not visitors."

I scoff. "He's my brother."

Declan places his arm around me and says, "Come on, Christine."

I feel my tensing shoulders relax at his touch. I reluctantly give in to him as he guides us out of the building.

This is the fourth time that we have tried to see Tallen. We even wrote a song about Parker that Declan is convinced will bring some cheer to Tallen's life. But after the last encounter, I'm not so sure Tallen will ever feel cheerful again.

It's been months since the last time I saw him. He's been avoiding all contact with anyone besides our mother. And even that is brief contact via a phone call.

I can't help but think part of this is my fault since I was the one that pushed him too far. Maybe if I hadn't forced him to tell me why he didn't want to go back home, he wouldn't still be here. Or maybe he would. I don't know, but what I do know is that he's missing out on his life.

I take my phone out and call Tallen.

It rings twice, then goes straight to voicemail.

"He's still screening my calls," I say. The only contact I've had with Tallen is a string of replies to my texts of him telling me to leave him alone or give him space. I'm not giving up on him, but I think he might need some tough love. I just don't know what that looks like coming from me.

Declan is staring up at the building as we pause outside. "He's been screening my calls too."

I send a text since it's the only contact I still have that Tallen hasn't rejected completely.

Me: Answer.
Tallen: Not ready yet.

I know Tallen has gone through a lot in the last several months. But summer is approaching. I'm about to graduate and leave for Papua New Guinea in the fall. And Avery is getting married in two weeks and he's going to miss *everything*.

How long does a guy need to grieve before he moves on with his life? How long until he talks to us again?

When we reach the car, Declan sits in the driver's seat quietly for a moment. I'm sure he's disappointed we drove all this way just to turn around again.

I place my hand on his leg to comfort him. "I'm disappointed too," I say.

He shakes his head slowly as he releases a breath. "I wish there was a way we could get that song to him."

"Me too."

When he looks at me, I smile, but the smile he returns to me is full of hope. "What if we play it here."

"Here?"

"Yeah," he says, adjusting himself so he can look at me better. "Right outside his window." He looks back to the building. "It has to be one of those along that wall if I'm remembering from the last time I was here."

"Okay," I say. "Let's do it." I'm trying to sound as excited as him, but it seems like a lost cause at this point. Tallen seems to have made up his mind and there doesn't seem like there's much we can do to change that. Maybe in time he will get better emotionally, but I don't see that happening any time soon. "But what if he doesn't hear it from his room? It is on the second floor."

Declan lifts his phone and says, "We'll record it and send it to him. Then we'll be sure he'll hear it."

That makes me smile. I love how eager Declan is to share this song with Tallen. I love that he's so certain there is power in music that is so thick it will reach Tallen's heart. And I love that he cares so much about Tallen's well-being that he's willing to do anything to get him to heal.

But with all the wonderful things about Declan and how passionate he is, I'm also worried that if Tallen doesn't respond the way Declan is hoping, that Tallen's response, or lack thereof, might end up hurting Declan.

I follow Declan out of the car as he retrieves his guitar from the trunk.

"Do you think he'll watch it?" I say trying not to prematurely sound defeated.

Declan brings the guitar strap around his chest and moves the guitar so it's on his back. "Come here," he says, giving me his full attention.

I take his outstretched hands as he pulls me close to him.

He's craning his neck to meet my eyes with his when he says, "I can tell you're not completely convinced about all this."

My eyes widen. "Really?" I want to support and encourage him with whatever he's doing, but I also don't want him to think one song is going to cure Tallen's broken heart.

He nods with a smile that crinkles the corners of his eyes. "I'm not convinced it's going to help him either, but it's worth a shot. Tallen is worth fighting for. And I don't know what else we can do to help him and to show him we're not going anywhere since he doesn't want to let us in."

I nod in agreement, and relief. Hearing Declan say all this out loud makes me feel like I can relax, and that I don't have to worry about whatever happens after Tallen listens to the song.

"And since nothing makes me happier than singing with you," he says. "I thought maybe sharing that happiness with Tallen is the best shot we have at reaching him again."

I blink at the tears trying to emerge in my eyes. I'm smiling when I say, "We're both lucky to have you in our lives right now."

He presses his mouth to my forehead for a moment, then meets my gaze. "Are your vocals warmed up?" he says with a wink.

I let out a gentle laugh and follow him toward the building again. "I hope so."

I text Tallen again telling him to look out his window, but I don't see any movement from the second story windows.

Declan sets his phone on a bench. He looks back at me before he hits record and says, "Ready?"

I nod.

He starts recording.

I step into frame.

He takes a few steps backwards.

I stand next to him as he faces the phone and says, "Hey, Tallen. Christine and I wrote this song for you, and we hope you like it. It's called Parker's Song." He glances at me and strums the first chord. "One, two, three, four."

The beginning is upbeat, lighthearted, and fun.

Declan's voice is bold and confident as he rattles off the intro and I pat my leg, keeping in time.

Remember when we used to
Light our farts on fire?
Your flames were big,
But Parker's were higher.

Remember when we used to
Make fun of Creed?
Then we found Parker jamming out,
To them secretly.

Remember when I bought that,
Old truck with the sticky break?
And Parker drove us straight,
Into the lake.
Man, that was great.

I can't help but laugh and I can hear the way the memories are causing Declan to hold back his laughter while he's trying to sing.

I swallow back my smile, then hum gently as Declan strums the heavy drop in the chords that lead the song into the next verse. And I ready myself to harmonize with him.

Now these are memories,
That we can't escape.

The scars won't go away,
But that's okay,
that's okay.
Because if he could...

Declan looks at me as we both suck in a rush of air before belting out the chorus.

He would tell you to heal,
He would tell you to breathe,
He would tell you to let go,
He would tell you to be free,
And forgive yourself.
Learn to live again,
A little different.

As the song circles back to the next verse, then the bridge, followed by the chorus again, I find my mind drifting to thoughts of Parker. And thoughts of Tallen. And the way Declan was always with them. Even now.

I have an ache in my heart that I hope never goes away for Parker. It's a reminder that I still had so much love left for him. It's a reminder of the love that will never go away. I'm thankful that it aches, because it means I can give the overflow of love I still have for him to his memories. The sting in my heart is like a connection I'll always have to him. Even though it will always be a bittersweet ache, I'm grateful for it.

When Declan stops strumming, and our vocals end, I don't bother pressing away the single tear that's rolling down my cheek.

Declan retrieves his phone and ends the recording. "Well," he says. "The video is sent. Hopefully he watches it." He glances at me with a hopeful expression that immediately sinks into concern. "Come here." I can tell he senses my grief.

He approaches me, pulling me in for a hug. My aching heart must have leaked up into my face and through my expression.

"It's bittersweet," I say with my cheek pressed to his chest. "I miss Parker. I miss when Tallen was happy. I miss them both so much, but I'm okay."

He gives me a firm squeeze before releasing me. "I miss them both too. And if I hadn't sang that song a thousand times before, I don't think I would have made it through without getting emotional too."

"I wish he would have at least looked out his window."

His chest expands with his inhale. Scanning the building he says, "I was anticipating seeing him come through the doors the entire time we were singing."

I wish this was easier for Declan. But I can't imagine going through the most painful part of my life with anyone else.

I look up at him. "What do we do now?"

He takes my hand as we head for the parking lot. "We wait. Give him some space. If the song doesn't do anything, something else will." He opens the door for me. "All good things are worth waiting for."

I flip my head around to face him but he's already closing the door and unloading his guitar in the trunk. Part of me thinks that last comment was meant for me. And I'm not sad about it.

After he starts the car, his phone begins to ring but it's connected to Bluetooth, so he turns the volume up on his car when he answers.

"Hey Margaret," he says, glancing back to the building one last time, I'm sure, to see if Tallen is there.

He's not.

Declan continues, "Tell me you have some good news for me."

Her aged voice glides out of the speakers as she says, "I do," she chuckles, "we've gutted the building and they're ready for you to begin delegating."

Declan lets out a small polite laugh. "I'm not sure I would call it *delegating.* More like unraveling an idea."

"You're too modest," Margaret says. "I'm emailing you the details for housing and what not."

"Something nice, I'm sure."

I know that Declan has mentioned that Margaret is the director of the museum he's helping establish. But the mention of housing confuses me. I know that the museum is located in Washington, D.C., but I assumed Declan would be overseeing his ideas unfold remotely. The idea of him moving has my heart bounding up into my throat. But I don't want to jump to conclusions. Maybe it's temporary housing.

"Only the best for you, Declan. A modern apartment building with a gated entrance." Her tone grows serious when she says, "All I need is a good date and I'll get your plane tickets bought."

He inhales with a smile as if he's about to respond to her, but then he glances at me, and his expression shifts down. "Hey, Margaret?" His smile fades when his eyes focus on the traffic again. "Can I call you back in a minute?"

"Of course," she says. "Talk soon, bye now."

Declan pulls into a parking garage as the call ends and returns to the radio. Someone is talking about the weather when Declan mutes the station.

"I can't stand radio chatter," he says this more to himself than to me. But I can't help but notice the hint of irritation in his voice.

I fold my hands in my lap as Declan begins the scaling search in the parking garage for an open spot.

"Sounds like you'll be in D.C. sooner than later," I say, pointing to a car backing out.

Declan slows, waiting for the car to pull out and leave. "It's certainly sooner than I was anticipating." He pulls into the now open parking place.

I inhale deeply. Considering how things are going to change. Wanting to resist the heartache that's going to accompany his absence in my life. I could cry.

I don't want him to leave. I don't want to do life without him. I love him. *I love him.*

"Hey," he says, turning the car off and taking my hands in his. His voice is tender and pleasant when he says, "We'll make it work. We'll facetime, and text, and I'll visit you, and you'll visit me."

"Declan," I say, locking my widened gaze on his familiar deep golden-brown eyes.

"When you go to Papua New Guinea, we'll figure it out. I'll write to you, so you'll have a surprise every time you check your mail. We'll make it work." His grin is thick with sincerity. And a hint of desperation.

"Declan," I repeat, wanting his full attention.

He pulls my hand up to his mouth and kisses the back of it. When his expression reaches mine again, it's filled with something unfamiliar. Uncertainty. Fear, maybe? "Christine, please." His tone has shifted too. "I want to do everything right with you. I want to give you all the parts of me no one else knows or understands. I love that you're the somebody that understands me. And I—" He cuts his words short, folding in his mouth and looking away.

"Declan," I say again before his assumptions get the best of him.

"Christine," his voice is a whisper, as if he's defeated. I can tell he's misunderstanding my expression as soon as his grip slips in mine.

But I quickly lock my hands around his and say, "Declan, I love you."

His mouth parts as his eyes shoot over to meet mine. Stunned.

I know this is unexpected. It's unexpected for me too. I knew I cared for him. I knew I enjoyed our time together. I knew he was the kind of man I wanted to marry, someday. But I didn't wake up this morning planning to tell Declan that I had fallen in love with him. I didn't really know I was in love with him until the very idea of not being in his presence daily presented itself. I can't fathom it. It makes me sick to think about living our lives apart.

"I love you," I repeat. "I love being with you. And I hate that you're leaving."

He reaches his hand to the side of my face. His concerned expression vanishes and is replaced with admiration. "I've been in love with you since I was fifteen."

And now, I can't breathe.

He peers into my eyes deeper than I've ever seen him do, reaching through my entirety until he takes hold of my soul.

"*I love you, Christine.*" The words glide over his tongue as if he's perfectly packaged their delivery. Waiting for a moment like this one to hijack my heart and knot it together with his.

"I love you too, Declan."

He lets out a laugh mixed in equal parts of disbelief and relief. "I've been waiting almost a decade to hear you say that."

My smile has never been bigger. I close the space between us, but instead of reciprocating, Declan ducks his head down. Blocking my intentions with his forehead to mine.

He keeps his eyes on mine when he says, "I told you I wanted everything to be right with you. I owe it to your brothers. And to *you.*"

I fold my mouth in, exhaling my slight frustration out of my nose. "I know," I say leaning back in my seat again. "And you are doing everything right. But I don't know how denying a kiss from me is part of doing things right."

He sits up and leans closer to me as he says, "You deserve all the good things. Our first kiss should be the day we say *I do* and commit our lives to each other. I don't want to treat you anything less than perfectly. You deserve each milestone of our relationship to be an unforgettable memory. And I can't let our first kiss be in a dingy parking garage." He gives me a smirk. The same smug smirk he's been giving me since the day I slipped on the ice.

I raise my eyebrows. "And I'll always remember the day we confessed our love to each other as a day that was stained because you didn't want to kiss me."

This makes him laugh. "I'll kiss you when I marry you."

I raise one eyebrow in his direction. He's still holding my hands and brings one up to his mouth, twisting my arm slightly as he kisses the inside of my wrist. It sends a shock up my arm that causes me to suck in a rush of air.

"It's been my devoir to marry you," he says as he caresses the place on the inside of my wrist with his thumb where his mouth just was. *Torturing me.* "And until then," he continues, "you'll just have to wait."

I let out a groan. "Then marry me!" I can't believe I let the words pass over my lips. But at the same time, I can't help but say it. I can't imagine letting anyone else reach into my chest and take my heart from me like he has.

"I can't tell if you're being serious." He's still flashing his smug grin at me. Even though his question seems confused, he's just as confident as ever.

My eyes widen as my voice shifts down. "I can't tell if I'm being serious either. But…" I fold my mouth in then look down at our hands, collecting my thoughts.

"But what?"

"It's just," I face him. "Something Brent said."

"What'd Brent say?"

I feel the last bit of doubt evade me as I say, "*When you know, you know.*"

ELEVEN

"Heads or tails?" Declan says, flicking a quarter up in the air and catching it as I shift my weight to one side.

He's taking me out to eat.

Again.

Heads or tails is the deciding factor on which restaurant we'll be eating at tonight.

He's taken me out to eat every night since I graduated last weekend. I half expected him to pull a ring out after graduation. My family was there. We went to a fancy restaurant. I wore my nicest dress.

He pulled my father aside in private to discuss what I thought was permission for him to ask me to marry him. Not that my father cares or even feels any sort of protection over me. But I know Declan wants to do *everything right.*

Declan held my hand at our booth.

He seemed to be cherishing each smile and laugh I gave, whether to him or anyone else at the table.

When the evening came to a close, he gave me another ivy plant, different from the first one, and walked me to my empty house where Avery never is anymore.

He told me I was incredible. That he was proud of me and my graduation. And that, even though he was going to miss me more than anything, he couldn't wait to see the fieldwork I was going to do in Papua New Guinea in the fall.

It was perfect.

I thought it was perfect.

Until the second night.

The second night, I was sent roses at noon. Lilies at 2:00. A snake plant and bouquet of sunflowers at 4:00. Then Declan took me to a restaurant where our table was covered in irises.

No proposal.

No ring.

The third night was an all-day scavenger hunt that led me to the Space Needle where I was sure I would get a ring.

I didn't.

The fourth night he brought me to the roof of his apartment building where he had strewn rose petals and lit candles. He serenaded me in a love song that was meant for my ears only. And when he took my hand in his and kissed my ring finger, I was certain he was going to ask me to marry him.

But he didn't.

By the fifth night, I didn't bother with heels or a dress when he picked me up to take me to the lake for a moonlit dinner he made himself. But I still wore makeup and dressed up as best I could in my casual clothes. Just in case.

But nothing happened.

And last night he took me to the waterfall gardens where we ate cheese and crackers and snacked on popcorn while we did my favorite thing in the world. Which is people watching.

I loved the low-key environment and the personal touch.

I loved the sound of the waterfall sputtering out over the rocks.

I loved the table for two.

Still no ring.

And now that it's been a week of this, I'm exhausted.

I'm not sure what is stopping him from asking me.

Surely he's not nervous. Declan doesn't get nervous. He's confident and honest. So, I don't understand what's giving him cold feet.

I know he wants things to be perfect, but he's going to run out of ideas and end up settling for something less perfect. Plus, if he waits any longer, he'll be asking me to marry him at Avery's wedding reception. Which would be the farthest thing from perfect.

"Tails," I say, answering his question with a hint of fatigue in my voice.

He flicks the coin one last time before letting it drop to my kitchen floor then it rolls until it finds its way under the stove.

We are both staring at the place where the quarter disappeared under the stove when Declan says, "I bet it landed on heads."

"Definitely tails."

He raises his brow, folds his arms over his chest, and leans back against the counter as he crosses his legs at the ankles.

"What?" I say with suspicion of his body language.

He shakes his head. "Nothing."

"What are you thinking?"

He hasn't taken his eyes off me. And the enticing expression on his face is only growing thicker by the second. "That you don't seem real."

I laugh. "Oh, I don't think they make fake women look like this. I'm fairly certain that I'm as real as they come."

He uncrosses his arms and reaches for me to take his hand.

I do. And he pulls me close to him, wrapping his arms around me.

"I know you are, but I keep wondering when I'm going to wake up." I'm not sure how any of this seems unreal for him. I still haven't gotten ready for our date and we're standing in my kitchen flipping a coin to figure out our fate for dinner.

I scrunch my nose. "You're painfully awake."

He presses his mouth against the top of my head. The gesture almost makes me want to cry. Not because I'm sad, but because I'm plagued by this torture he's putting me through. We both know he's going to ask me. We both want it. So why is he taking so painstakingly long?

I pull away with a smile. *A forced smile.* "I'll be right back."

He looks like he's holding something back when he says, "I'll get that quarter."

I head for the bathroom. When I finish and wash my hands, I notice that my reflection in the mirror, like my tone, is obviously fatigued. My hair is thrown up in an unmanaged top knot. I'm wearing track shorts with a sweatshirt I've had since community college. And the only makeup on my face is whatever mascara is left over from yesterday.

No wonder he hasn't asked me to marry him.

When I leave the bathroom, Declan is no longer in the kitchen. I scan the living room. When I don't find him, I head back down the hall to my bedroom. It's the only other place he could be.

But when I find him on one knee in the middle of my bedroom where he very obviously has just strewn fairy lights and tossed my favorite color of peach rose petals around, I freeze.

He's holding a box that is much larger than an engagement ring box. So I'm not sure if he's about to do what I think. I've had too many close encounters this week to know what he's going to do when he proposes. But he's also on one knee, which indicates this is a very different situation than the false alarms I've experienced over the last week.

"Declan." I hang on to his name with a grin I can't contain, and say, "What is this?"

He's opening the box.

Is it a ring?

Why is the box so big?

Maybe it's a necklace.

My heart begins to accelerate.

I can't think straight.

I can't breathe.

I don't know if I'm excited or nervous.

I don't even know my name right now.

"Christine." His voice warms me.

And reminds me that my name is Christine.

"I can't even begin to tell you what you mean to me." He drags his tongue against his bottom lip as his grin grows. "You're in my past, my present, and my future." His smile stretches across his face even more. "Being with you breathes life into me. You encourage me and inspire me." His eyes lock on mine intensely when he says, "You've become my muse."

He reaches for my hand as I approach him.

"Will you do me the honor of becoming my wife?"

The box is open.

There is a beautiful ring in the center of a bed of drying leaves. Some, more dried than others. Some, still fresh as if they were just plucked from their stem.

I'm nodding.

I'm laughing.

I'm trying to catch my breath.

"*Yes,*" I manage to say.

He's sliding the diamond ring on my finger.

It's perfect.

He rises and lifts me from my feet, spinning me in a gentle circle with our foreheads pressed together.

He says, "I'm going to do everything in my power to give you the best life when we move to D.C. together."

I pull away to look at him better. "But I have my trip to Papua New Guinea," I say with penitence. And I also say this as a gentle reminder for him. I feel torn between my deep desire to do fieldwork and my heart's desire to spend my life with Declan. I'm sure there's a way I can do both.

Certainly he wouldn't want to keep me from my fieldwork. I know I don't want to take him away from everything he's working on with the new interactive museum he's curating. That's why I haven't even mentioned asking him to come along with me to Papua New Guinea. Although I know the linguistic side of him would find it intriguing.

He continues, "And I'll fly there with you when you move in, and come back to get you when you're done." He's still holding me in his arms.

"You're going to be okay without me for six months? Maybe longer depending on my research?"

He grazes the side of my cheek with his finger, then caresses it down my arm until he reaches my hand. Lifting my hand, now decorated in the finest jewelry it's ever worn, he kisses my ring finger. "Why do you think I bought you a considerably sized ring? I don't want you or anyone else confused about how much I love you."

This makes me laugh with teary eyes.

"Come here," he says, guiding me to the window.

The streetlights illuminate our faces when he pulls the curtain to one side. "Look," he says nodding to the moon. "I don't want you to forget that even though sometimes we'll be miles apart, I'll always be looking up at the same sky as you. And this ring is a reminder of my love for you that's encompassing enough to reach across the ocean to grasp you."

I nod. But that tiny voice that tells me fifty percent of marriages end in divorce hits me with the slightest bit of doubt. Just enough that I say, "No matter what happens?"

He sits on my bed and pulls me close until I find a seat on his lap. Enveloping me in his arms, he says, "I know we will argue. I know we will fight. I know we won't always agree on everything. But I also know we will work through it. I know we will figure it out. I know we both want the best for each other. I know marriage is work. And I know I'll love you even when I don't like you."

I press my forehead to his and shut my eyes tightly as a form of controlling my fierce impulse to kiss him. "I'll love you even when I hate you."

He laughs.

I stand and begin to look for my phone to snap a picture. "Where did my phone go?"

Declan motions for the dresser with his hand and I notice both of our phones perched upright.

He hands me my phone before taking his.

I tilt my head and give him a suspicious grin when I realize my phone camera is on. "Were you recording that?"

He nods. Unfazed. Then retrieves his phone from the dresser. "Yes. Now we can relive that moment for the rest of our lives."

I run one hand down my torso and slap the top of my bare leg, revealing my lack of fashion today. "I look like a hobo."

He closes the space between us, lifting his phone and pulling me close with one arm around my shoulders. "Don't say that, it's offensive." I'm not sure if he's serious when he says this since his grin is so wide and his tone is gentle. But maybe it is offensive for him since he was technically homeless when he left town after he blamed himself for that little boy that drowned. Whatever the reasoning behind his comment, I'm making a mental note to be more sensitive with my verbiage.

He says, "You're beautiful." Then we both grin up at his phone as he snaps a photo of us right as I hold my hand up, flaunting the diamond hugging my finger.

I watch him inspect the picture. Then he faces it toward me. I smile, even though I honestly do look like a person that doesn't own a shower or hairbrush. And my smile widens at Declan's expression full of genuine happiness.

I give him a slight pouty face. It's one I've used many times on my brothers. But it feels slightly different revealing it to Declan as I say, "Why couldn't you have asked me to marry you last weekend? Or at the Space Needle? Or in the park? Or literally any other night of the week when I had clothes on that didn't smell like enchiladas?"

He cracks a laugh and sits back down on my bed. He's messing with his phone now, I'm sure he's posting the photo on social media or sending it to his family. I'm not a vane person, but I imagined my proposal would be a little more glamorous than this. Heck, I would have taken the people-watching-in-the-waterfall-gardens night over this.

"Why did you take me out every night this week on the most romantic dates that would have been perfect for a proposal, and then ask me now when I'm not ready or expecting it?" I'm not upset, I'm more curious. Okay, I'm a little frustrated that this one and only milestone of my life is going to be remembered by everyone from a photo and video of me in my jogging shorts and outdated sweatshirt.

The glow of his phone screen on his face disappears as he clicks the button on the side of his phone, turning the screen off. Now the only light in the room is shining from the fairy lights he strung around my furniture and keyboard. And I have to admit, Declan seated on a bed full of rose petals with the orange glow of the fairy lights is very romantic.

"Christine." *I'll never get tired of the way he says my name.* "This week I wanted you to experience all the ways I already know how to love you. I wanted you to know that I can take care of you, treasure you, and speak your love language." He's standing now, taking my waist in his hands. "And *this* you. The woman standing in front of me in her most natural form. This is the woman I want to spend my life with. This is the *you* that I'm in love with and want to wake up next to every morning. This woman is comfortable and that makes you the most beautiful to me."

My mouth falls agape, but no words come out.

He presses his cheek into mine as he hugs me, and gently whispers next to my ear, "And can we please get married soon because I can't wait any longer to kiss you." Then he holds me as he falls backward onto my bed.

I let out a playful squeal then prop myself up on my arms on his chest. "Let's tell our parents before we decide on a date."

He groans. Then, "What are you doing tomorrow?"

I shrug.

"Let's leave a day early."

"We're already leaving two days before Avery's wedding."

"I know," he says. "But let's leave three days early so we can have one day to tell our families we're engaged."

I smile. "Okay." Then I laugh. "Avery's going to lose her mind."

He raises his eyebrows. "That's why we're telling everyone three days before the wedding, so we're not stealing any of the attention she's expecting over the weekend."

I search his eyes for a moment then, "What are you hiding?"

He draws his head back as much as he can while resting on my

111

bed, then twists his face. Perplexed. "I don't think I'm hiding anything."

"There's no way you're this perfect."

He grins, then begins to tickle me. "Really?"

I'm laughing.

"You can't fathom the idea that I might be just as perfect as you are?"

Now I'm squealing and shifting out of his grip.

"Is that it?"

He releases his hands and hugs them around me while I catch my breath.

"Christine?" He's still teasing me, readying his hands to tickle me again.

"Okay," I say, holding his hands so he doesn't try to tickle me again. Not that I could stop him if he really tried. "You're wonderful and perfect and there's nothing you're hiding."

He flashes me a grin then nuzzles his chin against my head.

I run my finger down his sternum. "You know what I've been wondering?"

"What's that?"

I exhale slowly and glance at him with interest. "Did you get that quarter from under the stove?"

"I did."

"Was it heads or tails?"

He chuckles, brushes a loose strand of hair from my face, then, "Tails."

"Oh good," I say with relief. "I won."

"What'd you win?"

I lift my head and smile at him. "We're ordering takeout for dinner."

TWELVE

I set my bag by the front door and switch my phone from one side to the place between my neck and other ear.

"Yes, I packed your rehearsal dress," I say into my phone to Avery.

I actually didn't pack her dress yet, so I quickly rush to her room and find the rehearsal dress in her closet and pull it from the hanger.

She continues, "And my makeup bag?"

I can almost hear her tapping her foot.

I close her bedroom door and hurry to the entryway to lay her dress over my bag. "You don't have your makeup bag?"

She lets out an irritated exhale. "My *other* makeup bag."

I don't want to turn her into a bridezilla, but I can't help but say, "Oh, right, because everyone has two makeup bags." Maybe it didn't come out as funny as I thought it would.

She makes an irritated growling sound as I search through the bathroom drawers on her side until I find a dingy turquoise bag full of makeup.

"When will you guys get here?" Her tone is beyond annoyed. It's too late. She already sounds like a bridezilla.

I zip her makeup bag into the side pocket of my travel bag. "Probably eight hours or so."

"Okay, tell Declan to drive safe." Then she hangs up before I can tell her bye.

I check the time and quickly calculate when we should be there. No later than 2:30 pm.

My phone vibrates and my home screen shifts from a photo of me and Declan, to a contact photo of me and Avery.

I answer. "What'd you forget to tell me to grab."

Her voice is more elegant when she says, "Could you grab Princess' white harness and leash too, please?"

"Yes," I say, heading for her bedroom.

"And her blanket with unicorns and rainbows?"

"There's not a blanket at the hotel she can use?"

"She likes the unicorn blanket, it's her favorite."

Then why isn't it already with her?

"Got it."

"Thanks! Text me updates so I know you guys are safe."

"Will do." Then I hang up. And stare blankly at nothing in particular for a moment to decompress from Avery's intensity.

This is going to be a long weekend.

Part of me wonders if she felt bad leaving the first conversation in haste, and after everything with Parker, she's being more sensitive about this road trip.

I finish packing a few other things, water my plants, then text Declan.

He responds immediately, saying he's a few minutes away.

After I lock the doors, I gather my things so I can meet him outside. When he pulls up, I hurry down the steps with an armload of things and my suitcase bouncing down the stairs behind me.

He jogs from his car to meet me on the sidewalk and help with my bags.

"I hope there's room in my trunk for all your stuff," he says teasing me.

I try to keep in stride with him, but he seems like he's in a hurry. "Yeah, well don't blame me, half of it is Avery's stuff. Plus, you have an entire backseat if you run out of trunk room."

He raises one eyebrow as he side eyes me. But instead of saying whatever is behind his suspicious expression, he faces forward and opens his trunk.

"What is it?" I say knowing there's more to his secrecy.

He organizes the bags like a Tetris game until everything is rearranged to fit perfectly in his trunk.

He shakes his head. "Nothing." But his grin says otherwise.

"Declan," I say narrowing my gaze and pulling my mouth to one side.

"What?" He's getting into his car. So, I follow.

When we're buckled, I say, "Declan," again.

This time he lets out a quiet laugh. "Christine." He mimics the same tone I'm using when he says my name.

I shift in my seat so I'm facing him better. "I know you well enough to see that you're not telling me something."

He runs his tongue across his bottom lip, before folding his mouth in.

"Tell me," I say in my pouty voice.

He glances at me, then back to the road. "We're going to take a little detour."

"Okay? And why are we taking a detour?"

He takes my hand in his without looking and gently rolls his thumb over the diamond on my finger. "We're going to get Tallen."

We pull into the parking lot of the rehabilitation center and a million questions bounce around in my head while my heart sinks with the same discouragement I've felt every other time I've come here and been rejected by Tallen.

Is he going to throw his words at me again?

Will I be able to look at him without wanting to cry because he's in a wheelchair for the rest of his life?

Will I be able to handle his hardened expression.

Can I accept the angry man that's replaced my brother?

"Hey," Declan says slipping his arm around my shoulders. "I told you, he's changed."

I keep my gaze forward on the minivan parked in front of us. I wonder if it belongs to a woman visiting her brother. Or maybe a husband visiting his wife. Or a mother visiting her child. I wonder what happened to their loved one and if every family goes through this process of pain, and grief, and struggle to normalcy again.

But does it ever *really* feel normal again?

Everyone in the building either has a prosthetic limb or will sit in a wheelchair the rest of their life. How long does it take for them to experience happiness again? How long until they feel comfortable enough to wear their prosthetic in public? Or spin around in their wheelchair with grace?

I press my hands together nervously. "I know you said he's different now, but you didn't see him fall out of his wheelchair like I did." I turn to face Declan and rest the back of my head against his arm that's still wrapped around my shoulders. I feel remorse when I say, "Seeing him like that did something to both of us. Like it fractured our relationship or something. He was so vulnerable and angry. Maybe a little embarrassed. He told me he didn't want to see the world at that level from his wheelchair, and I think he was scared for the world to see him at that level too."

Declan pulls me close to him and presses his mouth against my forehead as he releases an exhale. Then he looks at me with compassion and understanding as he says, "There's something your brothers told me once after we lost a football game. I was really torn up about it because I fumbled the ball at the last second. It was the playoffs, and I really beat myself up about it for weeks after. I wanted that win so badly and felt like I let the team down. I know losing a high school football game is nothing compared to losing your ability to walk, but what they said still applies to this situation."

I keep my eyes on him in anticipation.

He lets out a breath through his nose, then faces me with a soft grin. Even his brown eyes seem like they're smiling. "I kind of hid from the world in my bedroom. I was disappointed in myself. I kept replaying the last five seconds of the game in my head and wishing I had done something different. Your brothers noticed I was pulling away and instead of giving me space, they invaded my life. I mean, like seriously wouldn't leave me alone. I turned them away, but they wouldn't listen. They were like leaches."

I laugh gently, thinking about my brothers together. Bouncing their positivity off of each other.

Declan lets out a laugh too, then says, "They said, *you never give up on your friends. Sometimes you'll be the one telling your friend to grow up, and other times you'll need your friend to say it to you. And sometimes you'll have to pick your friend up when they're down, and other times you'll need them to pick you up. You show up for your friends. No matter what.* I know he's your brother and not your friend, but all you have to do is replace the word *friend* with the word *brother* and the statement applies to you too."

He's right. Or I guess my brothers were right. It's interesting to hear that even when they were teenagers, my brothers had big hearts. And a sense of wisdom I didn't realize was there. It's as if Declan saw the raw brotherhood behind the humorous façade Tallen and Parker showed to everyone else.

"Come on." He turns the car off and motions out of the door as he says, "Let's go get your brother."

I smile. "Let's go get your friend."

Before we fully exit the car, I notice Tallen is already headed in our direction. The smoothness and control of his movements in his wheelchair is the complete opposite of how I saw him struggling to maneuver in it the last time we were together.

Declan meets Tallen first and they lock their hands before Declan leans down and embraces Tallen, patting his arm on his back.

I'm a little nervous and unsure what I should do. I still feel the sting of Tallen yelling at me. I know he was struggling, broken, and traumatized in that moment. But so was I, not in the same intense way as him, but I was hurting too. And when I reached a hand out to help him when he was down, he rejected me in the same way our father rejected us after the divorce. So, I'm a little nervous and unsure what I should do.

"You look good, man," Declan says to Tallen.

"Wish I could say the same for you," Tallen says with a smirk. "I guess, congratulations are in order after your engagement." He shifts his gaze between mine and Declan's. "Well, congratulations."

I don't know how to respond.

Declan responds for the both of us when he says, "Thanks. We haven't told our parents so act surprised when we tell them tonight."

Tallen nods. "Will do."

Declan takes Tallen's bag from his lap, and Tallen tries to hold on to it.

"I've got it," Tallen says, in his normal familiar voice.

Declan pulls it even harder. "Give me that," he says, playfully ripping it from Tallen's grip. "You don't know where it fits in the trunk. Plus..." he glances at me, then back to Tallen. "I think you two need to have a conversation." Then he shoulders the bag and strides over to his car.

I pull my hair to one side and wait for Tallen to stop looking at Declan and face me.

At first, he lets out an exhale and drops his head down. He looks just like the old Tallen, only in a wheelchair. The strength has returned to his body, his hair is trimmed and styled, and he's clean shaven. Healthy. And alive.

I clasp my hands together in front of me and say, "When did you two start talking again?"

He flashes his eyes to meet mine, then focuses on Declan in the parking lot again as he says, "A month or so. After the song, he wouldn't leave me alone."

I perk up. Straightening my posture. "You listened to it?" His comment makes the rejection I've been feeling begin to dissipate.

He looks at me, and even though I know he's Tallen, he looks just like Parker when he smiles. But the reminder of Parker doesn't make me want to cry this time, because I can tell I'm getting at least one of my brothers back. "Of course I did," he says gently, "it was hilarious, and heartbreaking, and everything I needed to hear that day."

I bite my smile.

He continues, "And everything I needed to hear the next day, and the day after that, and the day after that."

My eyes widen at his honest comment. "Really?"

He nods. "Of course. I've already told Declan, but I think I need to tell you too." He makes sure our eyes meet before he says, "Thank you for not giving up on me."

I can't tell if I feel like cracking a sob or laughing. I'm shook by this moment. My emotions are reaching for a comfortable place to flow out of me, but I'm not sure which emotion I'm feeling.

"And, Chris, I'm sorry." His expression is filled with remorse, and hope. "I'm sorry for everything. I'm sorry for Parker. I'm sorry for me. I'm sorry I missed your graduation. And I'm very sorry for the way I treated you and for being so selfish." He shakes his head, looking down, then, "I was trying to figure out how to keep going without Parker. Seeing you and mom just made me sad and I was tired of being sad and angry. So I pushed you all away. I blamed myself for the crash. I had to forgive myself and it just took a lot of time." He looks up at me, hopeful. "It's not an excuse, but it is what was going on and I wanted to be honest with you about it. I didn't think anyone knew how to deal with a loss like mine. But I got into group therapy and learned a lot, especially about how I wasn't alone. And what I was feeling was normal. And I'm sorry I left you alone in your grief, but I'm here now."

My smile shifts into a line as my eyes widen even more. Something triggers in my heart. Making me feel connected to Tallen again. Knowing that he's been listening to the poorly recorded video of the song I sang with Declan makes me see Tallen as my brother again. Not a broken angry stranger like he was the last time I saw him. And I understand now that his absence in my life had nothing to do with me or anything being wrong with me, but was something he needed to go through for his own healing.

I swallow, then say, "Thank you. I'm sorry too. I pushed you when you weren't ready. It came from a good place in my heart, but I don't think it was the kind of tough love you needed at the time."

He smiles. "Thanks, Chris. And thanks for seeing that I needed to be alone with myself and face my own stuff before I could see you. Maybe there was a better way to handle it, but I wasn't prepared for any of it so I did what was easiest for me at the time. And I'm sorry it hurt you."

"I know," I say. "It's okay. There's no blueprint or manual that explains how we should deal with grief or pain. I think we're just supposed to feel it and figure it out the best we can."

"I think you're right," he says with relief.

I smile genuinely. "Is it okay if I hug you?"

"Yeah," he says tossing his arms up. "I can't walk anymore; it doesn't mean you can't hug me."

I'm surprised that when I wrap my arms around his shoulders and hug him, everything feels the same. Even though I have to slightly bend down to reach him, he's still my brother. He's still Tallen. Things are a little different, but we'll get used to it.

I release him and he keeps up with me as I walk to the car. "I missed you," I say.

"Don't get mushy," he says. Then he purposely rolls off the curb in one articulate and continuous motion. Almost like he's showing off or making up for the last time I saw him struggle with his chair. "I missed you too." Then he rolls up to the car and steals the front seat from me. Without even checking the tires or locking his seatbelt into place.

I don't get upset that he took the front seat because I'm proud that he's come so far in the last several months. I'm grateful he's found confidence in who he is and has adjusted to what's happened to him.

I climb into the backseat, and we leave the building.

For the next two hours as we make our way down the state of Washington, I learn that Tallen made Declan promise not to tell me about the progress he was making or that they were talking. I don't hold it against Declan. I'm honestly impressed by Declan's loyalty to my brother. What a great quality to have in a future husband.

I also learn that group therapy sounds amazing, and I wish I could do my fieldwork with some of the people Tallen met. Or maybe even hang out for a therapy session.

I learn that Tallen wanted to feel ready for the world again before

119

he introduced his new self to it. Which is why he spent a couple of extra months at the rehab center instead of moving back home. He wanted to make sure he was back to himself mentally and prepared physically before leaving.

And I learned that, his and Parker's marketing company supported itself even while no one was running it. So he was able to pay for all the help he got while he was healing and recovering in full.

"Perks of a pyramid scheme," I say.

Tallen turns in his seat to face me. "It's an MLM, Chris. There's nothing *scheming* about it."

"You make profits off of everyone in your *downline*, aka, all the people at the bottom of the pyramid dishing out money."

He looks forward and ignores me.

"So, when's the wedding?" I think he's directing this statement at both of us, but I don't know how to answer so I look at Declan.

Declan smiles as he glances up at me in his rearview mirror. "As soon as possible."

Tallen nods once. "You could save the family the hassle of traveling again and get married at Avery's wedding."

"Not a half bad idea," Declan says.

I blow raspberries. "Can you imagine? She would disown me."

Tallen laughs. "That would really piss her off wouldn't it?"

"I don't want a big wedding anyway," I say. "I would be happy with a cookout in the backyard with our parents honestly."

When I glance at Declan, I can see him chewing on this information.

"It's weird you two met again after all these years, isn't it? I mean what are the odds?" Tallen says. "Same campus. Same town. Same day. Same time."

It is bizarre that everything happened so perfectly in that moment. But I don't give it too much thought.

Declan releases a short laugh, then, "Yeah, even after you tried to keep us apart, destiny had our best interests in mind."

I gently hit Tallen's shoulder with the back of my hand. "Is it true?"

Shifting just enough so I can see the side of his face and his eyes straining to focus on me, he says, "Is what true?"

"That you told him to leave me alone in high school?"

Tallen and Declan both share a look, then facing forward Tallen says, "Yeah. I mean, it was mostly Parker. But yeah, we were both protective of you."

I smile. It gives me a sense of safety and comfort knowing they had my back. Even though most of the time they were teasing me or lighting their farts on fire. It especially makes me feel secure since our father was so absent. Not just physically but emotionally as well. At least my brothers cared about me in their own way.

I lean forward so my head is between the front seats. "Is it true Parker pushed Declan against the wall and told him to forget my name?"

Tallen laughs. "Oh yeah, I forgot he did that."

Declan draws his head back and says, "I don't know how you forgot that, Parker was always pinning guys against the walls for talking about Christine."

Tallen nods as he raises his eyebrows in agreement. "That's true."

"You were too," Declan says facing Tallen.

"Nah, Parker was more physical. I just used my words to threaten them. And if I had known you were going to marry my sister in the future, I wouldn't have got in the way of *destiny*."

"Yeah, you would have," Declan says.

"You're probably right."

I'm so confused. "Guys were talking about me?"

Tallen shrugs. "Don't let it get to your head."

I feel like there's a whole side to Parker and Tallen that I'm just learning about for the first time. Hearing Tallen admit that he was keeping guys away from me makes it real and makes everything Declan said more real too.

I hit Tallen's shoulder again. "You're the reason I never had a boyfriend. Everyone was too afraid to look at me!"

"I'm glad they were protective of you," Declan says. "They saved you from a lot of unnecessary heartache and drama. Most high schoolers don't know how to be in a committed relationship or be mature about it."

I smile at him.

"Yeah," Tallen says. "You should be thanking me."

I roll my eyes and sit back in my seat.

How did I get so lucky?

THIRTEEN

"Christine, my goodness, it's beautiful!" My mom is adjusting her glasses from the top of her head and places them on her nose to better inspect the ring on my finger.

"Thanks," I say with a grin. "You should have seen the presentation when he proposed." I glance at Declan whose eyes are glued to me with a yearning expression, then I look back to my mom.

"I know, I saw the video!" She pulls her glasses off as she releases my hand. Then to Decan she says, "You're one of a kind Declan. Truly."

"Thank you," he says. "I could say the same about your daughter."

I tuck my arm around Declan's and say, "Well, we still need to make our rounds and let everyone know we're engaged."

"Have you told Avery yet?" she says this with a downward inflection.

I shake my head. "No, I'm still trying to figure out the best way to go about it."

"Life doesn't always go the way we plan it to." My mom nods with a smile. "That's a lesson Miss Avery still needs to learn."

I couldn't agree more. She's been comfortably the center of attention since the day she was born. Not that I want to be the *center* of attention. But sometimes I would like a moment of attention to talk about myself.

My mom continues. "And your father?"

I shake my head. "Not yet."

"Will he walk you down the aisle?"

"I haven't thought about it, but I'm sure he will."

My mom tilts her chin to one side, considering my statement.

"You know, you always have Tallen if your dad can't make it."

Tallen yells from the kitchen. "I'm not doing that. Dad would be heartbroken."

It took my mom and Tallen about ten seconds to get back to how they always were. I guess their relationship didn't need as much mending as his and mine did.

Mom waves his words away with her hand. "You have to have a heart in order for it to be broken," she says referring to my father's lack of compassion and empathy.

"*Mom*," I say. I know she and my dad can barely stand each other. I know he's a hard person to love. But I can't let her talk about him like that when he's not here to defend himself.

She covers her mouth briefly, as if she didn't mean to say the words out loud. "Well don't let me keep you any longer. I'll see you later tonight then?" I know she's asking this to make sure I'll be staying with her and not at Declan's. Not that she would mind if I did stay with him, but I can tell she's eager to discuss wedding plans and spend more time with me while she still can before my life relocates me the farthest I've ever been from her.

I nod and motion for the door as I get ready to leave. But not before I give her a reassuring smile.

"Good to see you, Declan," Mom says giving him another hug. She's not a big hugger so this is equally awkward as it is intriguing to see.

"You too," he says.

She takes the door, holding it open as she watches us leave. "Tell your folks *hello*," she says to him. "And that I'm looking forward to seeing more of them soon." She's smiling at herself as she closes the door. I'm sure she's daydreaming of grandchildren and family gatherings already.

When we reach the car, Declan opens the door for me and says, "I've never seen your mother so happy."

I duck my head and plop into the seat. "That makes two of us."

When we arrive at his parents' house, I notice a shift in his demeanor. I'm not sure what it is, but I can tell something is off.

He takes my hand as we make our way up the sidewalk to the front door that swings open before we reach it.

"*Declan!*" His mother's arms lock around him and she begins to...

Wow, this is a lot.

123

...she's sobbing.

Not wistful, teary eyed, cries that say I've-missed-you-so-much-my-wonderful-son. But instead, this is full blown, uncomfortably loud, sobbing.

I know it's been a while since Declan has been to Nevada to see his family. But his mother is acting like her prodigal son has returned unexpectedly. Which is odd, since she's known for months he was coming to town as my date to Avery's wedding.

I'm standing awkwardly behind him when Winnie, in a pair of oversized denim jeans and a toddler on her hip, appears in the doorway.

"Mom, stop," she says in an unfazed tone which makes me realize their mother's behavior is normal for them. And that it's apparently normal for Winnie to talk to her mother in such a commanding way. I can't imagine speaking to my mom with that tone. I also can't imagine my mom acting as intense as their mother either.

When their mother finally makes eye contact with me, it only lasts about two seconds before she spots the ring on my finger and gasps. "Did you two get married?" She covers her twisting face and begins to sob again, turning to Winnie and burying her face on Winnie's toddler free shoulder. "He got married without telling us."

Declan takes my hand to reveal my ring better. "Mom, we're not married yet. We wanted to let you know in person that we got engaged last night."

She faces us with widened eyes, and in a quieter voice says, "You're not married?"

He exhales out his nose. Seemingly frustrated. "No. Not yet."

She turns her attention to me. Which makes me feel uncomfortable because I don't know what to expect from her.

"Are you pregnant?" she says.

"*Mom!*" Both Declan and Winnie say her name with disbelief.

I shake my head with wide eyes. "No, I'm not pregnant."

"Thank God." She overexaggerates her sigh before she gives me a hug and says, "I'm Val." She kisses my cheek and I wonder if her lipstick smudged off on me. "Welcome to the family."

"Thank you," I manage to say without sounding too confused. I rub my cheek, just in case she left any of her lipstick residue there. I wouldn't want my first impression to be remembered by a lipstick stain on my face in the shape of Val's mouth. Although, I get the feeling his family wouldn't notice if I did.

I wish I had a notebook with me right now so I could jot down a few observations I've made in the last thirty seconds of meeting Val.

> *Val (i.e.. Declan's mother)*
> *-wears too much perfume*
> *-wears too much makeup*
> *-intense, unnatural reactions to normal life*
> *-no boundaries physically or emotionally with her children or*
> *people she's just met*

"I would have introduced you properly if you hadn't jumped to conclusions," Declan says to his mother. Then, "Mom, this is Christine. Christine, my mother, Valentine." Declan retrieves me from his mother by slipping his hand around my back and guiding me into their house that seems as normal as any other house I've been to. I'm not sure if Val's odd behavior made me think their house would be as odd her, but I welcome the normalcy of the home's interior.

Winnie smiles at me when we're inside and says, "Hey Christine, I hope you know you just signed up to marry a mess."

I laugh politely, but really, I want to sit alone with her and ask her to elaborate on that statement.

"Don't scare her off before they're married," Val says. "Why don't we all have a seat and you tell me about the engagement. Where did you meet? How long have you been dating? I just have so many questions. It seems my son has been keeping secrets from me."

I find a place on the couch and Declan makes sure to sit next to me and scoot me as close as he can to the armrest. As if he's protecting me from something. In this case, I think it's his mother.

Winnie places her toddler on her lap and begins bouncing him gently. To Val, she says, "Declan told us about her the last time Maverick stayed with him."

"No," Val says. "He told us about the Malloy brothers' little sister he was trying to get together with."

I look at Declan and flash him a smile. Knowing he's been talking about me all this time makes me smitten. Despite his mother's confusion that I am the Malloy brothers' little sister, it makes me feel valued that I haven't been a secret subject. It's validation in a way I didn't know I needed from him.

He tips his face close to the side of my head and softly says, "I promise I'm nothing like them."

I clasp my hand around his and laugh quietly to myself.

Winnie's eyes almost pop out of her head with irritation when she says, "Christine *is* the Malloy's sister, Mom!"

"What?" Val whips her head around to me. "But she's a woman." Then to me she says, "You're a woman! When did you turn into a woman? I've still pictured you as a high school girl."

Winnie twists her face. "You thought Declan was pursuing a teenager?"

Val throws her hands in the air and rolls her eyes. "I didn't know. I hoped not."

Suddenly a thundering sound rolls through the house until a brown-haired little boy runs into the living room and jumps into Declan's arms.

"Uncle Dec, guess what? Guess what?" the boy says eagerly.

Declan smiles for the first time since we've been in his parents' home, and says, "What? What?"

"Grandpa gave me a gun!"

Declan smiles and widens his eyes in an animated fashion. "Did he?"

"Yeah, a *real* gun."

The room instantly goes quiet.

I have a sudden awareness of everyone's growing concerned expressions, and it makes me uneasy. Surely his nephew is talking about a nerf gun or a toy. Maybe their family doesn't believe in owning guns, real or toy guns, so this is a taboo subject for them.

Declan sets his nephew down in front of him and places his hands on his small shoulders. "Ty, look at me, what kind of gun did Grandpa give you?"

"A war gun that goes, *bang bang!*"

Val and Winnie rise and begin rushing around the house instantly.

Surely Ty is not talking about a real gun.

Ty's smiling face falls to worry. "Am I in trouble?"

"You're not in trouble," Declan reassures him. "I promise you're not in trouble and you're not going to be in trouble. Just tell me where the gun is."

Ty's voice is shaky, as if he's trying not to cry when he says, "In the backyard. With Grandpa. We were going to shoot targets."

I'm starting to worry that he's talking about a real gun.

"Stay here," Declan says in a serious tone. "I'll be right back." I know he's speaking to Ty, but I feel like I should listen to his instructions too.

Winnie rushes back into the living room.

Declan's on his feet and brushing past her when he says, "He's in the backyard."

Everything seems so serious.

The energy instantly rises in the home and I'm feeling just as frantic as they are even though I haven't moved.

Winnie nods in response to Declan's statement, then hands the toddler to me and says, "Hold him for a sec, will ya?"

I nod, then grip him on my lap.

Winnie leaves.

The toddler takes one look at me and starts crying.

Of course.

Ty is standing in the middle of the room wide eyed and with a frown that makes me want hug him.

I have absolutely zero experience with kids, so I'm not sure what to do here.

Especially with the screaming toddler who's trying to escape my lap by turning into a jellyfish in my arms.

"Hey, Ty," I say, trying to get his attention over his screaming brother. "My name is Christine, I'm really good friends with your uncle and we're going to get married soon." I'm trying to figure out how to gain his trust instantly in a high stress situation. If that's even possible to do with a child.

He looks at me as a tear drops down from his big brown worried eyes.

"Is this baby your brother?" I say over the crying.

He nods, still with the widest eyes full of fear and a frown that could rip a heart in two.

"What's his name?"

Ty wipes his face with the back of his arm and slowly takes a step towards me. Then says, "Bud."

That's an odd name, maybe it's a nickname. "What's his real name?"

Ty takes a step closer to me and rubs his hand along the top of his brother's head. "Buddy."

Why do I bother?

I'm still not sure if that's a nickname, but I'm desperate to get this baby to stop screaming so I say, "What does your mommy do when Buddy is crying?"

He's still petting his brother's head. "She gives him booby."

I close my eyes gently, and inhale. Reminding myself I'm asking a child for help.

"Does he have a toy or something he likes to play with?"

Ty nods.

"Can you go get it for me?"

He nods again and runs out of the room. Then returns with a diaper bag.

I set Buddy on the floor which seems to calm him as he and Ty begin to rummage through the diaper bag together.

Ty pulls out a pacifier and shoves it into Buddy's mouth.

Before I can let the relief sink in, I hear what sounds like a gunshot come from the backyard that makes me jump.

FOURTEEN

"Did you hear that?" I ask my new friend that can't be more than five or six years old.

Ty nods as he hands his brother a diaper wipe to play with. "That's my gun. Grandpa said we could shoot in the yard. Did you know Grandpa gave me a real war gun?"

I believe that now that I've heard what sounded like a firework exploding way too close to their backdoor.

Then he finds a light up seahorse and squeezes it until it starts singing *You Are My Sunshine.*

Something about Ty's statement and the way the adults were acting is not adding up.

Val's home is on the edge of town, but her neighbors are close enough that I can't imagine they would feel comfortable with her husband doing target practice outside.

I'm not even sure it's legal to do that here.

Anyone else in my situation might have bailed by now, but the curious anthropologist in me wants to discover the family dynamics here. And the woman in me that's in love with Declan, wants to support him with whatever is going on.

I hear the back door open, and Val is in hysterics.

I leave my spot on the couch and sit in a chair closer to the threshold separating the living room from what looks to be the kitchen and backdoor. In this spot, I have a much better view of what's going on. And what I see is Val coddling a man on one side, and Winnie holding his arm on the other.

No one seems to be injured. That's a good sign. But I don't see Declan with them, which makes me a little nervous.

"Nobody was going to get hurt," the man says seemingly

irritated. He and Val both have their backs to me.

I'm assuming this is Val's husband, and Winnie and Declan's father.

This whole scenario is equally interesting as it is alarming.

Winnie catches my gaze, then helps her father sit at the table and directs him to stay put.

Val seems beside herself and I can't understand a word she's blubbering through her overly dramatic sobs.

Winnie makes her way into the living room. "Sorry about that. Thanks for sitting with the boys," she says, taking the diaper wipes and loading everything back into the diaper bag.

I lean back against the chair, trying to see out the backdoor window to where Declan should be. "Of course," I say, as if I've helped her out like we're friends and everything that's just happened in the last few minutes is completely ordinary.

"Do you like kids?" she says.

I face her. "Um, I haven't really had an opportunity to hang out with kids before today."

She smiles, scooping up Buddy and adjusting him on her hip. "You seem like a natural."

Ty pats Winnie's leg, and says, "Mommy, can I shoot my gun now?"

"Absolutely not," she says. "Grandpa never should have given you that gun to begin with."

Ty's voice burst into hysterics that put Val to shame when he cries out with, "But Grandpa said I could have it. It's my war gun!"

Winnie takes his hand, and they head down the hall. She turns back to me and says, "I better take care of this."

I nod with a polite smile, then lean back in my chair again to search for Declan.

Val's hysterics have gentled and now she is telling her husband that he's been acting incredibly irresponsible. I'm not interested enough to stay and listen to their conversation. Honestly, the anthropologist in me has left the building, so I'm feeling very out of place. Which forces me to make a decision to abandon all intentions of seeming polite in front of Declan's parents. Without making eye contact, I quickly walk past Val and her husband to exit through the backdoor.

I nearly trip over Declan as I back up with more force than I intended while closing the door. As I turn the blinding sunset forces my eyes shut.

With a lack of grace, I stumble to a seated position on the porch step with the help of Declan's balancing arms.

"Are you okay?" I say trying to ignore the fact that I nearly toppled over him.

He's sitting on the back step with his elbows resting on his spread knees. He clasps his hands together as he gives me a forced smile that quickly returns to a firm line. With his inhale, he says, "I'm okay. Are you?"

I cup my chin in my hand and balance my elbow on my thigh as I look at him. "Yeah," I say with an evoking grin. "Your sister told me I was a natural with the kids, but she missed the whole part where Buddy was screaming in my face, and I had to convince Ty to help me."

This makes him smile a little. "That was witty of you."

"Is his name really Buddy?"

He nods. "Yeah, it was Jake's father's name."

I watch him, waiting for him to continue and elaborate on who Jake is.

"Jake is Winnie's husband. His father died of a heart attack before Buddy was born."

"That's so sad," I say. "But really sweet of them to name him after his grandpa."

"Yeah."

I'm not sure why he's not talking about his reaction to Ty telling him that his dad gave him a gun. Or why he forgot to come back inside and get me. Or why I heard a gunshot. No one seems hurt, so that's reassuring. But after ten minutes at their house, I'm starting to realize why Declan valued his friendship with my brothers and spent so much time at our house when we were teenagers. My life and childhood seem boring compared to the chaos at this house.

I place my hand on his leg, and he interlaces his hand with mine.

"What happened?" I finally say.

He can only look at me with an expression filled with remorse.

It's starting to make sense why his demeanor changed as soon as we got here.

"What's going on with your family?" I say in a gentle voice. I don't want to offend him, but I'd like to be prepared for what to expect from them the next time we're visiting.

He runs his tongue along his bottom lip and folds his mouth in.

After a moment, he shakes his head and looks up into the sky as he says, "You don't know what a normal family looks like, until you see one." He glances at me. "And even though you grew up with a single mother, your family was the most normal functioning family I had ever been around. I loved how normal you guys were."

I don't move, or blink. I want to give him space to continue, and time to think before he puts his thoughts into words.

He looks down at his side, and with his free hand he lifts up the gun.

I don't know why it makes me gasp when I see it. But I do. Maybe it's because, like my lacking experience with children, I have no experience with firearms either.

He releases my hand, and in one fluid motion he slides a long metal piece filled with bullets out of the grip of the gun and sets the two pieces between his shoes.

"This isn't normal," he says to me with his attention on the gun parts. "And it's getting worse." His voice is pained when he delivers this sentence.

I place my hand on his shoulder, trying to comfort him. Trying to support him through whatever it is he's going through.

"My dad's always been a little quirky," he says looking forward with a slight hint of a smile curling in the corner of his mouth. "It's what made me see him as my hero. He was a fun dad. We did fun stuff together that was out of the ordinary. It made spending time with him so special for me when I was a kid. Then the affair happened, I didn't know about it at the time, but I could tell something changed between my parents. And between us. Maybe it was because I was becoming a teenager and my interests changed and the quirky stuff wasn't as enticing anymore. But something changed, nothing I can specifically dictate with words, but it was a feeling and we all felt it."

I stay quiet. Giving him a moment to sift through his memories and what he's trying to explain to me as he hashes it all out in his mind.

"Then," he says, blowing a puff of air out of his mouth. "Maverick came into our lives and my dad seemed himself again. Quirky and fun. He loved to make Maverick laugh and have a good time while he was here. Then after a few years, the same thing happened. An unexplainable shift." He locks his hurting brown eyes on mine, and I can't help but see the same worried expression that

Ty had on his face in the living room plastered on Declan's face now. "And it happened right around the time Maverick turned twelve. Except this time, it's worse. Like my dad can't be trusted alone with himself. Like he makes poor decisions. Sometimes when he's talking, he doesn't make sense. I don't know what to do. Today is the worst it's ever been. I mean, if something had happened to him or if he had given the gun to Ty and Ty had accidently..." He shakes his head. Unable to complete his sentence.

He doesn't have to. I know it's unbearable to think that one of them might have been shot by accident today. And even worse to utter the words out loud.

I don't press him. Instead, I say, "I'm glad we were here and that you were able to get to your father in time before anything bad happened."

"I don't know," he says, nodding toward the fence. "He put a hole in my mom's bird feeder and destroyed the fence post."

My eyes widen at the evidence that a gun was fired in their backyard in a setting where someone could have been hurt.

"What happened?" I say, knowing that the gun was fired but unsure of the details on *how* it put a hole in the fence.

Declan rubs at his forehead, then, "My dad didn't want to give me the gun. He was explaining to me that he taught me to shoot, and taught Maverick to shoot, and now it was Ty's turn. I tried to reason with him. Tell him that me and Maverick were twelve when he taught us to shoot a gun and we were at the shooting range, not standing around in our backyard with a piece of paper stapled to the fence post. He didn't want to hear it. He tried to defend himself, but he wasn't making any sense. Finally, he pointed the gun out at his side and said nothing was going to happen with the safety on. But the safety wasn't on, so when he pulled the trigger, it fired. I know he knows better. I know he knows how to operate a firearm. I know he is a safe person with a gun. None of this makes any sense. Even he was surprised by his actions. Thankfully he was in such a shock, that it didn't take much effort for me to take the gun from him after that."

I wish I had the answers for him about why his father is acting erratic and unresponsible. But since I don't, I say, "That sounds like something serious is going on with your father. Has he been to the doctor recently?"

Running one hand through his hair, he says, "I'm not sure."

"Maybe it would be a good idea to call up his doctor and figure out what's going on?"

He faces me and his mouth curls up slightly on one side. "You're probably right."

I'm not sure why no one has thought of taking him to get evaluated by a professional sooner than this. Then again, his mom is frantic and a little odd. I wouldn't be surprised if she's avoiding the doctor because she would rather be ignorant to her husband's condition than have to face the truth. Whatever the truth might be.

"What do you think is going on with him?" I ask.

He shrugs. "I don't have a clue. I worry about cancer in his brain. But I remind myself that he's always been a little quirky, so if it was cancer then it would have been an issue decades ago. I also wonder if he's just getting old, but he's only fifty-eight. I wonder if he's always been this way and only recently I realized how alarming his behavior is." He rubs at the back of his neck and gives me a remorseful expression. "What do you think it is?"

I shake my head slowly. "I wish I knew."

The back door opens and Ty pokes his head out. "Uncle Dec?"

Declan flips around to face Ty with a grin. I'm not sure if the grin is forced for Ty's sake, or natural because of Ty's innocent presence. Either way, it's nice to see his full smile.

"Yeah, what's up, little man?"

Ty looks at me, then back to Declan, as if he's not sure how to say whatever he's trying to say while I'm sitting here witnessing their conversation. "Are you really going to marry her?" he says, referring to me.

Declan picks up the gun in one hand, and slips the clip into his pocket. Then scuffling Ty's hair as he heads back inside the house, he says, "I sure am. Do you want to help me tell Grandpa?"

Ty nods and opens the door wider for Declan to enter.

I follow them both back inside to the kitchen. Val is now mixing something in a bowl at the counter with a grin on her face. Like everything is completely normal again. But Declan's father is no longer seated at the table where I last saw him.

Val begins to pour the contents of the bowl into a pan. "I hope you two are sticking around for cake."

Ty climbs onto the counter next to Val and runs his finger alongside the bowl. "I want to stay for cake," he says as he licks the batter from his finger.

"You are staying for cake," Val says to him in a sing-song voice. It's interesting she was able to shift from hysterics to joy in such a short amount of time. Then to Declan she says, "Well?"

Declan creases his forehead and says, "We still have more of Chirstine's family to visit tonight."

Val's smile falls into a noticeable frown.

"Another time?" Declan says. Then he scans the living room and doubles back to where Val is. "Where's Dad?"

She nods her head to one side, and with a downward shift in her voice, says, "Bedroom." The one-word statement leaves me feeling uncomfortable. I hate to think negatively of his mother after just *officially* meeting her, but something about her makes me feel uneasy. I'm not sure if it's her tone. Maybe it's the way she's avoiding eye contact with us. Or it could be the fact that she seems noticeably upset after Declan denied her invitation to stay and eat cake. As if he's a six-year-old boy that she can manipulate into staying at her home a little longer by offering sugar in place of responsibility.

Declan motions for me to follow him. The home is a ranch style house on one level, but it feels like a maze as we weave through the kitchen, living room, foyer, and hallway to get to the far side of the home where the master bedroom is. And the same bedroom where Declan's father is standing in front of a bookcase with his back to us.

"Dad?" Declan says approaching his father and putting his hand on his shoulder. I'm not sure if I should enter the room, so I stand in the doorway. Watching.

His father turns slightly and notices Declan. With an almost childlike and surprised expression he says, "Hey, Dec, you're home." He puts his arms around him and gives him a hug. "Oh, I've missed you. It felt like you'd never come back from college."

This encounter is odd since I know they were just outside together. I think Declan might be right about something more serious going on with his father's mind.

Declan pats his father briefly then says, "You mean *work*? I've been out of school for years, Dad."

His father nods and turns his attention to the TV on the dresser. "Oh, I know that. I've just missed you is all." He picks up the remote and points it at the TV.

Declan has the most concerned expression on his face as he watches his father. It only lasts a brief moment, but it's enough to break my heart for Declan.

He takes the remote from his father and clicks the TV screen off. "Dad, are you okay?"

His father looks up at him with a glazed-over expression. "Of course I am." Then he glances at me. At first, he smiles politely then turns to face Declan again. But then something must register in his mind, because he whips his head back to me with widened eyes and brushes past Declan.

He places his hands on my shoulders and looks at me in a panic. "Andrea, what are you doing here? If my wife sees you in my house, she'll have both our heads!"

Declan motions towards us. "Dad, she's not Andrea."

He faces Declan with his eyes still wide and worried. "You have to get her out of here, Dec." Then to me he says, "Andrea, please, you need to go. Now!"

I'm so startled, his words cause me to take a step back. I'm sure my eyes are doing everything they can to stay secure in their sockets.

Declan quickly takes his father's arm to get his attention. "Dad, this is Christine. Not Andrea. Christine Malloy. My fiancé."

His father's disturbance flashes between me and Declan. Then confusion sets in, and he takes several uneasy steps back to his bedside where he sits down in a slump.

"Dad?" The concern is thick in Declan's voice. I wish there was something I could do to help.

Maybe there is.

I approach Declan's father and sit next to him on his bed. "Hello," I say, reaching my hand out. "I'm Christine."

He blinks several times before taking my hand. "Sean Price."

"Nice to meet you," I say. I'm trying to sound confident and polite. There's obviously something going on. Sean's memory is smudged in a way that's causing him to confuse me with some other woman. And leaving him to make irresponsible choices, like giving his young grandson a handgun.

Maybe if I'm calm and confident, he won't get upset or worried when he realizes that something serious is going on inside of him.

"You too." His expression is shifting between confusion and vacancy. He faces Declan and says, "She looks like Andrea so much, doesn't she?"

"No, Dad." Declan shakes his head. "They don't look anything alike."

Sean looks down at the dark blue carpet and in a quiet voice he says, "I could have sworn she was Andrea."

Declan takes a few steps forward until he's standing in front of Sean. "Dad, is everything okay?"

Sean nods, his eyes still glued to the carpet.

With a defeated exhale, Declan reveals the gun he's been holding to his father and says, "I'm going to take this with me."

Sean nods, as if he knows he doesn't have a choice.

"And I'm going to have Winnie take you to the doctor, okay?" Declan places the gun between his lumbar and belt. I know it's unloaded so the placement doesn't seem concerning.

Sean nods, again.

"We're going to figure out what's going on, alright?"

This time, Sean doesn't nod. He continues to keep his eyes down, but it looks as if he's already checked out of this conversation. And given in to complete vacancy.

In one motion, Declan wraps his arms around his father's shoulders and squeezes his eyes shut with his hug. In almost a whisper, he says, "I love you, Dad."

He approaches me, standing next to me for a moment with his focus on his father. Then he takes my hand and leads me out of the room.

I turn my head around to look at Sean once more before he's out of sight. He looks like a lost child. A confused, lost, and lonely child. I hate that we are leaving him with Val. She seems in denial of reality, and unstable. She quickly gives in to dramatics that put Avery to shame. I don't know much about Winnie, so I don't know how helpful she'll be. I'm worried that there are children in this house where the grandparents are unreliable. And I'm sad that Declan would rather run than deal with the issues in his parents' home. But at the same time, I don't blame him. He's an adult with a life of his own. Is it his responsibility to take care of his parents?

Winnie is gently closing one of the bedroom doors when we file down the hall.

"Winnie," Declan says in a tone that seems interrogating.

She presses her finger to her pursed lips and says, "Shh, I just got Buddy down for a nap. He's been taking late morning naps, it's completely screwing up his sleep schedule."

Declan ignores her comment and says, "Winnie, you need to take Dad to see a doctor."

Her brow creases and her face twists into disbelief. "Why?" She sounds defensive.

"Just do it."

She folds her arms. "You think Mom is going to let me take Dad to the doctor just because you told me to?"

"Mom can get over whatever she has against doctors, and you can help Dad get a proper diagnosis."

Winnie begins to look angry.

And I'm feeling more confused by the second.

What is going on with Declan's family? Why won't his mom go to the doctor? Why is Winnie acting angry instead of concerned for their father's wellbeing? Why did Sean think I looked like Andrea? And who is Andrea?

"Why?" Now Winnie is raising her voice despite her concern for her restless baby.

Declan moves into her space. His towering appearance above Winnie is intimidating. Probably not intimidating to Winnie since she knew Declan before he towered over her. Then in a low voice he says, "He thought Christine was Andrea."

Winnie's mouth parts slightly as her eyes widen. She glances at me, then back to Declan. "I'll call the clinic tomorrow."

"Good," he says. Then to me, "Don't say anything to my mom about what happened with my dad in there, alright?"

"Okay." I respond in this way, because I don't want to add more stress to this already chaotic situation by questioning him. And because I'm ready to leave. I feel like I've been in fight or flight mode since I got here. That could be from the anxious energy Declan was putting off since we pulled into the driveway. Or it could be the simple fact that neither of his parents seem stable or safe to be around. Probably a combination of the two. Nonetheless, this atmosphere is making me want to bolt.

We say goodbye to Val, who insists we come back this weekend when Maverick is in town. Declan promises to come back for Maverick. Winnie quietly reassures Declan that she's going to take their father to the doctor. Ty cries when we leave. He's upset he didn't get to play *Guess Who* with Declan. Winnie picks up Ty and closes the door.

When we're back in Declan's car, the silence is louder than the chaos that was circulating in the house.

"Who is Andrea?" I finally say.

Declan faces me. "Christine, I'm so sorry. My family is a little out there. Believe me, I know, I lived in it for eighteen years. I'm not blind. And I know, I should have warned you. But I thought I could ease you into it. I didn't think we were walking into a ticking time bomb today. Honestly, it's not normally that bad."

I take his hand in mine. "Listen," I say with a calming voice. "You don't need to apologize for your family. I get it. Every family has their stuff, okay?"

"I know." His head falls back against the seat. In a less intense voice, he says, "Promise me something?"

"Okay."

He rolls his head to the side so he's facing me. Lines outline his smile and crinkle at the corners of his eyes when he says, "Promise you won't leave me because of my family?"

Laughter escapes my throat. "I promise I won't abandon you or your family. Don't forget I'm the one person that understands you better than anyone. Nothing could scare me away."

His shifting eyes land on my mouth, then he says, "I can't wait to marry you."

"Me either." I smile. Then tilt my head and say, "So, who is Andrea?"

A burst of laughter leaves his mouth as his hand slaps against his forehead. His brown eyes fix on mine as he raises one brow, then, "Are you jealous?"

I shrug. "I'm not sure, yet."

His smile widens, pleased with my response. "Andrea is Maverick's mother."

"I don't think I'm jealous."

He shifts back in his seat and starts the car. "Yeah, well, there's nothing to be jealous of anyway."

"Do I look like her?" I'm curious how his father could confuse us.

He heads down the road closer to the city where Avery is staying with her parents at a hotel. And where we still have to break the news of our engagement to them.

"Not at all," he says.

I give him a suspicious expression until he glances at me.

"Seriously." He seems honest. "She bleaches her hair, fake tans, and is almost forty."

"What color are her eyes?"

"I don't know." He takes my hand in his. Glances at me. Then looks back at the traffic. "Your eyes are the only ones I pay close enough attention to to know the color."

I don't hold back my enormous grin.

I cannot wait to marry him.

FIFTEEN

"Find her?" Avery says with apparent terror in her voice.

I crawl out from under the tiny bridge where Avery and Brent were posing for wedding photos three hours ago.

"Not yet," I say brushing the dirt from my dress. I doubt when the designer was picking out fabric she was anticipating I would be crawling around on my knees outside in the dark while looking for Avery's dog, so when I wipe at the dirt it sort of just spreads around more into the fabric instead of dusting off.

"She's probably lost in the woods or drowned in the lake by now!" I'm not sure if Avery has had too much champagne from the wedding reception or if I've forgotten how dramatic she can be when she's upset.

I begin to trek down the path toward the lake. "She's probably made friends with an armadillo and she's just fine."

Avery takes my arm and whips me around. Her grip is hard enough that I instinctually rub my arm where she was gripping me after she lets go. Her expression is plagued with fear when she says, "She's never been to the country, Christine! She's meant for the city! This place is Narnia to her!"

Before I can respond to her or calm her down, Brent and Tallen are on their way down the path from the reception followed closely by Declan. Brent and Avery take each other's arms and Avery begins blubbering about Princess running off.

"Well, the DJ just told everyone to line up for the bouquet. You should come back inside because I think you're supposed to throw that," Brent says pointing to the flowers choking in her hand.

Avery draws her brows together in anger and says, "I don't care about the bouquet, Brent. My dog is missing!"

Tallen and Declan share a look, then Tallen says, "You get back in there for your guests and we'll find Princess."

Avery pierces her eyes into them. "Promise?" Her shrill voice is making me want to plug my ears.

Tallen takes her hand briefly. "Yes, I promise we won't stop searching until we find her."

Avery reluctantly agrees, then hikes her dress up so she can keep in stride with Brent as they head back inside to the reception.

I nudge Tallen. "What if we don't find Princess?"

He shrugs and grips the wheels of his chair as he begins to roll forward. "Then I guess we'll never see Avery again. Not that that's the worst thing."

I let out a laugh of disbelief. "Tallen, don't say that, she's our cousin."

"I'm joking, obviously."

Declan falls in step with me. But my stride is anything but graceful with these heels on.

"So, this is where you've been for the last half hour?" Declan says to me.

"Yeah. Here, and over there, and back there." I throw my thumb over my shoulder. "I swear if that dog ran off and died, I'll never forgive her for ruining Avery's wedding."

Tallen coughs out his laughter. "Yeah, because you would never hear the end of it."

"Can you blame me for trying to live a peaceful life?" I take Declan's arm and stop him from walking. "Hang on a second," I say using him to brace myself. "I can't keep walking in these heels. They're deforming my feet and rubbing in all the wrong places." I remove the ridiculous shoes from my feet and set them on a nearby bench with no intention of ever retrieving them.

Tallen shifts around in a circle to face us. "I think I'll search for Princess in the parking lot, if you guys want to walk around the garden?" He taps his wheels with his palms. "I didn't know I was going to be off roading, or I would have brought my mudding tires."

At first me and Declan stare at Tallen, perplexed by his comment. Then, he says, "I'm joking, obviously."

Then we sort of force a laugh for him.

He waves his hand and says, "No, no, it's alright. It's too late for laughter now. It's not funny if I have to explain it to you."

"I'm sorry," I say. "I didn't know you were allowed to joke about your…condition."

He shakes his head, "Just stop," and begins to motion past us toward the parking lot. "Text me if you find Princess."

I smile. When I know Tallen can't hear us, I say, "You know, as difficult as it is to see him without Parker to bounce his humor off of, it's nice that he's acting more like himself again."

Declan locks his arm around my shoulders and I hang on to him as we walk through the grass. "It is nice." He glances at me for a moment then back at the trees and flowers lining the path in the moonlight. "You know what's not so nice to see?"

"What's that?" I say, curious.

"My date crawling around on her knees in the most peculiar dress I've ever seen. You should be dancing in there with me and pointing out all the things you want and don't want at our wedding."

The fact that he *wants* me to detail our wedding out to him makes me sigh with a wedding daydream in my mind. "Did you really call this dress peculiar?"

He nods with a smirk.

"I think you meant to say *hideous*."

He's laughing now. "You make it beautiful. Even with the dirt."

Now I'm cackling at his observations. "I can't wait to be married to you." The sentence leaves my mouth without warning.

Declan stops walking and faces me. His hands run down the backs of my arms until they are laced in my hands. "Then let's get married."

I release my left hand and lift it between us, revealing the ring he gave me. "I think that's the plan, isn't it?"

"Yes," he says, taking my hand back into his and closing the space between our faces by stooping down. "But I want to marry you right now."

"Right now?" I raise my eyebrows cynically.

He lowers his head so our eyes are level. "*Right now*."

Shocked laughter bursts up my throat and out of my mouth.

He smiles and presses his forehead to mine. "Tomorrow then? You did say you wanted a backyard wedding with a barbeque. We can make that happen tomorrow."

My mouth is open, and I'm still smiling. But I don't know what to say. I thought I would have time to sort out the details. I thought I would have a dress. I thought the *thought* of being married would have time to sink in. I mean, we just got engaged.

And I can't deny a tiny part of me is worried that this is all too good to be true. That the rug is going to get ripped out from under me at any second. That maybe all men are like my dad and abandon their families for their own selfish success and greedy wallet. And if they're not like my father, maybe they're like Declan's father and after decades of marriage, cheat on their wife with a younger woman.

These thoughts stem from only the tiniest bit of doubt, but it's there digging in my stomach and making me look at Declan in a way that I haven't allowed myself to entertain. Mostly because I don't want to believe he's capable of such things. But at the same time, I know I need to consider them and consider if his potentially heartbreaking human nature is worth the risk.

Declan pulls back slightly to inspect my expression. "What is it?"

I inhale deeply through my nose before letting the exhale flow out of my mouth. "I don't know. It just seems kind of fast."

"Tell me what kind of wedding you want, and I'll make it happen."

My eyes widen at his comment.

He must sense my lack of commitment to this idea since he says, "Today. Avery's wedding. Brent's vows. Her mother crying. It made me want that for us more intensely than I can explain. I want *you* more than I can explain."

I have no words. He seems almost pained by the thought of going another day without being married to me.

His voice is gentle yet firm, when he says, "You make me feel like I can do anything. That I can *be* anything. You make me feel like the best version of me."

I decide to ignore my doubts. Afterall, that's all they are. Just doubts trying to invade my happiness with Declan.

Wrapping my arms around him and pressing my cheek into his shirt, I say, "Then let's get married. *Tomorrow.*"

His arms tighten around me, then he lifts me from my feet as he spins me around.

My squealing laughter echoes above the trees, and is instantly followed by a yelp and high pitched whimpering.

Princess.

Declan sets me down on my bare feet. "You heard that too?" His expression is surprised, like he's the only one with ears that can hear between the two of us.

"Of course, I did. I think it was Princess." I say, taking his hand

and leading us toward the sound.

We call out Princess' name until her shrill cries are unbearable, revealing her whereabouts in the thick trees. Declan uses the flashlight on his phone until we find Princess.

Her harness is pitifully tangled in the branches on the ground. I don't have to work very hard to untangle her. Which leads me to believe she didn't have a clue how to help herself.

And I hate to admit that Avery was right, Princess belongs in the city.

SIXTEEN

"I spent the last week doing my best to convince you of the love that occupies my heart for you."

Declan Price is holding my hands.

He's had his eyes locked on mine since I walked down the short aisle that's the length of my mother's backyard.

Because it is my mother's backyard.

His smile has never been wider.

His confidence and love have conquered my doubts; lighting a flame under my feet that makes me want to do whatever he wants to do.

Just as long as we're together.

And, his voice is gliding through my ears and into my soul as he recites the vows he scribbled inside of a pocket notebook while I was trying on wedding dresses with my mother this morning.

"Christine," he says my name with the same depth I've grown accustomed to. And at the same time, it feels like the first time I'm hearing him say my name. His voice will never stop making my heart feel full.

He's standing so close to me I can see my reflection in his eyes, as he continues, "I promise to give you my endless patience, that I know love demands. To speak with purpose when words are necessary, and to share the silence with you when words are not. I promise to be loving and love you to the best of my ability...

...when life is easy, and when it's not.

...when our love is simple, and when it takes effort.

...when we're young, and when we're grey.

...when we're full of life, and when we'd rather be taken by death."

I'm glad I've already said my vows, since his are causing me to catch my breath and blink the welling tears away before they ruin my makeup.

He releases my hands. I assume to retrieve the wedding band. He takes a box from his suit pocket. The same box he proposed to me with. And when he opens it, the same leaves are sitting there. Only they are a little more dried and crumpled now.

He says, "I've saved a leaf from every flower and every plant I've ever given you."

My eyes flash up to his. Shocked. It makes sense now that some of the leaves were fresh when he proposed. Then my brows fall to the sides of my face as my stunned expression shifts to gratitude. Because of how thoughtful this man, *my husband,* is.

"Each leaf is a memory," he says, lifting one. "This is from the ivy I gave you on New Year's Eve."

My heart stings, but only a little, remembering the car crash that took Parker from both of us that night. The same crash that seemed to pull us together in our grief. Allowing us to lean on each other during the most painful parts of our lives.

"This one," he says lifting a stiff green leaf, "is from the night you graduated. This one is from when I sang to you on the roof. And this one is actually from a jade plant inside the museum, from the day I saw you outside the yoga studio. I picked it because I didn't want to forget that day with you."

I don't even mind that my mascara is burning my eyes at this point.

He takes the wedding band out of the box, slides it on my finger, and pulls me closer than he ever has as he cups my face in his hands and presses his mouth to mine.

I close my eyes and give in to him. *Finally.* The kiss is gentle and sweet and makes me want to cry more than his vows did.

Then, Tallen's voice interrupts the most vulnerable moment of my life when he says, "I didn't say kiss her yet."

Declan slowly pulls his mouth from mine. With his face merely millimeters away from me, he shifts his eyes to Tallen and says, "What are you waiting for?"

Our mothers, fathers, Winnie, and Maverick laugh at Declan's comment, since they are the only ones witnessing at the ceremony.

Tallen clears his throat, as if he's apprehensive in commanding his best friend to kiss his little sister. Understandably.

Then, he says, "Do you guys promise to love each other forever?"

Declan is looking at me again.

"*I do*," we say in unison. But only because Tallen told us that we had to say it to be official; according to his twenty-minute crash course in online ordained wedding officiant training we talked him into signing up for last night in the parking lot of Avery's wedding reception.

"Then go ahead and kiss..." he says with a hint of reluctance, "...again." I know he's saying it in that tone because he's my brother. And despite the fact that he's slightly reluctant, I also know he's glad his best friend just turned into his new brother.

Declan kisses me again, and this time everyone claps for us. It's a little sad how quiet the celebration is in my mother's backyard, but I wouldn't have wanted it to happen any other way.

The only parts I wish I could change, would be the dates for the tickets Avery and Brent bought for their honeymoon to Costa Rica. Which is where they are now.

And the other part I would change, would be waiting so long to connect with Declan. Because if I had given him my number after I slipped on the ice, I would have fallen in love with him a lot sooner.

And if I had fallen in love with him sooner, Parker might have still been here to see us get married.

PART TWO:

THE INNER BATTLE

SEVENTEEN

I wrap another one of Declan's sculptors in a towel and place it in a box then tape it shut and write *bookshelf stuff* on the side.

"I'm going to start on your bedroom," I say, peeking my head into the kitchen where Declan is packing the dishes.

"Sounds good," he says with his back to me. "I'll be in to help you when I finish in here."

It's been a week and a half since our wedding. And adjusting to living together has been easier than I expected. Although we have been busy.

So far, we've done a lot of packing. Since Avery is going to be living with Brent and I'm moving away to D.C. with Declan, neither of us needed double of anything. I'm happy to use Declan's things, especially since most of his stuff is in better condition than anything I own. So, after Avery made her claim on a few personal items, I posted the rest of our shared belongings on a classifieds page where I was able to get rid of almost everything and where I was more than happy to get rid of my old washer.

My landlord gave me until the end of the month to move out, but that won't be necessary since the house is empty, cleaned, and ready for new tenants. All I have to do is drop off the keys.

I place an empty box on the bed and scribble, *bedroom*, on the side. Then I take my iPad and find a playlist to listen to before digging into the depths of Declan's closet.

Declan's bedroom is organized, like the rest of his home. The only things out of place are my laundry strewn on a corner chair, my moisturizer and deodorant on his dresser, and my wallet and iPad on his nightstand.

I begin filling the bottom of the box with shoes. Then in a

bottom drawer of his closet organizer, I find several spiral ringed notebooks. I flip the top notebook open and discover that it seems to be a journal.

It's organized with headings at the top of the pages. Some labeled *journal* and others labeled *lyrics* and *poems*.

I flip to a journal entry dated a couple of years ago when Declan was still in college.

EIGHTEEN

Journal:

It's been months since I've had any creative thoughts of my own. Grad school is consuming my time and any chance I might have at a social life.

But more than school, my thoughts are consuming my mind in the worst way.

I can't go to a sports bar or even the diner without returning home feeling like someone has been screaming in my ears.

I expressed this to Winnie last weekend when I returned home for Maverick's birthday party. I don't know if it was the echo of vociferous children's chatter or the fact that I've turned into an insomniac, but I was having trouble being present—physically and mentally—at the party.

Winnie noticed.

She always notices.

And when I expressed my hammering mind's concerns, she reminded me of my goals. She reminded me that my mind is powerful, but perspective controls the negative voices in my head.

That's why I'm sitting here now, with a notebook and pen. Reminding myself that this is my life to take hold of. And releasing myself of the unproductivity. Making my life what I want.

And what I want is steadiness and consistency.

Because when I don't have that. When I'm left to my own blaring mind. I'm plagued with doubt in my abilities.

And nothing good ever comes of it.

Lyrics:

dancing shadows make me
wince
misunderstood is my new
circumstance
the rest of me
is silent
voices trap me
in the silence

NINETEEN

"Ready for some help?" Declan's voice causes me to jump and slap the notebook shut.

I flip around to face him. "I didn't hear you come in. You startled me."

He's leaning one shoulder on the doorframe, watching me with his arms folded over his chest and a smirk on his face.

I lift his notebook with a sheepish grin. "I found your writing."

He pushes off the doorframe and reaches a hand out for the notebook. "Which one is this?" I place it in his grip and he flips the notebook open. Then his grin fades as his eyes scroll across the pages. He glances at me, then closes the notebook and gently taps it against his palm. "How much did you read?"

I shrug. "Not much. A journal entry from when you were in grad school and feeling down."

His grip tightens on the notebook.

"And a short blurb of lyrics," I quickly say making sure I'm being fully honest.

His expression isn't hard as he continues to stare down at me, but it's not gentle either. Maybe I should have asked before invading his old thoughts scribbled on the pages of his notebook.

"I'm sorry," I say, rising to my feet. "I probably should have asked before reading anything."

He shakes his head and creases his forehead as he looks down at the notebook in his hands. "No," he says. His eyes meet mine and all the concern vanishes in his face. "I told you that I would share my writing with you." He tosses his notebook into the box on the bed without looking and grips my waist. "You're the somebody that understands me. I want you to know everything. But I also want you to know that the person that wrote in those notebooks was lost and hurting. I'm not the same person that I used to be."

I nod in understanding, and lift my chin up to him.

He takes my face in his hands and presses his mouth against mine with sweet passion. *I love his touch.* When he releases me, his eyes are bouncing between mine. "My life changed once I found you again. You saved me, Christine. And you gave me back my creativity."

I flash him a sweet smile. Then, "Those lyrics," I say this with hesitation, still unsure of how much he wanted me to read. I swallow my nerves down before continuing, "They were so sad."

He gently pushes my hair behind my shoulder, avoiding my eyes, when he says, "I had a hard time immersing myself in school and balancing the things I enjoyed." His eyes meet mine with seriousness. "Like writing songs. The lyrics you read, I wrote that because I was feeling lost and alone. I don't like remembering those times. I had friends, but my life was lacking a real connection with anyone. Then," he grins, "I found you." He kisses me again. When he releases me, his eyes are smiling. "And you've been the muse that I didn't know I needed."

I smile, feeling flooded by the simple fact that I'm wanted. I'm also curious to know the man he was before me, and why I seem so inspiring to him now.

"I'd love to read more of what you've written," I say, biting at my words and my smile.

"You can."

I rise on my tip toes to kiss him again but his phone rings, pulling his eyes to his pocket.

He retrieves his phone and glances at me. "It's Winnie," he says, answering her call.

I sit back down on the floor and begin pulling the rest of the notebooks out before I pack them away. Declan leans down, his chest pressing into my shoulder, as he slides a thick five subject notebook out from the bottom of the pile and sets it in my lap. Kissing the side of my face, he says, "Start with this one."

Then he stands, and to Winnie he says, "No, I was talking to Christine." He leaves the room and comes back with an empty box, then begins loading the contents of his dresser into the box as he continues his conversation with Winnie.

I set the large spiral ringed notebook next to me. Even though I want to dig into its contents right now, I know I have a long trip to

D.C. Which will allow me to give my full attention to reading it.

"What?" Declan's voice is suddenly low and concerned. "What does that mean?"

He faces me with a bereaved expression then sits on the bed. Noticing his concern, I quickly find a place next to him and I'm sure my eyes are mirroring his bereavement because I don't know what's happening and I'm concerned about what Winnie has said to cause such pain to rise in Declan's eyes so suddenly.

He pulls his phone from his face and turns it on speaker. "Winnie, you're on speaker now."

"Hey, Winnie," I say, trying to sound okay since I'm not sure what's happening.

She clears her throat. "Christine, hi, how are you?" I can tell she's been crying.

"I'm good," I say, facing Declan who drops his forehead into his other palm. "Is everything okay?" I try to keep my breathing steady when I notice Declan struggling to remain composed. The last five seconds have my pulse rising.

She lets out a steadying breath, before she says, "Not really. I took our dad to the doctor. They've been running some tests over the past week and..." Her voice cracks.

I don't say anything. My eyes are flashing between Declan's creased brow and his phone trembling in his hand.

"Sorry," Winnie continues after clearing her throat. "And, they are pretty sure he has early onset dementia."

My mouth falls agape. Shocked.

I don't know much about dementia, but I do know it feels like a loss. And loss is something Declan has already experienced too much of in the last year.

"I'm so sorry," I say, unsure how to go about the rest of this conversation. Especially because it seems as if this information has debilitated Declan. I don't want to ask the wrong questions. I don't want the answers to hurt Declan anymore than he's already hurting. So I ask a general question. "What are the doctors going to do now?"

"We have to figure that out," she says sniffling. "There's different medications we can explore. And memory therapy we can try. Right now, Dad is still in denial and Mom is...well, you saw how she can get. Plus, she doesn't have any trust in medical professionals. So right now, we're still figuring everything out."

It's quiet for a moment. Then I say, "Winnie, how are you

handling all this? Do you need us to come help you?"

"U-um—" Her words are cut short by a sob.

I hate this. I hate this for their father; having to live with such a horrible disease. I hate this for Winnie; having to bear the burden. And I hate this for Declan. It's crushing.

Winnie continues. "I just don't want to make the wrong choices for my dad. This diagnosis explains everything that's been going on with him. But it doesn't make it easier to know that's what the problem is. Especially because dementia can be so aggressive."

At this statement, Declan gets up, handing me the phone, or fumbling it into my lap before he exits the room.

"I know," I say, wanting to follow Declan but staying seated because he obviously doesn't want to hear the rest of this conversation right now. "If there's something we can do, please don't hesitate to tell us, okay?"

"Okay, thanks, Christine."

"And if we should reconsider moving to D.C. or—"

"No," she says firmly. "You guys keep living your life. I know my dad wouldn't want you to put your dreams on hold for him. I feel confident speaking for him about that too."

"Okay."

She's not crying anymore when she says, "Seriously, Christine. Promise you guys will finish what you started."

I let out an unsure breath, then, "Okay, I promise."

"All of it. Papua New Guinea. The museum. Marriage. Everything. Promise me that you guys will finish *everything* you've started."

"I promise, Winnie."

After the call ends with Winnie, I find Declan pacing around the boxes in the living room. His hands are clasped on the top of his head and his jaw is set. As if he's biting down the pain inside.

My hands automatically press against my chest. Trying their best to cradle my own heart. Because seeing Declan in this state, holding back his pain, resisting his heartache, is soul shattering.

When he reaches the wall and flips around to pace the length of the room again, he notices me and his eyes lock on mine as his arms drop to his sides.

I hurry to him, locking my arms around his torso.

He wraps his arms around me, entirely. Hugging me deeper than he ever has. Then his sob hits my shoulder in one solid crack.

I feel the fracture in his heart.

And I feel so helpless for him.

Then he says, "I should have took him to the doctor sooner. I knew something was wrong."

His pain makes me hurt, and his tears make me cry. But I want to be strong for him. "Declan," I say gently. "You can't blame yourself. You didn't know. No one did."

He balls up the back of my shirt into his fists, hugging me so tight I feel like I might not be able to breathe.

But I don't stop him.

And I don't say anything more.

I wish we could go back to seven minutes ago, when the biggest stressor was packing our belongings and moving to D.C.

Seven minutes ago, when he was kissing me and telling me I was his muse.

Seven minutes ago, when we were still oblivious.

TWENTY

I retrieve what looks to be a ceramic sculpture of a man's head, and set it next to Declan's laptop on his desk. Declan told me once it was a philosopher, but the name seems to have escaped my mind.

I take the, now, empty box and flatten it with the others near the entrance.

Declan approaches me as he examines one of my smaller spider plants in his hands. "We're running out of places for all your plants." He pulls his eyes from the plant to meet mine with a grin. "Where did you want this one?"

I take it from him. "I think it would look nice in the bathroom. Maybe on the window ledge?"

His phone rings. Before answering, he kisses my cheek and says, "That sounds like a perfect spot."

He takes his phone call to the back patio.

I take the plant to the guest bathroom and place it on the window ledge. Then I focus on the city that expands so far into the distance that my eyes have trouble focusing on the buildings.

We took the metro around the city yesterday and walked by the capitol. A large gathering of high schoolers were instructed by their teacher to not even think about touching the fence or security would jump down from the trees and arrest them.

The fear inducing instruction made us laugh, but I wouldn't be surprised if ninja security guards are staked out in the trees and bushes surrounding the White House.

The outings have been a nice distraction from the heaviness of Sean's dementia diagnosis that cast over Declan for days after Winnie told us.

I know Declan is still hurting, but he seems to be trying to live his life as normally as possible. And I'm trying to support him in that.

This morning we met Margaret at the museum. She told me if I wanted a job before I leave for Papua New Guinea, she had connections at the Smithsonian. I thanked her, but I'm already busy enough without a job right now.

She took us on a tour of the abandoned school she and Declan are turning into a one-of-a-kind interactive linguistics museum. Margaret is a lot smaller, and a lot older than I imagined. But I can tell she is an intentional person with a caring heart. I don't have any problem leaving Declan in her hands while I'm gone.

When we walked up the several flights of stairs it takes to get to the top of the building, I asked what she was going to do with the stairs.

"I haven't decided yet," she said.

"Rip them out and modernize them with the rest of the building's renovations," Declan said.

I squatted down and wiped at the dirty blue and orange flower decorated tiles. "You could clean them and leave them in their original form. It'll give the museum some character."

They both gave me blank stares.

I shrugged. "I mean, it's part of the original history of the building."

"I like that." Margaret smiled. "I've just decided we're going to keep the original tiles on the stairs."

This entire city is full of history that my mind is craving to see.

But the jetlag has yet to subside, and I've been so tired lately.

"Christine?" Declan calls out to me. The ceilings in the apartment are very high and the open floor plan creates an echo with his voice.

I meet him in the living room.

"That was Margaret." He's putting his shoes on. "She wants to go over some things with me at the museum."

I slump down on the couch. "We didn't spend enough time there this morning?"

"You're welcome to stay here if you'd rather."

I rise to gather my things. "No, I'll go. If I stay here and try to finish unpacking, I'm afraid I'll fall asleep."

I find my purse in our bedroom and double back to toss Declan's old journal in there. I still have yet to open the book. I thought I would read it on the long trip it took to travel from one side of the country to the other. But I quickly learned reading in a moving vehicle makes me sick.

My phone begins to ring as I follow Declan out and wait for him to lock up.

"It's Winnie," I say with excitement. I like that his sister is calling me instead of him.

As I answer, Declan whips his head around to say, "Don't answer."

My eyes widen and I whisper, "Too late."

"Hello?" Winnie says. Then after a moment she continues, "Christine?"

I'm looking to Declan for direction but he's shaking his head with a stern look on his face, then whispers, "I'm not here."

I finally say, "Yeah, hi, I'm here." I hope she's not suspicious of my delayed response.

"How are you?" She laughs to herself. "I mean, besides busy with married life and moving into your new home?"

I draw in a deep breath, trying to sound as normal as possible, then, "Yeah, super busy moving in. And there's so much going on with the museum. How are you guys? How's your dad doing?"

"We're good. Dad's good, considering the circumstances." She pauses for a moment, then, "Hey, so Declan wouldn't be there by chance would he?"

I'm looking to Declan for some sort of direction, but he's just staring at me like he's already given me enough direction.

"He actually just left," I lie. And I hate that I'm lying to her about something so trivial.

"Shoot, he did?"

"Yeah, he had to go down to the museum for something." It feels wrong to lie to her, but I'm sure there's a good reason Declan is avoiding her right now. At least there better be.

"I've been having a hard time getting ahold of him. Could you have him call me when he gets back?"

"Of course."

When she ends the call, I look to Declan for some sort of explanation.

But he averts his eyes and moves past me, leading us down the staircase.

When we're outside of the apartment building, I can't take it anymore. I've given him enough time to explain himself. But since he's not talking to me about what just happened, I take his arm and say, "Hey, what's going on?"

He tries to continue forward but I grip his arm tighter and pull him to a stop.

When he faces me, I say, "Why don't you want to talk to your sister?"

"Can we not have this conversation right now, Christine?" He flips around and motions forward again when I release my grip on his arm. I don't know why right now isn't a good time for this conversation. I don't think it would take much time for him to explain it.

I'm sure it has something to do with not wanting to talk about their father. But I wouldn't know for sure since he doesn't want to *have this conversation right now.*

I decide to let it go and wait for another time to talk about it.

Our apartment is just minutes away from the museum, so it doesn't take long for us to get there. When we're inside, Margaret and Declan disappear to the third floor, and I find a comfortable couch in Margaret's office where I debate on napping.

This jetlag is no joke.

I set my purse next to me on the floor and remember the notebook I packed. Now is as good a time as any to dig into Declan's writings.

I lay on the couch and prop my head against the armrest with the notebook in my hands. The first page is dated ten years ago, which was the same time my parents divorced, and we moved.

TWENTY-ONE

Journal:

I'm writing.

My thoughts are jumbled in my mind—so I'm writing.

Hopefully it helps disentangle my mind. Winnie says it helps her. So I'll try it.

It's better than listening to all the arguing in the kitchen.

I've met twin brothers. They are new to town. Parker and Tallen.

They're a year ahead of me. They like sports. We get along. And the best part is that they don't know my family.

After football practice today, Winnie gave us a ride to their house. She said she would pick me up after she got off work at ten.

We played Zelda and then watched YouTube videos of skateboarding bloopers.

Then...

I heard her play.

I heard her sing.

I watched her play.

I watched her sing.

She mesmerized me.

I had to know her.

But before I could know her, Parker pinned me against the wall and told me if I ever looked at her again, he would curb stomp my teeth in.

I can stop myself from looking at her.

But I can't stop myself from thinking about her.

Or thinking about her singing.

Her voice, it makes me want to write music.

Lyrics:

```
    Eb
one look
        Eb
and nothing comes between us
     Bb
your voice
     B
dreams, finally wake up
 Ab    Bb     Gm
i can't think straight
     Eb
i'm pacing
 Ab Gm
your song
 Ab   Bb      Eb
has my heart racing
```

Journal:

This morning my mom and dad were arguing.
They've been doing that a lot lately.
Which makes me want to avoid being home.
So I do.
I avoid home with football and hanging out with Parker and Tallen.
I got a ride with their mom after the game Friday. I sat in the back next to their sister. But I didn't say much to her when Tallen introduced us. I didn't really look at her—even though I wanted to.
I follow their rules and keep my eyes off of her.
But they never told me to shut my ears off when she's singing. And she spends a lot of time doing that.
So I don't shut my ears off.
I listen.
I feel it.
Her parents recently divorced, and I feel it in her music.
I want to ask her why she's playing that song, so I can tell her it's going to be okay.
I want to tell her we should play music together.
But if I did. I wouldn't have a place to run to.

I wouldn't have a home where I felt welcome.
I wouldn't have a place of solace.
So I just listen to her play on the other side of Tallen's
bedroom wall. And pretend everything is okay.

Journal:
Today I broke the rule.
Today I looked at her.
I spoke to her.
I couldn't help it.
She answered the door when Winnie dropped me off.
I said hello.
She said hi. Then she invited me in.
She said her brothers were upstairs.
But I didn't care.
I wanted to stay there and talk to her.
I wanted to tell her I sing and play guitar too.
I wanted to touch her hand.
I wanted to ask her a million questions.
But when she smiled. I walked away, and met her
brothers upstairs.
I didn't look back.
But I couldn't stop seeing her face in my mind.
Her mouth makes me want to study poetry.

Poetry:
i want her so much sometimes
i want to disappear

-mark anthony

TWENTY-TWO

I shut the notebook and press it against my chest.

I'm awestruck.

It's bizarre and flattering and interesting and alarming that his mind was plagued with thoughts of me for three years. And he didn't do anything about it because he didn't want to lose the security of our home and the friendship he had with my brothers.

I know we were only kids, but he seemed beyond his years.

He was writing songs with chord progressions that are so complex an adult would struggle to come up with it on their own.

I continue reading through the journal. I find that he quotes Mark Anthony often. And he begins to fill more pages with song lyrics and produces less journal entries as the notebook unfolds.

I like getting to know his young mind.

Margaret enters the office as I'm finishing reading about when Declan, Tallen and Parker all snuck into the school the night before my brothers' graduation and decorated the gym with toilet paper.

"I know there's not much to do in here," she says maneuvering past me. "But that couch is pretty comfy isn't it?"

I sit up, place the notebook in my purse, and give her a smile. "It really is. And I have a feeling I'm going to get to know this couch a lot better."

She smiles then opens a drawer at her desk and pulls out a file. "We're just about done here and then I'll give Declan back to you. We still have a few more things to go over with the contractor if that's alright?"

I nod. "Of course, take your time. I don't have anything else to do."

"Well, feel free to explore if you'd like. Just be careful in the auditorium." She winks. "It's a mess."

After she's gone, I debate on reading more of the journal. But then settle for wandering around the first level of the building.

Margaret has taped a piece of paper to the wall of each room designated for various exhibits she plans to provide for the community. All her ideas are based on words and language. What she's doing here is going to impact the children, and adults that visit, in monumental ways. This might be the first museum that people will learn something new about language and will want to visit repeatedly.

I walk around the first floor and find the auditorium on the far side of the building. It's an enormous open room that's been completely gutted. There's a pile of scrap wood and garbage in the middle of the room. And the only light is the orange sunshine bursting in from the windows on one side of the room.

When I step into the room, a piece of glass crunches under my shoe, the sound echoes throughout the auditorium. And I can't help but think about how Margaret is going to use the acoustics in here for her museum.

The echo and natural acoustics give me another idea.

I slide my purse strap from my shoulder and take the notebook out, flipping to the end of the journal entry where Declan wrote a song with chords. I hum the notes quietly until I can progress through them without thinking. Then I begin to add the lyrics.

After a few minutes of quiet humming, and fumbling through the lyrics, I sing.

And I *really* sing.

I'm not normally moved by my own voice, but the fact that the song came from Declan moves me.

The growing intensity of my voice reverberates through the room, expanding to every crevasse.

I sing the lyrics over and over until my voice has grown so loud my ears are ringing.

Then...

I stop.

Then...

The echo of my voice in the room hums to a stop.

And a gentle applause causes me to flip around where Margaret, Declan, and the contractor are watching me at the entrance to the auditorium.

I slap my hands to my cheeks and hope they don't see the embarrassment rising in my face. I don't know why I'm embarrassed, of course this was going to happen. Even though I hoped they wouldn't hear from the third floor. But how could I belt out that song without them hearing?

When I approach them, Declan is beaming. As if he's forgotten all about the tiff we had before we got here. He lifts me in his arms and kisses the side of my face.

"You're incredible," he says, setting me back on my feet. Then facing Margaret and the contractor he says, "Isn't she incredible?" Facing me again, with the widest grin, he says, "You're incredible! You're flawless! *You're perfect.*"

Margaret's smile is so big she seems to be shaking. She takes my hand in both of hers. "Forget the Smithsonian. Hell, forget Papua New Guinea! Come and work for me. I have a whole section on the second floor I want to dedicate to music and song lyrics. It would be the perfect exhibit for you."

From behind her, the contractor says in a monotone voice, "I thought you wanted kids to sing Karaoke upstairs."

Margaret waves her hand hushing him. Then to me, she says, "I'm not serious about you missing out on the opportunity you've been given to explore the culture in Papua New Guinea, but I am serious about giving you a position to work for me here at the museum when you come back."

I look at Declan, and I'm not sure why since I don't need permission to accept what Margaret is offering. But I also can't help feeling like I might be overstepping into his space. Afterall, this museum is like his baby. But maybe it could be *our* baby.

"I don't know," I say, unsure if I want to commit to anything.

"Please think about it." Margaret releases my hand. Then with a peculiar look, she says, "That song was beautiful. Did you write it?"

"No." I smile at Declan. "Declan did, a long time ago."

He laces his fingers in mine as he says, "Although, when I wrote it, the tempo was a lot faster." He looks at me, and with a soft voice says, "But I liked the way you slowed it down better."

When we return home, Declan is so elated by what happened at the museum that he finds his guitar and begs me to play my keyboard with him.

We sing his song.

We sing covers of other songs.

We play everything.

And I've never seen him happier.

I've never seen him more full of life and passion and joy. It's contagious.

We don't stop singing until it's almost midnight and I worry we're going to disturb the neighbors.

If I don't stop soon, I'm afraid I'll pass out from exhaustion, or starvation.

"One more," Declan says. He's seated right next to me, facing the opposite direction on my small makeshift piano bench that I bought at a garage sale. I'm pretty sure it was originally a sewing machine bench because it's a little shorter than I'd like it to be for playing my keyboard.

I power down the keyboard and lay my head down against the speaker. "I can't play another song. I don't have anything left in me."

When he looks at me, his eager expression shifts to understanding. He sets his guitar down and slides his legs around the bench so he's facing the same direction as me.

Brushing my hair out of my face, he says, "It doesn't help that we skipped dinner, does it?"

I can't even furrow my brow, I'm so tired. "Is it too late to order something?"

He presses a kiss to the side of my mouth. "I'll find something for us in the kitchen." He takes my hand and lifts me to follow him. "Come sit with me while I cook for you."

He's amazing.

I find a place on the counter in the kitchen that's out of Declan's way. He's tossing all sorts of things on the counter next to me, but I'm not sure what he's going to make. I honestly don't care, but I don't want to tell him that I'm past the point of hunger and just want to go to bed.

I check my phone, although I'm not sure why since I'm certain I'm incapable of forming a complete sentence right now. I have a text from Avery, another from Tallen, and a missed call from my dad.

I'm sure my dad is making his quarterly phone call to me, which typically means I listen to him talk about himself for an hour. I'll save that phone call for later.

Avery's message is a photo of her and Brent in scuba gear. I'm not sure if this is from their honeymoon or something she's doing for her new job.

I don't bother asking. Instead, I lift my phone and snap a selfie of me on the counter and Declan tossing a couple of chicken breasts into a pan, then send it as a reply to Avery.

I open Tallen's message and decide to text him back too since it's only 9 o'clock in Nevada.

Tallen: Dad's going to call.
Me: What'd he say?
Tallen: Big news. He's dating the new morning reporter.
Me: Thanks for the heads up.

I can sense the sarcasm in his text. Glad I decided not to call my dad back.

While Declan is plating our food, I check my email and find a message about my trip. It makes my stomach sink. I'm starting to feel pulled in two very different directions.

"This one's yours," Declan says with a grin.

I smile back, halfheartedly, and with complete exhaustion.

I want to stay here with him. I want to carpool to the museum and be a part of establishing it with him. I want to stay up until midnight creating music with him. I want to fall asleep in his arms. I want to eat dinner in the middle of the night with him. I don't want any of this to end.

I was so hesitant to commit my life to him, but once I did, I can't think of anything else I would rather be doing. I would even go to the extent to say that I would give up the opportunity to go to Papua New Guinea just to stay here with him and do whatever he wants to do. My old dreams just don't seem to matter as much as being with him does.

He's about to take a bite when he must notice something is off with me. He lowers his fork to inspect the food. "Is it the chicken?"

I shake my head and take a bite. "No, it's great." I don't want to ruin his mood with my teetering thoughts.

He tilts his head as his posture slumps. "Christine," he says my name as if he's annoyed. Which makes me a little sad since he usually glides my name past his lips. "If this is about Winnie, it's nothing. She's been pestering me with phone calls, and I'd like to live my life without her breathing down my neck." He fixes his eyes on mine and takes my hand in his. "And telling you to lie. I won't ask you to do that for me again, alright?"

I force a small smile, then say, "Thank you, but it's not that."

He forces a breath from his nose, as if he's trying to keep from getting upset. "Then what is it?"

I feel like I could cry. Maybe I'm just sleep deprived. Maybe adjusting to the reality of my new life is sinking in. I don't know what's making me feel weepy, but I can't push down the tears rising in my eyes.

I drop my fork to my plate and cover my face with my hands. "I don't know. I feel torn about going to Papua New Guinea and staying here. I'm excited and scared to be married. I can't believe it, but I even miss Avery." I pull my hands away and meet his apathetic expression with my confusion. "And I'm very, *very* tired and just want to go to bed."

My statement causes him to soften his expression and makes him laugh gently. He looks at me with a sympathetic expression. "Christine." Now when he says my name, his tone is relaxed. And filled with the sweetness I'm used to hearing. "You're going to Papua New Guinea. No one, not me, not Margaret, not even our marriage is going to take that from you. Okay?"

I nod and wipe my face.

"Come on, I'll take you to bed."

"Really?"

He nods and takes my hand, guiding me to our bedroom and abandoning the half-eaten meal at the table.

I don't waste a second slipping out of my jeans and climbing into bed. Declan curls himself behind me. Enveloping me in his arms. I'm already shutting my eyes and falling into tranquility. Sleeping. *Finally.*

Then, he quietly whispers against my head, "Thanks for staying up with me tonight."

I try to open my eyes, but they only flutter briefly before forcing themselves shut. I make a sound instead of saying, *you're welcome.*

He continues, "I can't wait to see the way you interpret the next song you find in my journal."

A gentle airy laugh escapes through my nose. "I think you were obsessed with me in high school."

He kisses my shoulder. "I still am."

TWENTY-THREE

"Do you have your passport?" I ask standing in front of the check-in machine.

"Yes." Declan lifts his passport. "I have my passport."

"And your phone charger?"

He nods with a reassuring grin.

"And an adaptor? The charger is useless without an adaptor. You know the prongs to the outlets are different there."

He takes my hands and says, "I know. I have the adaptor for the charger. Now, look at me."

I do and relax in his brown eyes.

"We are fully packed. And we're both prepared. So, stop worrying and calm down, okay? Remember, this trip is supposed to be fun." He kisses me.

Then he pulls me in close to him, and *really* kisses me. As if no one else is in the airport watching.

When he releases me, I cover my mouth. I'm still getting used to kissing him in public even though we've been married for months. My eyes flash around to the bystanders, some of which are still looking at us. The embarrassment begins to rise up my neck.

Then Declan takes my face in his hands and gives me a small kiss without ungluing his eyes from me.

"Declan," I say, as if I feel how uncomfortable we're making some of the people standing in line behind us.

My eyes are flicking between the people around us and his eyes.

His grin spreads across his entire face, as if he's glad people are watching. Which is slightly unnerving for me.

He says, "It doesn't matter if we're in the middle of blaring traffic. No distractions will take my attention from you when we're together."

I fold my mouth in, stunned that I'm actually married to him.

"Excuse me," an airline employee says. "If y'all are finished here, could you move your romance over to the security check? There're other people tryin' to get checked in."

"I'm so sorry," I say squirming as I pull myself from Declan's grip. "We'll get out of the way."

After we're through security, explore the airport, and file into our seats on the airplane, I feel a sense of worry wash over me.

Am I making the right decision? What if I'm kidnapped while I'm gone? Or murdered? What if something happens to Declan's dad and I'm not there to comfort him? What if me and Declan grow apart? What if he finds another muse?

"Hey," he takes my hand. "Why are you being so quiet?"

I shrug, not wanting to discuss the unnecessary anxieties swirling in my head. Because I know that's what they are. And I'm not going to let doubt creep in now. I've made it this far by being brave and determined. And if Declan waited a decade to be with me, six months will be cake.

"You're not afraid of flying are you?" he says teasingly.

I shake my head and laugh quietly. "No," I say under my breath.

"Christine." He still melts me when he says my name. "I know you. And I know something is off."

I smile. "It's just nerves. But I'm fine."

He gives me a suspicious look before shoving his satchel under the seat at his feet. The longer we're married, the more connected we seem to become. It reminds me of the twin superpowers Tallen and Parker had. I'm starting to wonder that maybe they were able to sense so much about each other not because they had superpowers, but because they spent decades of their lives together—even before they were separate fetuses.

After take-off, I stare at the screen in front of me and watch the little airplane journey across the ocean at a snail's pace. Declan falls asleep reading a book called *Caring for Loved Ones with Dementia.*

I open my purse and take out the journal I've kept tucked away. He knows I've been reading it. I feel weird reading it in front of him though. Which is why I'm just taking it out now while he's oblivious to my actions.

My progress has slowed way down since I've discovered pages and pages of songs that we've breathed new life into during our late-night jam sessions.

Declan is taking this whole music thing a lot more seriously than I am. For me it's a fun hobby, and a beautiful way for us to spend our time together.

But Declan wants to make our songs public. He even bought a couple of microphones and a recording system for his computer so we can start recording together when I get back.

It's been fun making music with him.

But I'm not sure my heart is in it as much as his is.

I flip open the journal and pick up where I left off the summer before Declan's senior year.

TWENTY-FOUR

Journal:
   My parents were both at work when my dad found out he had another kid.
   I guess I have a little brother.
   I hate my dad for cheating on my mom.
   I don't know why she doesn't leave him for doing that to her.
   The whole afternoon was weird.
   Winnie came home. Our parents sat us down. My dad told us he had an affair with a woman named Andrea four years ago.
   Mom knew.
   And he said Andrea showed up at his work and told him he had a son he forgot to pay child support for.
   Mom didn't know about that.
   Dad didn't either.
   Dad, being kindhearted to a fault, said he would provide child support but also wanted to be a father to his son. My half-brother.
   So now we're going to meet Maverick next weekend.
   My poor mom is shattered.
   I hate that things are broken.
   I hate that my parents have been arguing for years.
   I hate that Parker and Tallen are going to college three hours away.
   I hate that Winnie is getting married and moving in with Jake.
   I hate that I'm alone.

Lyrics:

this anguish takes over
making my soul strain
i forget
that there was ever a time
i was not in pain

Journal:
    Parker and Tallen stopped by to say goodbye yesterday.
    I left my journal open on my bed.
    Stupid.
    Parker found it.
    He read a poem.
    He laughed.
    He read a song out loud.
    He teased me for it.
    He doesn't know how much I love words and language.
    He skimmed over a journal entry.
    I tried to take it from him.
    Thankfully I've never written her name.
    He encouraged Tallen to tease me.
    But Tallen didn't.
    Tallen wouldn't.
    Because Tallen knew.
    He knew who I was writing about.
    He knew I was writing about her.
    He didn't have to tell Parker.
    Parker knew just by looking at Tallen's face.
    They pushed me onto my bed. Pinning me down.
    I didn't fight back.
    I told them it wasn't her.
    They called me a liar.
    I told them I liked Jess Thompson.
    That I was obsessed with Jess Thompson for years.
    I lied.
    And they knew.
    They told me to prove it.
    They demanded that I prove it.
    So I texted Jess Thompson.
    And I invited Jess over.
    And I proved it.
    And it killed me.

Then, when I went to work today.
I saw her at the pool.
HER.
And it killed me.
When I saw her, her hands made me want to wring my
own neck.
And it killed me.
I don't deserve her.
And it kills me.

Poetry:
i hurt myself today
to see if i still feel
i focus on the pain
the only thing that's real

the needle tears a hole
the old familiar sting
try to kill it all away
but i remember everything

what have i become
my sweetest friend
everyone I know
goes away
in the end

and you could have it all
my empire of dirt
i will let you down
i will make you hurt

-johnny cash

Journal:
My ambition is gone.
I'm trying to coast the rest of the year out until I leave
for college.
Everyone here is stupid.
I'm beyond this town.
I'm beyond this school.
I'm beyond the sports.
I'm beyond the girls.

AURORA STENULSON

I'm beyond the teachers.
I'm beyond the parties.
I'm beyond my parents.
I'm beyond it all.
And I can't wait to leave.

Lyrics:

i've burned the bridge
before i got to it
how do i say sorry
when you don't know my folly

one day closer
to the end of it
drowned in guilt
that i alone built

my carelessness is
my demise
i can't look into your eyes
for failure is my prize

TWENTY-FIVE

The island is beautiful.

The guest house I'm staying in is more of a large hut that shares a wall with a kitchen that I have to walk outside to get to. And my neighbor, Tila, is a native Papua New Guinean who is the nurse on this side of the island.

I can hear the ocean from my bedroom. Today, I woke up to my seventh day in Papua New Guinea and last day with Declan before he flies back to D.C.

So far, I've met with a small tribe that spoke a language that no one but my guide, Carlos, understands. But they seemed friendly enough that I'm not worried about visiting them again on my own.

And the Lukas family that lives down the road invited us to explore Port Moresby with them two days ago. We spent the evening at a concert until my feet hurt from jumping and dancing. We had a blast seeing the modernized parts of the island. But because we didn't get back until the early morning yesterday, and my body is still adjusting to the fifteen-hour time difference, we're just now rising out of bed for the day.

Declan rolls to his stomach and covers his head with his pillow. "I'm not ready to get up," he groans.

"Me either," I say, curling up next to him. "And I don't want you to leave."

He faces me with sleepy eyes. "I'll quit my job at the museum. Move to PNG with you in this room. We'll learn all eight hundred languages and visit the tribes in the bush and live happily ever after."

I laugh. "Don't tempt me."

He smiles, then rolls out of bed. "Or we can both abandon anthropology, move to L.A. and become famous musicians."

"Now, there's an idea."

He heads for the bathroom, which isn't anything more than a toilet and a tile covered drain with a bucket of water for a shower. There's running water, but it doesn't work half the time. So I have to boil water and fill up a bucket if I want a shower.

What have I gotten myself into?

I hear someone yelling outside, so I quickly get dressed and make my way out to the road.

I see two teenagers walking up the road. They wave when they see me, and I wave back. It's Thomas and Antonio, they are the oldest sons in the Lukas family.

"Christine," Thomas says before fully reaching me. "Is Mr. Declan gone?"

I smile, happy to have already made a few friends, even if they are teenagers. "Nope, not yet. But he's getting ready to leave soon. Carlos is coming to pick him up and take him to the airport."

Antonio kicks at a rock in the dirt. He keeps his eyes down as he scratches the top of his curly blonde hair, and says, "Our mom wants you to come over for dinner."

"Thank you. That would be great," I say. "Let her know I'll be there."

They nod in unison. Thomas is a little older, taller and darker than his fair-skinned and blond-haired brother. Antonio must have gotten the recessive gene some of the Melanesians have that turns their hair blond and their eyes blue since he's the only one in his family with light eyes and hair.

It's quiet for a moment then Thomas flashes me a wide full grin and says, "Hey, so, Christine?"

I let out a soft laugh at their awkward and forward teenager communication style.

"Yeah?"

Thomas and Antonio share a look. It reminds me of the way my brothers used to look at each other. And it makes me smile. "We were going to Tuvalu in a few days if you wanted to go?"

I tilt my head. "Tuvalu? Where is that?"

Thomas points out in the direction of the ocean. "It's a secret island over there. Our Bubu Keela and cousins live there." He's still grinning from ear to ear. I'm starting to think his smile is a constant part of who he is.

I shrug. "Sounds fun. How do we get there?"

"An airplane flies there every three days," Thomas says with an expectant look in his eyes. "Bring cash and we will get you a ticket when we go to the airport." The airport is at least an hour drive away from here and besides the single motor bike their family owns, Carlos is the only one nearby with transportation.

"Okay," I agree. I feel like I should be asking more details. But I've learned most of the things that go on around here, especially in the rural villages, are more of a go with the flow type of planning.

Antonio's eyes light up when Declan exits the hut and meets us outside.

"Mr. Declan, I wanted to give this to you before you left," Antonio says handing Declan a beautiful seashell necklace.

Declan seems surprised. "Antonio, wow." He gives him a hug. "Thank you. I wish I had something to give you. Did you make this?"

Antonio shakes his head. "No, my mom did."

Declan grins, then pats Antonio's shoulder. "Well, thank you. Tell your mother she's very talented. Man, I'm really going to miss your family. And I wish I could stay longer."

Thomas approaches him and they grip each other's hands before thrusting their arms around each other, hugging. "Won't you come back for a visit soon?" Thomas says with his wide grin, but I can tell there's a hint of sorrow in his expression.

Declan blinks at me, then to Thomas he says, "I think I'll be back sooner than you think."

The boys make Declan promise to come back before I complete my fieldwork. Then they head back down the road in a sprint. Racing each other.

"I'm going to miss them," Declan says, wrapping his arm around my shoulders. He kisses the top of my head. "But not as much as I'm going to miss you."

I fold my arms around his torso. "It's going to be no fun at all waking up without you in the morning."

He shifts his other arm around me so that he's holding my waist and tucks my head under his chin. "You'll be so busy with your fieldwork and finding tribes in the bush that you won't even notice I'm gone."

"Speaking of fieldwork, Thomas and Antonio invited me to visit their family in Tuvalu in a few days."

He draws his head back to look at me curiously. "Tuvalu?"

I nod. "It's an island. I guess an airplane flies in every three days so it must not be much of an island."

He chuckles. "So you're having a sleep over with a couple of teenage boys in Tuvalu?"

I pull away from him and give him a wide-eyed expression. "I didn't even think about that."

We look at each other until we're both laughing. I don't want our laughter to stop, because I know when it does the sadness and reality that he's leaving will immerse us.

I help him gather the rest of his things trying to keep myself from feeling sad that I'll be spending the next six months or so without him.

Then, we hear Carlos' truck coming up the road.

Declan pulls me in for one last hug, then, "Before I forget." He unzips his suitcase, rummages to the bottom, then hands me a journal.

His journal.

I look up at him. "You brought the next journal? But how did you know I would finish the first one?"

"I didn't," he says, pulling me in for a kiss.

Carlos honks the horn. He's a little more aggressive than I would like for a guide. But he has connections with the tribes, so I deal with it. And because his English consists of Tok Pisin, we don't really understand what he's saying unless Thomas is around to translate. So, instead, he does things like honk the horn on his truck to get our attention.

"I better go," Declan says, kissing me again.

I hug him hard and keep my face pressed to his. "I love you."

He smiles with his kiss on my mouth, then, "I love you *more*."

Carlos honks again. He holds the horn longer this time and he's not looking at either of us. At Carlos' gesture, Declan takes his suitcase and bag, then heads for the truck.

"Have a safe trip. And leave me a message when you're home!" We decided to use an app that allows us to text each other for free. And if I walk half a mile down the road, I can get enough cell service to send and receive messages.

He waves, as Carlos wastes no time stirring up a cloud of dust into the air as he pulls down the dirt road.

I head back inside my hut that feels more like a sauna than a home, and toss the notebook on my bed.

I can't help but feel like Declan just drove off with my entire heart. The same heart that used to daydream about fieldwork, Melanesians, grass skirts and head dresses dancing around a fire, and tribal chanting.

But now it seems consumed with linguistic museum construction, harmonizing with Declan's voice until three o'clock in the morning, and daydreaming about a future together.

"Christine," Thomas' voice wakes me from a nap I didn't mean to take.

He's standing in my open doorway with a bowl full of sago that, for a second, looked like a stack of pancakes before my brain registered to the country I'm in. And he's masked in his friendly familiar grin. "My mom wanted us to bring you some sago. In case you're hungry."

I can see Antonio's frizzy blond hair as he peers in behind Thomas in the doorway, but I'm not sure he wants to be acknowledged.

"Thanks," I say, sitting up on my bed. "I didn't miss dinner, did I?"

Thomas smiles. "No, we won't have dinner until later."

"He told our mom to make sago for you," Antonio blurts out.

Thomas elbows him.

Antonio doubles over after the blow, then, "What? You did."

Their sibling bantering makes me smile.

Thomas faces me and sets the bowl on the ground in front of the doorway. Like he's unsure if he should come into my hut or not. "I thought you might be hungry since you don't have any food here."

He's right. I don't have much food besides some chicken crackers I bought at the market at his mother's insistence.

"Thank you," I say. "I'm starving, so I know my stomach will appreciate it."

Thomas' smile widens, then he begins to say something. But his words are overpowered by a subtle rattle that grows into a roar under our feet.

The sound that accompanies the shaking earth under me, is like nothing I've ever heard before. And the aggressive rumbling would have thrown me off my feet if I had been standing.

Before the far wall crumbles before my eyes, I see Thomas jump back and protect Antonio with his body. Shielding him.

Then, everything goes black.

185

TWENTY-SIX

"Look, she's waking up." The voice I hear is familiar, but my mind seems so boggled and confused that I can't put a name to the voice I hear.

When my eyes flutter open, the first thing I see is a window. I can't bring myself to sit up because my head feels like it's grown into the size of a boulder.

"How are you feeling?" It's Tila's voice.

I press my eyes closed tightly, then open them. "My head," I say pulling my hand up, then hesitate, afraid of what I might feel when I touch my head.

Thomas and Antonio are standing behind Tila in her orange floral dress.

"What happened?" I say.

"There was an earthquake." Thomas says. "Your house fell on you." Even though my head is pounding, I can't help but notice his grin seems out of place with his statement.

Tila flips her head around to face them, and she makes a sound then shoos Thomas and Antonio away.

"Where am I?" I ask.

Tila forces a smile that doesn't match the rest of her downcast expression. She sits next to me on the bed and takes my hand in hers. "After the earthquake, Thomas and Antonio pulled you from the rubble and carried you to my house. A board fell on your head when the wall collapsed. You were lucky nothing worse happened to you."

I touch the side of my head and wince.

Tila's voice is gentle. "Careful, you have a good size bump on your head. But I think you're going to be okay."

Then, as if I've just been struck by reality I sit up and say, "An earthquake destroyed my house?"

Tila nods. "Yes, I don't know how my house is still standing. The earthquake probably reached a hundred kilometers from here."

My pulse accelerates so intensely that it feels like my veins are about to burst out of my skin.

"No, you don't understand." I grip her soft arms. "Declan was flying out today. If that earthquake reached that far it could have collapsed more buildings. And maybe it collapsed the airport."

"Please, try to stay calm." Tila's dark brown eyes widen. "I'm sure he's okay." She says this so unconvincingly I could cry.

My heart is pounding so violently in my chest, I'm sure my sternum is going to break.

"I need to get out of here," I say in a panic. "I need to get to Port Moresby and call Declan." Before I know what's happening, my stomach twists and I begin to throw up over the side of the bed at poor Tila's feet.

She stays seated as if she's not fazed at all, and with a careful voice she says, "I think you need to get to Port Moresby and make sure you don't have a concussion first."

I don't care if I have a concussion. I don't care that my body is hurting. All I can think about is if Declan is okay.

And if he's not, I don't think I'll survive without him.

His last kiss burns at my mouth.

And his last words reverberate in my ears.

I love you more.

I don't know what time it is. But the moon is out and shining enough light in through the window to bother me. Not that I can sleep right now anyway. Tila won't let me sleep until I see a doctor.

I turn to my other side to face the entrance of Tila's house when I hear something outside.

Thomas jogs in with a flashlight in one hand and my purse in the other. I'm not sure if his expression is tired from running or if he's worried about Declan too. Especially because they seemed to bond so quickly this past week.

"You found it," I say, reaching for my purse to retrieve my phone.

"And this," he says, digging his hand into his pocket and revealing my phone.

When he hands it to me, it's apparent his expression was full of grief because it's obvious my phone is broken.

I just wanted to check my app and see if I had a message from Declan. I'm sure Tila's house is far enough down the road to get service from here. But having service doesn't matter now when my phone is useless.

I only want to know if he's okay. Is that an unreasonable request? Because with my broken phone and head injury, it feels like it is.

The unknown is causing my anxieties to amplify.

It's as if all the same feelings of fear and uncertainty are returning just like before we got to the hospital before we learned that Parker had died.

My breath begins to intensify, and I feel the urge to vomit again.

I rush past Thomas and fall to my knees outside.

Then, I get sick.

Then, I begin to cry.

I don't know how I'm going to go on like this.

My head hurts. I'm alone in a foreign place. I'm injured. And I don't know if my husband is trapped under the rubble of a fallen airport.

Tila and Thomas are speaking in Tok Pisin behind me, and I don't know the language well enough to understand it fluently so I'm only able to pick up on pieces of their conversation.

Tila asks about his family.

Thomas says they are good.

Tila asks something about my house.

Thomas says something I don't understand.

Tila asks something about the radio at his house.

Thomas says the earthquake damaged it.

I don't understand the next few statements, but I hear Carlos' name and something about a doctor. And then just as I'm about to give up eavesdropping on their conversation, Tila says Declan's name. Which makes my ears perk up. But nothing they say for the next few minutes after that makes any sense to me.

Thomas gently says, "Excuse," before walking around me. He squats down in front of me and places his hand on my shoulder. "Christine, I'm going to get my moto and find Carlos, okay? He should be home by now. He can give us information about Mr. Declan and take you to the doctor in his truck. Okay?"

I lift the neck of my shirt to wipe my face and say, "Thank you, Thomas." Because it's the only thing I can say in my state of nauseated agony. I never thought I would be at the mercy of a teenage boy in a foreign country like this. But I can't imagine going through any of this without his generosity right now.

Then he patters away, running up the road toward his house.

Tila takes my arm and helps me up. "Can you try to drink some water?"

I sit on the edge of her bed and hold my head in my hands. "I don't know."

She brushes my hair out of my face. "With your vomiting, there's a chance of dehydration. And it will be a while before Carlos is here. I don't want you to feel worse than you already do, so if you can drink some water…" Her words trail but I know she's anticipating an answer.

I stay in my same position, and barely make a sound when I say, "Okay," and reluctantly take the water.

When I open my eyes, the first thing I see is the flimsy wooden wall of Tila's bedroom. Reminding me that I'm still in her home. Injured.

Then I hear birds and the distant sounds of the ocean.

I roll over on my side. My head is still hurting, but not as bad as last night.

Last night.

It's this thought that makes me realize it's morning. Did Thomas come back? Where is Carlos? And where is Tila?

I sit up and leave the bed. Like my home, Tila's hut doesn't have much to it besides a large open room with her bed, a small table, and an area for preparing meals. And because there's not much of a home to investigate, I quickly realize that Tila isn't home.

I walk outside.

Nothing.

I walk a ways up the road.

Nothing.

I walk down the hill toward the beach.

Nothing.

I walk toward my house, but not the entire distance.

Nothing.

When I get back to Tila's, I feel an eeriness emerge in my core.

It shouldn't have taken Thomas very long to reach Carlos since Carlos lives in the bay. On his moto, it shouldn't have taken more than fifteen- or twenty-minutes tops to get to Carlos' home.

189

Unless something happened to Thomas.

And that's why Tila isn't here. Because she's looking for him.

My pulse begins to accelerate. Because if something happened to Thomas, I would feel completely responsible. He only left because of me. And if Tila did go looking for him. How long should I wait for her until it's okay for me to worry?

"How are you feeling?"

I flip my head around to see Thomas.

I don't know why, but I rush to him and hug him. He seems stiff. Understandably. An American woman he's just met is hugging him, it's probably a little awkward. I don't hug him for very long though.

When I step back he clears his throat, and his natural grin seems just as stiff as his posture when he says, "Does that mean you're feeling better?"

I let out a soft laugh. "Sorry," I wave my hand, waving away my emotions with the gesture. "I thought something happened to you, and I was starting to worry because you hadn't come back and I couldn't find Tila, and Carlos wasn't here either. And I thought you were going to get him." I tilt my head, then, "Where is Tila? And why didn't Carlos ever come back for me?"

"Tila is at my house. She told me to come check on you. My mom is having the baby." He says this as if it's just a normal event occurring on a regular day. Then he shifts his mouth to one side with a shrug. "And Carlos wasn't home."

My mind spins. "Your mom is having a baby? Right now?"

He nods. And this time when he smiles it's genuine.

My hands shoot to grasp the sides of my head, and I wince from the pain that reminds me I was under my fallen roof yesterday. And it also reminds me of Carlos.

"And Carlos," I begin to say as my hands clasp against my chest. "He wasn't home?"

Thomas shakes his head but he's still smiling, like he's trying to keep me from worrying. "He might have stayed in Port Moresby. Especially after the earthquake. He might have wanted to be safe. There was damage from the earthquake along the coast. Fallen trees mostly, but enough to block some parts of the road to his house."

"You don't think something happened to him, do you?" I normally wouldn't be so transparent with a teenager, but he's the oldest of his siblings and more mature than any teenager I've ever met. I think he can handle honest transparency from a physically and emotionally injured woman like me.

He shakes his head. "Carlos runs on his own timeline. He probably met some friends in the city and then stayed with them after the earthquake. He doesn't have a family, so he wouldn't want to hurry home."

I nod. I can't tell if he's just telling me what I need to hear right now to not freak out. But I know there's not much more that he knows. It would be pointless to press him.

"But I left a message with his neighbor," Thomas says. "So, when he gets back, he knows to come here."

I nod. I wish that made me feel better. But I'm afraid nothing is going to calm my racing mind until I know Declan is okay.

I wish Thomas or Tila had a cell phone. I don't understand how anyone would want to live without one. If they had a phone, I could contact Declan that way. He should have landed back in the states by now. He might even be back in D.C.

I hope he's back in D.C.

Because if he's not back in D.C., that means that something happened. And the one image I can't shake, is Declan crushed by the cement walls at the airport.

TWENTY-SEVEN

The roaring sound of Carlos' truck has never been a welcoming sound until this moment.

I'm not sure if he knows I'm inside Tila's house, so I hurry to the road and wave him down with the last bit of strength I have.

There's a cigarette hanging out of the corner of his mouth when I approach him. The smoke makes my stomach lurch.

His brows are drawn together, as if he's angry. But I've spent enough time with him to know that that's his normal resting expression. "You sick?" he says in his broken English.

I point to my head. "I hurt my head." I annunciate my words, knowing his understanding of English isn't great.

He nods and takes the cigarette out of his mouth and flicks it at the road. He looks at me, squinting one eye from the sunlight blaring into his face, then, "I take you to doctor."

I lift my finger. "Hang on." I turn back inside Tila's house and dig in my purse to retrieve a pen and the journal Declan gave me before he left.

I flip through the notebook, but every page is full of Declan's handwriting. I can either destroy the back cover or erase one of his memories. I opt for tearing off the back cover and writing a message for Tila on it. I wish I hadn't sent Thomas away earlier. Then he could give Tila a verbal message for me. But I thought he should be with his family when he meets his new sibling.

I write on the stiff paper and let Tila know I'm with Carlos and going to the city to see a doctor and find out where Declan is.

Declan.

I place my cup of water over the note to make sure Tila finds it on her table. Then I rush back to Carlos. I have to find out if he knows anything about where Declan is.

"Carlos," I say, approaching him.

He's lighting another cigarette and doesn't bother looking at me.

"Carlos, do you know where Declan is?"

He raises one brow in my direction as he drags in a smokey breath. "Mr. Declan?"

I nod. "Yes, where is he? Do you know if he's safe? Did the earthquake reach the city?"

The lines between his brows deepen as he draws his eyebrows down even further than they normally are. I'm not sure if he's irritated by my questions or confused.

"No," is all he says. Then he blows out a puff of smoke that returns the retching feeling in my stomach.

I realize I've been speaking frantically, so he probably doesn't understand what I'm saying. I'm not sure how I'm going to communicate with Carlos. If my phone was working, I could use my translator app to talk to him.

Then, I remember that Carlos has a phone.

"Phone," I say.

He responds with, "I take you to doctor."

I nod. "Yes," then I put my hand out, "but I need to use your phone." He has the same messaging app I have. So, if I can convince him to let me use his phone, I can add Declan's number and send him a message.

Carlos shakes his head. "No."

I grip my hands around the opening of the truck door urgently. "Carlos, please." I'm begging, but I'm not sure if he understands my pleading. "Please, I need your phone."

He shakes his head again and looks forward. "No," he repeats. "I take you to doctor."

I feel a sense of despair rising inside of me. Is he saying *no* because he's selfish? Or does he just not understand me?

He blows out another smokey puff of air and it stings my eyes. But my eyes are also stinging with the tears that are rising in them from the defeat and frustration brewing in my core.

"I take you to doctor," he says again. "Or I go home."

His words are like a sword thrust into my internals. "No!" My tone is frantic. "I'll go." I rush around to the passenger's side and open the door. "You take me to the doctor," I say with the same broken English as him as I buckle myself in his truck.

193

He keeps his gaze forward and puts his truck in gear without another word. His cigarette is hanging at the corner of his mouth again as we begin to circle around to drive down the road. Then, before I feel completely ensnared in this truck, and in this country, Thomas appears on the far side of the road on his moto.

And I've never been more relieved to see a person in my life.

"Wait," I say to Carlos. I point toward Thomas up the road. "Wait for Thomas."

Carlos gives me an ill-tempered look before stopping the truck and waiting. I'm not sure why he's a guide, he's not personable in the least. In fact, I would go as far to say that he doesn't really like people at all. It reminds me of my fifth-grade teacher who hated students. I've always wondered if the money was worth the headache for people like them that are stuck in the wrong profession.

When Thomas reaches us, he stops at Carlos' side of the truck, and they begin speaking quickly in Tok Pisin.

Thomas finally looks at me with a smile and says, "He's taking you to the doctor, that's good."

I nod, "Yes, it is. But Thomas, can you please ask him about Declan."

His smile grows more serious with his nod, then when he faces Carlos, he asks about Declan.

Carlos glances at me, then responds to Thomas in a mumbled grunt.

Their conversation goes back and forth for a minute or so. Then Thomas exhales and grins at me. His smile fills me with a small sense relief, because I'm hopeful his smile will accompany some good news.

"The earthquake did not damage the city," Thomas says. "Mr. Declan was at the airport and Carlos is sure he made his flight safely."

I let out a breath and try to keep myself from bursting into sobs of relief. "Thank you," I say to Thomas. Then I touch Carlos on the shoulder and contain my tears as I say, "Thank you, Carlos."

His expression softens briefly as he gives me a nod and says, "You're welcome."

I look between Carlos and Thomas, and I'm sort of talking to Carlos but also to Thomas for a translation when I say, "Can I please borrow your phone so I can message Declan and see if he's landed yet?"

It seems Carlos suddenly understands me, because Thomas doesn't have to translate since Carlos opens the messaging app and hands me his phone.

I thank him and scramble to add Declan's number and send him a message, letting him know my phone broke and I'm using Carlos' phone to make sure he's landed back home safely. Then I hand Carlos his phone. If Declan is home, he's probably sleeping since it's after midnight in America.

Carlos puts the truck into gear and Thomas says he's coming with us.

"What about your mom?" I say.

He gets in the back and waves his hand with a smile, "After Antonio was born, I did not care to be there until after my brothers and sisters were born."

I nod, understanding how a teenage boy wouldn't want to hang out with his laboring mother. "Will she worry about where you are? I can leave a note for Tila that you're with us."

He shakes his head. "She won't worry." He pats Carlos' shoulder. "Let's go."

As Carlos pulls forward in a rush, it sends Thomas flying back against his seat.

The truck is so loud there is no point in conversation. It doesn't stop Thomas from patting my shoulder every few minutes to point to various landmarks and tell me their names and significance. The information goes in one ear and out the other since I'm fighting a headache and some slight nausea from the bumpy ride and intense heat. The only relief I'm getting, if you can call it that, is the hot breeze blowing in my face from the open windows.

I slouch down in my seat and look up into the blue sky where I can see buzzards circling around when we begin to slow down.

I sit up and look out the windshield. There's a huge tree that's fallen across the road.

"That's not good," Thomas says with one hand on the back of my headrest and the other on Carlos' seat. He looks at Carlos, then to me.

Carlos is glaring straight ahead when he puts the truck in park.

I'm looking at both of them for an answer but they're not giving me anything. "What are we going to do?"

Carlos gets out of the truck and inspects the tree before walking around in the thick grass.

Before opening the door to get out, Thomas smiles at me and says, "We'll have to make a new route."

"What does that mean?"

Thomas closes the door and gives me one last smile with a shrug before following Carlos. I watch them point at the fallen tree. Talk. Point at the road. Talk some more. Point at the grass. Talk again. Then Carlos points at me.

I feel my eyes widen, then I look down at my purse and pretend to busy myself with the contents inside.

Carlos struts over to my side of the vehicle, lifting his knees over the grass with each step, then hands me his phone. "For you," he says without meeting my eyes.

I suck in a rush of air when I see a response from Declan. "Oh my gosh, thank you, Carlos!" Thank God Declan is okay. My chest is expanding with my inhale and deflating with my exhale as I let the reality of Declan's safety sink.

I see Carlos in the side mirror as he takes a machete from his truck bed and begins hacking at the grass and smaller trees lining the road, apparently creating a path for us to drive around.

I drop my head to read Declan's message on Carlos' smartphone that looks as if it's ten years overdue for an upgrade. I'm still trying to catch my breath as my eyes scroll over the words.

Declan: How do I know this is Christine?

I smile. Of course he's concerned and cautious. I would be too. I'm sure he's tried contacting me which probably made him begin to worry after I didn't respond for an entire day. How can I convince him that it's me? I think for a moment, then remember the first poem he wrote to me. It's the perfect evidence.

Me: Of all forms of caution, caution in love is perhaps the most fatal to true happiness.
Declan: It is you. Thank God! I was beginning to worry when I didn't hear from you at all. I was sick to death when I read about the earthquake in PNG. Are you okay? What happened?
Me: I'm okay. My roof caved in and fell on my head, but going to the doctor now. I don't think it's serious, but seeing a doctor will give me peace of mind.

Declan: I'm so sorry that happened to you. And I'm more sorry I wasn't there with you. I hate that we're apart. I'll come back and keep you safe from falling ceilings and earthquakes.

Me: You're going to save me from natural disasters?

Declan: Yes. I want to hold you and never let go.

Me: I can't wait to be with you again. But you're going to be busy with the museum. We will be together again soon. What time is it there?

Declan: 4 am.

Me: Can you see the moon?

Declan: Yes, and it makes me miss you even more.

Me: Me too. I'll be home again before you know it. Until then, we'll share the same moon☾

Declan: I'm counting down the days and losing sleep staring at the slivered moon out our bedroom window, waiting to hold you again.

Me: I love you! I'll call when I get a new phone.

Declan: I love you more.

I set the phone in the empty driver's seat and lean my head against my headrest, looking past the buzzards that seem to have accumulated as I stare up at the tiny, slivered moon in the day sky. Missing Declan so deeply that my heart hurts.

TWENTY-EIGHT

"You're going to be fine," the doctor says. "I recommend resting for the next couple of weeks."

I nod. Thankful that nothing worse happened and that I'll be able to get back to the bush in a few weeks.

"You are a little dehydrated and sunburnt," he continues. "Make sure you're careful to drink water and minimize sun exposure until you've acclimated to the climate. Especially with your pregnancy."

My jaw drops to the floor along with my stomach. "What?"

He raises his brows with a frown then scans the documents briefly before looking at me again. "I assumed you were pregnant since your last period was well over eight weeks ago. Are your cycles normally irregular?"

I haven't thought about it. With the excitement of marriage, the museum, the late-night music sessions, and preparing for my trip, I completely forgot to pay attention to my own body's biology.

I shake my head. "No, they're typically regular."

"Have you been under extreme stress?"

I shrug. "Just busy."

He doesn't say anything when he looks at me, expressionless.

"Maybe a little stress," I say. But anyone that's newly married and going to a foreign country for an unknown timeline would feel some sort of stress. I just didn't think it was enough to cause my body to get so out of its normal rhythm.

With his inhale he says, "We can do a quick blood draw to check your hormone levels. Then you'll know."

"Okay," I nod anxiously.

When he sends me back to the waiting room, I must look as if I've seen a ghost since Thomas shoots out of his chair and says, "Is it a concussion?"

I sit down with my eyes fixed on the floor.

Thomas is still standing when he says, "Worse than a concussion?"

A thick woman steps out of a room and says my name as if I'm an inconvenience.

I stand up with my heart in my throat and say to Thomas, "I'm okay. I just have to do a blood draw, then we can go."

He nods, without smiling. I've known Thomas for a week and I've already learned that when he's not smiling he's really worried or scared.

So I say, "I might be pregnant," to ease his mind.

And it works. His eyes light up and his grin returns. "That's amazing!" I'm glad one of feels excited.

I meet the woman in the small room where she makes her way around a desk full of papers and a large, outdated computer, to sit next to me in the empty chair beside the one I'm seated in. With the door ajar, she wraps a thick piece of rubber around my arm until my arm goes cold and I can feel my pulse throbbing in my hand. Without warning, she thrusts the needle into the center of my arm. I feel fine until I look over at the small tube of blood in her hand.

The room starts to close in on me and I suddenly feel dizzy. "I don't feel so good," I say as my body gets heavy.

"Wait, wait, wait," she says pulling the needle from my arm and scrambling to find a place for the needle and vial. "Lean back." She props my feet up and begins to fan my face with a folded document.

"Is she okay?"

I lift my head slightly until I can see Thomas.

The woman gives him an annoyed expression, then she says, "She's a fainter."

I don't defend myself, even though I could. Because normally I'm not a fainter. I've given blood on several occasions during blood drives at the college. Every time, I was fine.

The woman instructs Thomas to trade places with her. As he takes over fanning me, the woman exits the room and returns with a small apple juice.

"Drink this," she says, handing me the juice, then she takes the document from Thomas which instantly stops the breeze in my face. "I got enough blood to check your hCG levels. I don't think I'll need to poke you again." *Thank God.*

I sit up to drink my juice while the woman exits the room again, this time with the vial of my blood in hand. The queasiness returns to my stomach but this time I don't feel like I'm going to pass out.

Thomas stands awkwardly in the center of the room. He looks as if he can't decide whether he should stay in the room with me or return to the waiting area.

I make the choice for him. "Sit." I pat the seat next to me.

He joins me, tapping his fingertips together in a steeple as he awkwardly prepares his statement before delivering it. "Are you excited?"

I'm assuming he's talking about the possibility of pregnancy. I grin from one side of my mouth, unsure. "I don't know. It's unexpected. And part of me thinks this is all just stress and I'm not really pregnant at all."

He turns to look down at his fidgeting hands again as he nods with a serious expression. Then he faces me again and says, "But would you be excited?"

A full grin spreads across my face at the thought of mine and Declan's child. "Yeah," I say. "I would be really excited about that."

As instantly as the excitement fills me, the onset of reality stomps it out of my mind as I remember I'm in a foreign country without my husband. And my heart stings at the thought of possibly leaving this beautiful country before my fieldwork has gained any momentum.

If I am pregnant, I could still do my fieldwork for another few months. Women work while they're pregnant all the time. It's completely normal.

The woman, who I'm still not sure if she is a phlebotomist or a nurse, returns with her same tired expression.

Thomas and I both straighten in our chairs with eagerness as she licks her finger and shuffles through several papers in her hand before tossing a pamphlet in my lap.

I don't bother looking at it before I nervously roll it in my hands until I've nearly rolled it into the size of a pencil.

The woman clears her throat, sits behind her desk, then finally looks at me, then Thomas, and back to me. I wouldn't say she looks irritated, but something about her expression tells me she expected us to leave by now. And something else tells me she either never learned bedside manners, or they don't teach that to phlebotomist-nurse-receptionist-hospital-workers here.

I can't take it any longer. "Am I pregnant?"

Her mouth barely moves when she says, "Yes. You can take a seat out there now," she points out her door, "and the doctor will be with you."

Her response hits me in the stomach. I don't know how I make it to the waiting room without my eyes popping out of my head or a bug flying into my gaping mouth of disbelief, but I do.

Everything makes sense now. Extreme fatigue. The nausea. Loss of appetite. Why do extreme stress and pregnancy have the same symptoms?

Thomas is filled with excitement when we take our seats, but I can't hear what he's saying. Because I'm in literal shock. It doesn't help that I'm dehydrated and I just had my blood taken. I want to have Declan's babies, but I thought I would have more time. I guess if I were to wait for the perfect timing I may never do it.

Excitement begins to flutter through my core. If Declan loves our baby the same way he loves and cares for his nephews, this child is going to have the best father in the world.

"Miss Price," the doctor says as he approaches me; I'm sure to hash out the details of my pregnancy hormone levels and whatever else doctors talk about with pregnant women.

"*Misses*," I correct, and as I do, I realize I can't deliver this news to Declan over a text message from Carlos' phone. This is one of those things you tell people to their face. Mostly out of respect, but more-so because there is usually a hug and a moment of emotional celebration to follow. And I can't help but wonder if Declan will get teary-eyed when I tell him that I'm carrying his baby.

TWENTY-NINE

As I rush down the terminal toward the baggage claim, my nausea turns into full blown ejection. Covering my mouth, I burst into the restroom.

Of course the airport bathroom is packed. Wasting no time, I find a garbage near the sink and puke.

A subtle sound of disgust rolls over the women standing in line. I ignore them, just as I ignored the men sitting on both sides of me on the plane when they made the same sounds at my retching on my last flight. I can't help that nausea accompanies pregnancy.

After I rinse my face, and my mouth, I exit the restroom. There's nothing fun about the first trimester of pregnancy and a twelve-hour flight.

As I squeeze between a couple of young men at the front of the baggage claim, I gently say, "I don't mean to cut in line, but I'm pregnant and need to get out of this airport as soon as possible."

The man making eye contact with me raises his brow and says, "Not my problem." Then closes the space I was trying to squeeze into.

"Rude," I say, walking to the other side of the baggage claim belt. Even Carlos wasn't this disrespectful. And he's one of the most firm men I've ever met.

As I retrieve my luggage, a voice behind me says, "I could have saved some money on parking if I had known you were ready."

I meet Winnie with a smile when I turn around to face her, my luggage in hand. "Sorry, my phone died on the plane, and I didn't bother charging it. I've been so preoccupied with feeling nauseous the last few weeks and the plane turbulence didn't help."

Winnie waves her hand and shakes her head. "Don't worry, you can start looking forward to swollen feet and heartburn soon." She takes the largest suitcase and wheels it to the exit.

"Somehow, that doesn't make me feel better."

She's the only one that knows about the pregnancy besides Thomas and Carlos…and Tila. After the hospital visit, I purchased a new phone, and called Declan immediately. I almost decided to tell him about the pregnancy over the phone so that I could continue my fieldwork until I was seven months pregnant. But as soon as I heard his voice, I knew I needed to come home and tell him about the pregnancy in person. And end my dream job just as it was getting started. It felt like the right thing to do for Declan and the baby. Even though it's not ideal for me.

I didn't contact Winnie until the extreme exhaustion set in and I had some cramping one evening when it was too late to walk to Tila's and was just the right time for a phone call to America.

After Winnie reassured me that I was fine, and everything was normal. I made her promise not to tell Declan or their parents. It was in that same conversation that she told me she was already planning to visit Jake's parents in New York. She offered to drive three hours to the airport in D.C. just so she could help me surprise Declan.

Which is exactly what's unfolding now.

I let out a steadying breath through my mouth as I press the back of my head against the seat and close my eyes, trying to get through this next wave of nausea before I barf all over Winnie's car.

"The glovebox," Winnie says rounding her way out of the parking garage.

I keep my eyes closed as the pull of the car makes me feel worse. "What?"

"In the glovebox, there's some candy that helps with the morning sickness."

I blink my eyes and open the compartment at my knees. There's a small plastic container with a picture of a cheerful pregnant woman. I read the label, "*Preggie Pop Drops*?"

Winnie shoves her sunglasses on her face. "Don't hold the ridiculous name against them. That's the only thing that worked for my morning sickness."

I twist the lid off and take one of the candies out. Inspecting the pink color through the crunching wrapper between my fingers. "I'm not sure I can stomach anything right now."

"Try one," her tone is insistent, "and thank me later."

If these little candies can make me look as happy as the woman on the label, I'll give it a try. I pop the candy into my mouth. "I don't understand why they call it *morning sickness* when it lasts all day."

Winnie lets out a laugh. "It's so misleading, isn't it? I was sick throughout the day with Ty until the end of my second trimester."

I can't even imagine what that was like. "I hope that doesn't happen to me." I shift in my seat and look in the back of her car at the empty car seats. "Where are your kids anyway?"

"They're with Jake at his parents' house."

I nod. "That's right. How is the visit going in New York?"

She shrugs. "It's fine. His parents are older."

I'm not sure what she means by that. But I feel like I might be overstepping if I ask her to elaborate. Instead, I change the subject entirely, and say, "Have you visited Declan yet?"

She shakes her head. "Not yet. We invited him Upstate for dinner." Her eyes glance over at me from the side of her sunglasses. "But you know how busy he's been with the museum."

I nod with understanding.

"Plus," she continues, "he's been a little off-putting since my dad's diagnosis."

This causes me to catch my breath. "I'm so sorry I forgot to ask about your father. How has he been?"

She shrugs. "It's fine. He's fine, considering what's going on. And don't worry, that pregnancy brain just gets worse."

I chuckle politely, but inside my mind I'm disturbed by all the pregnancy facts I'm learning from her. "How's your mom handling everything with your dad?"

She lets out a quiet laugh to herself. "Aside from berating the doctors, she's doing surprisingly well."

It's no secret that Val has trust issues with the healthcare system. I want to ask her more about her mom, but Winnie seems to only want to talk about pregnancy. So, the remainder of our conversations are mostly fixed on that.

When we finally get to the museum where Declan is working, I hesitate before unbuckling my seatbelt. There's something surreal about being back in D.C. There's something surreal about being thirteen weeks pregnant too. Maybe it's jetlag, or maybe it's pregnancy, but I feel as if I'm floating in a dream and the only thing that will pull me back down to reality is being held in Declan's arms once I tell him he's going to be a father.

"How are you feeling?" Winnie says.

I face her. "I'm not sure. A mixture of elated and terrified."

She pulls her sunglasses on top of her head and fixes her crumbling mascara under her eyes as she checks her reflection in the rearview mirror. "I meant, the preggie drops. Do you still feel nauseous?"

"Oh." I should have known we weren't on that deep a level of communicating yet. Afterall, this is only our fourth encounter we've had as adults. "Yeah, I do feel better. Thanks for sharing them." I smile. "I guess they do work."

"I told you," she says with confidence. She looks as if she's about to say something else, but her phone begins to ring. She checks it and says, "It's Jake."

I nod and begin exiting the car. Before closing the door, I duck down and open the glovebox to retrieve another candy. I don't want to kiss Declan with the rancid stench of old vomit breath.

Before she answers the call, Winnie says to me, "Good luck. I'll wait for you here."

I smile. "Thanks."

As I'm making my way up the cement steps to the museum entrance, I smile as I pass a mother and her elementary aged child with her husband following behind, holding their baby. I can't help but feel a wave of excitement run through my core daydreaming about the family that Declan and I are beginning to create.

At the ticket office, I inform the scrawny guy behind the counter that my husband works here and I'm trying to surprise him. But he seems suspicious of me. Probably because the last shower I had was two days ago from a bucket of water I heated myself and poured over my head. And because I've been on three airplanes in the last twenty-four hours, I'm sure I look like a disheveled woman off the street.

"Can you call him to meet you down here?" the ticket office guy says.

I shift my weight to one side. "I know this probably sounds weird, but my phone is dead, and I left it in my bag which is in the car. But I promise, I'm Declan Price's wife. Plus, I don't want to call him because I'm trying to surprise him."

His fingers pad across the counter as he decides what to say to me next. "I'm new here, so I'm not sure if I'm allowed to let you in unless you purchase a ticket." He picks up his phone and begins dialing. "One sec while I call my supervisor."

As I fidget in my pocket, I feel for the candy from Winnie's glovebox. I take the candy from the wrapper and plop it in my mouth. The hint of ginger mixed with the sweet taste of lemon infuses my mouth. Where were these things two months ago?

The ticket guy forces a smile at me, then as he places the phone back on the receiver he says, "I'm sorry, no one is answering. Would you like to take a seat and wait until my supervisor comes back from her break?"

I look at him blankly for a moment, then as if all my frustrations and stressors from the last week erupt inside of me at once, I say, "I came straight here from the airport where I got off an airplane where I had been smashed and barfing between two large men for twelve hours. I'm supposed to be in Papua New Guinea living out my dream job and doing fieldwork with the Natives. But because my house fell on top of my head during an earthquake, I had to see the doctor who didn't even congratulate me when he told me I was pregnant."

He holds his hands up. "Ma'am, please take a seat."

I lean forward into his space when I say, "And I flew all the way back to America where the smog infused my lungs while I was thrust down the landing strip, and now I'm dealing with guys like you that feel some sort of entitlement by standing behind a ticket counter." Maybe he didn't deserve that, but I feel better getting it out.

He waves his hand toward himself as he looks over my shoulder and says, "Security."

I take a step back, shocked that he's making this situation into a bigger deal than it is. I didn't raise my voice. Okay, maybe a little bit. But I'm tired, cranky, pregnant, and I just want to see my husband. I should be allowed to have at least one hormonal outburst while I'm sharing my body with a tiny human.

A thick, muscled security guard approaches. With his bellowing voice, he says, "What's the problem?"

Before the ticket guy can say anything, I say, "I'm just trying to find my husband so I can tell him that I'm pregnant."

The security guard says, "Did you purchase a ticket to enter the museum?"

"No." I shake my head as my irritation begins to rise. "My husband works here. I'm here to see him, not tour the museum."

The security guard and ticket guy trade looks before the security guard reaches for me, clasping his hand entirely around my upper arm; tightly. "I'm going to have to ask you to wait outside."

I'm shocked, and confused, that he's treating me this way. I'm not acting like a criminal, and all they need to do is bring Declan down to the ticket office to know I'm telling the truth. I don't resist the security guard's grip, even though I'm boiling inside. "Declan Price is my husband."

"I'm sure he is."

He doesn't believe me.

I've never felt more like a foreigner in my own country. I've never felt more unheard. And I've never felt more disrespected as a human being.

I'm feeling more and more defeated when I hear, "Arty! Let go of her!" The voice comes from the other side of the ticket office. And it belongs to Margaret.

The security guard—apparently his name is Arty—releases my arm and faces the direction where her voice came from. "This *woman* is claiming to be Declan Price's wife." My mouth falls agape as he says *woman* as if it's an insult. "Can you believe it?" And now he's turning this into a joke.

A rush of relief infuses me when Margaret takes several quick paces towards me. She slips her arm around mine and holds my hand. To Arty she says, "Did you ever think that maybe she was telling the truth?" She leads us in the direction of her office.

I could cry. Not only because a tiny frail *woman* in her sixties just rescued me like a hero, but because within the first hour of being back home in my own country I've been more mistreated than I've ever been in my entire life.

Arty's expression twists into confusion. He thrusts his large, fanned palm in my direction, "Declan is married to *that?*"

I've never felt the urge to spit on someone, but in this moment, it's taking everything out of me to keep from hawking a righteous load of spit directly at his chauvinistic face.

Margaret stops in her tracks. Facing Arty with a forced smile, she says, "Arty?"

He folds his arms over his wide chest, then tips his chin up. "Yes, ma'am."

"You're fired." Then she gives my arm a tug as we roll forward into her office.

I take a seat on the couch and blow out a breath that causes my mouth to tremble. "Wow," I say. "Thank you, Margaret. But you don't have to fire him, I mean, I do look like I'm homeless." I smell the inside of my shirt and scrunch my nose. "And I kind of smell homeless too." I'm not sure why I'm not happier about her firing a disgusting person like him. Maybe it's me hoping that Arty is a better person than the one I just encountered.

She laughs as she places a mug under the Keurig spout and presses the start button. "I've been waiting for an excuse to fire Arty. He's more trouble than he's worth. I'm just sorry it was at your expense." She leans against the counter as she turns to face me while the coffee drips down into her cup. "But enough about Arty. Did I hear you say you're pregnant?"

My eyes widen. I meant for Declan to be the second person I told in America about the baby, but somehow I've managed to blurt it out to several complete strangers and a sexist man in the last hour.

A smile grows on Margarets face as she clasps her hands together enthusiastically. "How far along?"

I release an exhale. "Almost fourteen weeks."

She takes her coffee in her hands and sits next to me on the couch. "Ah, I'm guessing you've been plagued by morning sickness and fatigue?"

"That's an understatement."

Her voice is reassuring when she says, "It'll pass. And once you're holding your baby, you won't remember any of it."

"Thank, God." I let out a small laugh. "Do you have kids?"

She sips her coffee, then nods. "Four."

My eyes widen in astonishment. "Wow."

"And six grandchildren," she grins, tilting her head to the side, "so far."

"I don't know how you did this four times."

There's a knock on her office door. She stands to open it, but before she does, she says, "When you're my age, pregnancy will seem like a blink in your memory."

Before she reveals who is at the door, I hear his voice. The warmth and familiarity of his voice reigns over the parts of me that were lost without him; making me feel whole again.

"Declan," Margaret says opening the door further, "Come in."

His eyes are fixed on Margaret as he combs his worried hand through his hair while the other hand hugs his hip. "Arty told me you fired him. Is that true?"

It's taking everything out of me not to jump into his arms before he sees me.

She nods. "It's true."

"And he said—" Declan notices me and glances away, but quickly takes a double take as his eyes lock on mine. Wide in surprise. I rise to my feet. His shocked expression sends a blazing fire down my ribcage, and I have to catch my breath. It's only been a month since I've seen him, but it feels like a lifetime.

"*Christine,*" he rushes to me with the same expression of disbelief, but it's accompanied by an expanding smile. Scooping me in his arms, he buries his face into my neck and holds me tightly. "I missed you so much."

I hug him back, dragging in his familiar scent through my nose. "I missed you too."

The door closes and we both look up to see that Margaret has disappeared. I'm grateful that she wants to give us some privacy.

Declan takes my hands in his and we sit on the couch together. "What are you doing back?" His eyebrows crease with concern. "Did something happen? Are you okay?"

I smile. "Everything is fine. I'm fine."

He holds my face in his hands as his eyes flash between mine. "I can't believe you're here." He presses his mouth against mine and my smile is so wide I'm having trouble kissing him back.

He pulls me in for another hug, completely enveloping me in his heavy arms.

"Declan," I say, resting the side of my face against his shoulder. "I came back early to surprise you because there's something I have to tell you."

Releasing me, he gazes down into my eyes as if he can't wait to kiss me again. "You stopped your fieldwork to come all the way back here just so you could tell me something?"

I nod reassuringly.

He kisses me, then, "It must be really important." He kisses me again. "Okay, you have my undivided attention."

A shudder of excited anxiety spirals down my torso and dances around in my core. I inhale deeply, then smile. Trying to balance the feelings of fear and elation.

His hand wraps around the back of my head as he gently pulls me closer to him, then he kisses my forehead. "Whatever it is," he kisses the tip of my nose, "I'm so glad," he kisses one cheek, "that," then the other cheek, "you're h—"

"I'm pregnant!" I blurt the words out with excitement before he finishes his statement.

He hesitates in front of my mouth, stopping himself from kissing my lips. It's a brief hesitation, but long enough to cause the dancing anxiety in my core to spin into a full-blown tornado.

Pulling back, he runs his tongue along his bottom lip. "You're what?" he says, inspecting me curiously with his tilting head.

I smile. Shrug. Swallow my nerves down. Then, "I'm pregnant," I look up at the ceiling and squint remembering that it takes two to create a life. "Well, we're pregnant."

His jaw sets as his mouth falls firm. Something is off about his reaction.

I continue, "I know we weren't planning to get pregnant right now, but—"

"How could you do this?" His voice is low and cold as his words hit me.

My mouth parts, as I fall short of words. Shocked and confused by his question. As if I did this on my own.

He releases my hand and rises to his feet, pacing the short length of Margaret's office. After a moment, he places his hands on his hips and faces me with a look of abhorrence. "How long have you known?"

My eyes are flicking frantically between his darkening gaze. "A month."

He drops his head back and rakes his fingers through his hair, pulling his hand into a fist at the top of his head. I can see one of the scars on his head from the accident at the pool when he does this. In a whisper, he says, "A month." His voice grows louder as he says, "You could have taken care of this a month ago, but instead you felt it was necessary to prolong the inevitable and *surprise* me at work?"

This isn't the reaction I imagined at all. He's turning my daydream into a complete nightmare.

In this moment, I don't recognize him. And because I can't figure out who is standing in front of me, I also don't know how to respond to him.

He begins pacing again. "It'll be fine." I'm not sure if he's talking to himself right now. "Abortions are still legal in D.C.; we can take care of this as soon as tomorrow." He takes his phone out and begins scrolling as he continues striding back and forth across the room.

I clasp my hands together, and I'm surprised by the calm that floods over me at the same time my heart breaks in two. "I'm not getting an abortion."

He stops pacing and lifts his gaze, staring at the door. Motionless.

Through clenched teeth, I continue, "Like I said, I know we didn't plan for this. But I want to be a mother. And although your heart seems to have dropped out of your chest, I still want you to be our child's father." I rise to my feet and make my way to the door. Before exiting I face him, and say, "Even if we have to raise our baby separately."

With his back still facing me and in a quiet, stern voice, he says, "I told you that I never wanted to bring a kid into this world."

I don't react.

I don't respond.

I don't wait for an apology.

Instead, I exit Margaret's office without a word.

But inside, between the crushed pieces of my heart, I find the strength to compose myself as I make my way out of the building and back to Winnie's car.

THIRTY

"Are you sure you don't want me to stay?" Winnie says, placing a cup of tea on the coffee table in front of me. "It's kind of nice having a conversation without being interrupted by a diaper change or tantrum."

I drag my finger through the steam billowing out of the top of the teacup. "I don't want to keep you from your visit with your in-laws." I lift my chin slightly to look up at her. "I'll be okay."

She nods and begins gathering her things around my apartment. "Okay, well if you need anything you have my number." Her voice is gentle. Which I appreciate since I'm sure this is difficult for her empathizing with me as a woman and juggling her concern for her brother.

I force a smile.

She smiles back, but it looks as if she's unsatisfied. As she shuts the door behind her, I can hear her phone ringing while she heads down the stairs.

I release an exhale and adjust myself so I'm laying comfortably on the couch with my feet propped up on the armrest. I close my eyes, promising myself I'll only take a short recovery nap before I unload my luggage and shower. But before I doze off, there's a knock at the door.

Winnie must have forgotten something.

I see Winnie through the peephole and open the door.

Before I can ask what she left behind, she rushes past me, her hands waving around in the air as her words begin flying out of her mouth. "I know Declan is my brother. I love him," she glances at me, "I do," then she looks back at her waving hand in front of her, "and my loyalty is with him. I mean he is family." She's almost gasping for air she's talking so fast.

I finally shut the door. "Here," I say guiding her to the couch, "sit down."

She nods and follows my instructions.

I push the chamomile tea she just made for me towards her. "I think you need this more than I do."

She nods then picks up the cup and takes a sip. "I'm sorry," she says rolling her eyes. "I was just talking to Declan on the phone, and I realized sometimes he can be..." she runs her tongue along her bottom lip, and I can't help but notice it's the same mannerism Declan does when he's thinking too. She squints, then, "I want to say *callous* but that seems a little harsh."

We both laugh. Then after a moment, I adjust myself so I'm facing her better and say, "So you care about your brother, but you also understand he can be a real jerk sometimes. Was that what you came back to tell me?"

She glances down at the teacup in her hands and places it on the coffee table. Then, looking back to me, she says, "I know growing up with him was different for me than being married to him is for you."

I nod in understanding.

"But," she continues, "I know that at the beginning of a relationship, and especially the honeymoon phase of marriage, things are so fun, and blissful, and romantic. But it's not always like that throughout the entire marriage." She's talking so fast. "In reality, we have arguments and disagreements. People don't always see eye to eye in marriage." She adjusts her purse onto her lap. "What I'm trying to say is that, when things get hard in marriage it doesn't mean it's the end or you should give up. And in the same breath, I know that when Declan doesn't get what he wants, he can pull himself away."

I tilt my head. "What do you mean he pulls himself away?"

She inhales deeply and holds her breath for a moment before releasing it, then, "He gets things stuck in his head, and sometimes that makes him unreasonable."

"Okay," I say. "What am I supposed to do about it?"

She shrugs. "I don't know. I want to defend him and say that he has a lot going on with his new job, and his wife moving to a different country right after their marriage, and right after they moved to the opposite side of where their families are, and right after he found out his dad was suffering from dementia."

Her words sting. I look down at the dark maroon rug under the coffee table. I know her words weren't meant to hurt me. I can tell she's trying to be honest with me as gently as she possibly can. But I still feel the sting, which is accompanied by a sense of guilt. Maybe I haven't been considering his feelings as much as I should have been.

"You're right," I say pulling my gaze up to hers.

She places her hand on my knee. "But I also know it's lonely and isolating when your husband isn't on board with having a baby. And that's not fair to you."

My eyes widen. "Jake didn't want Ty?"

She shakes her head. "Jake didn't want the responsibility of a baby while we were still in college." She shifts her mouth to one side. "It's different for guys. They don't really get it until they feel their baby kicking behind that big belly wall. And for Jake, he didn't love Ty until he was holding him in his arms."

My mouth parts but no words come out. Just shock and a little frustration. How is it that I already have such a deep love and bond for this baby that is no bigger than a ripe peach, but my baby's father might not fall in love with them until he's holding the watermelon sized baby in his arms?

"It's not fair," I say. "We sacrifice everything to house a child, and men can't even show up until they're born?"

"Not all men," she says with a grin. "My dad was so excited to be a dad."

"How do you know?"

She rolls her eyes. "He documented every second of my mother's pregnancy on a box load of home videos. And I've grown up under his protective wings. He loves being a dad."

I grin in response to her statement. Hoping some of that paternal instinct will kick in for Declan too.

Winnie's phone begins to ring in her purse. She pulls it out and answers; her gaze fixed in front of her. "Yeah, mom…..I'm not with the boys right now…." She glances at me then back down to the rug. "I'll have them call you when I get back….I'm sorry this is messing up dad's schedule….Okay, bye."

I press my hands against the tops of my thighs, anticipating if Winnie is going to elaborate on her phone call or not.

She scrolls at her phone, and I notice her pinky sticks out on one hand as she does this. "My mom," she begins, "she calls the boys every night before dinner, but with the time difference it's screwing up her schedule. Which inadvertently screws up my dad's schedule." She blows flustered raspberries then finally tucks her phone back into her purse. "Anyway…"

"How is your mom doing with all…" I gently motion my hand in a circle, "…that."

"I'd say she's moving towards acceptance."

"That's good, right?"

She places her hands in her lap. "I mean, she's always been leery of doctors, but she's coming around. Especially since she's seeing how helpful they've been with my dad."

Earlier Winnie had mentioned Val berating Sean's doctors. My curiosity gets the best of me, and I have to know *why*.

So, I say, "Has your mom always been like that with doctors?" I'm trying to sound as casual as possible. Especially since I'm still not sure what are hot topics for Winnie. I'd hate to offend the one person that seems to be able to talk sense into Declan.

She presses her mouth together in thought as she makes a humming noise in her throat, then, "Not always. It started after Declan wrecked on his bike when he was a kid."

I give her a curious look. Remembering Declan mentioning a bike wreck once, but unsure of the details. "What happened?"

Winnie grips the teacup with both hands and sits up straighter. "I think Declan was nine or ten. He and a couple of the neighbor kids were riding their bikes off some jumps." She sips the tea, then sets the cup down as she arches her hand in a flying motion. "They somehow made the jumps higher and higher. Declan got his bike going pretty fast off the jump, but he lost control. His tire hit just right, catapulting him over the handlebars."

When she smacks her hands together, it causes me to jump in my seat.

"Our mom rushed Declan to the hospital, and she was certain there was something wrong." She rolls her eyes and lowers her voice slightly. "I mean, something more wrong than road-rash and a bleeding head wound."

I nod with understanding.

"Anyway," she continues, "the doctors cleaned him up and sent him home. My mom insisted on a second opinion, a scan, something to see what was wrong. But they said he was fine aside from a minor concussion." She shakes her head. "I remember when they got home, Declan seemed okay at first." She twists at her necklace. "At dinner that night, my dad was asking him about joining the basketball team at the YMCA." She cuts her eyes to mine. "Declan couldn't remember what basketball was. My dad asked him about school. Declan couldn't remember anything about school. My mom started flipping out. She said she knew something was wrong, but the doctors wouldn't listen. My dad didn't understand how the doctors could miss this."

I cover my mouth. Shocked at the horror his parents must have felt.

"I remember," she narrows her eyes, "when I asked him if he remembered me and mom, and dad, he did. I asked if he remembered what happened when he was riding his bike, but he couldn't remember who he was or anything before that day."

I scoot to the edge of the couch. "That's terrifying. How did he get his memory back?"

"My parents took him back to the hospital. The doctors said that sometimes kids get temporary amnesia when they hit their heads hard enough. They ran some scans and tests to be sure, and everything ended up being fine. He fully recovered and gained all his memories back in the following days." Shaking her head she says, "But my mom never recovered." She slumps back against the couch and crosses her arms over her chest. "It completely traumatized her. I mean, we didn't even go to the doctor for check-ups after that."

I begin to muster up the courage to ask another question, but the lock on the door beeps, then the door drags open.

Declan halts his entry into the doorway as his eyes adjust to the sight of his wife and sister chatting on his tufted sofa. After a month of solitude, he's probably gotten used to coming home to an empty apartment. I'm sure this is strange, even if he was partly expecting it.

Winnie meets Declan on his way to the kitchen. "Let her in, Dec," she says in a quiet voice as she places her hand on his shoulder.

He cuts his vexed eyes at her. As if her words are betrayal to his ears.

She continues, "All the way in." Then she says goodbye to us and leaves the apartment.

When she's gone, there's something about the way Declan avoids looking at me that makes me wish I had tried to keep her here a little longer as a mediator. I'm sure she could have talked some sense into him.

Declan untucks his shirt as he pours himself a glass of wine. Before he takes a drink, he leans his hip into the counter and raises his chin as he looks down at me, where I'm still seated on the couch.

I refuse to speak to him. I wait patiently, knowing he won't be able to stand the fact that I'm staring at him, wordless, for much longer.

And just as I expected, it doesn't take very long. "I hope you don't find me rude for not offering you any wine." He raises one brow. "Correct me if I'm wrong, but you're not supposed to drink while you're pregnant."

I purse my lips and bite at my tongue to keep myself from spitting insults at him.

He gulps down the rest of his wine and places the empty glass on the counter before approaching me and crossing his arms over his chest. "Are you going to sit there and stare at me all night, or do you have anything to say for yourself?"

My nostrils burn with my exhale as the tears rise into my eyes. Angry tears.

"I don't know what you were expecting, Christine." He pulls one hand up to his face and rubs at his forehead. "I mean, I told you I didn't want to have children."

I let out a harsh breath of disbelief. "You *never* said that."

His eyebrows rise in surprise. "Yes. I. Did." He pauses between each word, as if he's tired of repeating himself.

"I don't remember the topic of children ever coming up before today." My pulse is throbbing in my throat, and I can hardly get the words out. I'm hurt he's being so mean about this.

He begins pacing, which I'm starting to realize is a gesture he does when he's angry or upset. "The day we went to the ocean," he pulls at the top of his hair with one hand, while the other is fanned out harshly, adding more intensity to his words. "When I told you about Eli."

"When you told me about who?"

"When I told you about the boy at the pool."

I cross my arms, trying to steady my intensifying emotions. "You're going to have to be more specific."

He lets out a frustrated groan, as if he doesn't want to revisit the memory. Then he finds a place on the couch, but not too close to me. Letting me know he's still upset with me. His elbows are resting on his spread knees as he cradles his head in his hands before saying, "*How could anyone bring a child into this broken world*," he turns to face me, but his eyes won't meet mine. "That's what I said that day, *How could anyone bring a child into this broken world.*"

I feel my anger shifting, as if it's being overridden by a new feeling of empathy for Declan. I don't want to feel sorry for him in this moment. He was cruel to me today. But hearing the story Winnie told about his bike wreck and knowing the pain he felt after Eli drowned at the pool—not to mention the insufferable damage it caused Eli's parents—I can see why Declan wouldn't want to bring an innocent baby into the world.

My voice is gentler when I say, "I didn't interpret your statement as seriously as you meant it."

His expression is anguished as he says, "I thought we understood each other, Christine."

"We do, but sometimes we have to talk through stuff." I inch closer to him. "I knew we weren't planning for a baby, and I would have been fine without one. But having children was never out of the question for me, and I'm sorry I didn't express that better to you before."

Staring down at his hands with a creased brow, he says. "You've always been enough for me. Just you." His eyes cut to mine. And I notice his chest rising with each breath. "I thought I was enough for you." His words are pained as they drop out of his mouth. And out of his heart.

My mouth falls agape. Stunned by his words. I blink rapidly as I speak gently. "You are enough." I shake my head, trying to jostle his statement to make some sort of sense. When it doesn't make sense, I say, "Why would you ever think that you're not enough for me?"

"I thought," he looks down at his hands again, and I notice he's twisting at the silver band around his finger. "I thought that when you read my journals you would understand that you're all I've ever wanted. That by marrying you, I was achieving the greatest treasure. And that, together, we would live our dreams. Just you and me." He yanks his ring off over his knuckle, then forces it back down his finger. It's making me nervous. "I thought it was going to be *us* until death parted us. I thought I was the only one that you would give your entirety to—and all your attention."

I narrow my gaze, trying to understand him. "I felt the same. But, just because we're going to have a baby doesn't mean our life ends or that we'll love each other less." I take his hand in mine so he stops pulling his ring off and back onto his finger. "If anything, our love for each other will grow with a baby in our lives. I mean, look at Jake and Winnie and your nephews. Can you imagine life without them?"

When he looks at me, his expression melts into understanding. "No," he scoots closer to me and takes my other hand in his, "I can't imagine my life without them."

"You love them."

He nods as his hardened expression relaxes. "I do."

"And you'll love our child with their big brown eyes even more," I say with certainty.

He swallows hard and glances down at my stomach, then back to my eyes. "I want to believe that's true."

I reach for something in my heart to help ease his doubt. "Remember when you were ready to marry me, but I wasn't ready to commit to you?"

A glimpse of a smile hits the side of his mouth. "Of course I remember."

"Just like you waited for me to be ready. I don't mind waiting for you to fall in love with the idea of bringing a child into this messed up world."

He pulls my arms gently wrapping them around his torso and he encapsulates me in his arms. "Thank you." He kisses the side of my head. "Do you forgive me for acting like an ass today?"

I close my eyes and tighten my grip around him, relieved we found a way to move forward—together. "Of course I do."

"Thanks for being the somebody that understands me."

I've wanted nothing more than to be that for him.

Somebody that understands him.

THIRTY-ONE

"I think you were a little flat in the second verse," Declan says biting his guitar pick between his teeth as he plays back the track on his computer.

I pull my hair to one side and twist it into a loose braid. I let out an exhale of fatigue and place my hand on my visibly growing belly. "I'm sure I am flat. Try using your abs to sing when they're splitting apart."

It's only been a few weeks since I've been back, but my belly has expanded, and I need a new wardrobe to accommodate its growth. I know I'm only going to get bigger.

Declan maneuvers around his computer desk and strides over until he's standing behind me where I'm seated at the keyboard. "Can we do one more run through?" He gently massages my shoulders and kneads his thumbs into the back of my neck. It feels incredible. "And I promise we'll take a break after."

I've never seen him with this much passion for anything. Not even with the museum. Of course he loves running the museum with Margaret, but he could create music with me for endless hours, not eat, or drink, or sleep. It's as if he works outside of the limits of time when he's making music.

But I don't work outside the limits of time. And I do need to eat, drink, and sleep.

I tilt my head pressing my neck deeper into his massaging hand and groan.

His hands come to a stop as he rests them against my shoulders. "Nooo," I plead. "Don't stop, that feels amazing."

He lowers his face to the side of my head and says, "Run through the song one more time, first?"

I groan again. Only this time it's not because I'm feeling relief. I'm feeling like a rundown racehorse. "Fine," I say, unsatisfied.

He kisses the side of my face. "I'll make it up to you later. I promise."

"You better."

We run through the song several more times until Declan is satisfied with the recording, and I'm brutally exhausted.

While Declan is making a few adjustments to the song on his computer, I begin to leave the room. It's no easy task singing while pregnant, but singing while pregnant all evening and into the middle of the night is impossible.

"Hey," Declan rises from the desk to face me as the computer lights up his face with a blue glow. "You didn't want to listen to the final master track?"

I give him a wistful smile. "I'll listen some other time. I need to get some sleep before work tomorrow."

He makes his way over to me, wrapping his hands around my waist. "You know you don't need to work. I make enough to support the two of us."

Thankfully Margaret held true to her word and kept a position open for me at the museum. I thought I would be on the floor, helping with visitors or leading tours. But I'm more behind the scenes with this position. She has me in the tech room making sure the karaoke room is functioning adequately. It's not ideal, but it keeps me busy enough.

"I know. But I like working, and I sort of need it for my sanity. There's only so much talking to plants I can do in one day when I'm home alone." I lift my arms, clasping them around his neck. "And soon it's going to be the three of us."

His smile ever so slightly shifts downward as he winces as if I've poked him with a needle. It's small and subtle. But nothing he does goes unnoticed since we've been married. I wish I could ignore it, but I can't. And since I can't, I feel the subtle frustration rise inside of my heart.

I'm trying to be patient.

But I don't get it.

Even though he apologized. Even though he said he would accept fatherhood. And even though I told him I would wait for him to love our child; he doesn't seem to be making efforts to acknowledge this pregnancy; despite the fact that it's staring him in the face. Literally.

He ducks his head to look at me. "You're right." Then he kisses the top of my head and says, "I just have a couple more things to work on and then I'll come to bed."

As he makes his way back in front of the glowing computer screen, I can't help but feel disappointment. I don't want our child growing up feeling unwanted or in the way like my father made me feel.

I refuse to accept any sort of thoughts that might allude to the idea that Declan is anything like my father.

When I toss the covers off of me in the morning, just when the sun rays are gently peeking through the window curtains, I realize that Declan's not in bed. Nor does it seem as if he ever came to bed since his pillows are still neatly placed. And even though we share blankets, his side seems untouched.

I check my phone to make sure I don't have a missed text on my way down the hall.

Surely he wouldn't go into work this early without me.

Then, I find him lying on the floor in our living room. The sight of him on his back slightly startles me because I wasn't expecting him to be on the floor, but it doesn't jar me enough for concern. At least, not at first anyway.

Since we've been married, there's been an indescribable connection developing between us. As if I can sense his feelings and emotions before he says anything. It's like being locked together with someone in a way that intertwines every cell in our bodies.

"Declan?" My voice is low and quiet.

Even though his eyes are closed, I can sense he's not sleeping. And although I can sense he's awake right now, I can't quite figure out what's going on in his mind.

Normally, I might attribute his behavior to sleep deprivation, and maybe that's part of what's going on. But I can also sense a distancing that's growing between us that I don't want to acknowledge.

"Declan?" I repeat, hugging my arms around my chest with my growing concern.

This time, when I say his name, his throat rolls but his eyes stay closed as he stays in the same position with his hands clasped over his chest, that's rising and falling with each breath. "Hmm?" The noise he makes comes out annoyed.

"What are you doing on the floor?"

He drags in a deep aggravated breath through his nose, then, "I'm concentrating." He flips one hand gently in the air, gesturing with his words. "Praying…meditating…call it what you will—essentially I'm focused deeply on my thoughts."

I press my mouth together, unsure of the voice coming out of his body. I know he's Declan. I know it's his voice speaking to me, but at the same time, it's not him. I know it's strange, but he sounds different and it's unsettling.

I take a step closer to him and kneel on the floor with my hands in my lap. "What kind of thoughts?"

He presses his palms at his eyes cantankerously. "It's everything and nothing and it doesn't matter."

Maybe it's time to revisit the conversation about becoming parents. "Are you feeling worried about the baby?"

He finally opens his eyes and gives me a look of disgust as he pulls himself up onto his elbows. "No, it's not *that.*"

"Then what is it?"

"I said it doesn't matter."

"Why didn't you come to bed last night?"

"I wasn't tired." He shifts to one side as he faces me. "And I was working on our song that you don't seem to really care about."

I'm hugging my arms around myself again. Protecting my heart as best I can against his verbal blows. "How can you say that? You know I care about your music."

"Then why don't you help with editing or creating the master take? And if you care so much, why do you refer to it as *my* music and not *ours?*"

I gentle my voice and my expression. "Declan…"

"What?" He sits up completely, his unrecognizable voice is accompanied by his unrecognizable eyes. It's as if they've changed color and turned black overnight. "Let me guess, the pregnancy is making you too tired."

"Declan…please…" I'm begging him. I don't know how much more I can take. He's going back and forth with the same conversation, and I can't take the uncertainty anymore.

"The pregnancy is making you tired. It's also making you flat when you're singing. I told you we should have taken care of this when you first told me about it."

I'm shocked he's prioritizing his music hobby over our child. My voice is grated when I say, "Stop! Okay, please, just stop. You're being so cruel."

He rises to his feet, heading toward the bedroom then stops with his back to me. Turning his head just enough so I can see his profile, he says, "And I don't want to hear you complain about being tired or not fitting into your pants. You did this to yourself, so you can deal with it yourself." Then he walks away.

"I didn't do this by myself, Declan!"

I cover my face as a sob cracks out of me. How could he be so ruthless? Why doesn't he accept our child? Why is he rejecting the very thought of its existence? And not owning the fact that it takes two people to create a life? We weren't being careful or trying *not* to get pregnant. How does this all fall on me?

I don't have any idea how I'm supposed to ride to work with him and spend the day pretending like he didn't just shame me for carrying our child.

THIRTY-TWO

"Everything okay?" Margaret says as she stirs creamer into her coffee during the lunchbreak.

I take the last bite of my sandwich before tucking it into my cheek and saying, "Yes, I'm good."

"Looks like pregnancy is treating you better." She points at my empty sandwich bag.

I smile and sip at my water. "Yeah, I hit the second trimester and my nausea disappeared."

She nods with satisfaction. "See, didn't I tell you, it'll seem like a blink." I hope this entire pregnancy turns into a blink. Picking up her mug, she says, "Tell Declan to get some rest and feel better soon for me."

I nod with a pinched grin. Knowing if she knew what he said to me this morning she might not be wishing him warm thoughts.

Then she leaves the room.

I gather my things to retreat back to the dark tech room. Where I'm left to mindlessly check screens for the next few hours. And since a monkey could do my job, my mind wanders back to Declan.

He ended up calling in sick just as I tried to revisit our conversation this morning before I left. He wasn't having it. And so much so, that he couldn't be in a car with me for the short drive it takes to get to work.

Maybe spending the day by himself will shift his priorities into the right place again.

꒰꒱

As I head towards my apartment from the parking garage, I can see two men struggling to maneuver a legless baby grand piano. I'm not sure if they were trying to match, but they're both wearing sweatpants and white t-shirts.

I quickly realize one of the men is Declan, and upon closer inspection, I recognize the other man as Arty, the security guard that was fired from the museum.

I decide I'm going to march inside the apartment and pretend like I can't see either of them. Even though I can't deny how attractive Declan looks in his casual attire. The only problem with my decision is that I have to walk right by them since they're inching closer to the building entrance.

"Hold on," Declan says to Arty when he sees me approaching. They stop what they're doing and Arty holds the piano steady on the small rolling device it's perched on. Moving heavy things seems to be a fitting job for a neanderthal.

I keep my stride quick as I pass them without looking.

Declan jogs over to meet me in the stairway. "Christine, listen."

I stop on the first step and flip around to face him. We're almost eye level and there's something that gives me a little more confidence than normal at this height.

He searches my expression and with his exhale he says, "Look, I know I was being an idiot this morning."

"That's putting it lightly." I fold my arms over my chest.

"Okay," he leans his shoulder into the wall, shoving his hands into his pockets, "I deserved that."

"Is that all you wanted to say?" *Because I'd like to get out of these tight clothes and into a hot bath where I can pretend like this day never happened.*

"No," he holds my gaze gently. And I can't help but notice that his eyes seem to have returned to their normal deep brown. "I'm sorry. And I meant for the piano to be a surprise for you when you got home but it's a lot heavier than we thought, so we wasted time back tracking to find a piano dolly…"

I purse my lips and tighten my grip around my arms. A surprise piano isn't going to fix our problems. And I really don't want to hear about the trouble it took for him to get it here.

He must recognize my uninterested expression since he says, "Anyway…" His gaze shifts down to my mouth, then back up to my eyes. "I told my parents about the baby."

I blink in disbelief. "You did?"

He draws his hand up to caress a finger against the side of my face. "I did."

I want to jump into his arms and kiss him, but I also want to push him away because this morning was the second argument we've had about this. And I don't know what makes this apology any different. Other than the fact that it's accompanied by a giant gesture. I spent the entire day broken over the words he shot at me this morning. Not to mention the anger I festered while I was at work. How do I know he's not going to get upset about it again?

His expression is hopeful when he says, "Do you forgive me?" I love the way his mouth curls up into a grin on one side.

I want to stay mad at him for a little longer, but what good would that do? My heart softens as I remember what Winnie said about marriages having ups and downs. So I say, "You have to stop being mean to me when you're upset and just talk to me."

"Is that a *yes*?"

"Yes. I forgive you." I think that's true; I know I wanted him to be excited about the baby and he seems to be taking steps toward that direction by sharing the news with his parents. I have to meet him in the middle, and this feels as close as I'm going to get to the middle.

He inches closer to me. Since I'm still on the first step, our noses are almost touching without him having to crane his neck to meet me. Then he gently presses his mouth to mine and I reciprocate his gesture. Even though I'm still not certain we won't have this argument again.

"Are we moving this pig or what? You've already butchered my entire day." Arty's bellowing voice is more irritating than ever. Or maybe I just think that because of the way he mistreated me before.

Declan turns to face him. "I butchered your day?" He laughs quietly. "You don't have any place to be. If anything, I made your day more eventful."

Arty spits at the cement, which makes me loath him more. "Whatever. Let's get this over with." The ostentatious tattoos of topless women covering his arms are just as revolting as he is.

"Alright," Declan says, which makes Arty exit the stairwell. He turns to me again, dragging his hand down my arm until he laces his fingers in mine.

I can't help myself when I say, "Why are you friends with him? He's a creep."

He shrugs. "He's not that bad." He kisses the side of my face. "Plus, who else was I supposed to hang out with while you were gone?"

I scrunch my nose. "Margaret?"

He drops his head back with his laughter, which makes me laugh too. "I didn't think you would be very happy if I was hanging out with another woman while you were in a different country."

I bite at my lip. "I appreciate that. But, I'm not very threatened by you hanging out with Margaret." With my smile I say, "Plus, I'd pick Margaret as your friend over Arty any day."

He grins, then pulls my hand up to his mouth and kisses my finger, along with the ring he put there. "I talked to Winnie today too."

"Yeah?"

"Yeah." His expression falls serious. "She's good at putting the important things into perspective for me."

"Maybe call Winnie the next time you start having second thoughts about this baby?"

His lip curls in thought as he drops his gaze. "I'm not going to fight about it anymore." When he looks up and locks his eyes on mine, he says, "I promise."

He seems sincere. In a quiet voice I say, "Okay."

A loud slap from the other side of the building startles me enough to make me jump. It's followed by Arty's loud muffled voice as he says. "Price! I'm walking home if you're not out here in three seconds!"

I roll my eyes. "You better go before your muscle leaves and I have to help you haul that piano into our apartment."

"Alright." He smiles, then as he exits, he says, "I'll see you up there."

"I'll be in the tub."

I turn and scale the stairs. I don't waste any time drawing a bath for myself when I get inside. And I decide to pick up the next journal in Declan's collection to read while I'm relaxing in the tub. Hopefully the content is lighter than the last one. Which seemed to be a dialogue of negative thoughts and self-loathing on repeat while Declan finished grad school. I don't know how he got through it.

Right as I step into the warm water, my phone rings. I debate on ignoring it, but then I see it's my mom. We've sent several strings of text messages, but I haven't spoken to her since before I left for PNG. I even told her she was going to be a grandma over a text message. *Worst daughter awards goes to...*

I answer.

"Hey, Mom."

She draws her words out with an upward inflection. "Hey, Chris. How are you doing? Adjusting to being back in the states yet?"

"Yeah…" I let my words trail.

My mom is quiet for a moment, then, "Chris…"

I twirl my finger in the bathwater. "Mom…"

"I'm your mother, I can tell something is bothering you."

How can she tell over the phone? "It's just…" I groan uncomfortably. "We keep having the same stupid fight. It's like, we're fine, then Declan just gets mad again and I get mad that he's mad. Then he apologizes and we're fine again. But somehow we always circle back to it."

"I see." She exhales and her tone goes upward as she says. "Have you thought about giving counseling a try?"

"No. Declan doesn't seem like the counseling type."

"Well, you'll never know unless you ask him."

I process this for a moment. If she's right, there's nothing to lose. "Okay. I'll bring it up to him."

There's a lull while I pull a stray hair off my knee and stick it to the side of the tub.

Then, my mom says, "Can I tell you something about marriage?"

Her question is a little strange. "Yeah?" I say uncertain.

"Marriage is hard work."

It's quiet again.

"I mean." She mumbles something to herself. Then, "I've been doing a lot of reflecting on my life. And I know that I could have tried harder with your father. Not that I'm regretting the way things turned out. We probably would have ended up divorced regardless. But, I do feel like I could have explored more options to work for our marriage before we separated."

I'm a little shook by her words. From the time I can remember, they were arguing. We couldn't have a family dinner without an argument. Luckily for us, my father often worked late. But when my father was home, it seemed that my parents couldn't be in the same room for more than two minutes without arguing. And their augments were nothing short of a verbal bomb.

I love my father, but I always respected my mom for leaving. He's pompous and arrogant. He didn't even congratulate me when I told him I was pregnant. Instead, he said, *Don't expect to start calling me gramps, I'm too young for that.*

My mom continues, "I don't want you to make the same mistakes I did is all. And I want you to know that arguments are a normal part of marriage. It's just *how* you argue that makes or breaks your marriage."

I smile. "Thanks, Mom."

I admire her strength and am grateful she taught me how to be a strong woman. "And if it's any consolation, I think you made the right decision leaving him."

After our phone call, I place my phone on the bathmat and retrieve the notebook from the floor.

There's a gentle knock on the door then it opens slowly.

"Hey," Declan says. "I'm going to give Arty a ride and then—" His eyes shoot to his notebook in my hands.

I lift the notebook and begin to say, "I finished the last journal and thought I would help myself to the next book. If that's okay?"

Actually, I think he's looking at my belly. "Wow," he says with his exhale. He drags one hand over his mouth and down his shoulder until he's rubbing the back of his neck. "There really is a baby in there, huh?"

I twist my face, perplexed.

He shakes his head, then, "I mean obviously you're pregnant, it's just..." he runs his tongue across his bottom lip, "...there's a real baby growing inside of you."

I smile. "Yeah, that's how it works."

He approaches me and kneels. When his eyes finally drift from my belly to meet my face, he says, "Is it okay if I...?"

I nod with widening eyes. Shocked at the extreme shift from his aggravated attitude this morning.

He rubs his hands together, warming them. Then he slowly sinks his hand down into the water and around my belly. His hand is cooler than the water and causes chills to spread up and down my body.

He looks expectant when he says, "We made this?"

I smile and nod. "We sure did."

I place my hand over his, then a sudden internal twinge happens inside of my stomach.

A sharp breath escapes his throat with his smile.

"Did you feel that?" I ask, unsure what we just experienced.

He nods, still in awe. "Was that a kick?"

"I don't know, I've never felt it before."

230

He leans his face down toward my stomach. "Hey buddy," he's speaking to my stomach, "I'm your dad."

I.

Could.

Die.

And I think I may have just fallen in love with Declan Price all over again.

"Don't kick your mom too hard, okay?"

The tears well in my eyes.

He continues, "You're going to be the strongest punter, aren't you?"

I laugh. "Football?" I roll my eyes with the welling tears. "Why football?"

He looks at me and notices a tear escape. "Hey, what's the matter?"

I shrug as my smile deepens and another tear falls. "I've just been waiting for this."

He kisses my mouth, then presses his forehead to mine with his hand still on my belly. "I'm sorry it took me so long to get here." He kisses the top of my head then releases his hand from my stomach and rises to dry his hand with a towel. "I hate to go right now, but I should probably take Arty home before I owe him a day of my time."

I nod, blinking rapidly as I draw in a steadying inhale.

He begins to open the door, but I stop him with, "Hang on a second."

He shuts the door again and faces me.

I scoot up in the tub and press my mouth together, trying to figure out how to say this without sounding like something is wrong. "What do you think about counseling?"

He shrugs his shoulders and folds his arms over his chest. He purses his lips in thought for a moment before he says, "I don't know. If you think it would help you, then I don't see why you shouldn't go."

I nod slowly, realizing he misunderstood what I was asking. I meant for us both to go to counseling, but now that I realize that's not even in the forefront of his mind, I think I'll wait to have this conversation another time.

His eyebrows rise. "Was there something else?"

I force a smile. "Nope."

"Alright. Enjoy your book." He winks. "I'll see you in a bit." He closes the door as he exits.

I let out an unsettled exhale as I sink down into the bath again and flip the notebook open.

THIRTY-THREE

Journal:

My stomach is in knots.

KNOTS.

I hate to imagine I've just lost an opportunity.

Time stopped.

STOPPED.

When I saw her, time stopped.

It's unexplainable.

You hear it all the time. People say that time stopped for them. You don't realize it's literal until it happens to you.

Today, I took Maverick to the fair. Dad was working, and it was a nice day for the middle of summer. Too nice to stay cooped up indoors.

We stopped to get fuel at the gas station.

And there she was. One gas pump away from us.

She'd aged beautifully into a woman.

I couldn't move.

I couldn't stop looking at her.

Her existence rendered me speechless.

And time stopped.

In that moment I knew I had to leave Zoe.

We've been dating for four months.

But I knew we weren't going to turn into anything serious.

And in that moment, frozen in time at the gas station, I knew I was going to marry Christine Malloy.

Then...time went on.

Suddenly, we weren't frozen anymore.

She got in her car and drove away.

And time kept moving forward while I was stuck wondering why I didn't say anything to her.

Lyrics:

did i miss my chance
the opportunity gone
did i wreck your plans
with my missed love song

fate brought us together
the timing of this dance
fate will make forever
in another circumstance

i've wrecked myself
by turning back time
only it was a dream
lost in my mind

Journal:
Zoe took the breakup well.
Apparently I wasn't the only guy she was seeing.
It made it even easier to imagine being with Christine.
I made an Instagram account to see if I could find her.
I didn't.
In fact, I didn't find her on any social media platform.
It makes me fall for her even more. Knowing she's not caught up in that world of nonsense and distraction.
Instead, I found Parker and Tallen. They seem to be doing well. Almost every photo looks like they're on vacation.
I could reach out to them.
But I won't.
Our friendship was in the past.
Which is fine.
I don't want to do anything to hurt my chances with Christine.
They didn't want me to be with Christine before. What's to say they've changed their minds now?

Journal:
Maybe it's all in my head.

Maybe I've created this ideal relationship with Christine that will never exist.

Maybe she's already with someone.

Maybe she's happily married.

Maybe she is better off without me.

Afterall, if anyone knew the thoughts in my head, they would run scared.

Lyrics:

shifting this way
shifting back
my pulse is racing
heart attack

i'm sorry for
waiting too long
to take you seriously
i was wrong

Journal:

Winnie said she ran into Parker at the grocery store.

How convenient.

It's been months since I saw her.

Apparently, Christine is going to school here in Washington.

The same campus I went to.

The same campus I've done research at.

I think I'll call and see what sort of linguistic artifacts they have that might need a specialist's eye.

Helping fate reach its destiny.

Journal:

I've been spending more of my free time at the campus.

I need to see her again.

I don't want to look back ten years from now wishing I had said something.

Wishing I had tried harder.

The only thing that silences the darkness in my mind is monopolizing my thoughts with the idea of seeing Christine again.

Is this healthy?

I don't know.

I don't care.

Lyrics:

obsessed is the understatement
of the decade
possessed by the lingering
image of her parade
back into my life
the last knife
in my back
i've done it to myself
it's the last attack

Journal:
It's turned into agony.
The waiting is agonizing.
The unknown is ripping me in two.
The what ifs are tormenting me.
The want for her is murder to my soul.

Journal:
Winnie broke into my mind again.
She always knows how to pry her way into my head.
I should be grateful. She's saved me from myself more times than I can count.
Today, I drove down the coast to meet her, Jake, and my nephews at the beach.
The drive was long. Mostly because I was wrestling with the destruction in my mind.
As soon as Winnie saw me, she knew.
I denied her accusations.
Tried to play it off as burn out from work.
But she saw through me.
I don't know why I pretend like nothing is happening.
She knows.
She always knows.
But, I didn't tell Winnie about Christine.
She wouldn't understand.
I did tell her about the plaguing drumming in my head though.
She mentioned medication.
She thinks because Jake is a doctor she knows what

she's talking about when it comes to medical advice.

I don't need medication.

I need Christine.

Journal:

I found her.

A damsel in distress, fallen on the snowy campus sidewalk.

It feels like my heart has a rhythm again.

I'm looking forward to seeing her more than anything I've ever looked forward to in my life.

Now, to convince her to fall in love me.

THIRTY-FOUR

I slap the book closed.

My mouth has fallen agape, and I don't even know when it happened.

I shouldn't be alarmed.

Right?

I should be flattered that he felt so passionately about me.

Right?

Or did I marry my stalker?

I laugh out loud at that ridiculous thought.

If I had a diary or a journal, I could have had the same sort of things written in there about him.

But there is one thing I can't shake. One thing that reoccurs throughout all his journal entries that does seem to be cause for concern.

What does alarm me, is the constant mentioning of whatever negative thoughts were going on inside his head. Which is something even he didn't want to mention permanently on paper. But he did mention one person that knew exactly what those thoughts were.

I pick up my phone from the floor to call Winnie to see if I can get some more information about all of this. Especially because I've seen the uglier parts of Declan after he's admitted to concentrating on nothing more than his own thoughts. But my phone begins to ring before I can dial Winnie.

It's Avery.

And she's trying to facetime me.

I quickly grab a towel and wrap it around myself.

I walk out of the bathroom and straight into my bedroom when I finally answer.

Her hair is wet and she looks like she is wearing a wetsuit. She's probably at work. "Oh my gosh, are you naked?" Her voice is echoing behind her like she's in a locker room or open hallway.

I laugh nervously hoping no one heard her. Although whoever she works with is probably used to her loud personality. "No," I say extending the phone to show her I'm wrapped in a towel. "I was in the bath."

"Aren't you *not* supposed to go hot tubbing while you're pregnant?" She shakes a cup that sounds like it's full of ice.

I roll my eyes. "I was in my bathtub not hot tubbing in nuclear chemical water."

She pops an ice cube in her mouth and begins crunching it while she's talking. "So, like," the sound her teeth are making against the ice cube is almost unbearable to my ears, "do you know if you're having a boy or a girl?"

"Not, yet. That appointment's not for another couple of weeks."

I get a twinge of excitement imagining what we will have. And now that Declan seems to be more on board with the pregnancy and fatherhood, I'm also excited to discuss baby names and nursery decorations with him.

"Yay, maybe you'll have twins and get one of each!"

"I'm not having twins."

"You never know, sometimes one is hiding during the ultrasound." Avery's eyes widen with surprise and her smile spreads across her face. "Want to see something amazing?"

"Sure."

She starts jogging inside the building. And all I can see is the eagerness in her expression and the dim blur of the ceiling lights. When the screen flashes with blinding light, I can tell she's outside. The contrast adjusts on her beaming face so that I see her again. Then she flips her phone around and says, "Can you see the pod of orcas out there?"

Her job as a marine biologist seems so fun and exciting. I hope she can hear me over the rushing ocean. "Yeah," I say. "I can." They are specs on her screen, but I can see them surface and roll over the water before plunging back down again.

"That's the disappearing J-pod," she says this with apparent sorrow in her tone. "We spotted them while diving today. There's not very many left in the pod and we're not sure if they're going to last."

She flips the screen back to herself, and I've never seen a more genuine expression of remorse on her face.

I give her a look of sympathy. "I don't know what a J-pod is, but I'm sorry the orcas are disappearing." And I am sorry. Even though I don't have the same connection to marine life that she does, I can sense her angst and that's enough to make me feel sympathy.

She's squinting into the distance. The sunset is turning her entire face bright orange. She finally looks down at me and begins walking back inside the building she ran from.

With a smile she says, "There's a pregnant female out there. She lost her baby last year and went into such a state of grief that she carried him around for two weeks after he died. But she's pregnant again, so that's good news for her and good news for the pod."

I place my hand over my protruding belly. "I didn't know they felt grief."

She's inside now and still walking. "Of course they do. All living things can feel grief. Just like they feel happiness and sadness." She shrugs and her tone goes up an octave. "Anyway, I wanted to show you the pod because she reminded me of you when I saw her."

A sad pregnant orca reminded her of me? I process this thought for a moment, then, "Thanks for comparing me to a whale."

She laughs a deep gut busting laugh.

Which makes me laugh too.

Then she says, "I miss hanging out with you."

I never thought I'd say this, but, "Me too."

She snaps her fingers. It's so loud that I jump. "Maybe I can fly out for a visit sometime soon? You can show me the museum. I'll take you shopping. We can find the best crib and jogging stroller."

"Jogging stroller?"

She nods. "Yeah, it's what moms use to push their babies around in."

I roll my eyes. "I know what a jogging stroller is."

She makes a sort of squealing noise, then, "I should come for the delivery! I can help you. When's the due date? I'll clear my schedule."

"I don't know if you're going to want to be here for that."

"It's the least I can do after I missed your wedding. Not that that was my fault since you guys decided to get married the day we left for our honeymoon."

I'm starting to feel a little overwhelmed by her intrusion even though I just told her I missed hanging out with her. Which is the truth, I do miss hanging out with her. But I also don't want her invading the earliest moments after my baby is born. "I'll have to text you the due date when I look at my planner." I lie. I know the due date. It's April 10th, but I'm not telling her that.

I can hear someone yell her name from a distance and invite her over for some sort of creature analysis. "I'll be right there," she says looking up at them. Then she faces me again. "I gotta go. Duty calls."

I smile. "Keep me updated on my spirit animal."

She tilts her head.

"The orca that's expecting," I say.

She laughs. "I will. And send me your due date. I'm serious about visiting you."

"I will," I say waving goodbye.

After that conversation and realizing the planning I'm going to have to do to ensure she's not here for the birth submerges the last bit of brainpower I had left, any desire I had to talk to Winnie on the phone has been replaced by the desire to watch TV and think about nothing for the rest of the evening.

I begin to change into my silkiest pajamas until I feel too restricted. Instead, I settle for wearing one of Declan's t-shirts as a nightgown. There's a lot more room in his clothes anyway. I seriously need to go shopping.

I heat up some leftovers and curl up on the couch to watch a documentary series on something about Mayan treasures.

After the show, I begin to wonder how far Arty lives from our apartment. I didn't think to ask how late Declan would be. Hopefully he grabs something before he gets home since I'm eating the rest of the leftover alfredo. I send him a text and start up another episode.

I must have fallen asleep on the couch since the TV screen has a pop-up box asking if I want to continue watching. I turn the TV off and drag myself from the couch.

As I'm rinsing my dishes, I catch a glimpse of the time and wince. As if the stove clock has just slapped me in the face.

Declan should be home by now. I walk over to the couch in search of my phone and find it wedged between the cushions and unlock the screen.

No missed calls.

No texts.

It's after midnight and Declan still hasn't called or responded to my text. I call, but it goes straight to voicemail.

Now I can't help but worry.

I don't know Arty's number, so I can't even call him. Maybe I can text him from Declan's computer. He might have his contacts connected to it.

I rush to the office, fling open the double French doors, and sit at his desk. When I open the computer the light is blinding from the screen. I turn the desk lamp on, and when I do, I notice the baby grand piano on the far side of the room. It's perfectly set up right between the windows. And there's a bouquet of roses decorating the piano lid. Apology flowers. He must have set them there before he left.

I feel the panic rising. Imagining that if something unspeakable happened to Declan—that if I might not ever get to see him again— I didn't ever tell him *thank you*. I was frustrated with him, and angry, that I didn't take a moment to even thank him for the piano.

Why is my mind going straight to the worst possible scenario?

Turning my attention back to the computer, I begin my search for any trace of Arty's contact information. There are several tabs open on Declan's desktop so I click through them, quickly realizing that he's posted our song all over every major social media, video and music library platform that exists.

And people…*love it.*

Before I can look any further through the content, the front door opens and I hear Declan's voice.

I close my eyes briefly with my exhale of relief. Thank God he's okay.

I'm surprised to see Arty and another man standing in the entrance with Declan. They're all in good spirits and talking about getting together again.

As I make my way over to Declan, wanting nothing more than to throw my arms around him and tell him I'm happy he's safe and home. And that I'm so grateful for my piano that I can't wait to play. I become overly aware that I'm wearing nothing more than Declan's oversized t-shirt in front of his friends.

Since Declan's back is to me, Arty and the other guy notice me first. Arty's grin fades as he nods his head in my direction and says, "Looks like we woke up the old ball and chain."

He's disgusting.

Declan jerks himself around to face me. "Baby-y! Heyyy!"

I'm not exactly sure what gave his inebriation away first. The fact that he's never called me *baby* before, or his sluggish posture and squinty eyes accompanied by exaggerated raised eyebrows.

"Where were you all night? I was really worried about you." I fold my arms over my chest not because I'm upset, but because I'm trying to hide myself from his friends. "Did you get my text?"

He takes several heavy steps toward me and hangs on to my waist. He's not exactly looking at me when he says, "We were just hanging out for a jam session." He takes his phone from his pocket in a less than smooth manner. "I was recording the songs with my phone and it died." His alcohol infused breath makes me want to gag.

"How much have you had to drink?"

His lip curls up into a smug grin on one side of his face. I used to love that smug grin, but right now I sort of loath it. To Arty he says, "I told you we shouldn't have started drinking."

Arty flexes his shoulders back and extends his neck, lifting his chin at us. "I told you she was a ball and chain. We could still be jamming out if you weren't so worried about getting back home to her."

The other guy laughs at Arty's statement. I don't bother looking at either of them. I don't want them to think I care that they exist.

Declan drops his hand from my waist and faces them. "Don't talk about her like that." He stumbles toward the door and manages to open it. "She's beautiful. She's my beautiful ball and chain." I know this is the alcohol talking, so I let it slide and try to focus more on him calling me beautiful—which makes up for the other thing he said.

This makes Arty and the other guy laugh more. I don't understand why Declan would want to be friends with guys like them. They're disgusting. But at the same time, I know it's probably been difficult not having any friends here. I'm glad he's found some guys to play music with, but I just wish they weren't guys like Arty.

Before Arty files out the door, he looks me up and down with the worst expression. I turn my head away as if cutting eye contact will somehow make me less visible.

Once Declan locks the door, he shuffles past me to our bedroom and flops on the bed face first. I wish I had told Declan about the encounter with Arty at the museum before today. Maybe then he wouldn't have went out with him. Now's not a good time to bring it up either, I'm not even sure Declan would remember later if I told him now anyway. So, I'll save the conversation for another time. He should know what kind of cretin he's befriended.

Since I've never seen him drunk before, I'm trying not to hold the last several minutes against him. Far be it from me to judge a drunk person. But I can't help but feel a sense of insecurity. Not because I'm afraid of Declan, but because I'm in such a vulnerable state carrying our child. I don't know if Arty or that other creep were drinking or not, but I do know Arty doesn't mind being aggressive with a woman when he's sober. Who's to say he wouldn't get angry with me and try to hurt me when he's not? And if he did try something while Declan was drunk, I don't think Declan would win that fight.

I head for the kitchen to retrieve a glass of water and Advil for Declan. I suppose I should be thankful that nothing did happen. And that my husband is silly and not aggressive when he's inebriated.

When I retreat back to our room, Declan is pulling his shirt off and drops his head with his eyes closed as he sits at the edge of the bed.

I sit next to him and take his hand to place the cup in it. "Here," I say guiding the cup to his mouth. "Drink this. And then take these," I hold my palm open with the Advil. "Hopefully it helps with the hangover tomorrow."

Staring at my torso he says, "That's my shirt."

I look down, then back to him. "It's the only thing that fit."

"It's super hot." *Hot*, another word I've never heard him use to describe me. He chuckles to himself, then takes the Advil and drinks the entire glass of water. When he meets my eyes with his glossy gaze, he says, "I love you so much, Christine." Dragging out the word *so*. "You're my favorite person ever."

I take the glass and set it on the nightstand. "I love you too." I pull the duvet down for him. "Let's get to bed. If you keep calling in sick Margaret is probably going to fire you."

He blows raspberries as he rolls under the covers. "She would never. Margaret *loves* me."

I turn the light off and slip into bed next to him. "She told me to tell you to feel better soon."

He curls his body behind mine. He's warm and comforting. And I'm thankful he's alive, even if he stinks like alcohol. I feel bad for ever considering he was my stalker earlier.

"*You-know-what-we-should-do?*" he says slurring the statement together into a long-jumbled word as he whispers it next to my ear. Except his whisper isn't really a whisper and it's more like a loud rushing of air mixed with his words.

I fold my mouth in so my laugh doesn't escape. There's a sort of child-like innocence to him right now that makes me want to giggle. "What should we do?"

He tucks my head under his chin and closes his arms around me. "We should quit our jobs at the museum and just make music together."

A quiet short laugh escapes my nose. "Sounds like a pipedream."

He scoffs dramatically. "It's not at all." His voice is quieter when he says, "You're my muse. As long as I'm with you, I can do anything."

My eyebrows crease as I think about this statement. And when I consider it with his other statements he's made before about being *obsessed* with me and calling me his *muse*. I have to wonder if there's some deeper, *darker*, truth to it. Or maybe it's just in my mind. Nevertheless, maybe my mom is right about counseling. Even if Declan doesn't want to go, it might be helpful for me to detangle everything going on in my own head.

THIRTY-FIVE

"Are you almost home?" Declan asks, his voice reverberating through the speakers on the Bluetooth in my car. "Your brother is starving and wants to go out to..."

I hear Tallen yell in the background. "Old Ebbit Grill! I can't believe you guys haven't checked it out yet."

Declan says, "Apparently he's dying for some calamari."

I smile, then turn my blinker on and merge onto traffic. "I'll be fifteen minutes tops."

"Alright," he says.

"Did you guys finish putting up the crib?"

"Uh—" I hear some muffled talk before Declan says, "We'll knock it out before you get here."

"You didn't get it done yet?"

Tallen is yelling again. "It'll take five minutes!"

Declan says, "It'll be finished when you get here."

When I get off the phone, I reflect on my counseling session with Kaleb today and come to the conclusion that he's not going to be a good fit either.

This is the third first-session I've been to in the last few weeks. And I'm starting to wonder if a good therapist exists. Or at least one that I can relate well to.

I sort of feel like I'm wasting everyone's time by not committing to a therapist. I'm wasting the therapists time by going to one or two sessions and then dropping them. I'm wasting my time by repeating the same dilemma over and over. And I'm wasting Declan's time by leaving to drive however far I need to in order to sit on a couch to talk with a stranger I have no intentions of talking with again.

And because of this, I'm getting nowhere. I'm just a hamster on a wheel. A tired, pregnant orca-sized hamster running and getting nowhere. Left with only my thoughts circulating in my mind.

When I get to the apartment, I take the elevator. I can hear Tallen and Declan laughing before I even open the door to the apartment. "Sounds like you two are having a good time," I say, tossing my purse on the kitchen table and taking a seat. "Did you finish the crib?"

"Yep," Declan says with his welcoming smile.

"Don't get too comfortable," Tallen says, sliding my purse toward me. "We're about to leave for lunch. Remember?"

Declan stands behind me and rubs my shoulders. "How'd the session go?"

I drop my arm on the table and lean down, resting my forehead against it. Then I make a whimpering sound.

"That bad?" Declan says.

Tallen taps my arm. "Why don't you save yourself a trip and try online counseling?"

I lift my head. "Is that a real thing?"

Tallen shrugs. "Probably. Everything is online since the pandemic."

I tip my head back to look up at Declan who is still rubbing my shoulders. He shrugs too. Then he says, "It wouldn't hurt to look into it."

"What is it, like a zoom call or something?" I exhale wearily, then pull my phone out of my purse to see if I can find anything about it. "It sounds kind of sketchy."

Tallen begins reaching for my phone, but my younger sibling reflexes cause me to pull away from him. I draw my eyebrows together with suspicion. "What are you doing?"

His voice is defensive, but in the sibling sort of way when he says, "What am I doing? What are *you* doing? Let's go, I'm hungry!"

"Okay," I say, shouldering my purse and tossing my phone into it. "Let's go, then." I rise from the table and lead the way to the door.

Declan laughs. "You two have always been so different compared to me and Winnie."

Tallen rolls his chair toward the couch to retrieve his jacket. "That's because your sister is way older than you. It's like having another mom. Chris, is like having a mosquito for a sibling."

"Hey," I say. "I never bothered you. You and Parker were always picking on me."

247

Declan retrieves his phone from his pocket. He's still gently laughing when he says, "Speaking of younger siblings. My brother's calling. I'm going to take this real quick, then we'll go."

Tallen throws his hands in the air then slaps them to the tops of his thighs. "Are you kidding? Can't you take this conversation to the car?"

Declan shakes his head with a smile and leans back against the counter in the kitchen as he answers his phone. He crosses his legs at the ankles and presses the phone to his ear.

I fold my arms over my chest and partially on top of my belly. I raise one eyebrow at Tallen when I say, "Some things never change, huh?"

"What do you mean?" he says tilting his head.

"You're like a garbage disposal. Always hungry, never satisfied. I thought your metabolism was supposed to slow down when you became an adult."

He lifts his eyebrows and blinks gently as he raises one hand to his chest. "I guess I'm just blessed."

Just as we begin to express our laughter, Declan lifts his hand in our direction indicating he wants us to stop. Then with his phone still pressed to his ear, he says, "Woah, woah, woah, hold on, Maverick. Where are you guys?"

Tallen's grin falls into concern and we both look at each other, alarmed.

"Okay," Declan says to Maverick, but directs his attention to me. He pulls the phone down to his neck for a moment and says, "Get ahold of Winnie."

I nod and take my phone out.

Tallen quietly says, "What's going on?"

"I don't know." I shrug dialing Winnie as quickly as I can. Her phone goes to voicemail so I leave her a text telling her to call me as soon as she can. "She's not answering," I say to Declan.

"Try my mom," he demands.

I do as he says, but she doesn't answer either. I give Declan a remorseful expression and say, "She didn't pick up."

His eyes are wide and full of panic. Pointing to my phone he says, "Look this up." Then he turns his phone on speaker. As soon as he does, all I can hear is Maverick's gasping breaths. "Alright, Maverick," Declan says. "You're going to be okay. I just need to know where you are so I can help you."

I can tell Maverick is holding back tears as he says, "I don't know. Some frozen yogurt shop." Then, in almost a scream he says, "Dad, come on! I'm ready to go!"

The complete dread that fills Maverick's voice causes the hairs on my arms to rise.

Maverick continues the dreadful screaming with, "Dad! Get up!" Then to Declan he says, "He won't get up, he's just sitting on the curb by the road." He lets out a quiet sob. "I'm scared he's going to get hit by a car."

Declan's mouth falls open as if he's going to speak, but nothing comes out.

Maverick screams at their father again, begging him to take them home.

I approach Declan and crane my neck over the phone. "Hey, Maverick? It's Christine." I'm trying to sound calm even though my heart is drumming in my chest. "Is there a sign somewhere that says the name of the store? Or maybe someone that you can talk to?"

"No. No one is here. The store is closed." He's gasping for a breath between each sentence.

"Okay," I say with the same forced positive ring to my voice. I'm not sure what's going on with their dad. But I can probably make an accurate assumption, leading me to believe it would be pointless to try and talk to their father right now. "We're trying to help you," I say. "Is there a sign? Or another store close by that you could tell us the name of? Maybe the street you're on?" Too bad Maverick doesn't have an iPhone, facetime could really come in handy right now.

"It's uh…" Maverick sniffs. "It's called Honey Treat."

"Perfect," I say punching in the name of the shop into my phone in search of the address in Nevada.

Declan says, "You're being very brave, Maverick. You were smart to call me."

"I just want to go home," Maverick cries. It's heartbreaking hearing him like this. Even though he's thirteen, he still has the fear of a child. But Declan is right, Maverick is being incredibly brave.

When I finish the search, my jaw drops. "They're in Reno," I say. My eyes are just as wide as Declan's when I face him. It's unbelievable. It means that they drove there alone. And I'm not sure if Sean is supposed to be driving with his condition. "That's over an hour away from your house."

Declan flips his head to Tallen. "Call the police," he says. "Give them the address so they can meet my dad and Maverick there."

Tallen nods and begins calling the police station in Reno and delivering the details.

I try Winnie and Val's phones again, but there's no answer.

Declan drags his hand through his hair and says quietly with irritation, "Where are they?" Then to Maverick he says, "Listen, I'm not going anywhere. Okay?"

Maverick squeaks out a short, "Okay."

"You're going to be safe. Just stay right where you are, help is on the way." Declan cuts his eyes to me as his face goes pale. Still speaking to Maverick he says, "And promise me something. Okay?" His voice is grim when he says, "If Dad gets too close to the road or walks into traffic, promise me you won't go after him."

I can't believe what I'm hearing.

Maverick lets out a short sob without answering.

No kid should have to think about something like this. No kid should be in this situation.

"Promise me, Maverick. I can't let anything happen to you." Declan's voice breaks as he says, "Promise me you won't go after him!"

Maverick cracks another sob.

I take the phone from Declan and place my hand on his shoulder seeing that this is escalating quickly. He presses his palms to his eyes.

Tallen is still on the phone with the dispatcher.

I circle my hand between Declan's shoulder blades, providing the best comfort I can right now. Then to Maverick I say, "You're going to be alright, Maverick. The police are going to be there any minute. You can relax, it's going to be fine."

Maverick lets out a quiet cry when he says, "Dad..." My heart breaks.

My phone begins to ring and Winnie's name pops up on the screen. I shift my phone in Declan's direction, and he takes it from my hand to answer.

"Where are you?" Declan says into the phone as he strides abruptly toward our bedroom.

I hear the faint echo of police sirens from Declan's phone. "It sounds like the police are going to be there in no time," I say to Maverick.

Maverick exhales deeply. "Yeah." His voice is nasally from crying. "I can see them coming."

Tallen tells the dispatcher that the police are arriving.

"You're going to be okay now," I say. "And I'm so sorry this happened today, but I'm really proud of you for calling your brother. And I know he is too. That was a smart decision."

"Yeah," he says with a sniff. The sirens grow increasingly louder until I can hear a police officer speaking. Then to the officer, Maverick says, "Yes. That's my dad right there. I'm talking to my brother's wife on the phone." Then to me, he says, "The cop wants to talk to you."

"Okay," I say. "Good job today, Maverick."

THIRTY-SIX

Nothing has been the same since the incident with Maverick. The last several weeks have been hell.

I don't know much about Andrea, but she doesn't want Maverick having unsupervised visits with Sean anymore. And she contacted a lawyer about it, so there might be a judge involved. Which means court for Sean. Even though that doesn't seem fair considering he has dementia.

Andrea's also trying to sue Val for being negligent. Apparently Winnie and Val had taken Ty and Buddy to a fall festival at the preschool. Leaving Sean and Maverick at home. They didn't expect Maverick and Sean to leave. They didn't expect Maverick to get in the car with Sean, knowing his condition. And no one expected Sean would drive all the way to Reno.

The entire thing devastated Declan.

Tallen couldn't get Declan to open up about his feelings, even with Tallen's own devastating experiences. Declan didn't care when our song began going viral. It didn't even cheer him up when we found out that we're having a girl.

"Hello there," Margaret says, peeping her head inside the tech room where I'm sitting in the dark by myself. "How are things going?"

I open a tab on my monitor that reveals several small screens showing the surveillance footage throughout the museum. Technically that's not part of my job description, but once I learned that I had access to the cameras, I've made a habit of people watching. "It's good." I say, revealing the screen to her. "Looks like it's a pretty busy day out there."

She grins. "I meant with you."

252

"Oh," I let out an embarrassed laugh. "I'm okay."

She enters the dim room, closing the door behind her. Which causes the room to get darker as the screens light up our faces.

"Is everything alright with you and Declan?" She motions her hands in a circular manner. "I don't mean to intrude, but if there's something I can help with please let me know. The perks of being old is that I have a lot of wisdom to share."

Would I be in violation of professional boundaries if I asked her to be my unofficial therapist?

"Thank you," I say. "But we're okay. There's some other stuff going on with his family and I think it's just a little stressful for him." A little stressful is an understatement.

She nods, unconvinced. But I can tell she won't press me any further about our personal lives. I love that about her. "Well, I hope things get better for him soon." She smiles as her eyes find him on the surveillance screen. "He's such a good man. I hate to see him unhappy."

I turn to look at the screen where my eyes adjust to Declan setting up a ladder in front of the massive globe in the World Language Room.

"Look at him, there," she says, lifting her palm toward the screen. "He's switching the burned-out lights on the globe. I told the maintenance man to do that last week."

I place my elbow on the desk. Resting my chin on my fist as I give her a smirk and say, "I think he needs a raise."

She laughs and rises as if she's going to leave. "I think you need to get back to work," she says this with humor.

When I turn back to the screen, I see two teenagers pushing each other near the ladder as one shoves the other hard enough to knock him against the ladder.

The ladder doesn't wobble.

It doesn't rock.

But instead, it shifts completely to one side. Tipping over in one rapid motion. I suck in a rush of air and reach my hand out in front of me as if I'm able to catch the ladder and stop the scene from unfolding before me.

But I can't.

And I'm left helpless, as I watch my husband catapult down, bouncing his head off the hardwood floor.

"No!" The word escapes my throat without my mind having a

chance to decide on it.

"What is it?" Margaret notices the terror in my voice and rushes to my side, planting her face in front of the screen. "Oh my goodness." She slaps one hand over her mouth.

My eyes are glued to Declan's body sprawled on the floor as Margaret hurries out the door and begins hurling commands to the security guard and some other workers.

When she returns after a few moments, she says, "Christine, don't look at that screen."

I know I should turn away, but I can't.

There's something waiting to erupt inside of me. My pounding heart is heavy in my chest but hasn't quite made the decision to thrust up into my throat yet. Because I'm waiting to know what to do next while my attention stays focused on the bystanders circling Declan.

I'm waiting. Part of me is waiting for Declan to stand up and be fine. The other part is waiting for the dark flow of blood to pool from his head.

Suddenly, a security guard reaches him as Declan rolls to his side and a sharp exhale makes its way out of my mouth. And almost immediately after, I let out another sharp exhale that's accompanied by an uncontrollable sob.

Margaret wraps one arm around my shoulders and gives me a brief squeeze. "He's going to be fine." She reassures me. "Now walk with me so I know you're going to be okay too."

"Are you sure you don't need to see a doctor?" I ask, placing an icepack against the back of Declan's head.

He holds the icepack against his head and gives me a halfhearted smile. "I didn't fall that hard. I'm fine." Margaret sent us both home after his fall. She made sure Declan was okay and could walk a straight line before she let us go. And she asked me several times if I was stable enough to focus on driving.

"Do you need anything else?" I ask.

"No." He gently closes his eyes and rests his head against the couch. "Thank you, though." His voice is low and numb. It's been this way for weeks now, and this new depressed tone makes me miss the confidence and sophistication in his normal voice. I'm desperate to hear that voice again.

I sit next to him on the couch, tucking my feet under me as I get comfortable. Draping one hand over the top of my belly and lacing the other one in Declan's hand, I inspect the shape of his pouting lips. The natural way of his frowning mouth and remembering when I noticed his mouth for the first time when he rescued me after I slipped on the ice and hit my head.

"Are we okay?" I say gently.

Without moving from his position, he slowly raises his brow as he looks over at me. "Yes," he says drawing in a deep breath and turning away, "we're fine." Then he pulls his hand from mine, switching it with the hand that was holding the icepack.

I know he's going through a lot, and I shouldn't make this about me. But I can't help but feel this growing distance between us. And I can't help but feel like I'm the only one that cares.

He is experiencing a tremendous amount of stress. His father's dementia is increasingly worsening. He might not see his brother again. His mother might be sued. He's becoming a father. And he just fell off a six-foot ladder and hit his head.

I dig my elbow into the couch and hold my head in my hand. "Thanksgiving is coming up soon," I say trying to sound happy. "We could go home and visit our families."

He doesn't say anything.

I bite at the inside of my cheek for a moment, trying to figure out how to make him feel better. "Or we could take a vacation? Travel to Mexico someplace where we have no cell service?"

He draws his eyebrows down and grimaces as if he's in pain. Then pulling his hand up to his face he opens his hand and rubs his temples with his thumb on one side and index finger on the other. "Christine, please." He stops rubbing his temples and drops his hand over his eyes. "Can we talk about this some other time?"

I drop my gaze, defeated. "Yeah, that's fine." I rise from the couch, hoping he'll ask me where I'm going, or encourage me to stay on the couch with him. When he doesn't, I say, "I'll let you get some rest."

"You were supposed to make everything better," he says this in a low voice. It's the same tone of voice he had when he was lying on the floor submerging his mind in his own negative thoughts. If there's anything I've learned from the past several disagreements we've had, it's that when he gets in these sort of moods he just needs to be left alone.

I ignore his comment and go to our bedroom. Closing the door

255

so I don't disturb him. I get my laptop and Declan's journal, then sit in our bed. I have every intention of searching for flights to Mexico, but somehow my heart isn't in it, and I quickly abandon the Mexico idea all together.

Instead, I push my laptop aside and open Declan's journal to begin reading. But I can't focus on that because my mind is elsewhere.

So, I switch the journal for my laptop again and begin typing in the search bar for online therapists. If I'm going to continue circulating the thoughts in my head, I may as well find someone who can help me understand them.

THIRTY-SEVEN

I quietly scoot out of bed to use the bathroom, which is something I do several times a night now that there's a baby growing above my bladder. But when I return, I notice Declan's not in our bed.

It's almost 3:30 in the morning. I look down the hall and see a glow from his office.

I begin to lay back down in our bed, but there's something unsettling about being in our bed at this hour knowing he's on his computer.

I try to fall asleep for a few more minutes. It's useless. I toss the covers off and head down the hall where I find Declan at his desk.

He immediately notices me. "What are you doing up," he says flatly, looking back to the screen.

I cradle my arms over my chest, hugging myself, and walk around to see what's keeping him from coming to bed. "I had to pee. What are you doing up?"

He has one tab open on YouTube. There's a pop-up box asking if he's sure he wants to delete his account. "I couldn't sleep," he says.

I flip my head to face him with concern. "Are you deleting your channel?"

He nods, looking back to the screen and drawing in a deep inhale. "Yep. And not just on here."

I watch him. Noticing the dark shadows under his eyes and the intensity in his expression as he continues deleting the account. I fold my hand over his shoulder to get him to look at me.

He flinches subtly at my touch, then faces me. "What is it?" He almost sounds as if he's annoyed by my intrusion on his middle of the night solitude.

I press my mouth together as my eyebrows draw apart with

concern. "Why are you deleting everything? You had a huge following. I thought you wanted to pursue this. To pursue your music."

He looks back at the screen. "No. Like you said, it's a pipedream."

I gently close my eyes and exhale. Regretting ever saying that, even if I was joking when I said it. I didn't think he would remember since he had been drinking, but it must have hit the memory box inside of his brain and implanted itself there.

"I never would have said that if I knew it was going to deter you from pursuing what you love."

He rises from his chair like he's going to leave the room. "It doesn't matter anymore, Christine." He heads for our bedroom. "Nothing does." His voice is dark and defeated when he says this.

He's been distancing himself further from me lately. And he's been avoiding his parents and Winnie since the fall. He doesn't even want to play music. Or hang out with Arty—which I would normally be ecstatic about, but in this case, I'm beginning to worry.

Tomorrow, or I guess today, is Thanksgiving and we've had the entire week off but his reluctancy to discuss any plans has left us with the decision to stay in our apartment. I was hoping for relaxation, but I feel more like a hostage in my own home. Walking on eggshells with Declan constantly fifteen to twenty feet away.

"What does matter to you?" I say as he's about to close the door to our bathroom.

He pauses at the doorway and turns his head just enough to see me from the corner of his eye. "You wouldn't understand." Then he flicks the bathroom light on, closes the door, and starts the shower.

I release a long exhale full of defeat and remorse. I don't know how we got to this place. I've invited him to join me in my online counseling sessions, but he refuses. Counseling is helping me understand myself and my reactions, but I'm struggling to heed my therapist's advice and accept Declan where he's at. Because he's stuck in this negative state, and for some reason he thinks I should be able to guess what he's thinking.

The house is silent.

Vacant of any trace of another human besides me and the baby in my belly.

The keys are on the counter. Which means the cars are here.

All of Declan's things are here.

His guitars.

His computer.

His clothes.

His toothbrush.

His wallet.

His phone.

But Declan is not here.

It's Thanksgiving and he's gone. And I don't understand why he's gone or where he went.

I responded for the both of us in the group texts sent to us from his family this morning wishing us a Happy Thanksgiving. And my mom and Tallen called early enough that I was able to lie and tell them Declan was in the shower when they asked to talk to him. I hate to lie, but I'd hate to make something out of nothing when I'm unsure where Declan is.

In the last five hours since I searched high and low for Declan, I've been growing increasingly concerned that maybe he's done the one thing he's done before when life seemed too unbearable, and he's run away from his problems.

After the little boy at the pool drowned, and Declan left everything behind without hesitation, no one did anything to find him. And since his parents didn't send a search and rescue for their eighteen-year-old missing son, I can't help but wonder if maybe he ran from his problems before. Maybe his absence was a normal thing.

Declan said that his family didn't even question him when he came back from his hiatus. Except Winnie.

I pick up my phone and dial Winnie.

I'm determined to get some answers.

Like, why did Winnie tell Declan to *let me in*. What did she mean? What does Winnie know about what's going on inside Declan's mind? And why do I feel like they're hiding it from me?

Who is my husband?

The phone rings so many times I'm already preparing for what to say in my voicemail to her when she finally answers, "Hey, Christine. Happy Thanksgiving." She doesn't sound chipper, not that she normally does. But I was expecting pleasantries since it's a holiday.

"Winnie, hi. Are you alone?"

"I—uh," my to-the-point question must have caught her off guard, "is everything okay?" The confusion is apparent in her voice. I exhale, clinging to the betrayal I feel so I don't slip into the terror buried in my throat. The last thing I want to do is create chaos for their family on Thanksgiving. And if I'm sobbing and terrified about my missing husband, that would create a commotion.

"Yes," I say, making sure I sound convincing. "There's just been some things going on and I wanted to see if you could help."

I hear a door close as Winnie gets quieter. "Of course. It's not the baby, is it?"

"No, no," I say. "She's fine. It's actually..." I feel the quiver in my stomach creeping up into my throat. So I swallow it down, clenching my teeth to make sure it disappears before I continue. "I don't want to alarm you, but I don't know where Declan is."

It's quiet for a moment before she says, "What does that mean?"

I close my eyes gently, keeping the tears from rising. "I haven't seen him since late last night. He hasn't been sleeping lately and he hasn't been himself since everything happened with Maverick. Normally I wouldn't be alarmed, but all his things are still here. His car, his phone, everything."

"Would he go on a walk?"

"A walk in the freezing cold without his phone?"

She lets out an exhale. "I'm trying to help."

I gentle my tone. "I know," I drop my head into my hand, "I called because, I know he's run off before when things get tough."

"And you think that's what he's doing now?"

I don't say anything. Mostly because I get a feeling that I'm somehow irritating her by making assumptions and asking these sorts of questions. Declan may be her brother, but he's my husband and somehow that seems to trump her relationship with him. I think I've earned the right to know what exactly is going on.

I can hear the door open on the other side of the phone, and someone say something to her, she whispers something in return before the door closes. Then to me she says, "I don't like speaking for my brother. He's a grown man and he can do that for himself. With that said, yes, he's run off before. And, yes, he was under tremendous amounts of stress, just like he is now. I might be his sister, but that doesn't mean I know what's going on in his head all the time."

I'm nodding, although I don't find her statement entirely true since Declan and his journals have specifically identified Winnie as the *only* person that gets inside his head. "I understand that. All I'm asking is if you think that I should be calling the police or if I should get the turkey in the oven and expect him home for dinner."

I hear Winnie laugh subtly, then, "If he's not home in a few days, I wouldn't judge you for calling the police."

This doesn't make me feel better, but it's better than nothing and gives me some sort of direction to take. "Thanks, Winnie."

After the phone call, I begin to preheat the oven for the turkey, but quickly turn the oven off and decide to take a drive to the museum. It's only a few miles away and he could easily get there on foot. Even if it is freezing.

My winter coat is too small to zip up when I put it on, so I rummage through the closet on Declan's side to find something more fitting. I pull his old winter jacket on and zip it up with ease before grabbing the keys from the counter and heading for the parking garage.

My phone rings from the car's Bluetooth, and I contemplate answering for a moment since it's my father. I don't remember the last time we spoke on the phone. It had to have been before I moved to D.C. I don't enjoy talking to him, but since it's Thanksgiving and he is my father, I feel obligated to answer.

"Hey, Dad," I say approaching the vacant museum.

"Chris! I'm so glad you answered. You're a tough girl to get ahold of."

I'm not glad I answered. Because by the tone in his voice he's about to tell me about his new girlfriend, or a promotion, or relocation. All of these topics are things he manages to drag out into an hour-long one-sided conversation where he talks about himself and how great he is.

I decide to make sure he knows the conversation needs to be quick and say, "Dad, I can't talk long—"

He cuts me off with, "I know it's Thanksgiving, I'm sure you're with your mom." I'm not but he wouldn't know since he's too preoccupied with himself to ask. "I'll keep it quick."

"Okay, real quick."

"We're having a baby!"

A baby?

A real life human?

Good thing I'm already parked, since I'm sure that statement would have caused a car accident if I were still in traffic.

Instead of congratulating him, I say, "Who is *we*?"

His voice is disappointed when he says, "Chris, you know good and well that Natasha and I have been together for six months."

I instantly feel sorry for that child. And for that unborn baby's sake, I pray that Natasha is a good mom. It's the only opportunity that kid has at a decent chance at life. I know my mom's the only reason I turned out as good a person as I am.

"You and Natasha will be pregnant together, isn't that great? Everyone at the station couldn't believe I already have kids in their twenties, they thought this was my first because I look so young."

I'm baffled by the words that I'm hearing. And I can't help but feel like this is some sort of game for him. Maybe he's hoping I'll regurgitate the conversation to my mother. Which I won't. He wasn't happy at all about becoming a grandfather, but having a baby the same age as his grandchild seems to make him feel elated. It's just another one of his narcissistic games. And a terrible attempt at obtaining his youth.

All I can bring myself to say is, "That's great, Dad. I hope you and Natasha are happy."

"I thought you'd be more excited."

Why? Because I'm going to have a sibling the same age as my daughter?

The last thing I want to do is get in the middle of his games. "I'm ecstatic. But I'm right in the middle of something and I need to go. I'll call you later," I lie, "Bye, Dad."

I exhale as I end the call before he can say anything else, unsure why today I'm more irritated with him than normal. Maybe it's because I blame him a little. Because I'm worried I may have married a man that's like him; charming, charismatic, driven, sophisticated, selfish, abandons his children, as close to an adulterer as someone can get without being one. *An adulterer.*

The only reason Declan would go anywhere in the freezing cold without his phone, wallet, or car, would be if he was getting a ride somewhere. With someone.

In the same breath, things haven't been going so well. And I've been feeling distant from him. I can't imagine him doing that. I can't imagine him destroying our marriage like that. He hated that his father fractured their family in that way. Surely he wouldn't stoop to that level.

I shake the thought and hurry to the back of the building. I quickly punch the code into the electronic keypad, unlocking the employee entrance door.

The building is dark. Quiet. I search every floor, calling Declan's name to no avail. The entire building is empty. And why wouldn't it be? It's Thanksgiving. Everyone is home with their families. Except for missing persons and probably adulterers.

I shouldn't jump to conclusions. But when Declan told me that I was supposed to fix everything, I didn't take him seriously. Now, I can't help but wonder if maybe he's second guessing our marriage. Maybe he thought I was more than I am, and I failed him.

I drive toward Presidents Park. We love to stroll around that area. But he's not there. No one is. Because it's Thanksgiving.

I look for him around the Fashion Centre at Pentagon City. But he's not there. No one is. Because it's Thanksgiving.

I head over to Chinatown, mostly because I'm starving at this point and craving some almond chicken. And I know that area of town is still open, and probably full of people that don't celebrate Thanksgiving or don't have anyone to celebrate with. Like me.

I order almond chicken at one of my favorite smaller dine in restaurants, but take it to go so I don't have to sit at a table alone. Instead I sit alone in my car and devour my meal. Somehow it feels worse eating alone in my car than eating inside the restaurant.

I take the fortune cookie and place it in my coat pocket before I buckle my seatbelt. And I feel something else inside of the pocket. When I pull it out, it's a USB. Maybe there's something on the USB drive that might help me figure out where Declan is.

I shove the USB back into Declan's coat pocket and drive back to our apartment.

When I get back, I feel a subtle sickness rise in my stomach. What if there's footage of his affair? What if there's something horrific my eyes won't ever unsee?

Before I open the front door, I have a quick sense of hope that I'll see Declan in the kitchen cooking our Thanksgiving dinner. Not that I'm hungry anymore. But I would eat again if it would bring a smile to his face.

I swing the door open. No one is here. Declan's things are still where he left them. And there's no trace he's been back at all.

I take his phone on my way to his office where his computer is. Before I take a seat I'm already logged in and shoving the USB into the port. There's three folders. Each of them labeled:

Journal.
Her song.
Nova.

My eyes widen as my heart begins to race at the last folder labeled *Nova*. Who is Nova? And is *Her Song* for me? Or is it for Nova? I'm beyond jumping to conclusions. My mind is already picturing him in bed with another woman named Nova. And I might vomit all over his computer.

I skip the *Journal* folder and the one labeled *Her Song* and open Nova's folder. There's a lump in my trachea that's making it difficult to breathe correctly.

My hands are cold and stiff trying to find the button that makes the icons bigger. I click on the first photo, and close my eyes tightly before opening them.

When I see the photo of Nova, the lump in my throat drops down to the bottom of my lungs and my mouth falls agape with a rush of air. I cover my mouth with my hand as the tears pool into my eyes. Because I realize that Nova isn't some woman on the side.

Nova is our daughter. And the photo is the first ultrasound picture we received at thirteen weeks.

I click on the next photo, and the next, and the one after that. The entire folder is full of every ultrasound image we've taken. And he's named our daughter Nova. And I love it.

I finally slump down into the computer chair. Dropping my face into my hands, I begin to cry. Helpless.

I don't know what to do. I don't understand what's happening to my husband or our marriage. I don't understand where he is or why he left. I don't know if I should be angry or worried.

After a moment, I take Declan's phone from his coat pocket and unlock the screen. I search through his texts first. I don't think he's having an affair, but I want to be one hundred percent certain before I rule that out. As I scroll through his messages and skim through his text strings, I don't find anything alarming.

His email is the same.

And so are his apps.

But when I skim through his search history, I'm unsure how to decipher what he's been researching.

First, he searched for a few open mic nights downtown. Not very alarming considering his passion for music. But then, there are searches for music opportunities in L.A. and several searches for music producers, agents, and band members. He's even gone as far as to search for apartments for rent in and around the L.A. area. But he's never mentioned wanting to move to me. Maybe he was looking for the sake of curiosity.

The search history is from a few weeks ago. Before everything happened with Maverick and their father. I can't help but wonder if he was serious when he told me we should quit our jobs and make music together. Maybe he was looking into it financially. But then everything with Maverick happened, and he hasn't been the same. Maybe he lost his ambition for music. Maybe that's why he deleted the songs we recorded.

I decide to do a search history on his computer too. But there's nothing out of the ordinary.

Next, I open the folder called *Her Song*. It's a single page document with words falling down the center of the page that says,

your thoughts are
draining
they've got a heavy hold
on you
your mind is
racing
these thoughts won't lead you
to the truth

but I—
I—am
yours
I—am
yours
yours…for now

I read over the lyrics several more times, trying to find what he's saying. Trying to read between the lines. Trying to understand the message.

But just like his journals, there seems to be a missing piece.

His journals.

I open the last folder labeled *Journal*. I know that I originally planned to read through all his journals in chronological order. But the last journal I read was leading up to the time that we met again.

And I'm fairly certain I have an idea of what he was thinking during the time he was pursuing me. And I feel fairly certain, because he was saying them to me. Things like, *you're my muse, you're stunning, you're flawless, perfect, it's been my devoir to marry you,* and *you're the only person that understands me.*

If I read the journal from his computer, I might understand how we managed to get to this place. Where instead of calling me *flawless,* he's telling me that I was supposed to fix everything.

THIRTY-EIGHT

Journal:
   She thought it would be a surprise.
   Even after I told her I didn't want children.
   I told her I didn't understand how anyone could bring a kid into this messed up world.
   She was standing right there, agreeing with me while the ocean waves slammed into the rocks behind us. Now she gets upset when I'm not happy about bringing a life into this world. A life that I'm certain will be tortured.
   Just as I'm tortured.
   Tortured that I couldn't save Eli from drowning.
   Tortured knowing that Maverick is growing up in a broken home.
   Tortured by the death of Parker.
   Tortured by watching my father deteriorate into a man I don't recognize.
   Tortured by the thoughts creeping up again.
   Tortured by the noise.
   Tortured by the fact that I might have been wrong about Christine.
   Maybe she's not the muse I thought she was.

Journal:
   I've been talking to Winnie.
   She always brings up medication.
   I still don't think I need it.
   She doesn't understand that I can handle my life. I know what I need to function.
   When I'm sleeping well and creating music with Christine, I'm at peace.

I can't begin to describe the way our voices sound together. It's like being on a cloud at the gates of Heaven. So close that angels can touch us.

She's steady.

Her steadiness keeps me tethered to the world in a way that allows me to stay grounded, but still provides the freedom I need to reach up into the sky and touch Heaven's door.

I love her so much it aches in my heart.

And I'm afraid to love anyone else as much as I love her. Because I'm afraid if we bring a child into the world as perfect as Christine, it might destroy me if something ever happens to our child.

It destroyed me when I couldn't save Eli.

It destroys me every day knowing Maverick is growing up without the life he deserves.

Winnie told me to open up to Christine.

I thought when she read my journals she would understand.

I thought she would see that she's the only woman I've ever wanted to be with.

That she's the only person that makes my heart sing so loud that the words rupture up out of my windpipe, serenading her with every ounce of my existence.

She's supposed to be the person that understands me. That understands that I need her.

But she doesn't seem to understand this.

Without her, the darkness claws its way back into my mind. And every time she brings up the baby, I hear something telling me to run.

Journal:

When Tallen visited, I felt like myself again. There's something about having a friend that knows your history and still wants to be your friend when you haven't spoken in years.

Just as I felt like myself.

Just as I wanted to be a father.

Just as I began to really consider a music career.

Just as I opened my heart to Nova.

Just as I saw Christine as my muse again.

Something shifted in the worst way.

And I can't come back from it.

I can't stop the thoughts parading in my mind.
Telling me to run.
Telling me I'll ruin Nova's life. That I won't protect her when she needs me.
Telling me I'll let Christine down.
Telling me I don't deserve good things to happen to me.
Telling me I'm an imposter.
Telling me my music is worthless.
Telling me I'm not a good brother.
Telling me I can't save my father.
I don't want to think anymore.
I just want to shut it off.
I want the noise to end.
I need the noise to end.
And there's one thing that turns it off.
When I'm no longer Declan Price.
When I'm no one.

Poetry:
    love can sometimes be magic
    but magic can sometimes...just be an illusion

    -javan

THIRTY-NINE

It's been four days since Declan left.

And today is my breaking point.

After reading the journals, I'm convinced he's run off. But I'm also convinced there's something going on that I don't understand.

When I read the journal from his computer. It seemed obvious that he's suffering in his own mind. I just wish I knew what was causing it and I wish I knew how to fix it.

I've debated calling Winnie again. But she's made it apparent that she doesn't want to speak for her brother. I wonder if it would change her mind if she knew that I've read his journals and I know that they've talked about whatever *darkness* is plaguing him to the point of making him feel like the only relief he can get is if he abandons his family without a trace.

I feel sick wondering if he's okay. Wondering where he is and if he's safe.

I feel exhausted from waking up every hour wondering if Declan is going to ever come home.

I feel angry that he left. That he didn't tell me about what's going on in his mind. If he's depressed, we can figure it out together. I only wish I had paid more attention to the warning signs that led up to this. But I didn't think he was suffering. I thought he was selfish.

And I feel guilty for not taking the warning signs more seriously.

The oven timer goes off, pulling me from my thoughts back to reality.

I finally decided to cook the turkey. I was hoping Declan would be back by now. Then we would cook it together. I've never cooked a turkey before, and he's a much better cook than I am. It was supposed to be our first Thanksgiving as a family. Now our first

Thanksgiving is a tainted memory I'll never forget.

When I examine the turkey after pulling it from the oven, I can tell it's going to be dry by the way the crispy skin has tightened and split. I guess it doesn't really matter if it's dry since I'm the only one that's going to eat it.

I begin making some instant mashed potatoes from a box in the back of the cupboard because peeling and cooking real potatoes seems like a lot of work for a meal for one. Or two, I guess, if I'm counting Nova.

I wish Declan were here so I could ask him why he decided on the name Nova. I wish he had never left. I wish his dad never had dementia. I wish everything was different.

I don't stop the tears from streaming down my cheeks as I stir the water into the powder mix. I drop the whisk in the pan and give up on the instant potatoes so I can lay in my bed and cry.

Cry is an understatement. So is *sob*. I'm confused about how I should feel or what I should do. I don't know if my husband wants to be gone. Can you report a missing person if they want to be missing? I don't know what state of mind he's in. I don't know if he has any intention of coming home. Did he just want a break? I don't know if he was taken against his will. What if he was taking the garbage out and was struck by a car? What if someone captured him? That would explain why he's missing. That would explain why all of his stuff is here.

I hear something that pulls me from my miserable state of mind. I wipe my face on my pillow and roll out of bed, carrying my belly in my hands like a package.

When the front door closes, my pulse begins to accelerate, and my feet move faster toward the entrance.

It takes a moment for my brain to adjust to what my eyes are seeing. I don't believe it at first, but once I'm gripped in his arms, I know it's him.

I know it's Declan, but he looks disheveled. And dirty.

"I'm so sorry, Christine," he says with his tightening grip. "I'm so *so* sorry." His voice shudders on the last part of his statement. I hear the remorse in his broken words. I *feel* the remorse in the way he's consuming me in his arms.

And I'm crying. Again.

I'm relieved, but I'm also confused, and a little angry. But more than anything, I'm worried about him.

My voice is gentle with concern when I say, "What happened to you?" My head is pressed to his chest, and he smells like a metro station. "Why did you leave without telling me? Where were you?"

His chest begins to tremble as his voice breaks with, "I don't know." He cracks a sob that rips my heart. "I don't know," he repeats, wounded.

I hug him tighter and take his hand, leading him into our bathroom.

He still hasn't looked at me since he walked in the door. As if he's too ashamed to face me after what he's done. And what he's done, I still don't know what that is.

I start the shower and pull his jacket from one arm and then the other. He lets me do this and partially helps me while he stares at the floor. He doesn't look depressed. He looks *broken*.

I've never seen him like this before. It breaks me, because I don't know how to help him. His eyes are red rimmed and swollen. Vacant while full of pain.

I pull his shirt up over his unmanaged hair. Even though he was only gone for a few days, he looks as if he's been homeless for years.

Once I've helped him fully undress, he steps into the shower. And *weeps*.

I can't take the tortured sight of him. I don't bother undressing when I step into the shower. I clasp my arms around his torso, hugging him with the side of my face pressed to his back. His shattered weeping makes me breakdown with him. I continue to hold him in my arms as the water pours over us. The water at our feet is tinged with brown from his dirty body.

I want to ask him what happened. I want to ask him why he left and where he was and how I can help him. But I don't think he even knows the answers to those questions. So instead, I hold him while he grips my arms tightly in his, and continues to break open the most tortured parts of himself through his painful sobs of remorse.

The only thing he manages to say is, "I don't know what's happening to me."

FORTY

I draw a finger down the side of his face. He's been sleeping for eighteen hours straight.

He seemed trapped last night. Like he couldn't get out of the guilt he felt for leaving. When I would ask where he went, he could only say *I'm so sorry*, and *I don't know*.

I don't know where my husband has gone, but I'm determined to help this man heal until he returns.

His eyes flutter open as he turns to lay toward me with the side of his face against his pillow. "Hey," he says with a hint of a smile in the corner of his mouth. "What time is it?"

I trace his relaxed deltoid with my hand and rest it there as he wraps his arm around my lower back.

"It's almost one in the afternoon," I say, hoping he wants to get out of bed and talk.

Instead of talking, he looks at me. Inspecting me, as if he's painting a mental image of me in his mind. Shifting his intense gaze from my forehead, to my hairline, down to my mouth.

I crease my eyebrows with concern. I don't want to be a mental image in his mind. I want him to look at me like he's going to see me every day for the rest of our lives, and that's not how he's looking at me. He's looking at me like he might never see me again.

"Do you want me to make you some coffee?" I ask.

He finally locks his eyes on mine. "Christine." I miss when he used to say my name with a honeyed voice. Thick with his yearning for me. Now he's saying my name like its painful.

I clench my jaw shut. Worried in anticipation with what he's going to say next.

He runs the tip of his tongue along his bottom lip in thought.

Then he says, "I was watching the highlights from the Detroit game on NBC yesterday."

I exhale, wondering why the first full sentence he's said to me since he's been home is about football. "Did they win?"

He shakes his head flatly. "No."

I draw my eyebrows together curiously. "Where did you watch the highlights? I know it wasn't on your phone, because your phone was here."

"I went to the library," he presses his mouth together, thinking. "You can use the computers there for free."

I nod, still curious to know more about where he was. And even more curious to know *why* he left in the first place. But I'm trying to be patient and understanding until I get the answers I want to know.

With his inhale he says, "Your father commentated between games."

I'm surprised my father didn't remind me to watch the game when he called. Not that I gave him much of a chance with our clipped conversation.

He continues, "And he announced to all of America that he's expecting a child."

I fight the urge to roll my eyes. "He called to tell me on Thanksgiving. It was kind of difficult to hold it together since I was in the middle of trying to find you."

His solemn expression shifts as his eyes brighten. "You went looking for me?"

I give him a look of anguish. "Of course I did." I touch the side of his face. "You're my husband, I was worried something happened to you."

He flicks his eyes between mine then presses his mouth to my lips suddenly. Kissing me with intensity.

After a moment, he presses his forehead to mine. Then in a whisper, he says, "I'm so sorry I did this to you, Christine."

"It's okay." I know he's sorry. It's all he's been saying. I forgive him. But I still want to know why he left. "You're here now, and that's what's important. You came back."

"That's the thing." He releases me and shifts to his back. Resting his bent arms at the sides of his head and looking up at the ceiling. "It's like I couldn't stop myself. I knew what I was doing, but I couldn't control it. I walked out the door and kept walking." He looks at me from the corner of his eye. "And I didn't snap out of it until your father said he was having a baby. Then I remembered you. I remembered our baby. I saw how excited your father was, and it made me want to feel excited about our baby again."

I'm not sure how to interpret what he's saying. How does someone know they're doing something, without having any control over what they're doing?

He presses his palms to his eyes. "I'm so sorry, Christine. I don't know what happened."

I pull one hand from his face, and shift so I'm seated cross legged on the bed next to him. I lean forward, looking directly at him when I say, "What *did* happen?"

He shakes his head with an expression full of anguish. "I don't know. I really don't know."

I exhale, feeling the frustration rising despite how patient I'm trying to be. "But what *did* happen? What was happening before you left? What were you thinking about?"

He sits up, scooting up against the headboard. His mouth opens but nothing comes out. His eyes are shifting, searching the duvet in thought before he says, "I took a shower. I hadn't been sleeping very good for weeks, it was the same story that night. Then I saw you, the city lights were shining through the window on your face. So I went to shut the curtains, but when I looked down at the traffic below. It was like the streets were calling me."

I crease my brow, not understanding. "What do you mean, the streets were calling?"

He pulls his eyes from the duvet to meet mine. When he notices my unsettled expression, he presses his hands to his face and runs them to the sides of his head, up into his hair. He exhales hard, turning his head away from me. In a low, disappointed voice he says, "I don't know how to explain it." He shakes his head. "You're supposed to be the person that understands me."

I take his hand. Feeling the familiar distance and *darkness* returning. "Declan," he looks at me, "I am the person that understands you. But can you blame me for not being able to read your mind? That's not fair. I'm not a mind reader."

"How do I explain something to you that I don't even understand?"

"Try."

"I can't!"

"Why did you delete your music?"

"It's not going anywhere."

"Where do you want it to go?"

He shakes his head, frustrated and confused. "I don't know."

I drop my head back and exhale, vexed by his lacking memory. "I know you were searching for places in L.A."

He looks at me with widening eyes for a moment. Taken aback.

I continue, "If you really want to pursue music and move, just tell me."

"I don't want to move. That's what makes this so difficult to explain. Sometimes I want to be a musician. But most of the time I just want this. Us."

"Then why did you leave?"

He pulls his brows together, hardening his expression. "I. Don't. Know." He pauses, enunciating each word to get his point across.

Since I don't want this to turn into a fight, in a gentle voice, I say, "Okay. I'm trying to understand. So, what happened next?"

He keeps his eyes on me for moment, noticing I'm not dropping the subject, but also that I'm not getting defensive. He drops his head back against the headboard, pulling his gaze from me. His bare chest rises with his inhale as he says, "Then I walked out the front door. And kept walking. I don't know why, other than the fact that as soon as I was gone, I felt better. I felt like I was supposed to be hidden in plain sight. That I wasn't a failure anymore. That I wasn't anyone or anything."

His inner monologue burns me. I want to shake him, and demand he never talk to himself like that ever again. Even if it's just his thoughts. How could he think that he's a failure?

"You're not a failure," I say not stopping my voice from wavering. "You're gifted and creative. You're successful at everything you do."

His eyes flash compassion toward me, but he doesn't move or say anything. I can tell he doesn't believe me. His journals repeat it over and over. His negative thoughts consume him. And the one thing he thought would fix it was being with me.

And I'm going to show him he was right. I'm going to show him he's stronger than his mind.

"I wish you could see yourself the way I see you." My jaw tightens as the tears burn my eyes. "So badly, I wish you could see what I see. Because you're everything to me."

FORTY-ONE

I make my way to the kitchen where Declan is pouring batter into the waffle maker.

Glancing at me and with a grin he says, "What are you doing up so early?"

I approach him. "If I smell food, I'm out of bed. Remember, I'm eating for two?"

He grips my hips and kisses me. "I was going to bring you breakfast in bed."

"You're too sweet."

He kisses the top of my head. Then turning around, he pulls a small box from the cupboard above the refrigerator. It's the perfect place to hide a gift from me, since I can't reach up there without standing on a chair.

Facing me again, he says, "Don't expect anything less on Valentines Day."

I smile at him, taking the box from his grip and opening it. There's a pearl ring. My mouth falls agape with my smile. "It's beautiful."

He kisses the side of my face, and takes it from the small box to place it on my finger. "Just like you."

I laugh. "Stop, that's so cringey."

He laughs, knowing I hate cliches. Then he forks the waffle from the waffle maker onto a plate. "Fruit or syrup?"

I roll my hands over the top of my belly, feeling like a queen with the pearl garnishing my finger. "Both."

He begins drizzling syrup and decorating the massive waffle with strawberries and blueberries when he says, "Go back to our bedroom."

"Why-y?" I say drawing out the word curiously.

"So I can serve you breakfast in bed." He turns to retrieve the milk from the fridge.

A short breath of laughter escapes my nose. I take a strawberry from the top of the waffle before retreating to our bedroom. Smitten by my husband.

"I saw that," he says as I head down the hall.

I maneuver myself back into bed, but I make sure I'm sitting upright and place a pillow on my legs to act as a table for me to set my breakfast plate on. Not that I need it since my belly will suffice.

When Declan arrives, he's holding the plate with the waffle and a glass of milk in one hand. And in the other hand, he's carrying his guitar.

A grin spreads across my face. "Did you come to serenade me while I eat breakfast?"

He kisses my cheek and places the plate on the pillow in front of me. "It wouldn't be Valentines Day if I didn't."

I take a bite of my waffle and watch him as he adjusts himself on the corner of our bed near my feet. Then he begins to sing,

One look into your eyes,
and I see mine.
Two hearts
beating synchronously.
I notice
and can't catch my breath
until I'm complete.

My soul's on fire
like the loudest choir
all shouting from Heaven
in a serenade session.

The flames all rise
look into my eyes
when I say, "Again
you're my only person."

I've let you see
into my core.

The broken parts
that lead to poor
choices that rock
your world.
Nothing about it's
beautiful.

My soul's on fire
like the loudest choir
all shouting from Heaven
in a serenade session.

The flames all rise
look into my eyes
when I say, "Again
you're my only person."

I burn for you.
Listen to these words,
these last four words,
I love you more.
I burn for you.
You are my muse.
These last four words.
I love you more.

My soul's on fire
like the loudest choir
all shouting from heaven
in a serenade session.

The flames all rise
look into my eyes
when I say, "Again
you're my only person.

My love, your heart
a never-ending part.
Listen, what we swore:
The one who understands,

I love you more.

I nearly knock my plate over, while I spill the glass of milk as I lunge toward him with tears of complete joy.

He notices the tears and says, "Hey, don't cry, it's just a little spilled milk."

I laugh at his attempt at humor during such a sweet moment. "I'm absolutely in love with you," I say crashing into him. "I don't know how you do that."

He's flashing me the familiar smug smile I fell in love with years ago, when he says, "It just comes naturally."

My smile widens. "You *have* to record that song and post it immediately. I think it's your best work yet."

He shakes his head, setting his guitar across the bed and locking his arms around me. "That song is for you."

"What's it called?"

He grins smugly. "Four Words."

"Why?"

"The one who understands." He dips his head toward me and says, "That's you. And…" He raises one brow. *"I love you more.* They're four simple words, but hold so much depth, and history to them."

I kiss his mouth and rest my nose on his before I scoot backwards to find a towel to clean up the spilled milk. As I reach the bathroom, I take a towel from the cupboard. When I face him, I lean my shoulder into the doorframe and cradle the towel in my arms.

"What?" he says approaching me.

I hand him the towel, staring at him intently. "Thank you," I say with a small but fully grateful voice. "I can't imagine doing any of this without you."

He smiles, then, "Thank you."

I narrow my eyes, trying to figure out what he's thanking me for.

He pulls his lower lip into his mouth, then releases it with his smile. "Thank you for loving me when I'm hard to love."

I hug him. "That's what marriage is for."

He tucks my head under his chin, hugging me back. "You've loved me through the ugliest parts."

I hope it's been the ugliest parts.

It's been three months since he walked out and only returned because of the plaguing guilt he felt after seeing my father proudly announce that he and Natasha are expecting.

Since then, I've finally found a therapist I can connect with. She's been helpful in so many ways. She's a big believer in balance. Balance in the aspect of health and wellness. She believes it's important to have balance in body, mind, and soul. Which I appreciate about her and have seen a drastic change in our marriage since we've prioritized balancing ourselves. Together.

Declan came to a few of the first sessions with me. But once we figured out how to *balance* he didn't think there was a reason for him to continue therapy.

I guess that's what people are supposed to do. Go to therapy to get help. To heal. And then to move forward in their lives. Balanced.

But I still go once a week. Maybe as insurance, just in case we struggle. Or if I find Declan on the floor meditating on his dark thoughts again. I hope those parts of him are dead. But I'm not going to pretend like I don't worry it will happen again.

"I'll clean this up," he says motioning toward the spilled milk. "You get ready for the appointment."

I smile. Grateful for his help. It's no easy task bending over to do anything these days. "I love my midwife, but I'll be glad when we don't have to see her anymore."

"Only one more appointment before she's here," he says referring to our baby while wiping the towel over the hardwood floor. "And I wouldn't be sad if she decided to come sooner."

"Me too." My eyes brighten. "Maybe we can do a water birth in the pool at the birthing center? I think that would be relaxing."

※

"Can you turn that down?"

I glance at him, then twist the volume knob until the voices from the radio quiet through the car speakers.

He has seemed slightly agitated since we got in the car. I'm not sure why. Maybe it's because it's Valentines Day and I didn't get him anything.

It's not that I didn't get him anything. I have a reservation at Marcel's for dinner tonight. I was waiting to surprise him after the appointment, but maybe I should've told him sooner.

"Are you okay?" I ask.

He keeps his eyes forward and his grip tight on the steering wheel. In place of a response, he lets out a harsh exhale.

I debate on keeping dinner a surprise. But since he seems upset, I decide to break my silence. "So I was going to surprise you later, but I have a reservation at Marcel's for dinner tonight." I smile, hoping for a reaction. "It's your favorite restaurant. I thought you'd be excited since we haven't been there in a while."

I'm not sure why he's not responding. But I don't want to press him too much, since it is Valentines Day and we're getting a 3D image of our baby at the appointment today.

I switch the radio station, maybe some music will change his mood.

"Christine," his tone is cold. "I told you to turn it down."

I tilt my head, creasing my brows in confusion. The volume isn't up that much. "It is down, I'm just trying to find a different station."

"Turn it off!"

I flip my head up in his direction. My eyes widen. Stunned. I can't speak because he's acting like a completely different person than he was this morning.

I notice his breathing is intense, along with his white-knuckle grip on the steering wheel. He begins to accelerate beyond the speed limit.

"Turn it off, now!"

I press the power button immediately, silencing the radio. "Okay, it's off. What's going on?"

He's breathing so hard that it's the only sound inside the car. Along with the increasing sound of the engine revving as we speed faster down the freeway.

My expression shifts to concern as I instinctually brace myself. "What are you doing? Slow down!" I notice we're weaving through traffic at an alarming speed. "Declan, you're starting to scare me."

Just then, he veers toward the left side of the road. He slams on the brake, causing the tires to screech on the road as we come to an abrupt halt.

Then, without warning, he lets out the deepest agonized yell I've ever heard.

I cover my ears. I'm not sure if it's so loud because I'm so close to him, or because we are contained in the small space of the car. Either way his painful shout reverberates past my eardrum down into my core where a Braxton Hicks causes my stomach to tighten.

I don't realize he's stopped yelling until I notice my ears ringing when he steps out of the car, slamming the door behind him. I want to get out and talk to him but I'm afraid to open my door since cars are speeding by on my side. I'm not sure why he pulled off on the wrong side of the road.

His back is to me as he presses his hands into the concrete road divider and leans forward, hanging his head between his shoulders.

It's not long before a police car pulls up behind us with his lights on. I try to lean over into Declan's seat to reach the button that rolls the window down. But it's no use with my belly in the way, not to mention my short limbs.

It only takes a few moments before the officer approaches the car and opens the driver's side door. He ducks his head down to speak to me. "It's illegal to park on the left side of the road," he says in a firm voice above the traffic outside. "I'm letting him go with a warning since he's not feeling well."

I nod even though I'm unsure of what Declan said, or his reasoning for stopping in the first place. It seems the officer knows more about that than I do.

He motions toward my door. "I'll move traffic and come around to let you out so you're safe to walk around the car and drive." I guess I'm going to be driving us to the appointment now. Not that I want to go anymore. I'd rather go home. Or to therapy. Or even to a parking lot where I can sit with Declan and figure out what just happened.

The officer gives me a nod before saying, "I'll give you a bag in case he gets sick again before you get home, and so you don't have to pull over in this kind of traffic again. It really is a hazard if a car is stopped on either side of the freeway here."

I nod in agreement. "Okay, thank you." I'm not exactly sure what I've just agreed to. Apparently, I'm driving us home now, instead of the appointment. And apparently Declan told the officer he got sick and that's why we're pulled over on the wrong side of traffic. Maybe he did get sick. I didn't have much time to ask him between his yelling and exiting the car.

While I'm waiting, I call to reschedule my appointment for today. There's no point in trying to get there on time now.

After the officer makes sure we've safely exited and entered the car in our designated places, he offers to follow us home, but I decline his offer. Ensuring we'll go straight there.

The car ride is silent.

The walk back up to the apartment is silent.

The house is silent.

I hate how silent it is.

Instead of demanding that Declan explain himself, which I really want to do right now, I decide to cool off before trying to speak to him.

Part of me knows his mind is consuming him again, but the other part is frustrated he doesn't just talk to me. How hard is it to tell me how he's feeling?

I close the French doors where my piano is and scoot the bench out so I have room to fit. It's been a while since I've played the baby grand piano he got me. Honestly with everything I've been juggling, it's been a while since I've played any instrument at all.

Since Declan re-activated his online accounts and started recording and posting music again, I haven't been helping him much with his music. Aside from singing back up or harmony from time to time.

It feels good to play the piano again.

Feeling the keys under my fingers like I never stopped playing.

I play several of the classical pieces I know by heart when I check the time and realize it's been over an hour. It's amazing how much a person's mood can change from one hour to the next, especially when they're doing something constructive like playing Beethoven's full Moonlight Sonata and Chopin's saddest pieces.

My mind feels clearer as I shift between the piano and the bench, readying myself to leave the room so I can have a calm discussion with Declan. If he's ready, of course. But when I stand to exit, I see Declan sitting on the other side of the room at my keyboard bench. The one that's a little too short for my keyboard. Which causes Declan's knees to stick up higher than they would if the bench were meant for a piano.

His elbows are resting on his raised knees as he cradles his head in his hands. I'm not sure if his posture indicates he wants me to continue playing, or if I should leave so he can be alone.

I decide to sit back down on the piano bench that fits my small grand piano perfectly. Only I'm sitting on it backward to face Declan.

Just as I sit down, he lifts his head, running both hands down his face. His dark expression I saw in the car has shifted to exhaustion and remorse.

I look at him helplessly. The one thing I've dreaded returning to our marriage is here. The worst part is that I don't even know what *that* is.

When we talked about it in therapy, our therapist attributed his behavior to insomnia, low self-esteem, and possible depression. She wanted to spend more time with him one-on-one for a proper diagnosis, but that never happened.

He folds his mouth in and keeps his gaze lowered before saying, "I can feel you when you play."

I keep my eyes fixed on him. My expression full of anguish. Because I know he's suffering. And I'm beginning to realize that when he's suffering, he can't stop his mind. I know he wants to, but he can't. I just wish there was a way to get ahead of it before it happens.

He rests the side of his head into his palm as he looks at me. "I felt it *all*."

I let out a sad exhale. "What did you feel?" I'm glad he can feel me, but I wish he would talk about the feelings he has going on inside of himself.

He looks down, blinking in thought. "I felt your anger. I felt your defeat. I felt your sadness." Shifting his eyes to meet mine, he says, "I felt your love."

He's right. I felt all those things while I played. Banging on the keys, striking them fiercely, only to fall into the trance of gently pressing the deepest chords, and gliding over the sweetest melodies.

In a quiet voice I say, "What happened today?"

Flexing his hands, he says, "I got caught up in my head." He scrunches his forehead and pulls his brows down, as if he's experiencing the pain all over again. "I was fine, until I wasn't."

"What changed from this morning? We were having such a sweet day together."

He clenches his hand into a fist and knocks it against the bench. With a slightly raised voice, he says, "I'm trying to talk about it, and comments like that aren't helping."

I keep my tone calm. "I'm not trying to hurt you. I'm trying to understand what happened."

He thrusts his arms at his sides before slapping his hands on the bench. "Something happened after you mentioned the birthing pool." He rakes his hand through his hair with a tightening jaw. "I don't know what it was about that, but I couldn't stop thinking about Eli once you mentioned it."

My mouth parts, but no words come out.

He shakes his head. "It spiraled from there."

I stand to make my way over to him, but he rises and makes his way to me before I meet him. "Thank you for telling me," I say.

He takes my hands in his. I can sense the regret in his expression. "I'm only sorry I didn't tell you sooner."

"We're going to figure this out," I say hoping we can keep coming up from this. "We are figuring it out."

He nods then looks at me deeply with a pleading expression. "Thank you for being the person that understands me."

I wouldn't say that I smile at him, but my expression is more amiable when I say, "Four words."

"You are my muse." If eyes could smile, that's what his are doing now as he says, "The one who understands, I love you more."

.

FORTY-TWO

Pineapple.

The smell of pineapple is infusing my nostrils before I'm even awake. I swipe my hand as it knocks against something.

"Hey! Be careful." It's too early for Avery's voice to be screaming in my ears.

I don't bother apologizing. She should be apologizing to me. I'm two weeks past my due date, and probably the same size as one of her orca whales.

"Don't shove food in my face and that won't happen," I say with apparent irritation. I should not be awake. I don't mean to sound irritated with her. It's not her. Okay, maybe it is a little bit because of her. But mostly, I'm just tired of being pregnant.

She picks a piece of pineapple out of the bowl with her fingers and plops it in her mouth. "I was reading that if you eat a whole pineapple, it induces labor."

"That's a load of crap. It sounds as legitimate as your castor oil method." Which obviously didn't work since I'm still pregnant.

She scoots next to me on the bed and plops another piece of pineapple into her mouth. "You won't know unless you try."

She has a point. And right now, I'm willing to do anything to get this baby out. "Give me that."

She grins and hands the bowl to me.

I hate to admit it, but I'm kind of glad she's here. I told her to come at the end of April, hoping Nova would be here before then and I would have already bonded with her. But Avery was afraid she'd miss the entire birthing experience—which I didn't want her here for—and the first week of Nova's life outside of my belly— which I also didn't want her here for. So she booked a flight and showed up early.

Well, early for the due date I gave. Which ended up being after my real due date.

She's been here for ten days already, and I've tried everything from spicy foods to light jogging to try and get this baby to budge. Nothing has worked so far.

She scoots off the bed and begins digging in my dresser. She's made it her job to feed me and pick out my clothing every day before she sets us out sightseeing for the day.

"Is there anything you haven't tried from the list?" She's also made a labor-inducing-list in my notes on my phone so I can cross them off as we try them.

I check my phone. "Looks like everything, aside from acupuncture and..." I scroll until my eyes meet the last three lettered word on the list. I let out a broody groan.

She tosses a maternity dress on my bed and takes my phone. "And what?" A line forms between her brows as she skims over the list. Then she raises her eyebrows up and down and tosses my phone on the bed next to me. "Maybe what gets the baby in there, gets the baby out too?"

I stuff a piece of pineapple in my mouth and finally slide out of bed. "Yeah, well, I need Declan for that and he's at work today."

After the last breakdown he had, he agreed to go to therapy with me again. But just like the time before, as soon as he felt normal and balanced, he stopped going.

He's been working more. Preparing for the busy summer season that's approaching at the museum.

"When will he be home?"

I shrug. "What's today?" It's a legitimate question since I haven't been to work in over a month, and I have no reason to pay attention to what day of the week it is.

"Wednesday."

I rub my eyes and realize I forgot to take my makeup off last night as my mascara smudges on my hand. "He usually comes home early on Wednesdays. So he should be here by two o'clock."

She flashes me a wide grin. "Looks like today's schedule includes acupuncture for brunch and afternoon delight for a snack."

I look at her for a moment to process what she's said, then we both throw our heads back in laughter at her ridiculous statement.

There's nothing I hate more than to admit Avery is right about something. But in this instance, I'm more than okay with it.

Nova Harmony Price was born late last night after seven hours of labor.

I can't get over how perfect she is. She looks just like a babydoll. All seven pounds and four ounces of her.

And the best part, is that Declan is absolutely in love with her.

In fact, he's holding her now while Avery is meeting the UberEats driver to get our dinner down in the lobby.

Declan sits next to me on the bed and smiles. His grin is captivated with how proud he is. "Can you believe we made this?"

I shake my head. "I thought she would never come out."

"Yet, here she is." Even his brown eyes are smiling proudly. "She's really cute isn't she?"

"She looks just like me."

I can't argue with him since she is his twin. Even my midwife and doula commented on how much she looks like him. And I don't mind at all.

Avery enters the room with an armload of Jimmy John's. "You won't believe who the UberEats driver looks like."

I reach for my sandwich. "Who?"

She hands me a bag, then begins unloading the rest of the food onto the table. "You have to guess."

I unwrap my sandwich and take a ravishing bite. "I don't know, Keanu Reeves?"

She shakes her head and takes Nova from Declan's arms so he can sit down to eat. "Mr. Bealey from sixth grade."

I laugh, holding my hand under my chin to catch any crumbs that might fall from my mouth. "How did you expect me to guess that?"

She shrugs. Then looking down, she gently sways Nova from side to side. "If a daughter ever looked just like her father, it would be Nova."

I roll my eyes with a grin. There must be *something* she got from me.

"Where did that name come from anyway?" she says, running her hand over the top of Nova's wispy brown hair.

Declan looks at me with a smile. He knows that I found his USB in his coat pocket while he was gone and figured out that he wanted to name her Nova. We've talked about it and his reasoning for naming her Nova made me fall in love with the name even more.

He shifts his gaze over to Avery and runs his hand over his mouth before saying, "Nova is Latin. It means *hope* and *new*. It's the same name given to the stars that suddenly appear in the sky without any indication or warning. These instant stars that come into existence also shine brighter than any other stars." His eyes shine when he looks at me with a reminiscent grin, as he continues, "Nova is a perfect name for her, since she came into our lives unannounced and in an instant. And I'm certain she will brighten every day of the rest of our lives too."

There's nothing more attractive about Declan Price, than watching him fall entirely in love with our daughter.

FORTY-THREE

"She doesn't fit in her outfit."

I flip my head around to see Declan holding Nova who is squeezed into the cutest Fourth of July outfit.

I press my mouth together, but the laughter bursts through.

He shakes his head. "Christine, it's not funny. She's grown out of all of her newborn clothes."

I turn back to adjusting the car seat again. Not only is she growing out of her newborn clothes, but she's growing out of her car seat. Thank goodness we purchased one that will adjust to her rapid growth until she's a toddler.

Nova coos up at Declan. She always coos for him. She rarely coos for me, if ever. I'm beginning to think she only sees me as a food source.

"What is she going to wear to the parade?" He sounds honestly concerned.

"She's a baby, she doesn't care what she wears."

He adjusts her in his arms. "She does. Or she will at least when she's older and looks back at photos from today. She'll wonder why she was celebrating the Fourth of July in a hippo onesie."

I shift to face him with a look of contemplation. "I love those hippo onesies."

He looks at me disappointedly. "Christine."

I lift my hands. "Alright, I'll run to Target and pick up a new outfit for the parade."

He takes a step closer to me and lowers his face so I can kiss him. "Thank you," he says, talking about the outfit I'm about to go out and buy, that's probably going to last ten minutes before it has spit up on it. Then he lifts Nova so I can kiss her too.

When I return with the new outfit, I can hear Declan singing and strumming on his guitar gently.

Nova is in her swing almost asleep.

He looks up when I close the door and winks at me. "I just fed her and she was getting restless so I put her in the swing."

I place the plastic bag with the outfit on the table. "Good thinking."

He meets me in the kitchen, standing behind me as he grips my waist. "I'm losing interest."

"In going to the parade?"

"Not that."

I turn to face him, wrapping my arms around his neck. "In what then?"

His eyes flick between mine, as if he's trying to tell me without words.

I tilt my head in confused anticipation.

With his exhale he says, "I'm not interested in working at the museum anymore."

"Why?" I crease my brow. Shocked he would ever want to leave. "What happened?"

He sways his head as he looks over my shoulder. "Nova happened."

I smile. "What were you planning to do instead?"

He shrugs with a smug grin. "Full time father?"

I laugh. "Try again."

He rocks his head from side to side, debating on how to say the next words to me. "I want to pursue my music. I want to take it seriously instead of playing for a hobby." He runs his tongue along his bottom lip. "Maybe I'll get famous, who knows."

I bite at the inside of my lip. Chewing on the information he's just shared while carefully choosing the words I use when I reply. "Let's do it."

His eyes widen. "Really?"

I nod with a smile. "Yes. But I think we should stay at the museum too."

"I don't know what to say."

I shift onto my tiptoes and kiss him. "You can start by telling me I'm the best wife in the whole world."

His picks me up and I laugh when his goatee tickles my neck as he kisses me. He sets me on the counter and looks at me with a grateful expression. "You're the best wife in the whole world."

FORTY-FOUR

"He's not responding to anything, Christine. I'm not sure what else to do," Margaret's voice is filled with terror. "He's been standing outside the building for a couple of hours, if not more."

I shift my phone to the other ear as I pick Nova up off the floor where she was playing. "Hold off on the ambulance. I can be there in ten minutes."

She exhales, as if she doesn't like that I'm asking her to wait. But she doesn't know Declan like I do. I'm certain he's having an episode. He's my husband and I know him. And I'm sure once I get there, I can talk to him and bring him back to reality.

"I'm walking out the door now," I say reassuringly.

When I get off the phone with Margaret, I hurry to my car and pack Nova into her car seat. She's pleasantly happy to look at herself in the mirror I placed on the seat for her on the car ride until we park at the museum.

I quickly unbuckle Nova. Gripping her on my hip, I rush down the sidewalk until I round the corner where I see Margaret waiting with Declan.

I slow my stride as I begin to approach them. There's nothing that seems too alarming about the sight of them standing together. Until Margaret rushes over to me in a panic.

Before she's completely reached me, she says, "Oh thank God you're here. I'm calling the ambulance now."

My expression shifts into confusion. "Margaret, please. I don't think that's necessary." Declan's not pacing with trepidation. He's not yelling or pulling at the top of his hair. He's just standing. Staring with his hands in his pockets.

Margaret is walking next to me now. She seems frantic. As we

294

approach Declan she says, "Let me know when you're ready for me to make that call." She reaches her arms out for Nova. "I can hold her while you talk to him."

I nod and hand Nova to her. She walks several steps away and lets Nova reach up into the trees, pulling at the leaves.

"Hey, what's all the commotion about?" I say with my smile as I reach for Declan's arm.

My smile suddenly fades to concern. He feels stiff. Even when I pull his hand from his pocket, it's as if his arm is packed with weights as it falls to his side when I let go.

"Declan?" Even my voice is full of concern now. This is different than anything I've seen with him before. "Are you okay?"

No response.

Just a silent vacant stare.

Like he's not there. His body is standing in front of me, but *Declan* is gone.

I remember a technique that my therapist suggested when he gets stuck in his mind like this, and I say, "Five senses."

I kiss his mouth. "Taste. What do you taste?"

Nothing.

I pick up his hand and press it to the side of my face. "Touch. What do you feel?"

Nothing.

I run my finger down the bridge of his nose. "Smell. What do you smell in the air right now?"

Nothing.

I lift myself up on my toes so I can reach my mouth to his ear. And in a quiet voice, I say, "Hear. What do you hear? Traffic? The birds?" I press my eyes shut. "*Me?*"

Nothing.

I take my phone from my pocket and turn the screen on. Showing him my lock screen, which is a photo of him blowing raspberries on Nova's cheek as she laughs. "See." My voice is weak. "What do you see?"

Nothing.

I stare back at him for a long moment. Hoping he will come back. Hoping he has enough willpower to get out of his mind and back into his body. But there's *nothing.* Which causes my heart to thicken with a heaviness I've never felt before.

"Declan, you're starting to scare me," I say noticing how

indescribably vacant and lost his eyes are. And *dark*.

No, no, no. Please, no. Not the darkness. I don't know how to reach him in the dark. I don't know where he goes. But he's unreachable. Even for me.

I place my hands on his shoulders and shake him gently. He barely moves. Stiff in his statue.

This feels…petrifying.

I don't know what to do.

So, I face Margaret who is forcing her smile for Nova. When she catches my imploring eyes, I give her a nod. Letting her know it's time to call the ambulance.

I fold my lips in as the corners of my mouth begin to quiver. I'm trying to keep it together. For Margaret. For Nova. And for whatever part of Declan is still here.

My knee is bouncing as I wait for someone to tell me what's going on.

Margaret took Nova to walk around the hospital in the stroller for me. She wanted to give me some privacy, but I liked the distraction of her company. And Nova's.

Now my pulse is pounding so heavily I can see my heartbeat through my shirt.

"Mrs. Price?"

I flip my head to see the doctor followed by a tall middle-aged woman with bright red curly hair and lipstick the same shade as her hair.

I inhale sharply. "Is he okay?"

The doctor nods. "He's going to be fine." He lifts his hand out to acknowledge the woman. "This is Dawn, she's with behavioral health and had a few questions to go over with you."

I raise my eyebrows, unsure what she needs to know since I already told the paramedics, two nurses, and the doctor what happened. Which isn't much.

I shake her hand. "Christine."

I feel better when she takes a seat next to me. It feels like we're at the same level now instead of having her towering above me. She smiles, and I notice she has a full, stained, crooked grin. "Nice to meet you, Christine."

I blink at her, hoping she explains how Declan is doing. When she doesn't I say, "Is he responding yet? Can I see him?"

She places her hands on top of a folder and clipboard on her lap. Then leaning forward slightly toward me, she says, "Declan is going to be fine. They treated his catatonic state with Thorazine, so you'll get to see him soon. I was hoping to ask you a few questions before we head in there, if that's okay?"

My leg begins bouncing again. "Catatonic?" I look at the doctor for an explanation, then back to Dawn when he doesn't answer. "What do you mean?"

She smiles pleasantly, without showing her teeth this time. I feel like she's trying to keep me calm, so I oblige her and straighten my leg. Forcing it to stop bouncing. And give her a similar grin.

"The state he was in when he got here," she says, "is known as a catatonic state. It's just as you described to the doctor. He was unresponsive but conscious."

I nod, and try to sound calm when I say, "I understand. So, is he back to normal now? And will he be able to leave soon?" If there's nothing medically wrong with him, I don't see why we can't go home.

She responds with, "Possibly."

That doesn't sound convincing.

She opens her folder and pulls a pen from the top of the clip board. "You just had a baby?" She is speaking with an upward inflection now.

I nod, realizing that the doctor brought her in for some kind of behavior questioning since she works for behavioral health. Which I'm still not exactly sure what that means. "Yes, her name is Nova. She's almost six months old."

Her eyes wrinkle in the corners with her crooked grin. "So sweet. That's a precious age." She scribbles something then, "Has that been stressful? Having an infant at home with late nights and changing schedules."

I exhale, realizing these are leadup questions to whatever she's really concerned about. "It's been an adjustment, but Nova is an easy baby. Declan adores her. I've never seen a better father, honestly." My expression goes flat when I say, "Is there something going on with Declan that I should be concerned about? He's had episodes before, but nothing like this."

Dawn's smile falls slightly. "What do his episodes normally look like?"

I fold my mouth in, searching the ceiling in thought. "Normally, he zones out, lays on the floor in silence, leaves for a few days, or yells at the top of his lungs in a panic."

"What sort of things does he yell?"

I shrug. "The last time he was yelling at me to turn the radio off, and then he just burst into a loud roar like I've never heard before." She nods and continues writing.

I fold my arms. "There's nothing consistent about his episodes either. It's like he gets a thought in his head that he can't shake until it begins to sabotage his entire mind."

"What kinds of thoughts?"

I lift one shoulder. "Negative thoughts."

Dawn meets my eyes as her hand freezes, holding her pen in position. "How long have these episodes been going on?"

I shrug. "I'm not sure, but..." I wrestle with the idea of telling her about the journals or not. I decide to be general about the information. "Since before we were together. A few years, I think."

She clears her throat before saying, "Any drug or alcohol use?"

"No drugs. We occasionally have wine with dinner, but nothing excessive." I don't mention the time he was drunk with Arty since it was only once and out of character for him.

"Any family nearby?"

I shake my head. "No. We've been in D.C. a year. We moved from Washington, but our families are both in Nevada."

"How would you describe his relationship with them?"

"It's good." Which I think is true. Or at least it was until his father started showing signs of dementia.

The sound of her pen etching across the paper is starting to make me nervous.

"Are either of you taking medication?"

I shake my head, no.

"In any sort of counseling? Or support groups?"

I nod.

"What kind?"

With my inhale, I say, "I'm in therapy. Sometimes Declan comes. Only it's usually after one of his episodes. And he typically stops going after one or two sessions, when he starts to feel like himself again."

"And how's that been going?"

I sit up straighter in my chair. "Good."

She nods with understanding. With her same gentle questioning, she says, "Any kind of mood disorders in his family?"

I tilt my head and say, "Mood disorders?" Unsure of what classifies something as a mood disorder.

"Depression, bipolar, post-partum depression, anything like that?"

I shake my head, no. But then I remember Sean. "Actually—"

She raises her eyebrows when she looks back at me with intrigue.

"His dad," I say. "It's not really a mental health thing, but he was diagnosed with dementia recently. Not really a mood disorder. But, I don't know if that's important to know."

Her eyes shift to the doctor, which makes me pull my brows together in confusion and turn to face him too.

The doctor has been quietly leaning back against the wall in the room with his arms folded over his chest. But when he hears my statement, he pushes himself from the wall and lifts his chin up with narrowing eyes that seem to be inspecting me. Maybe not inspecting *me* but inspecting my statement.

Now the doctor and Dawn are looking at each other with the same knowing expression. As if they've just found the missing piece to whatever is going on with Declan, but are both hesitant to say it out loud. And in front of me.

I wish I wasn't so good at studying people.

The doctor scratches at the stubble on his chin. With the best positive tone he can curate, he says, "Has your husband had any recent or past head injuries?"

Without breaking eye contact I say, "He's had more head injuries than I can count on one hand."

He keeps his eyes on mine until he fully inhales and exhales through his nose. Then he looks at Dawn and says, "I'll be back with Dr. Fidore."

She nods aggressively, as if she expected him to say this.

I feel my hands go cold as my throat tightens. I don't know who Dr. Fidore is, but I'm assuming the information I just gave requires a specialist of some sort.

"Why does Declan need another doctor?"

Dawn gives me a sympathetic expression. "Dr. Fidore is a research doctor and specializes with patients that have similar family history and symptoms as Declan."

I nod, without concrete assurance. "Is Declan still going to be okay?" I say, tensing my shoulders, unsure if I'll be able to withstand her response.

She gives me a subtle look of remorse with a small grin, then pats my arm before she says, "We're going to figure out what's going on with your husband as soon as we can."

My eyes dart to a leaf I've been twisting in my fingers. It's uniquely red with V-shaped angles. I took it from Nova earlier and thought maybe I would keep it and add it to the box of leaves Declan gave me. But now I'm not sure I want it as a memento of this day since it's going to remind me of the unfolding tragedy that's fracturing my life. And Declan's.

FORTY-FIVE

The clicking of Dawn's heels against the hospital floor are echoing as she pulls forward down the hall.

"His room is just a bit further this way," she says, motioning her arms in front of her.

I'm trying to keep up with her long strides.

She grins down at me. "Hopefully you'll get to see him before they take him back for the MRI scan."

My nerves are jittering in my throat so frantically it's making it difficult to take a decent breath. Not to mention how I'm rushing to keep up with her.

"It's right here," she says pulling at the door handle to reveal Declan sleeping in the hospital bed.

She holds the door open as I enter the room but when she doesn't follow me in, I turn back to face her. She says, "I'll be back later for an evaluation."

I nod. Then she closes the door and the sound of her clicking heels disappears down the long hallway.

I move a chair closer to the side of his bed where I can sit next to him. Making myself comfortable in anticipation of what's going to happen next.

Something comes over me and I can't catch my breath as the tears form in my eyes. Because even in his sleep, Declan looks like he's being tormented. The twisting look of pain infused in his resting expression is unbearable.

I blink the tears away as his eyes slowly open. But it's no use trying to hide my tears, since the sight of his bloodshot and sunken eyes shatters my anxiously beating heart.

Pulling his bottom lip in, he winces as he shifts in his bed. "I have to go." The words come out tired.

I'm not sure if he's disoriented from dehydration, but I know he can't leave so I rise and place my hand on his chest to keep him from trying to sit up. "You have to get an MRI."

Averting his gaze, his words come out slowly as he says, "You don't understand, I have to go."

I exhale. Still full of remorse and anguish for the state he's in and all the confusion coursing through both our minds. "We'll go home after the MRI." *Hopefully.*

He's shaking his head slowly and fixing his eyes on nothing in particular, but also concentrating on something thick in the front of his mind. "I have to go. I have to get out of here." His voice is quiet, yet far away. As if he's not saying this to me but someone else.

"Declan," I say, sitting on the edge of his bed as I press his hand over my heart. Trying to comfort myself with him, and comfort myself from him.

He glances at me. Then turns, looking past me again. "I have to go." His tone is quiet and haunted.

"Go where?"

His expression becomes vacant and lost. And what he says next sends a chill down my arms. "I have to suffer the consequences for what I've done."

I crease my brow. Not understanding what he's talking about. "What did you do?"

His eyes gloss over. "I have to go," his voice begins to break, "I'm so sorry."

I'm starting to worry. "Declan, what happened? What are you talking about?"

A doctor enters the room as Declan continues to quietly say that he has to go.

I approach the doctor. I press my palms together tightly in front of me. Unsure how to deliver the information to him about Declan's confusion.

"I'm Christine," I say with apparent fear in my voice, "his wife."

He nods and lifts a wrinkled hand in my direction. "Dr. Fidore."

I reciprocate his handshake. "He's…" I swallow down the cracking in my voice, then exhale. Looking over to Declan, but speaking to Dr. Fidore, I say, "He keeps saying he has to leave. I'm not sure what he's talking about. He's not himself. He seems distant and confused."

He adjusts his glasses and raises his bushy eyebrows. With his inhale he stands up straighter and without acknowledging my statement, he says, "I spoke with Dawn." He dips his head, glancing above his glasses over in Declan's direction when Declan repeats that he needs to go. Looking back at me, Dr. Fidore says, "We'll take him back for an MRI scan to see if we can figure out what's going on and get you some answers."

Then a technician comes in to take Declan away for the MRI.

Dr. Fidore exits the room.

And something feels so unsettling about this.

It seems as if everyone knows what's going on. Or at least has an idea about what's going on. But no one is telling me.

I sent Margaret home a few hours ago. She insisted she take Nova, but I don't want to burden her any more than I already have.

Nova is asleep on my chest.

Declan is asleep in his bed.

I wish I could sleep.

After the MRI scan, Dawn evaluated Declan. I took the opportunity to run home and gather a few things. Poor Nova is exhausted from all the shuffling around, and so am I.

No one is answering my questions in detail. So, I'm sitting here with a million different scenarios running through my mind while my husband and baby sleep peacefully. Or as peacefully as they can in a hospital room.

A gentle knock accompanies the quiet voice of Dawn entering the dark room. "Hey," she says with her familiar smile.

I give her a look of expectancy.

"I know you've been patiently waiting, but something came up that pulled Dr. Fidore away."

Nova shifts her head on my chest with a quiet whine. I rub her back gently and press her head back to my chest to encourage her to fall back asleep.

Dawn places her hand over her mouth. As if she realizes her voice has stirred Nova. Then she quietly says, "Sorry."

"It's fine," I say gently.

In a whisper, she says, "It shouldn't be too much longer. I'm sure you're ready to get home." Her eyes beam. "Dr. Fidore should be here soon."

With a nervous exhale, I say, "Is Declan okay?"

She nods. "He's going to be just fine." *I haven't heard that a million times today.*

I'm also tired of settling for that answer. So, I say, "But what *is* going on with him?"

Nova begins to fuss. When I can't get her to settle, I stand up, trying to keep from waking Declan. Dawn must sense my struggle since she pulls the door open for me then follows me to the hall.

To my relief, and Dawn's, Dr. Fidore is walking down the hall in our direction.

"Oh, good." Dawn waves him over. "Dr. Fidore, we were just about to discuss Declan's diagnosis."

Diagnosis?

He throws a thumb over his shoulder. "Sorry, I got hung up with another patient. I headed this way as soon as I could."

I'm swaying Nova back and forth in my arms, which has kept her from crying. And kept me from losing my mind. It's a form of unusual torture to make someone wait this long for information on their husband's condition. Especially since I don't know if I should prepare myself for brain surgery or his death. Which seems to be the only reasonable explanation for his random behavior and their prolonged elucidation.

I shouldn't scare myself. But I don't want to be naïve to the intense change in his behaviors. For all I know, he could have a brain bleed from falling off the ladder at the museum. This is all my fault. I should have taken him to the hospital the day he fell from the ladder. I should have taken his behavior more seriously. I could have avoided all of this if I had just pushed him to see a doctor then.

"Sorry to keep you, Mrs. Price." Dr. Fidore adjusts his glasses as he clears his throat. "So I'll get right to it then. Normally these things take quite some time to figure out. But with Dawn's evaluation, and what I've found on his scans—"

I suck in a terrified rush of air. "What'd you find on his scans?" Please don't say brain bleed. Or worse. *Cancer.*

"Well," he raises his eyebrows, "after comparing his scans with other patients of mine, I found that he has a brain abnormality in two areas of his frontal lobe, as well as a very small part of the hippocampus known as the CA1 that is found specifically in people with schizophrenia."

I stop swaying.

Chills run down my arms and the back of my neck.

My mouth falls open as my heart falls into the bottom of my stomach.

I don't pay attention to much of what Dr. Fidore says after that. Instead, I repeat the last word he said over in my mind. My thoughts fix on everything I've looked over and made excuses for in the last year and a half.

Declan's aversion to the radio *chatter*.

All the journal entries about the dark thoughts and screaming in his head.

All the lyrics he wrote depicting his haunted mind.

The insomnia.

The delusion of becoming a famous musician.

The ups and downs in his behavior.

Pushing his family away.

Running off without a trace.

I would have never guessed in a million years that all of it would point to this. To schizophrenia.

FORTY-SIX

I situate myself on the couch in Declan's room, which feels more like a dorm with all the furnishings than a hospital room. Earlier this week he was transferred to the psychiatric hospital to further explore treatment options.

Even though it's visiting hours, Declan is still sleeping. He's adjusting to the medication they've prescribed him but it seems to be affecting his sleep cycle.

My phone vibrates and I quickly check it. I'm not surprised to see a text from my mom. After I told her about Declan's diagnosis, she flew out to help with Nova. She'll never understand how helpful it's been having her here during all of this.

I smile when I open the text message. It's a picture of Nova grinning with a massive pastel orange bow on her head. My mom is taking full advantage of spoiling her first grandchild. We have more clothes, toys, and headbands with bows than I know what to do with since my mom has been here.

"You're happy about something."

I blink as I lift my face to see Declan pulling himself into a seated position on his bed. "You're awake," I say with relief.

The first few days he was at the psychiatric hospital, he was agitated, probably from coming off of the drugs they gave him at the hospital. Since then, he's been restless during visiting hours when I've come to see him. So now, I'm full of relief because this is the first time he's sounded like himself.

He stretches his arms over his head before shifting his body out of bed to sit next to me on the couch. "Well," he says, lifting his hand to affectionately push my hair over my shoulder like he's done so many times before, "what's putting a smile on your face?"

I show him my phone screen and he takes the phone to inspect the photo more closely.

"She's so cute." With a smile, he hands the phone back to me and says, "I can't wait to get out of here and hold her again." Then he fixes his eyes on mine.

I keep my gaze attached to his for a long moment. Savoring the fact that he's lucid. Savoring how he looks like himself again. And sounds like himself again.

Slipping my arms under his and around his torso, I hug him tightly. "I've missed you so much," I say with my face buried against his chest.

His chest rises with his breath as he envelopes me in his arms. In a deep whisper he says, "I've missed me too." As if he knows he hasn't been himself.

Lifting my chin, I look up at him but keep my arms locked around his body. "Why didn't you tell me what was happening to you? I would have helped you. I would have been more patient and understanding if I knew the reason for your behavior."

Running his finger down the side of my face with an apologetic expression, he says, "I didn't know something was happening to me."

I shake my head. "I have so many questions."

His eyes shine. "Ask them and I'll try my best to give you an authentic answer."

My mouth parts to speak as I begin to rewind each thought I've had since his diagnosis. "The voices. When did that start?"

He runs the tip of his tongue along his bottom lip as he looks up at the ceiling in thought. "I can't pinpoint it. But I think it was during grad school and the downward spiral my dad was on before dementia." He swallows, then, "At first, I thought it was my own thoughts. And for a long time, I assumed everyone could audibly hear their thoughts like I could. It wasn't until the voices got louder and more negative that I told anyone."

"Winnie?" I say.

Looking down at me he nods, then, "She assumed it was depression. Then later changed it to bipolar disorder. She encouraged me to get on medication, but I thought she was jumping to conclusions. Plus," his mouth curls up on one side into a small grin, "when I first saw you again at that gas station, it was as if you pulled back the clouds and showed me sunshine for the first time.

307

You lit up the dark world around me."

This makes me smile, but also worries me that he might still think of me as the antidote to his quandary. And I couldn't be less perfect for the position.

Placing his index finger under my chin, he gently tips my head back as he kisses me softly. He's kissing me as if he hasn't seen me in a long time. But it's also tainted with pain, as if he's never going to see me again. He pulls away then presses his bearded cheek to mine, as he says, "And nothing silenced the voices more than being with you did. Even the thought of being with you was enough to quiet my mind and inspire my musical creativity. That's why I wanted you to read my journals. So you could understand how deeply your presence affected me." He looks at me with a raised eyebrow. "I wasn't joking when I told you that you were my muse."

Hearing him call me that again washes tranquility over my ambiguity. But despite feeling a sense of peace, I still have questions. "The other day," I say. "At the hospital, you said something about facing the consequences of your actions."

He shakes his head with a look of remorse. "I don't really know what I was saying. Part of me thought I had taken you from a better life. One without me. One that was easier and more fulfilling. One that wouldn't cause you so much pain." Then his remorseful expression drops into complete agony. "I believed that my existence had made your life worse in every way. And part of me still thinks that's true. You were living your dreams before I inserted myself into your life."

"Listen," I say. My breathing is heavy with deep empathetic compassion as I place my hand against the side of his face where his growing beard tickles my palm. "This life is more meaningful than anything I ever planned for myself. Nothing is more important to me than you and Nova."

He nods, shifting his stinging brown eyes between mine.

"*Nothing*," I say again, reassuring him of the truth, "is more important than you and Nova."

His brow shifts downward with his apologetic expression.

I tilt my head with concern. "What's wrong?" I say, noticing the penetratingly sorrowful shift in his demeanor.

"I just want to be normal." His eyes are pleading, as if he's waiting for me to take it all away. Despite the medication, he still seems to be relying on me to choke out the storm clouds with the sunlight.

I don't know how to tell him I'm not the one for the job. I want to take it all away. I want to make his mind better. But I don't know how. All I can offer him is my love. I only hope that's enough for him.

His gaze shifts suddenly from me to the door where the chatter of passersby is heard. I can tell something about the people talking is troubling him by his panicked expression. So I get up off the couch and stand in front of the door. Invading his view and hopefully his thoughts too.

He drops his head, looking down at the cold linoleum. I can barely hear him when he says, "I don't know what's real or a delusion anymore."

I rush to him again, gripping his defeated face in my hands so he's looking at me. Then I say, "I'm real. Just focus on me and I'll always remind you of what's real."

FORTY-SEVEN

"Did you get a candle?" My mom says frantically icing the edges of the cake she's made for Nova's first birthday.

I place the paper plates I just bought at the store on the counter. "She's one. I don't think she even knows how to blow out a candle."

She pauses mid-icing to look at me with a face full of disappointment.

I exhale and take the baby monitor from the counter. "I'll be back in twenty minutes with a candle."

"You'll be happy you did," she sings.

One would think that when their mother offers to throw a birthday party for their daughter at her house, that she would have picked up a candle for the cake herself. I would blame her forgetfulness on the pressure of having Declan's family over, but my mother loves to have a house full of people to share a meal with. Maybe she thinks keeping me out of the house is giving me a break.

I smile at that thought.

Before leaving, I slide the backdoor open and wait for Declan to see me. He's laughing at something Tallen has just said. I beam at the sight of the full backyard. Our families together to celebrate Nova's birthday. It's a sweet sight.

Ty and Buddy are playing in the grass with Val and Sean. Jake and Brent are listening to Avery chatter. And Winnie is making small talk with Tallen's new girlfriend.

When Declan looks over in my direction, he gets up to meet me in the kitchen.

I give him a flustered expression. "I'm going to run to the store again. Apparently we *need* a candle for the cake." I hand him the baby monitor. "Nova's still napping."

He looks at the monitor with a grin. "She's adorable when she's sleeping."

"It's funny," I say. "I can't wait for her to nap, but when she does all I want to do is go wake her up." I rise up onto my tiptoes to kiss the side of his face. "I'll be back in a bit."

When my heels meet the floor again, I can see Winnie walking in our direction.

Declan flips around and finds his seat near Tallen and his disgustingly flawless girlfriend whose name I shamefully keep forgetting.

I turn around, leaving the door ajar for Winnie, but she stops me with, "Did I hear you say you're going to the store?"

I'm still walking when I look back briefly to say, "Yeah, for a birthday candle."

"I'll go with you." Her statement is direct. Not giving me a choice.

Winnie keeps the conversation light on the way to the store. Which is fine by me since Declan hasn't told his family about his last episode, diagnosis, medication, or therapy. And it's the only thing I want to talk about with Winnie.

"It's great seeing Declan be such a good father to Nova," she glances at me. "Especially considering how he reacted to the pregnancy in the beginning."

We're on our way back to the house. And something about her statement makes me want to drive faster so she doesn't figure out what I'm not supposed to tell her.

"Yeah, he's an incredible father."

She strums her fingers against her leg, gently tapping one at a time as if she's pondering whether she should continue the conversation.

"Remember when he walked out on Thanksgiving?" she finally says.

I know where this is going, and I have no idea how to stop it from unraveling. Maybe it will end on its own. Maybe we will get back to my mom's house before I have to tell her that her brother is living with schizophrenia.

"Yes," I say. "I remember."

"It's strange." She rests her elbow against the window and cups her head in her hand as she faces me. "When I asked him about it,

311

he didn't know what I was talking about."

I crease my brow, unsure why he would lie.

"So," she says, "one of you is hiding the truth. And I'm not one to get in the middle of other peoples' business. But you're parents now. There's no room for relationship games and if you're struggling, you need to reach out for help. I know we're going through stuff with my dad's dementia, but that doesn't mean you can't ask for help when you need it."

I nod and begin digging around in the center console suddenly in need of a piece of gum. Hoping my silence will deter her from continuing.

"I know I said I didn't want to get into my brother's personal life," she says this with a contrite tone. "But I can't help but think about how your marriage will directly affect Nova."

She's not stopping. And I can't seem to find where that pack of gum went.

"And," she continues, "we both know what it's like to grow up in a home...where..." She looks down at my hand rummaging around in the console. "Can I help you find something?"

I pull my hand up and grip the steering wheel. "Yes, there's some gum in that mess somewhere. Thanks."

She's digging under the receipts, pacifiers, and empty water bottles when she says, "As I was saying, I'm here for you guys. Just don't lie to me again, okay?"

I flip my head in her direction briefly before facing the road again with a scowling expression that I can't hide. Because she thinks *I'm* the one lying about Declan vanishing on Thanksgiving.

"Here you go," she says, handing me the pack of gum.

I take it. "Thanks," I say, tossing a piece into my mouth in hopes that it keeps me from doing exactly what I know I shouldn't do.

With a pleasant tone, Winnie says, "Are you still nursing Nova? Because I know she's a year old, but there are some major benefits to—"

"He's lying."

Winnie faces me. The car is silent for a moment before she says, "Excuse me?"

I'm chomping on the gum so intensely it's causing a clicking sound in my jaw. I exhale, already regretting what I'm about to say but I can't help myself. Part of me feels betrayed that Declan would let his sister think I'm a liar. The other part of me wants to accept the help she's willing to give.

So I say, "I told you the truth. He left on Thanksgiving for a few days. And he's been hearing voices." I glance at her directly. "And he said the radio says things to him too."

There it is. I said enough for her to put two and two together. If she can't figure it out, that's on her.

The car is quiet for a long moment. I'm sure she's trying to process what I've just thrown at her. And since she so quickly believed that I was lying before, maybe she's having a difficult time believing me now.

When we pull up to my mom's house again, I turn the car off and face Winnie. I expected to be met with a look of confusion or betrayal from her, but instead she looks sad as she keeps her gaze forward out the front window.

"Hearing voices? Like, schizophrenia?"

"Yes."

She nods slowly, without looking at me.

A long moment goes by again, and I feel like we should get out of the car. "Winnie?" I say in a quiet voice.

She exhales and faces me. "I told him to get help a long time ago." She must want to talk more about Declan. *Finally.*

"I know," I say gently.

She shakes her head. "He's been hearing those voices for a long time."

"I know."

"He was so successful, I didn't want to believe it was schizophrenia."

"I know, it's okay."

She rubs her forehead and looks up at the front door where Brent is waving us inside.

"I'm sorry, Christine, I shouldn't have kept any of that from you. He's your husband, and you had a right to know. Even if it was just my own suspicion. You had a right to know."

"It's okay, really," I say, wanting to lean over and give her a hug but also feeling like she's not an affectionate person.

Before I can talk myself into hugging her, Brent opens my car door.

"You guys gotta come inside," Brent's voice is hurried and panicked. Which is odd since Brent is never hurried or panicked and always takes his time when he talks.

313

I exit the car and follow him up the driveway. "Is Nova okay?"

He glances back at me while still pulling forward to the entrance. "Nova's fine." He looks at Winnie briefly. "It's your father."

FORTY-EIGHT

When we reach the backyard, Jake is kneeling on one knee in front of Sean who is seated in a lawn chair. He seems to be calming Sean down from whatever happened that we missed.

My mother is comforting Val in the kitchen while everyone else is circled around Jake and Sean.

Winnie hurries next to Jake outside but she doesn't say anything. The same remorseful expression that consumed her face in the car is plastered to her face now as she peers down at her confused father.

And I can't seem to find the one person I want to be nearby.

I face Brent and in a quiet whisper I say, "Where is he?"

He nods his head toward the staircase. "Upstairs with Nova."

I squeeze his arm gently and give him a small grin. "Thanks."

I stride up the stairs, expecting to see Declan in my room.

He's not there.

I peek into Tallen's old bedroom, but he's not there either.

I begin to head back downstairs when I catch a glimpse of Parker's bedroom door slightly ajar.

Surely Declan wouldn't go in there. No one has opened that door since Parker was alive.

I slowly creep down the hall and press the door open. I'm surprised to see Declan standing with Nova in one arm.

"What are you two doing in here?" I say feeling equally confused as I am curious.

He looks at me and smiles. He shouldn't be smiling. Something just happened with his father that has both our families in distress. Yet, here he is holding our daughter with a pleased expression on his face.

When I approach them, Nova reaches for me and says, "Mama!"

I take her and force a smile, then to Declan I say, "What happened with your dad?"

He combs one hand through his hair and stuffs the other in his pocket as he looks down at the grey carpet. He runs his tongue along his bottom lip and with a short laugh of disbelief he says, "I can't do this anymore."

I crease my brow. Confused. And concerned about what *this* is. "You can't do what?"

He drops the hand that was in his hair to his side then fans it out in front of him. "This! I can't keep doing this!" He looks at me and his eyes are dark. "Parker died. He made me laugh more than anyone I've ever known. And when I walked into his room, I honestly half expected him to be sitting in here playing one of his video games."

My mouth parts but no words come out. I thought we were past this. I thought the medication and therapy was working.

He continues, "And then my dad…" he drops his head back and blinks up at the ceiling, "he's never going to be the same. He's just going to get worse and worse. He was fine all afternoon, then in a split second," he snaps his fingers, "he had no idea where he was." He rolls his head to face me as he presses his mouth together to compose the pain trying to make its way into his expression. "He didn't know who we were. He was lost and confused. I hate seeing him like this, Christine." He can't hold his composure anymore, and the angry tears burst from deep inside of his core. "I hate that he has no idea who Nova is. I hate that I can't talk to my dad anymore without feeling like I'm looking into the eyes of a stranger."

His heartache shatters me and I can't help but let the tears fall down my cheeks. I take a step toward him and hug him with my free arm.

Nova leans her head on his chest too, and he places his hand over her head.

"I'm so sorry," I say, wishing there was more I could do to comfort him. "I hate this for you."

He clears his throat, but when he speaks I can still hear the pain in his voice. "And I hate that every time I look at Nova, I think about what I did to Eli's parents when I let him drown."

A chill runs down my spine and I pull myself from him.

When I look into his eyes, I can see the darkness that's consumed him. I don't want him to be tormented every time he looks at our daughter. I don't want him to be in pain when he's visiting his father.

And I don't want him to miss Parker so much that he never accepts his death.

"What can I do to help?" I finally say. "I'm right here with you."

He stares at me with those chilling dark eyes that tell me something isn't right. But he doesn't say anything, except, "I can't do this anymore."

FORTY-NINE

"Here you go," I say placing a sandwich next to the uneaten omelet I left for Declan from this morning.

He glances up and pulls his headset off one ear and says, "Thanks." Then looks back at his computer and begins clicking away at his mouse.

I place my hand over his and pull the headset down so it falls at his neck.

His brow furrows when he looks at me as if I'm irritating him.

I *hope* I'm irritating him, then at the very least he would be feeling something towards me other than numb.

He tightens his jaw. "Christine," he says my name with a downward inflection. He never says my name anymore in the fluid way he used to. "I'm working on a track for this new song and I can't be bothered when I'm feeling this creative flow."

He begins to pull his headset back on, but I stop him.

He gives me a look of irritated anticipation. As if I'm wasting his time. Then he finally thrusts a stabbing, "*What?*" at me.

I exhale. "You're not eating."

"I'll eat when I'm hungry."

"You haven't been back to work, and you were supposed to help Margaret with the open mic night project on Monday, but you didn't show."

"I'll give her a call later."

"It's Thursday."

He runs his tongue along his bottom lip as he leans back in his chair and locks his hands over his head with arrogance. "What do you want me to say, Christine?"

I want him to face everything he's running from. I want him to

318

care that it's been six weeks since he spoke to his family. I want him to answer Winnie's calls. I want him to talk to Margaret and go back to work. I want him to play with Nova and come to bed with me. And I want him to say that he's been skipping his medication and falling back into his old patterns of grandiosity.

I place his pills next to his food. "What I want you to say, is the truth."

His exaggerated exhale tells me I won't be getting the truth. "You're acting like my mother and trying to control me."

I keep my composure. Maybe because I'm too hurt to yell at him. "I'm acting like your *wife* and showing you that I care."

There's a familiar narcissistic behavior to his body language, the way he's positioned so comfortably in his chair, that's reminding me of my father right now and making me want to leave the room. "You want me to suppress all that is creative about me and take those pills." He thrusts his hand in the air as he says this, as if he's discovered the truth. Which he hasn't.

"I want you to take care of yourself."

He stands up instantly and towers over me with his neck craning down as he peers into my eyes with a look of fury. In a low shaky voice he says, "When I take those pills. I can't make music. And if I can't make music then I can't…"

I cross my arms. I don't ask him to finish his statement because I already know what he's thinking. He wants to be a famous musician. He wants to create music and forget about everything else. But I also know that he's not himself right now, so I'm not going to argue with him.

He sits back down and faces the computer screen. There's gravel in his voice as he says, "Life isn't supposed to be like this."

I exhale. "No one's life is *supposed* to be anything. No one knows what they're doing. We're just figuring it out along the way. But the one good thing about us is that we're doing life together. And I'm going to love you…even though I really don't like you right now."

When he doesn't respond, I walk out of the room. He doesn't bother trying to stop me. I'm not mad. I'm more…frustrated.

I go to our closet and pull out an empty journal I hid on the top shelf behind a box of my old college books. I was saving the journal to give to him for his birthday in a few weeks, but something tells me he needs it now.

I sit on my bed and open the leather-bound journal before I

scribble a message on the first page:

To my husband,

I hope you find this journal as a place to empty your thoughts. I also hope that ten years from now we can look back at this time and only remember the difficult parts as a blink in our minds.

Remember, I'll always be the somebody that understands you.

Four Words:

I love you more.

Love,

Your wife

I place the journal on his nightstand. Maybe getting his thoughts out of his head and on paper again will help him shift back into reality. It doesn't help that he's skipping his medication.

I know that if he could help it, he would. And I know that I can't be angry with him or blame him. It's not his fault. Life is difficult right now, but I actively choose to be with him through it all. Because I know if the situation was reversed and it was me in his position, I would pray to God that he stuck by my side.

It's just getting harder to stay positive…

FIFTY

I place bananas into the shopping cart and begin to make my way toward the baby aisle so I can grab some diapers for Nova.

Declan was still asleep when we left this morning. He's been staying up later and sleeping in longer. And meditating every chance he gets. If I'd even call it that.

I feel like I don't see him anymore. I've been focusing all my attention on Nova that I'm not even sure if Declan's been to his last few therapy appointments.

Nova reaches for a blanket with sparkling yellow stars when we approach the baby section. I hand it to her as my phone rings.

When I see that it's my father calling, I debate on answering.

"Dada!" Nova exclaims.

I smile at her. "Not dada…well, not your dada anyway."

I answer reluctantly, "Hey, Dad."

"Your baby brother is here," he doesn't waste a second getting to the point of the phone call, "and he looks just like me."

"Congratulations, Dad." I have a hard time getting the words out.

"You have to come and meet him."

I exhale, dreading the thought of being in a face-to-face setting with my dad. At least over the phone I can hang up any time I want to. In person it's a lot more difficult to leave. "Yeah, maybe we'll visit when we get some free time."

He clears his throat and in a more serious tone says, "I know you were just at your mothers last month."

I roll my eyes. Not that he can see.

Part of me wants to wring Tallen's neck since I'm sure he's the one who told our father that I was in Nevada. It's not that I don't want my father to know when I visit my mother, it's the fact that I don't want to have to deal with his narcissism and manipulation because I choose to visit my mother and not him.

He continues, "You never visit. You still haven't met Natasha and now you have a brother that you need to meet."

I toss the diapers into the cart and head for the self-checkout line. "You know, Dad, I have a lot going on right now. But I'll make an effort to visit as soon as I can." I'm not making any promises though.

"What's going on?" He seems sincere when he asks this. I don't know why, but I think I'll try to confide in him. Not completely, but maybe it will help talking to someone other than my therapist and mother about what's going on.

"I, uh…" I realize I don't know how to confide in my father. Which makes me a little sad. But also makes me want to make the effort to include him a little more in what's going on in my life. "It's just marriage stuff."

"Are you being kind to Declan?" He says this as if he's certain I'm the one to blame for any issues in the relationship.

"Yes, Dad, I'm being kind to Declan." If he only knew the lengths of kindness I was extending to Declan when he's been more than undeserving of it.

"Is Declan being kind to you?"

I hesitate before answering. Because it's not that Declan is being unkind, it's more that he's avoiding his real life and giving in completely to a delusion. Maybe if he wasn't avoiding his family and his job and his marriage then I wouldn't call his music a *delusion*.

I begin bagging the items as I scan them across the beeping light at the self-checkout. "We're both figuring out how to do marriage and realizing that it's tough."

"What's tough?"

I scan a bag of bell peppers. Ignoring his question.

"Chris, I'm your father and I know a thing or two about marriage." This statement makes me want to laugh because the only thing he knows about marriage is how to ruin one.

I pay for the groceries and head for the exit. Curiosity gets the best of me, and I want to know the answer to a question that's been rattling around in my head the last month. So, I reluctantly say, "How do you help someone who doesn't want to be helped?"

I hear my dad exhale, forming his thoughts into deliverable words, then, "You might have to wait until they're ready to accept your help." That was a better answer than I was expecting. Maybe he'll have some insight on marriage after all.

"I've been waiting for a long time…"

"Have you tried marriage counseling?"

"If I could only tell you how much therapy I've done in the last year."

His voice shifts down as he says, "Oh, Chris, why didn't you tell me?"

I unload the groceries into the trunk and blink away the tears trying to work their way out. It feels humiliating admitting this to my father. "It's not something I really wanted to flaunt about my marriage."

"You want to know what I learned from your mother?"

I'm taken aback. Surprised he's admitting to *learning* something from her at all.

He continues, "Your mother taught me that it's okay to let go."

I'm not sure what he means.

"She taught me that sometimes we marry the wrong people."

I'm starting to see where this is going.

"And she showed me that I married the wrong person." There it is. "If I had only waited for Natasha, then I would have never had to endure that divorce." As if the divorce was so hard on him.

I want to defend my mother, but I know it would go in one ear and out the other if I did. So instead, I say, "Thanks for sharing that."

"Natasha is the most incredible woman I've ever met. She's so talented and beautiful. You would know all this if you called me more." He laughs to himself, "And if you called, then I could give you a lot more advice."

I laugh too. It's more of a scoff, but I think my father interpreted it as a laugh.

I begin putting Nova in her car seat, but she starts to fuss and fight me. It's close to her nap time and I'd rather her sleep at home than in the car. "I better go," I say. "Nova's ready for a nap and it's probably going to get pretty loud in a second."

"Alright," he says. "And Chris?"

Nova continues squirming in her chair and pushing at my hands that are trying to fasten the buckle. "Yeah?"

"Remember, marriage isn't supposed to be hard, it's supposed to be easy."

I roll my eyes. "Bye, Dad."

I hang up before he can toss anymore *advice* out of his mouth.

323

Not that I would call it that. If there's anything I've learned, it's that my dad is selfish and doesn't *ever* give good advice. And marriage is hard work, especially in the beginning. And especially when you toss something like *schizophrenia* into the mix.

What he should have said, was that marriage isn't supposed to be hard forever.

FIFTY-ONE

It's been seven hours since we got home from grocery shopping. I've already made dinner, ate dinner, bathed Nova, and put her to bed. And in that time, Declan hasn't been home.

The familiar worry begins to ball up in my stomach when I call his cell and it goes straight to voicemail. Again.

I've already done the searching. The same searching I've done when he's left before. And I've been met with the same indications that reveal he *should* be home any second. But part of me feels that just like last time, he won't come home for another four days since his things are all still here, including his car. The only thing missing, is him.

I won't let my mind go there.

After I get myself ready for bed, I try to distract myself by reading a book. In the story, the woman's husband has just left for a work trip across the country and she's pregnant and alone. Did I mention that their marriage is not on good terms? Even reading can't stop my thoughts from jumping to the worst-case scenario.

I slap the book closed and try to close my eyes in a similar way. Rolling to my side, I try to get comfortable but when I open my eyes, I notice Declan's phone on top of the journal I left on his nightstand last week.

My heart drops so hard into my stomach that I feel paralyzed. The throbbing my pulse is doing is so loud my entire body feels as if a drum is pounding inside of me.

I don't want to believe this.

I don't want to do this again.

I want him to be out on a walk.

I want him to be playing music at Arty's.

I don't want him to have abandoned us.

I don't want to endure each second that he's gone.

What if he doesn't come home?

What if he needs to call me but his phone is here on his nightstand?

I can finally move again, although my heart is still vibrating in my chest. And I take his phone, turn it on, and try to figure out if there's any indication of where he might have gone. Last time he left, he came back smelling like a metro station and told me he'd been to the library. The library is closed and it's too late to check the metro stations with a toddler. So I have no other option than to go through his phone for information on his whereabouts.

After an hour of useless searching, I toss the phone on his pillow. What more can I do other than pray that he's safe until he returns?

If he returns.

I move his phone from his pillow and begin to place it back on his journal, but I hesitate. Maybe he's written in his journal, and I can figure out where he is?

Almost as quickly as I set the phone down, I'm already flipping the journal open only to be met with empty pages.

Until…the first page.

As I scan his familiar handwriting, my heart explodes into fragmented pieces that I'm unsure I'll ever be able to completely put back together again. Because the only thing he's written is a response to the message I left for him:

Christine,

I have to pay for what I've done. My actions cannot go unpunished.

And I have four more words for you:

You're <u>Not</u> My Muse.

No *Love, Declan.*

No *I'll see you soon.*

No indication of where he's gone or if he'll return.

I'm gasping for air when the sobs engulf my lungs. How has the mouth that's kissed me so gently turned into a sharp weapon against me? Why is he blaming me? I hate this delusion that's consumed my husband.

I read the words over again. And again. And again. And again. Hoping at some point they will change. Hoping that I'm mistaken and read them wrong. Hoping there's more that I've missed. Hoping I'll find an apology or an explanation for the heartless way he's destroyed every beautiful memory of us.

His words have ruined the only parts of our relationship that gave me any hope. I didn't want to be his muse, he made me that. I didn't ask for him to write me a song, he did that on his own. They were the things that I clung to. They were the parts of him that told me he still loved me. Nothing has ever crushed me more than what Declan has just done by writing the shortest most hateful words he ever could have written to me.

I cover my mouth and scream into my hand as I weakly toss the journal to the floor. Wishing I hadn't opened it at all.

My phone begins vibrating and part of me hopes that it's Declan calling to apologize for the agonizing pain he's caused. Because part of me knows that these words weren't written by my husband but by the part of his brain that's been abnormally developed to torment him. *And me.*

I tap the little green button unsure how I'm going to speak after I've been sobbing, but also not wanting to be alone in this heartbreak.

"Chris." Tallen's familiar voice runs through the speaker on my phone as he says, "Did Dad break the news to you yet and tell you that you're not the baby of the family anymore?" He's laughing subtly in disbelief. "I still can't believe they had a kid together."

But I can't go there with him right now. I can't laugh in disbelief with him. Our father's life seems so trivial in comparison to what's happening to me right now. I can't shake this. And then, I *break* when I can't hold the pain in any longer.

Tallen sounds farther away, as if he's pulled his phone from his ear at the sound of my cracking sobs, when he says, "Whoa, Chris, settle down. What happened?"

Another burst erupts from my throat.

I can hear Tallen's breathing intensify. The worry is apparent in his voice now. "Just tell me you're gonna be okay."

"It's Declan…" The words are broken as I deliver them with sharp breaths. "H-he left."

He's quiet for a long moment, then he gently says, "Let it out."

He blows out a long exhale, settling into the conversation. "Let it out for as long as you need." His voice is quiet with sorrow. "I'm not going anywhere. I'm right here for you, Chris. For as long as you need me, I'm right here."

My brother continues to sit with me on the phone for hours as I cry into the speaker in complete and utter torture.

And he doesn't go anywhere. Not even after I fall asleep.

PART THREE:

AGONY OF DEVOTION

FIFTY-TWO

The dark room is suddenly consumed by the eleven o'clock sunshine from my bedroom windows as my mother yanks the curtains open.

"That's better," she says to herself. Then watering my plants, she says, "I'm taking Nova to the indoor park, Magic Ground, so she can play without burning her little legs on the slide." Her voice shifts downward as she begins speaking from the side of her mouth. "I'm not sure how either of you survive the heat and humidity here."

I sit up and rub at my eyes. "It's only this miserable at the beginning of summer." I'm trying to sound normal and force myself awake although every part of me has wanted nothing more than to sink into my bed and never come out ever since Declan left.

My routine has consisted of holding Declan's pillow while I cry myself to sleep around two in the morning, and then sleeping in until right before lunch time. This is when my mother tells me what her and Nova will be doing for the afternoon, then I fall back asleep until they come home before dinner.

I don't eat, *because I'm emotionally suffering.*

I don't sleep, *because I'm in physical pain.*

I don't smile, *because it's too much effort.*

And I don't shower, until my mother turns the shower on and pulls me out of bed.

My mother pats my leg. "You should come with us today." Since she arrived a day after Declan left, she's pretty much been a full-time care provider for Nova. And nothing makes me feel worse. I feel guilty for being unable to get out of bed. And I feel even more guilty for wanting to cry every time Nova smiles at me because she looks so much like Declan; especially now that she has so many teeth.

I swallow down the shaking trying to rise in my voice as I say,

"Maybe tomorrow." This has been my response to my mother's invitations to join her and Nova on their shopping sprees, adventures, and outings for the last several weeks. Even though it might not seem like it, I'm glad she hasn't given up on inviting me. She rises from my bedside and begins to exit the room. "We won't be home until late this afternoon. I'm meeting Cecile later for dinner with her daughter." It doesn't make me feel any better that my mother's managed to already make more friends since she's been here than I have in the last year. She's heading into Nova's bedroom when she says, "Don't forget that your brother will be here today."

"I won't." *I probably will.*

"Text me later if you'd like me to bring you something to eat."

"I will." *I won't.* But I'm sure she already knows that.

I can hear my mother and Nova happily gabbing to each other as I bury myself back into the pillows and sink under the blankets in my bed. Because I feel abandoned and alone. And because even though I want to get up and live my life, I can't. I physically and mentally cannot bring myself to get out of this bed, and nothing makes me feel more like a failure.

I turn my playlist on my phone and set it next to my head as I fall asleep again. Aching in the memories of who Declan was before the inevitable pains of life triggered his mind into unlocking the dormant schizophrenia.

There's a tickling at my nose that I rub away with my hand. When it happens a second a time, I realize I can't open my eyes because they've been taped shut.

I groan and pull at the tape, knowing there's only one person in the world that would do something as immature as this to another human.

"There she is," Tallen's tone is pleased.

The dryness in my throat makes my voice sound scratchy as I say, "What are you doing here?"

With a disappointed humming in his throat he says, "You forgot I was coming to visit?"

I don't answer him since I don't have the heart to tell him I've been preoccupied with my own drowning sorrows to care about a visit. Which could easily translate to, I don't have the heart to tell him I'm avoiding my life by sleeping it away.

He lets me struggle with the tape until I peel it off, along with some of my eyelashes, and can finally look at him with dismay. "Aren't you a little old to be playing pranks on me?"

With a perplexed expression he says, "No." Then proceeds to tickle me.

I'm in no mood for laughing, and when I try to sit up and stop him, my head is instantly forced back to a laying position. I grab at my hair and say, "You did not," with warning.

Tallen stops tickling me and smiles. "I did."

"You tied my hair to the railing?"

He nods. "I did."

"*Ta-allen,*" I say in a familiar pouting voice.

He laughs, pleased with himself, then, "I knew you were still in there somewhere."

With my exhale, I say, "You didn't have to resort to juvenile pranks to find me, you know?" He's taped my eyes shut countless times when we were growing up, but he hasn't tied my hair to the railing since I was in middle school.

As he untangles my hair from the railing, he tilts his head to the side and looks down at me. "Really, Chris? Because Mom *hoping* you out of bed was working so well, wasn't it?"

I shrug. I still don't want to leave my bed, but something about having my brother around seems to lighten the deep despair I've been plagued with. I know my mother has been here to help me, but she's more of a security blanket that I sulk to. Tallen feels more like an Adam Sandler character from the 90's that I can't help but feel uplifted by.

"Ready to get out of here, then? I'm starving." He rolls himself backward and gives me an expectant look, as if he's waiting for me to follow him. "Well?"

I lean back against my pillow, rubbing at the place on my head where my hair was pulled. "I'm not feeling up to it today."

"Too bad," he says, pressing forward into the hall. "Meet you in the car."

I stir my latte and watch the foamy decorative leaf disappear into a swirl.

Despite his wheelchair, Tallen seems to have adapted to the world as if nothing ever changed. He locks his chair across from me at the small wire table outside the cafe.

The fries and club sandwich he ordered seem like a heavy meal for this time of day, but I remember although it might be breakfast time for me, the rest of the city had lunch hours ago.

"I might relocate here." Tallen's words are almost uninterpretable with the large amount of sandwich consuming his mouth.

I drop my chin into my palm and continue stirring the coffee that I'm not sure I'm going to drink. Without looking up, I say, "That would be nice."

"Yeah, I mean, I could be here to help you too." This makes me glance up at him without an expression. He shrugs. "You know, if you needed it or anything."

I do need help. But I don't want to burden Tallen. If he happened to move here and hate it, I would blame myself. And right now, I can't blame myself for anyone else's lives not going according to their plan.

He tosses a fry into his mouth. "What do you think?"

I finally sit back and scan the traffic while people are quickly passing by along the sidewalks. I wonder if any of them notice my unmanaged appearance. "What does your girlfriend think of you moving?"

"Sandi?"

I nod.

"She would love it."

"You haven't mentioned it to her yet?"

"She works remotely so she can travel without missing work. Plus, she loves trying new things."

I raise my eyebrow. "You would be okay with a long-distance relationship?"

He takes another humungous bite of his sandwich. With a mouthful he says, "I'm going to marry her so it wouldn't be long before we were living together anyway."

This grabs my attention. I sit up and lean forward to analyze his expression before pointedly saying, "You're engaged?"

"Not yet," he looks at me with a self-assured smile, "but I'm going to ask her soon."

"Wow." Leaning back again, I shift my mouth to one side in thought. Here I am with my world crumbling around me, and Tallen is probably eager to start this new chapter of his life. I'm sure my lack-luster attitude isn't making him feel very excited though.

He gives me a sharp look. One that says he's disappointed by my shortage of enthusiasm.

I drop my head to the side. "I'm sorry," I say quietly. "I think I've forgotten how to be happy." I force a small smile in the corner of my mouth and give him my best hopeful expression. "You're going to be a great husband...to...uh..." I can't believe I've already forgotten her name again.

He rolls his eyes and makes an irritated noise in his throat. "Sandi! S-A-N-D-I. Her name is Sandi."

"I'm so sorry," I gently laugh into my hand. "I'm just distracted by how pretty she is; it makes me forget her name."

"Well stop it." He raises one eyebrow and lifts his chin up. "You think she's pretty?"

"Disgustingly flawless."

He laughs, food in his smile and all. And it makes me finally crack a laugh that hurts my face.

"There she is," he says.

I shake my head with a grin.

"I mean," he continues, "there she *really* is. You weren't really all there this morning."

I press my mouth together with my fading smile, remembering how quickly I forgot about Declan for the first time in weeks.

Tallen sets his sandwich down. He leans against his forearms on the table. "Are we going to talk about you sleeping your life away while Declan's run off?"

I trace my finger against the lines of the metal table. "I don't know what to do."

His voice is quiet. "I don't know if there's anything you can do."

"Maybe if I report him missing to the Police..."

"But, Chris," he places his hand on my arm, which makes me look up at him. "He's not missing. He left you a message telling you he was leaving."

I wish I hadn't found that note he left in his journal.

I look back down at the metal lines on the table as Tallen says, "He wanted to leave."

FIFTY-THREE

I haven't been able to sleep since my conversation with Tallen. The fact that Declan *wanted* to leave is consuming me. And I'm not sure what's worse, sleeping my life away or not sleeping at all.

I peer out the window at the bright city lights below, wondering if Declan is out there. And wishing I had x-ray vision so I could find him. If I could just see that he was okay, I might feel a little better knowing he was under the same midnight sky as I am.

I quietly pad across the kitchen floor, careful to be as silent as possible with Tallen asleep in the office and my mother asleep in the guest room. I'm not worried about waking Nova at this hour, but I still tiptoe past her bedroom door just in case.

When I reach my bedroom, I feel my way around my dresser until I reach my bathroom. Safe inside the bathroom, I sit on the edge of the bathtub and pull my phone out to do exactly what my mother and Tallen instructed me *not* to do. Which is call the police department and report my husband missing.

My voice is quiet but loud enough for the woman on the other end of the phone call to hear me. "Hello, my name is Christine Price." I'm feeling determined and it's apparent in my voice. "I would like to report a missing person."

After answering several questions about Declan's physical features and what he was wearing the last time I saw him, we get into some deeper questioning.

"A-and," I can tell the woman is scanning a screen for the next question, "has your husband been diagnosed with any mental illness?"

"Yes, schizophrenia."

The line goes quiet for a moment, then, "Alright...and what

happened during your last interaction."

I clear my throat, thinking back to when we last had a conversation. "It's difficult to explain."

"All information is helpful if you can remember anything."

"It's difficult to explain because we didn't have any sort of real conversations for weeks before he left. And the last thing he said to me was a written message telling me that he was leaving."

Her voice becomes annoyed when she says, "It sounds like he voluntarily left."

"No," I'm beginning to feel the panic creep into my stomach, "he has schizophrenia and hasn't been taking his medication. He might have voluntarily left but I know he didn't mean to. His thoughts take over when—"

"I'm sorry, ma'am," she stops me from continuing, "but with his mental illness along with the fact that he's voluntarily left you and let you know he was leaving...this isn't a missing persons case."

I try to think of something to keep her on the line. But there's nothing.

"I'm sorry, ma'am," she says again. "Good luck with your husband."

After the conversation, I stare down at my phone in disbelief. What was the point of answering fifty questions just to be let down? There must be a loophole or another way to report Declan missing. I can't do this on my own. I don't understand why everyone thinks he left on his own. If he doesn't have control over his thoughts when he gets into that dark place, then he shouldn't be held accountable for his actions when he's in that dark place either.

I do a quick search on my phone for another police station. Maybe if I explain myself from the beginning, I can get some sort of help. Surely the authorities don't want helpless people wandering the streets.

I dial the police department on Park Rd.

They can't help.

I contact the Metropolitan Police Department.

They can't help either.

After seven more departments give me the same response, I begin to feel defeated. I begin to give up. I begin to experience the overwhelming pain in my chest that haunts me when I start to believe I might have to accept that my husband left me.

"WMATA Police," the woman says in an automated voice

through my phone speaker.

"Hello," I say with less intensity to my voice than I had at the beginning of my train of conversations, "can I speak with someone about a missing person?"

"This is the Transit Police Department, if you would like to report a missing person, you'll have to contact the Metropolitan Police."

I exhale. "I already have…" The defeat is heavy in my voice. I'm not sure why I'm still trying. The rest of the phone numbers I've pulled up from my search results are campus police, capitol police, and harbor patrol. I'm sure they'd direct my call to the Metropolitan Police too. I don't want to endure seven more pointless conversations so I tell the woman my desperate situation in hopes of being directed to the appropriate department—preferably the FBI at this point—so I can find my husband.

The woman silently gives me the time to unravel my struggle with the other police stations. And after a long pause, she says, "I'm going to put you on hold. Don't go anywhere alright?"

Even though she seems to be giving me false hope, I stay on the line. There's nothing left to lose at this point.

"Stay right there and don't hang up, okay?" she says this in a more direct tone than the first time.

"Okay, I won't hang up," I reassure her.

When six solid minutes goes by, I'm watching the clock, I'm beginning to wonder if she's forgotten that she left me on hold. Maybe I should hang up and call back?

"Ma'am?" Her voice startles me after sitting in complete silence for so long. "Are you there?"

"Yes," I say perking up a little. "I'm here."

Her tone is less automated from the first conversation when she says, "I have Deputy Hurst ready to speak with you about your missing husband."

My heart skips a beat. "Really? Thank you so much!" I'm trying not to get my hopes up, but this is the furthest I've come in the search for my husband, so I can't help but feel a tinge of optimism.

"You're welcome. Please hold while I transfer your call."

It's not even a millisecond before another woman's voice is on the phone. "This is Deputy Hurst."

I can't breathe as I begin unraveling the events that led to Declan's abandonment. And then, as I finish the conversation, I still can't breathe because I'm terrified she's going to tell me that she can't help me either.

I can hear her writing something before she says, "Mrs. Rice? Was it?"

"Mrs. Price," I correct her.

"My apologies," she says gently, "Mrs. Price, I'm gonna help you."

I exhale with great relief. "Thank you so much, Deputy Hurst. Thank you."

"But I wanna be clear about somethin'," she says in a firm tone. "If he's found and doesn't want you to know where he is, I can't give you his location."

"I understand." I don't understand, but at this point knowing he's alive is better than nothing.

After giving her the rest of the information she needs, I hang up with a new sense of hope that is quickly thrust to the back of my mind when a deafening pounding rattles me—reminding me of the earthquake I survived.

My heart is accelerating as I try to quickly pad down the hall, reminding myself that an earthquake in D.C. is a less plausible explanation for the rumbling sound coming from my door than an actual person knocking.

Another intense pounding at the door startles me before I swing it open. I'm not sure who I was expecting to see, but it wasn't Arty.

He marches through the threshold, and I close the door as I face him.

He's in my kitchen when he swings around to look at me. "Where is he?" The intensity behind his voice and his body language leads me to believe he's upset about something.

"Declan's not here," I say, glancing at the time. It's barely six in the morning now, everyone is going to be waking up soon, so I have to figure out how to get Arty out of here before then.

"If he's not here, then where is he?" He demands with a booming in his voice that rattles me in the same way his pounding fist on the front door did.

I tighten my robe around myself, then cross my arms. "I don't know."

He approaches me slowly, pointing an aggravated finger in my face. "Margaret won't tell me where he is." His jaw tightens as his eyes grow in anger. "Now, you're hiding him, and I really wouldn't want anyone to get hurt because your man doesn't know how a loan works."

The closer he gets to me, the more I notice the smell of alcohol on his breath. Which scares me. His unpredictability mixed with inebriation is the perfect combination for disaster. And the worst part is that I get a sense I won't be able to talk sense into him. I look down at my phone in my hand, formulating a plan in my mind to how I might call one of the officers that I was just talking to for help with a new crisis. And that new crisis is Arty.

Before I can make a decision, he takes my phone and slides it across the kitchen counter. Thankfully not very hard. "I don't think we need to involve anyone else." He takes both my wrists in his hands and backs me up against the door. I turn my head away from him when he closes in next to my face. "If he's not going to pay me back, then we'll have to arrange for payment another way."

"Get off of her," Tallen's voice is bold and demanding. I release a relieved exhale when I hear it, but quickly remember that he's only partially as intimidating as he used to be. And Arty's size is dangerous against Tallen in his chair.

Arty backs off away from me, then focuses on Tallen. My paranoid heartbeat is pulsing harder. I don't want Arty to hurt Tallen, but I know that there's nothing me or Tallen can do to physically to protect ourselves against Arty. So, I hurry to my phone to call for reinforcements.

"You're not Price the thief," Arty laughs maniacally. "You're not even half of Price." Arty keeps his feet planted when he twists his torso to face me. "Is this why you don't know where Declan is?" he says with his hand out in Tallen's direction, insinuating that I've replaced Declan with Tallen. Little does he know that we're siblings.

"How much?" Tallen says, ignoring his comment and lifting his chin up at Arty.

Arty lets out a short breath of sinister laughter as he approaches Tallen. "What was that?"

Tallen's stiff expression stands firmly focused on Arty as he pulls his wallet out. "How much does Declan owe you?"

Arty grunts as his lip curls. It's sickening. "Two thousand."

I'm gripping my phone now, unsure if I should follow through with the call I intended to make to the police.

Tallen writes in his checkbook. "I'll double that," he says tearing the check out and lifting it in Arty's direction. Arty reaches for it but

Tallen pulls it back, looking at him with only his eyes and without lifting his head up all the way. "The extra two thousand is to keep you from showing your face around here ever again. And if Declan comes to you for anything, you turn him away."

Arty's grimacing face is unconvinced. "How do I know that check isn't going to bounce?"

A smirk grows on Tallen's face. "It won't."

Arty snatches the check from Tallen, inspecting it for a moment before facing me to look me up and down. "If this is real," he says lifting the piece of paper in his hand, "I want nothing to do with you Prices from here on out."

"Done," I say tightlipped.

He points his finger in my face once more. "You tell Price he's never getting a cent from me again." Turning to open the door, he says, "And I'm keeping the guitar and mic he left at my house."

I don't respond, and instead wait for the door to slam closed. I hurry over and lock it. Noticing my pulse is still pounding.

Tallen shakes his head with disappointment. "What the hell is Declan doing hanging out with that guy?"

"They worked at the museum together and liked to play music sometimes." I exhale, frustrated by their friendship. "I had no idea Declan borrowed money from him." I pull my hair over my shoulder, trying to detangle it along with my thoughts. "I don't understand why he would borrow money. Do you think Arty would lie about that?"

"It really doesn't matter now," he says, adjusting one of the levers. "I took care of it, so let's just let it go." He approaches me with a concerned expression. "And, Chris, I think you should move. For yours and Nova's safety."

I shake my head hesitantly.

"Even if you move a block away, it's better than staying here."

"I can't."

"Why not? Who knows if that guy will come back for something else?"

"I'll get a restraining order. I promise. But I can't leave. I have to be here if Declan comes back."

Tallen's expression falls to remorse as his eyebrows drop to the sides of his face. "Chris..." he says quietly as he takes my hand in his and pats it with the other.

I can tell Tallen wants me to accept that Declan is gone. That he's not coming back. That he willingly left, along with his mind. But I can't abandon him.

I won't stop loving him, even when it hurts.

FIFTY-FOUR

I toss my hand over to Declan feeling for him for comfort as the nightmare that plagued my mind vanishes. Only when I reach for him, he's not there.

It's been eight months since I made that phone call to Deputy Hurst. She hasn't called with good news yet. But that hasn't stopped me from berating her with messages and phone calls asking for updates. And so far, the trail to finding Declan has been ice cold.

I get out of bed and meander around my home hoping that maybe my life in the last year has been the nightmare and I'm really going to wake up to see Declan next to me in bed.

I pinch myself, just in case. It hurts. Which means this is real.

I don't want to accept that all I have is the memories we shared. I don't want to feel the pain of not knowing whether he's alive or dead. The worst part of all this is that, if something happened to him, if I will never see him again—the memories we shared are going to last longer than the time I spent with him, loving him. The memory of him will be longer than the time we spent together. And that truth *hurts*.

"Mama?" I hear Nova call from her bedroom.

I blink away the tears I didn't realize were forming in my eyes and retrieve her. She's adapted well to the early morning wakeup call that's been our new routine since I went back to work at the museum. Margaret was a life saver when she established a daycare at the museum for all the employees with children. What would I do without her?

⁂

I have my playlist going quietly in the background of the security room. People watching has sufficed the anthropological longings I

344

have for fieldwork. Even after Margaret offered me a job on the music floor, I declined because I'd rather be up here watching people on the screens.

It's interesting seeing the way people interact in the museum. Or the way they don't interact. And every once in a while, I notice a familiar manly figure only to see them turn around and reveal their faces, which causes me to quickly realize that they're just someone else's father. They're someone else's husband. And they're not Declan.

"This is an interesting song," Margaret says appearing behind me. "Who sings it?"

I turn in my chair to face her better. "It's *In My Veins*, by Andrew Belle."

"I've never heard it." She tilts her head and listens deeply, tucking her chin into her palm. When she pulls her brows together, several lines form between them before she glances at me. "It's sad," she finally says with a wayward expression.

I nod and glance at the monitors, "This entire playlist reminds me of Declan," unable to look at her while I admit this.

She takes a few steps towards me and places her hand on my shoulder, comforting me as if I were one of her children. "Any luck with the search?"

I shake my head, keeping my eyes down. I'm afraid if I look at her, I might cry. And I might cry because the small sense of hope I was clinging to is beginning to fade away along with the sound of his voice and the scent from his clothes.

"Oh, Christine, I'm so sorry. This must be torture for you." I wish she would change the subject. "Is there anything I can do to help?"

I swallow down the growing rock in my throat that's making it difficult to speak, and say, "If I think of something I'll let you know." Which I know I won't have to do since she always seems to find a way on her own to help me when I need it.

She begins to exit the room before stopping in the doorway. "You know," she says with her palm clasped around the door frame, "Declan began this *open mic night* idea before..." she rolls her head as if she doesn't want to say the words out loud, and instead settles for, "...everything." She gives me a grin. "I can get you the documents with all the details, maybe you'd like to take that over? We were close to finalizing everything last year, but I'm not certain how to run

345

something like that. And as well as I knew Declan, I think you would be a better fit than anyone to run the show the way he wanted to."

I'm not sure if her handing this role over to me is her way of trying to make me feel better, or if she's trying to preserve Declan's memory. Either way, I'm hesitant to accept.

And she must notice since she says, "We'll visit more once you've given it some thought, alright?"

She turns around and heads down the hall out of sight.

It feels wrong to take on Declan's ideas. But it also feels right. Maybe reading through the documents and seeing his ideas will help me feel closer to him. Especially since I can't figure out if I'm supposed to give up searching for him and accept that he's gone, or if I should persevere and endure through the heartache; never giving up until I have the answers I need.

I check the monitors and when everything seems okay, I walk into the hall where a large window shines the greying sky light down the stairwell. I lean against my hands on the window ledge and look down at the street below where I can see a man on the corner. He's homeless and facing the other direction. I watch him intently, hoping he'll turn around to reveal his face. Pleading that when he does turn in my direction, that he looks like Declan. Begging God that that homeless man *is* Declan.

My phone vibrates in my back pocket. I answer it automatically, refusing to take my eyes off of the man until I see his face.

"Mrs. Price?" The familiar direct tone says through the phone speaker. "This is Deputy Hurst."

"Hello, Deputy Hurst."

The man turns slightly, but just enough that I can tell he's not Declan which causes me to let out a remorseful exhale and retreat back to my chair in the security room.

"Do you have a moment?" There's something different about her voice. It's still direct. It's still full of authority. But there's something in her tone I haven't heard before.

"Yes, I do." This statement comes out as more of a question since I'm not sure what she's about to tell me.

"I wanna let you know that a body has been found with the same description as your husband." And just like that, her words rip a hole right through me.

My mouth falls open but my lungs deflate as my heart shoots up into my throat, blocking any words from coming out.

She continues with a hint of regret in her voice. "If you could meet me at the mortuary, I'll take you in to identify the body."

FIFTY-FIVE

The same horribly gut-wrenching cries consumed my entire being as they did when I was told Parker had died. One of the upstairs security guards found me in a hyperventilating mess on the floor when I got off the phone with Deputy Hurst. I managed to tell him to get Margaret for me and by some miracle she was able to calm me down.

She reassured me that I didn't need to breakdown until I had answers. And as of right now, I don't have any answers. So, I should take this process one step at a time until I am face to face with the body they've found that could possibly be my missing husband.

Margaret was kind enough to offer to come, but I begged her to keep an eye on Nova in the daycare room until I regained my complete composure.

If I regain my composure after identifying the dead body.

When I pull into the parking lot of the address Deputy Hurst gave me, I remember what my therapist taught me. *Five senses.*

I go through my senses, telling myself to focus on the clouds subtly moving in the sky. And smelling the cold, fresh scent of rain about to fall from those same clouds.

Once I'm calm, I tell myself that there are plenty of men that I see every day at the museum that resemble Declan. This man I'm about to be face to face with is no exception. Although my mind reminds me that with all of the photos I've given Deputy Hurst, there's a slim chance they've found a man that looks identical to Declan without being him.

When I enter the building, Deputy Hurst is already inside talking with three other people, whom I quickly learn are a medical examiner, counselor, and pathology assistant.

The medical examiner introduces himself and then provides me with the description of the man I'm about to identify. "Brown hair. Brown eyes. Six foot four. Muscular build. Olive skin. Late 20's. No tattoos or piercings. Two scars. One on the back of his head, and one on top of his head."

I continue to remind myself of all the men I've seen that look like Declan just so I don't fall into premature hysterics.

But how could this not be him?

After a brief rundown of what I should expect while in the mortuary, I'm led through a door where a coroner is standing over a covered body on a table. At that moment, everything becomes slow motion.

Scanning the stale, sterile room where the counselor, pathology assistant, and Deputy Hurst file into is in slow motion.

The medical examiner gestures with his hands and speaks in slow motion.

The coroner responds in slow motion.

My heart thuds in my chest in slow motion, making the pounding unbearable to take a proper breath.

The coroner pulls the covering off the body in slow motion.

Revealing his dark hair first.

My heart continues beating through my chest, like a jack hammer.

His forehead is pale, but I can tell his skin is normally an olive color.

My stomach twists into a tsunami.

The covering continues to slide, revealing his eyebrows, then his closed eyes lined with thick eyelashes.

I cover my mouth with both of my hands and my breath rushes through my flared nostrils like an incoming derecho.

The straight bridge of his nose, then his mouth, and his chin are all exposed in one moment as the covering falls to his neck.

I brace myself against the counter. We're not in slow motion anymore. We're in real time. And not only can I feel my intense breathing, but I can hear it fill the entirety of the room. Along with my thundering pulse. And I'm hyperaware of the fact that everyone is looking at me except the pathology assistant, who's staring at the uncovered face of the pale lifeless body lying on the steel table.

Deputy Hurst steps in front of me, blocking my view of everything and everyone else in the room. "Mrs. Price," she says taking my trembling hands in hers.

I meet my eyes with her expression, full of dread and anticipation. And then the words burst out of me. "It's not him." I'm still trying to catch my breath. I can't tell if I'm hyperventilating because I'm in the presence of a dead person that I don't know. Or because that dead person is not my husband.

"Thank God," Deputy Hurst says quietly, dropping her head back while locking her hands on her gear belt.

"I'm sorry," I say, breathless. I don't know if it was the anticipation or relief or fear that got such a huge reaction out of me. "I prepared myself for it to be him, even though I didn't want it to be him." I place my hand over my heart, trying to settle my breathing. "I'm sorry."

With her hands locked on her belt, Deputy Hurst drops her gaze down to mine and with a gentle somber tone she says, "No, don't be sorry. This just means he's still out there."

Her words rattle in my mind the rest of the day. I expected I would shake the initial anxieties after I told Margaret that the body wasn't Declan's. I thought when I sang Nova to sleep and held her a little longer in the rocking chair that I might be freed of the unsettling turning inside of my mind.

But here I am, lying in my bed, haunted by the fact that I still don't know where he is.

Or when he's coming home.

Or if Deputy Hurst is going to call me up again to identify Declan's real body.

I don't know how much more I can take.

I don't know why, but I take Declan's journal from his nightstand and toss it at the box on my dresser. It causes the box to slide off the edge and hit the floor, spilling the leaves.

I don't bother wiping my face when I get out of bed to scoop the broken leaves back into the box.

And as I do, I realize that this box held every good memory that we had. And I can't help but be angry and blame him for ruining it.

Will another leaf ever go into this box? Should I start plucking leaves and making my own good memories again?

Then, as if Declan can hear me, I say, "We were supposed to be together through the ugliest parts. If this isn't the ugliest parts of us, I don't want to know what is."

FIFTY-SIX

I run the thermometer back and forth across Nova's forehead.

After a few seconds, the thermometer beeps and reads a hundred degrees. Not an alarming temperature, but enough to acquire lots of cuddles, rest, and fluids. And some normal mom anxiety.

I want to call my mom, but I know she'd tell me to put a cold washcloth on Nova's head and give her some Tylenol.

Instead, I text Winnie since she's recently been in the middle of toddler raising and might have some modern remedies I don't know about.

Me: Any tips on helping a sick toddler with a fever?
Winnie: What's her fever?
Me: 100°
Winnie: That's not bad. Keep her hydrated. See if you can get her to eat applesauce or chicken broth. Lots of rest for Nova and no work for mom.
Me: Is there anything that will work instantly?
Winnie: Nope. Welcome to motherhood, where sleepless nights are common, and nothing is easy for the rest of your life.
Me: Not the answer I was looking for. But I get it. How're things in Nevada?
Winnie: Jake's started his own practice, so we see him a lot more since he's in charge of the hours he works. Maverick hates high school but started a garage band. Mom's still in denial of Declan's diagnosis. And Dad is...the same. The boys keep growing. Bud turns four in a couple of months if you want to fly out for his birthday party.

Me: I should probably get my kid feeling better before I even think about making plans to visit. Tell everyone hi from us. And thanks for the help. I'll get some applesauce and broth delivered to the apartment today.
Winnie: No problem. Give my niece a hug for me.

Since Declan's been gone, I've been reaching out to Winnie more. Just to keep the family ties. And especially because we only get to see her and the boys when they visit Jake's parents in New York. She knows I won't leave until I find out where Declan is, but I appreciate the invite.

※

Everything I try to do to provide comfort is reciprocated with a whiney "*No*," from Nova. This goes on until after ten o'clock when the sky is dark and only the moon and traffic thrust their light through the kitchen window.

Once I get the humidifier working and gotten as much snot out of Nova as I can, she finally gives in to the exhaustion and rests her precious little head on Declan's pillow in my bed and falls asleep. I figure it will be easier to tend to her needs if she's in bed with me.

I want to let out a breath of relief, but I'm afraid if I make any sounds, it will stir her awake. But I also need to get out of this bed because, even though Nova has no appetite, I do. And I didn't get around to dinner with her glued to my hip all afternoon.

After I slip out of her warm grip, I spend a good thirty seconds closing the bedroom door as slowly and silently as possible. Then, I quietly tiptoe down the hall and over to the kitchen, settling for a bowl of cereal since it's quick and easy, and I need calories immediately.

My phone lights up on the counter as I'm spooning cereal into my mouth ravenously. I stand over it, expecting Winnie to be checking in on Nova after our text conversation this morning. But instead, I see an image from Avery.

I drop my spoon into my bowl and take my phone in my free hand, opening the message from Avery. And I smile when I see the photo she sent. It's an aerial photo of an orca and her baby. I don't have to ask to know who those whales are.

Another message comes in. This time it's a video of the mother orca and her baby. I wonder who mother orcas contact when they need help taking care of their sick babies?

I'm getting a call from Avery when I hear the lock on the door beep.

I answer her call. "Hey, Avery, how's my spirit animal adjusting to motherhood?" I set my bowl of cereal down and narrow my eyes in the direction of the door. Unsure if I really did hear something or if I just need to get some sleep.

Avery lets out a delighted laugh. "She's so maternal! The entire pod has accepted having a new baby around. It's great!"

"That's so sweet," I say automatically as the key code beeps from the other side of the door again. I'm not sure if I should yell at whoever it is that they have the wrong house and if they keep putting the wrong code in they're going to set off my alarm system, or if I should be calling the police.

"*That's so sweet?*" Avery repeats unimpressed by my lack of excitement. In my defense, maybe I would be more excited if I wasn't distracted by someone trying to get into my apartment.

"I'm sorry," I say, approaching the door, "but I think someone's trying to get into my apartment." And I hope it's not Arty again since Tallen's not here to pay him off this time.

"What?" Her voice—that just shot up several octaves—bursts through my eardrum in a shrill. "What are you going to do? Should I call the police? What are we still doing on the phone? I'm calling the police."

"Avery, wait," I say before she can hang up, "I think it's just someone who is lost or something. It doesn't feel threatening."

"Ha!" She's appalled. "How can you *feel* if it's threatening or not. That's ridiculous."

Just before I can look through the peephole, the door unlocks and slowly begins to open.

I step back quickly, unable to answer Avery's demanding questions about what's happening.

Before my eyes adjust to the silhouette of the ghost in front of me, I say, "Avery, everything is fine. I'll call you back." Then I hang up, taking another step back in disbelief.

FIFTY-SEVEN

"*Christine*," his honeyed voice warms my core in every possible way it could. His voice returns every memory of the countless smug grins he ever gave me. His voice breaks the cement that I poured into the cracks of my heart, trying to harden myself, and replaces the holes with love. "I'm so sorry," he continues, "I'm so, so, sorry for leaving. I'm sorry for what I said. I'm sorry for what I didn't say." His hands drag through the long toughs of hair that obviously haven't been trimmed since he's been gone. "I'm sorry for what I did. I'm sorry," his voice breaks, "I'm so sorry, Christine."

He collapses to his knees in front of me, taking my hands in his. His touch. His real life, physical, touch causes me to inhale sharply.

Pressing my hand to his cheek, he continues in a quavering voice, "I don't deserve your forgiveness, but I hope you extend it to me. I wasn't in my right mind. I've done so much soul searching and healing. I promise I won't leave you ever again. I promise."

I lower myself to the floor, not able to blink or pull my eyes off of him. My voice is barely a whisper when I say, "It's really you." I'm still in shock.

This was a complete surprise for me. I didn't know what I was going to find on the other side of that door. But it's different for him. He's not surprised at all, because he knew he would see me on the other side of the door. He knew he was going to see me again. He had time to prepare what he wanted to say. I'm still trying to grasp the fact that he's alive and standing, or kneeling, in front of me.

"I'm so sorry," he says again, pressing his eyes closed as the pain of his abandonment sinks.

Even though his eyes are red-rimmed and stained with remorse,

I can tell he's healthy. I can tell he's sincere. And I can tell he's present, and focused, and living, and real, and *here*.

He presses his cheek into my hand again, and with a pleading expression he says, "Please, Christine." If his expression could twist anymore into repentance, it does when he says, "Please forgive me."

I cup his face in my hands, his stubble tickling my palms, and I flick my eyes between his. Part of me is in disbelief that he's real. Part of me can't fathom that his return is here. So suddenly. And that he's *himself*.

"Please, Christine," he pleads. "I'll do whatever it takes to prove that I'll never do anything like this to you again."

My heart is beating so erratically that I can't focus. I thought I was going to meet him again in a body bag. I thought the man I married was gone. I thought he lost himself to the shadows of his mind, never to return again unless it was against his will or out of his control.

He doesn't ask me to forgive him again, but his eyes do. They beg me to forgive him. They promise he's willing to do whatever it takes. And they promise that he'll never leave again.

"I forgive you," I say. Then, wrapping my arms around his shoulders, I bury my face into him and say, "I can't believe you're alive."

He holds me, completely enveloping me in his arms. Everything about him feels familiar and comforting. And *right*.

He chokes out a laugh with his tears when he says, "I missed you so much."

"I missed you more than I can explain." My eyes burn with the tears forming in them, but it's the good kind of tears. The ones that were waiting to emerge for a time when I felt joy and relief again.

We stay in this position of embrace for a long time. Holding each other like we're afraid if we let go, we'll wake up from a dream. I don't know where he was, but he smells clean and looks as if he's been taking care of himself.

I'm the one to pull away first, mostly so I can take in his face again to make sure he's really here.

He is.

He pushes my hair over my shoulder and grins when his eyes meet mine. He rises to his feet and reaches his hands out to help me stand. Kissing the side of my face, he releases his grip and walks back to the open door.

"What are you doing?" I say curious as to where he's going.

He retrieves a bag he left in the stairway. "I brought some things for you," he says, shutting the door behind himself and locking it this time.

I fold in my mouth, wishing I had a welcome home gift for him. Although I wasn't sure he was ever coming back.

"This," he says, pulling a thick book from the bag. "I want to show you how this changed my life." He flips through the thin pages until one falls open stiffly and a leaf falls to floor. He bends down to retrieve the leaf, and I notice his hands look tough, and more rugged than I can remember. I'm sure he's been on the streets this entire time despite his appearance now.

Then he reads a line from the book. *"No one can serve two masters, either you will hate the one and love the other, or you will be loyal to the one and have contempt for the other."* He looks at me longingly as he hands me the leaf. "This was the first day I took back my life."

I hold the leaf in my hand. It's completely flat from being pressed inside the book. One side is dark green and the other is light grey and soft to the touch, almost fuzzy. I glance up at him, opening my mouth to speak.

But he holds his finger up, and says, "There's more." He flips through the pages again to where another leaf is, and hands it to me as he begins to read. *"Husbands, love your wives deeply."* He flips to another page, hands me a small, thin, pink leaf. *"I am my beloved's and my beloved is mine."* He continues flipping through the book, handing me leaves, and reading quotes eagerly.

Finally, as I'm holding the leaves in my cupped hands, he says, "Every day, I peeled off a layer of regret, and I focused on you." He runs his tongue along his bottom lip that sends a rushing wave through my core. "And every day I felt my soul more at peace, and I felt more love for you and less attraction for the delusions in my mind."

It's as if he's a new man. Completely changed from the inside out.

He flips the book once more, landing on a page with a pressed orange petunia. *"Children born to a young man are like arrows in a warrior's hands."* Looking at me he says, "This one is for Nova." He places the flower on top of the leaves in my hands.

I spread my hands open on the table, allowing the leaves and the single flower to fall into a pile. Then I pick up the flower and say, "I think she needs her own box."

His mouth curls up on one side into a smile that spreads across his face, wrinkling the corners of his eyes. Then he approaches me and gently kisses me with a heavy passion I've missed so much. It feels right, and comforting, and *real*.

I hug him again, pressing the side of my head into his chest. Drawing in a deep inhale, I say, "You smell like *you*."

He hugs me a little tighter and rests his cheek against the top of my head. "So do you," he says with an inhale.

My grin shifts into a frown and I pull my head up to look at him. His brown eyes—that seem awakened—flick between mine as his expression drops. "What is it?"

I shake my head. Not wanting to say the piercing thoughts that have plagued me since Nova started talking more after she turned two.

Placing one hand under my chin he kisses me, then, resting his nose next to mine, he says, "Four words."

My heart skips a beat and I give him a hopeful expression. *"The somebody that understands."*

With his grin, he says, *"I love you more."*

I let out a breath and hold him tightly again.

With his honeyed voice, he says, "I know you, and you know me. No matter how much time passes and no matter how far apart we are. That will never change. We can tell each other anything, alright?"

I nod. Instantly falling back into a rhythm with him, as if he never left. As if he is the same man I said *yes* to when he proposed to me.

"Tell me," he whispers.

"It's just…Nova…" I feel his body tense subtly, then he lets out a calm breath as he runs his hand up and down my back.

"I know," he says quietly. "I've thought about that too." He leans back and ducks his head down to meet my eyes. "If she doesn't remember me, I'll just have to convince her to fall in love with me again. Won't I?"

My mouth falls open and I blink at the tears forming.

His eyes shine when he says, "I'm serious, Christine." I love hearing him say my name. "I'm not going anywhere, ever." His voice shakes when he says, "I'll never be able to thank you for waiting for me. And for loving me when I broke your heart and turned your entire world upside down along with our innocent daughter's."

"You'll always be worth loving through every part of our lives.

When it's easy, and when it's not. You're worth it to me."

We hold each other again. Tightly.

Letting the emotions out that were bottled up for so long.

I breathe him in, hoping I'll never have to miss him so profoundly ever again.

After several minutes in this position, and once our emotions settle. He sniffs as he wipes at his face with his spread palms, then says, "Would it be the worst thing in the world if I woke her?"

I don't even bother looking at the time or mention she was sick. I smile and shake my head. "She's in our bed. In your spot."

His eyes light up with thankfulness and eagerness to get to our daughter. He kisses me, then heads for our bedroom.

Instantly, he returns, making his way past me as he digs into his bag. "Four words," he says, quickly kissing the side of my cheek, "*You are my muse.*" And just like that he's reversed the pain that tortured me from his last four words. Then he presses his mouth to mine before he hands me a notebook and says, "Four more words, *You are my home.*"

"That could be a song," I say.

He flashes me a smug grin, then says, "It already is," then heads for our bedroom again.

A short laugh of disbelief escapes my throat. Disbelief that he's home. Disbelief that he's better. Disbelief that he found a way to balance himself. Disbelief that in a matter of hours, he's seemed to heal the broken parts of me that I never thought would mend. And disbelief that all I had to do to find him, was wait for him to walk through the door.

I grin with appreciation and flip the spiral notebook open.

FIFTY-EIGHT

Journal:
I'm ready to go back.
The streets are unforgiving and have subtly stopped calling.
Music is in my mind without the voice of delusion and unreason fueling my actions.
And more than anything, I want to go home.
She's still waiting for me there. I hope she's still waiting for me. There's an elusive dread that accompanies my thoughts of her. And it makes me nervous that I've been gone too long. That another man has taken my place. That he loves my wife and is raising my child.
I don't deserve her, I know that.
I always knew that.
But I want her.
And I want to be in her life. I desire to be the husband she warrants. I desire to be the father Nova deserves.
If she has moved on. If too much time has passed. I won't give up loving her. I won't give up on being a present father for Nova. I won't give up on fighting for our marriage. I'll do whatever it takes to get her to fall in love with me again. And not because she's my muse, not because she fuels me with creativity, not because she's beautiful, strong, and talented. But because our souls are knit together. Because I made a vow when I told her that:

I promise to be loving and love her to the best of my ability...
...when life is easy, and when it's not.
...when our love is simple, and when it takes effort.

...when we're young, and when we're grey.
...when we're full of life, and when we'd rather be taken by death.

And I'm not backing out on that promise.

Journal:
I understand my mind can be a lethal weapon.
Which is why I'm trying to take care of my mind by taking care of myself again. Balanced in my mind, body, and spirit
I also understand that when I remind myself that that's not me. That those thoughts aren't real. Then, I'm not consumed by their weight. My thoughts don't trap me anymore.
I can hear my own real thoughts.
And I know that I can't do this on my own.
I need the support Winnie always gave. I need my therapist to remind me that I'm in control of my mind, and my mind is not in control of me.
I also know that I need the friendship Tallen extended to me. I need the responsibility of my job. I need the unconditional love of fatherhood. And I need the accountability and love that Christine always stretched out to me. Especially when I was difficult to love.

Journal:
Schizophrenia is not my identity.
I know that now.
I am Declan Price, child of God, son to Sean and Valentine. Brother and friend to Winnie, Maverick and Tallen. Father to Nova. And husband to Christine.
Christine, the joy of my life. The muse to my mind. And the wife that deserves the best of me.
I've been across America and I'm on my way home.
I'm planning to go back. But not just yet.
I still need to finish what I started when I left.

Journal:
The nightmares and regrets and loose ends are all tied up. Both, in my mind and in my heart.
I know my dad is sick. And I accept it.
I know this isn't my home forever, and I know this

world will try and break me down and betray me. I just hope it's not too late to make a few more memories with my dad before his mind is completely gone.

Through my transient travels and homeless hitch-hiking, I saw a lot of love and hate. I heard stories of tragedy and loss, of passion and rage, of missed opportunity, of growth, and of found peace.

I saw fathers lift their hands against their children. I saw fathers ignore their young child's cries. I saw fathers devoted to their children. And I saw children living with an absent father. And I learned that there's no perfect childhood.

And then I remembered Nova.

And my heart ached.

How could I do this to my innocent child. She didn't ask to be born into a family with an absent father. And the worst part is that I left on my own accord. Not completely. My mind had taken over every reasonable part of my judgement. But essentially, I was the one that walked away. That's how she will see it. And no kid should grow up unsure if their father loved them or not.

I'm going back soon, I already know that. I'm going home.

But I have to finish this process of healing. I don't want anything to pull me away again.

My only hope is that I come back before she has memories of her life without me in it. I know from this moment forward; I don't want a single memory without Nova and Christine in it.

Journal:

I went to the cemetery in Nevada.

The one where Eli was buried.

I thought it would help, with the healing process. Especially since his death was one that I've struggled to accept for over a decade. It's been more difficult to accept than losing Parker, who I knew for half my life. I wasn't ready for what I found at the cemetery.

What I was faced with was better than anything I might have expected.

If I'm honest, I've buried that tragedy. I've avoided the pain associated with his short life and the even shorter memory I have of him. It's always astonished me that I spent brief moments with Eli, and those moments are clearer than any other memory and more haunting than anything I've ever experienced. It's the negative things that seem to scream the loudest in our minds, isn't it?

I thought if I could face the memory of Eli's life, if I could find out who he was, then maybe I could face his parents who I had decided to find and contact to apologize to and extend my condolences.

I wanted to hear from them who Eli was while he was alive. I wanted to know his story. And when I walked through the tomb stones at the cemetery until I found Eli William Irving's tomb stone, I was shocked to see it set right next to Allan and Lilly Irving, loving parents to Eli.

To say I was surprised is an understatement. I was overwhelmed with so many different emotions.

Greif.

Gratefulness.

Pain.

Relief.

The list goes on. I felt like I was on a rollercoaster of emotions. Pulling me up into thankfulness and gratitude, back down to remorse.

Eli's parents had died two years prior to Eli's death. When I later found their obituary online, it said they had been in a tragic boating accident. I gathered they were well off and devoted parents. And Eli was their only son; their pride and joy.

It didn't seem like such a tragedy anymore. When Eli died, he didn't leave his parents behind to mourn and suffer in the loss of their son. Eli was brought home. He was reunited with his parents. If anyone was suffering, it was Eli growing up without his parents.

And I finally grieved and accepted Eli's death.

I felt relief for myself, and I felt relief for Eli.

All it took, was a change of perspective.

His drowning was a bittersweet tragedy that I needed to accept. I wish his life wasn't so short. I wish I hadn't been hung over and asleep when he needed me. But now that it's all happened. Now that there's nothing anyone can do to bring him back, I have to forgive myself. And forgiving myself is the most loving thing I can do for Eli to move forward in my life.

If it had been my child, I would want the negligent and

lost teenage boy to forgive himself too.

So, I forgive myself for Eli's death.

I forgive myself for leaving Christine and Nova.

I accept my father's dementia.

I accept Parker's death.

I am capable of loving.

And I am capable of being loved.

For the first time I feel hope in my life. And that hope tells me that I'll be home with Christine again.

And for the rest of my life, home is wherever Christine is.

EPILOGUE

"It's staw-ting to sting, Daddy," Nova says dropping her hand from the guitar strings and shaking it at her side.

Declan sets his guitar down with a smile and maneuvers around the table. "Let me see," he says, taking her hand for inspection, "Looks like you need to play a little more until you grow some callouses."

Nova leans her chest against her guitar. "It takes too long to gwow cow-ouses..."

I squat down near Declan and take Nova's hand. "Ooo," I say pressing at her fingertips, "Is that a...no it couldn't be."

"Couldn't be what?" Nova says inspecting her fingers.

Declan cranes his neck around Nova's hand. "Oh, I can already see it!"

"See what?" Nova's expression is shifting between confusion and concern.

Maverick slumps down in the bright floral chair across from us. "Don't let them fool you," he says pulling an Air Pod from his ear. "Your dad used to tell me I had little callous seeds in my fingers that were about to sprout when I was a kid too."

Nova covers her fingers with her other hand. "Thewe's seeds in my fing-ews?"

Margaret peeks her head in the door of the backstage room. "You better get out there, it's almost time to start."

We give her a nod before she disappears.

"It's not true, kid," Maverick says to Nova as he retrieves his guitar. "The only way you can grow callouses is practice, practice, practice. And practice what you like. No more of this *Twinkle, Twinkle* bull—"

"*Maverick!*" Both Declan and I say in unison.

"Bologna," Maverick says with an awkward grin as he raises his arms with his shrug. "I was going to say Bologna. Jeeze, what do you guys think I am a sailor?"

"*Yes,*" we say in unison again.

He begins to strum on his guitar. "Well, not around my niece I'm not."

Approaching Maverick, Nova says, "If I can't play *Twinkle, Twinkle, Little Staw*, what can I play to gwow cow-ouses?"

"Here's one," he says, strumming hard across the guitar strings, as he sings, "*Now you're messin' with a,*" two intense strums then, "*son of a bologna sailor!*"

I release the breath I was holding, knowing the lyrics to the real song, and laugh.

Maverick points at us. "Bet you never heard that song before!"

"Alright, save it for the microphone," Declan says motioning for us to head out of the room. "And fix your socks and shoes. I can't let anyone know my brother dresses like Kevin Federline."

Maverick twists his face into confusion and pulls his chin into his neck. "I don't know who that is, but he's fire if he's dressed like this."

Declan holds the door open as we file out. "I meant Kevin Federline from two-thousa…" he stops short on his words and draws in a deep breath as he runs his hand through the top of his hair, giving up on his explanation. "You know what, it doesn't matter. Wear your socks like that."

Maverick struts down the hallway with the band. "Oh I'm going to."

"Just don't tell anyone you're my brother."

I hold Nova's hand as we make our way through a side door, leaving Maverick backstage.

The lights are already dim when we find our table in the audience as a younger woman on the stage introduces the band.

"What took so long?" Avery says when we sit down.

Nova lifts her hands. "I'm twy-ing to gwow cow-ouses."

"Ohhh…right…" Avery smiles in confusion, then to me says, "What is she talking about?"

Tallen knocks on the table. "Girls," he says in a way he used to when we were kids. "Hush!"

I raise my hands in surrender, then point to Avery.

Avery shakes her head, unimpressed at my accusatory finger in her direction. "I'm not sending you anymore pictures of otters holding hands."

"No, wait," I say, pleading sarcastically. "Please don't take away the hand holding otters."

She holds her hand up, jokingly. "Too late."

"Auntie Ave-wy," Nova says abandoning her chair next to me and crawling onto Avery's lap. "Can I still see the sea ott-ows?"

Avery gives me a sinister look, then pulls out her phone for Nova. "Of course you can my favorite muffin, just don't show your mom."

Before I can laugh, Tallen is knocking on the table again with a look that says we better zip it.

Declan scoots into the empty chair next to me and wraps his arm around my shoulders, pulling me closer to him. "Ready to livestream?"

I nod with a smile. "Ready to call your parents?"

He nods, pulls his phone out, and facetimes Winnie.

She answers immediately with, "Hey! We're all ready for you here."

Her voice causes Tallen to furrow his brow in our direction. Sandi places her hand on his shoulder then whispers something to him that makes him smile. Then she rolls her hand over her protruding belly as she looks at me with her stunning smile and says, "He's done being grumpy now."

I raise my eyebrow at Tallen with uncertainty. Then he holds Sandi's hand, and to me he says, "I'm in a fantastic mood!"

I mouth, *thank you*, to Sandi for whatever she said. I'm not sure that I want to know.

Declan sets his phone up against a glass of water on the table so that it's facing the stage. "Can you see it okay?"

Winnie nods. "Yep, looks good." Then she hands the phone to Val.

Val extends her arms under her chin at an unflattering angle, and sits next to Sean. His expression is interested, but he doesn't talk much these days, so Val begins explaining everything that's happening to him. Not before she says, "Has Nova been checked out for her speech problems?"

Declan forces a smile. "She's seven, Mom. She'll figure it out."

"Ty and Bud never had those kinds of problems," Val mutters.

Winnie pipes in with, "Yeah but Declan had a lisp until he was nine, and then he grew up and got his Ph.D. in linguistics." This seems to shut Val up.

Setting the phone up with the tripod, I begin a livestream on Instagram and find my place under Declan's arm again. "Did you ever think your little brother would be playing at your open mic night?"

The stage goes quiet as the announcer exits and the band shuffles around in the dark.

With a growing smile and his reflective eyes fixed on the stage, Declan says, "I hoped he would." The spotlight flashes on Maverick. "But it's absolutely surreal."

Maverick adjusts the mic as his voice echoes out into the audience. "Welcome to the annual Open Mic Meet the Stars Night. I'm Maverick, and this is my band, Muse-Ick Box!"

The crowd screams with wild energy.

Maverick peers out into the audience, placing a hand against his brow to shade his eyes against the blinding stage lights. "I'm looking for my brother. Declan Price. Anyone seen Dec tonight?"

My jaw drops as my eyes widen and I turn to look up at Declan. He looks just as surprised as I am.

"What's he doing?" Avery says flipping her head around to face us.

Declan shrugs. "I don't know, but I don't trust him."

"Excuse me for a second," Maverick says pointedly. Then placing the mic into the stand he says, "I gotta do something real quick." He bends down, laces his shoes, and shoves his socks down. "Alright, *now* has anyone seen my brother?" He scans the audience again. "Come on, Dec, you can't leave your little brother hanging like this. Plus, check it out," he lifts his leg up and wiggles his shoe in the air, "I fixed my socks and shoes for you."

The crowd becomes hysterical with laughter.

I pull Declan's arm off of me and encourage him to stand by tugging on his hand. "Go," I say with a laugh, "It is *your* stage after all. What's he going to do?"

"I really don't want to find out."

Declan reluctantly makes his way to the stage and Maverick turns the entire march into a show. The audience is riled up by the time Declan approaches Maverick.

Maverick wraps his arm around Declan's shoulders, and I still can't believe they're the same size. "This guy right here," Maverick says, "Taught me everything I know about rock music. Years ago, he let me use his tiny recording studio in his office. And showed me the ins and outs of this ruthless thing we call rock music."

Right on cue, the crowd cheers.

"And I just wanted to bring him up here to say thanks." Maverick faces Declan then into the mic, he says, "Thanks for making me a superstar and creating Muse-Ick Box. You're the best big brother, Dec."

Declan nods and gives Maverick a hug. Then he leans into the mic and says, "You're welcome, now let's get on with the show."

Nova is clapping and beaming with excitement that both her dad and uncle are on the stage.

"Hold on," Maverick says, with a comical tone, "I think we should play a song together."

Declan folds his arms and shakes his head with his laughter.

Maverick points to stage right. "Anyone got another mic and a guitar?" He's holding Declan's shirt sleeve with one hand, making sure he doesn't try to bolt, and waving towards himself with the other. "Yeah! Bring that out here." He faces Declan again. "Don't worry, Dec, we're getting you set up."

Declan continues to shake his head and laugh as the crowd feeds into Maverick's humor with their amusement. And by this point, I'm joining right in along with their hollering and laughter.

When Declan has his own mic, he says, "Thank you all for not walking out on us. I have no idea what my brother's up to with all these spur of the moment antics."

"That's the kind of response I get for bringing you on stage with me?" Maverick lets out an exaggerated scoff. "You know I'm famous, right?"

"Yeah, I do. You know I'll always be older and cooler than you, right?" Declan says as he takes a guitar from someone with a headset running across stage. "And I'm pretty sure you just gave me all the credit for your fame too."

Everyone in the audience laughs at his humor.

"Alright," Maverick says subtly picking at his strings. "Let's give this patient crowd a show."

"Wait a second," Declan strums down the guitar. "Alright, I just wanted to make sure it was in tune. I thought you were going to pull a prank on me."

"No, that's not the prank," Maverick says, beaming. "The prank is that you get to pick the song."

Declan grins and begins to play the chords to a familiar song as he looks out into the audience until his eyes land on me.

"Well, Dec," Maverick says adjusting his guitar strap, "What're we playin'?"

"The only song worth playing."

Maverick throws his arms in the air to get a reaction from the audience; which he does as he says, "Which is-s-s...?"

Declan drags the tip of his tongue against his bottom lip before he says, "Four More Words."

CHRISTINE'S 'MISSING DECLAN' PLAYLIST

normal the kid - take a moment to breathe

favian villa - i've fallen to my knees

the paper kites - walk above the city (ft. maro)

katelyn tarver - you don't know

the broken view - all i feel is you

tom walker - leave a light on

andrew belle - in my veins

louis tomlinson - two of us

trading yesterday - shattered

ryan star - losing your memory

judah (dante bowe, aaron moses) - i love you

flora cash - somebody else

sasha alex sloan - dancing with your ghost

sam smith - to die for (acoustic)

nf - paralyzed

FROM THE AUTHOR

Includes spoilers. This section is meant to be read after the story.

If there is anything that I hope this story does, is that it brings hope and spreads awareness.

Hope for those struggling in similar circumstances. Whether that be a circumstance like Declan's; navigating life with a serious mental illness. Or one like Christine's; loving someone with a mental illness that's difficult to understand.

And awareness to those that might not understand what people are struggling with.

I also want to say that I know that no two people are the same or have the same story. The topics in this story are personal to me and a representation of what I've witnessed and gone through. It doesn't in any way mean that all people diagnosed with schizophrenia will share the same symptoms or respond to their symptoms in the same way.

Although I didn't mention it directly, Declan was struggling with some PTSD from the pool incident. I incorporated this into the story because sometimes schizophrenia can be triggered by something like PTSD.

I try to write stories that provide a means of resources, just in case one of my readers is struggling with a similar circumstance in their own life. In this case, I talked about various counseling and therapy tools that my characters used. Christine benefited from in person and online counseling. Tallen liked group therapy best. And Declan benefitted from a number of resources to heal, but ultimately needed to find balance on his own.

I also loved incorporating the aspects of marriage in this story. Because sometimes marriage is about loving someone else through their ugliness. And I wanted to show that, even though their marriage was young, Christine wasn't going to give up.

I knew I wanted to write this story for a long time, but I kept putting it off because I knew it would hurt.

And much like Declan refusing to face the parts of his life that made him feel pain, I didn't want to dig into those painful parts of my heart either.

I remember after writing the outline for this book, I placed a little post-it in the center of my outline and wrote a note to myself. It said, *Your heart will hurt the entire time you write this.*

And it did.

So much so that I didn't want to finish it.

This story was so raw for me because my brother was diagnosed with schizophrenia nearly ten years ago. And much like Declan at the beginning of the story, my brother was charming and self-driven. It was easy to enjoy his company. And I saw how easily the love of his life fell for him and I saw how beautiful they were together. Much like Declan and Christine.

My brother was also a talented musician and incredibly smart. So smart that, although he was two years younger than me, he used to help me with my homework. He could play any instrument he got his hands on and could make up songs on the spot. I remember his voice bringing our sister to tears at a talent show he played at once. He was gifted, to say the least.

I also witnessed the subtle changes begin to emerge in him in our adult life. We would talk about impulsive things he did and delusions of grandeur that invaded his mind. But even when me, or my siblings, or our parents would talk sense into him, he always seemed to slip back into the parts of his mind that were taking over the person that I knew as my brother.

After we learned his diagnosis, some of us were in denial. Some of us were in shock. Some of us were heartbroken.

And because he would seem okay, we often wondered if his diagnosis was a mistake.

My brother would get help, get balanced in his mind, body and soul. Something would trigger his mind, and then he would disappear without a trace. When he'd return, he would talk about the events that took place while he was homeless as if they were an adventure. They were horrifying to me; sleeping in trees, bathing in people's hot tubs at 2 am, stealing food so he didn't starve. I could see in his eyes that he was losing himself. For some reason, the delusion would always have more power than the treatment he was getting, the support he was getting, or the meds he was taking. Pulling him back into the life of a transient. Again. And again.

I *lost* my brother.

I don't know where he is.

I don't know if he's alive.

I don't know what's happened to him.

My brother has been *lost* for years.

And just like the way Christine wrestled with the unknown, I also experience the indescribable fear that I'll never see him again. Every day I battle with this. Which is heartbreaking because he is one of my favorite people and he was such a light to so many people that knew him.

In our last conversation, I told him that I missed my brother and I felt like he wasn't my brother anymore. He called me a name, and then we didn't speak in person ever again. A few texts here and there from ever changing phone numbers. A handful of Instagram comments. But I didn't see him in person ever again after that sad conversation.

It's been a tough memory to live with. It rips my heart out to even admit it. And I wish I had been more patient and understanding with him.

Despite everything, he's still my brother and I care about him. He was my best friend for my entire childhood on up into my adulthood. And I really miss him, our deep theological conversations, and the laughing we used to do together. I miss that.

It's the strangest and most heartbreaking sensation to live in this sort of torturous limbo.

Not knowing if he's okay.

I was hesitant to share this story, because it is raw. And

there's nothing pretty about it.

But writing it really has healed the parts of me that felt so much regret. And I want to thank you for reading it.

Without going into much detail on the parallels between Declan and my brother, I want you to know that this story was inspired by my brother's life. The only part that's unwritten for him, is the ending. And I do hope and pray that my brother has an incredible epilogue to his life.

Whether I know about it or not.

RESOURCES

This story mentions some heavy and sensitive topics. First of all mental illness is not something to be ashamed of. Schizophrenia, PTSD, and Dementia were all touched on in this story and present themselves in different ways. So it can be difficult to understand or pinpoint what is going on without seeking help. I don't write about these topics lightly. I write about them because they are real and raw and happening to people and their families every day. I think it is important to bring awareness to these kinds of illnesses that attack the mind because we are quick to blame the person, when oftentimes they don't understand what's happening to them and their actions are almost out of their control. And I also think it is important to share that there is hope for these situations. And that with positive support from friends and family, anyone can live a normal life.

If you or someone you know is struggling with delusions, confusion, obsessions, hallucinations, or disorganized speech, please schedule an appointment with a healthcare provider immediately.

If you are in crisis and/or panicking, please call or text **988**

To chat with a counselor, text **"HELLO"** to **741741** for 24-hour help.

ACKNOWLEDGMENTS

First of all, thank you, Jesus. Without salvation, I'd never have the courage to do any of this.

A humungous thank you to Michaela Burton, Cheyenne Tice, Ami Ohara, Monica Derrick, Rachel Clearwater, Lindsey Sanford, Giulie Darland, Kara Vaterlaus, Tracey Hazel, Cierra Geiger, Jordan, Lainey, Gabrielle, Emily, and so many more that have supported my writing and the message behind each story I publish. Ladies, to say you're amazing is an understatement!

Thank you to my daughters, Jai and Aims, for your constant eagerness in my writing. I love you both so much and am proud that you're my daughters.

Thank you to my sons, Des and Evan, for constantly checking in on my sanity when I'm hulled up in my writing corner. You boys mean the world to me and I love you.

Thank you to my wonderful husband, Kyle, you're my rock and my security blanket. I love you more than words can express.

A big thank you to my mom who is my biggest cheerleader. Mom, I'm so thankful you care enough to read the first draft of every story.

To my big sisters, Sarah, Amie, and Sandi. Thank you for always making sure I'm happy and healthy! I love the dynamic of our sisterhood and am grateful for the love and support you've given me through whatever endeavors I'm doing in life. I love you three more than you know.

To my niece, Ava, you're amazingly wonderful inside and out, and I'm so proud of the young lady you've transformed into. Thank you for your excitement and interest in my writing. I sure do love you!

I want to thank my little brother, Hayden, for being my childhood best friend and filling my memories with so much laughter. This story wouldn't exist without you. I miss you dearly…and hope you're okay.

Thank you to so many more of my friends and family that have supported and encouraged me through this entire journey. These stories keep growing because of you!

And thank you! Yes, YOU, my readers. Your enthusiasm and excitement for reading fuels me to create more stories. Thank you for all your thoughts and reviews. I'm always grateful to see new posts for my work on Amazon and Goodreads well after my books are released. Thanks a million for the time you take to read every word.

ABOUT THE AUTHOR

Aurora Stenulson has written two other novels, *The Consequence of Audrey* (February 2022) and *Your Drowning Heart* (December 2022). She enjoys writing contemporary YA and women's fiction with her own unique personal twist. She lives with her four wonderful children and incredible husband on their homestead in Wyoming.

For more information about the author and upcoming books, visit: aurorastenulson.com

Instagram @aurorastenulson
Email authoraurorastenulson@gmail.com

Printed in the USA
CPSIA information can be obtained
at www.ICGtesting.com
JSHW080213121023
50002JS00003B/5